WARDEN

NOVA ONLINE

ALEX KNIGHT

PORTAL BOOKS

Chapter One

Kaiden Moore didn't want much out of life. Not spending the next half-century in prison seemed about enough.

But it was the year 2074, and the Party were cracking down hard on crime. He'd always thought that was a good thing, being a law abiding citizen, but now he wasn't so sure. He wondered how many other innocents had been convicted by the Party's overzealous new policy.

Fifty years in prison with no chance for parole was a rather light sentence, the media had said. Some went so far as to say the judge hadn't been harsh enough. After all, Kaiden had murdered his neighbor, Fred Bernstein.

Except, of course, he hadn't.

Not that the judge had believed that. Or the media. Or the guards that had just sat him down in the state prison's processing center.

They said they had found his fingerprints on the murder weapon. And when he said he'd never seen it before, let alone touched it, they didn't believe him.

"Kaiden Moore," the clerk said, snapping Kaiden from his reverie. "That you?"

"Yes, but there's—"

Ding. The clerk tapped a screen in front of him and an all-too-cheerful green check mark flashed across it.

"Eighteen years of age?"

"Right. But—"

Ding.

"Sentenced to fifty years?"

"Ye–"

Ding.

"No parole."

"I–"

Ding.

"Listen to me!" Kaiden shouted, rising from his chair and slamming his hands on the desk. "I'm innocent!"

The guards behind him promptly took hold of his shoulders and forced him back down. The clerk stared at him for a moment, then spoke aloud as he typed.

"Additional comments: quick to anger."

"Best flag him with a code eleven, too," one of the guards said from behind. "I heard he tortured his victim before killing him."

"Good lord, did he?" The clerk shook his head, then typed a few more lines. When he was done he tapped the screen and another green check mark popped up.

Ding.

"Place your hands on the desk," the clerk said. Before he'd even finished the sentence, the guards forced Kaiden's hands onto the tabletop then mashed them flat so his fingers were splayed. A red light flashed as the desk recorded his biometrics.

"This might sting."

A needle pierced his shoulder and Kaiden hissed as a jolt of pain shot through him.

"This will sting."

A larger needle was jabbed into his forearm.

"Gah!"

"Aaand your tracker chip," the clerk said in a sing-song tone.

The hiss of compressed gas filled Kaiden's ears as a third needle plunged into his neck.

"I thought I was the one accused of torture," Kaiden mumbled, rubbing at the already swelling soreness.

The clerk rolled back in his chair and opened a drawer. A bundle of clothes smacked into Kaiden's face, then fell into his lap.

"Uniform."

Kaiden had just looked down at what appeared to be a crisp

white jumpsuit with "inmate number 1041293" stitched across it when a second bundle of cloth hit his face.

"Spare uniform, and..." The clerk turned to look for something else.

Kaiden winced and covered his face in preparation for whatever was going to be thrown next.

The clerk paused, one hand outstretched, and raised an eyebrow.

"Socks and underwear," he said, then placed them on the desk and slid them over. Assorted clothing arranged in his lap, Kaiden waited several long moments as the clerk double-checked his notes. He half thought to try to plead his case again – he was innocent; why wouldn't anyone listen? – but a guard behind him cracked his knuckles slowly, one by one, and Kaiden decided he might wait for a more receptive audience. Maybe the prison's governor?

"Alright then, Kaiden," the clerk said. "Looks like you're all good to go. Try to keep that anger in check, huh?"

Before he could respond he was pulled out of his chair and dragged toward a door at the end of the room.

"Oh, wait."

The guards stopped a moment, Kaiden hanging from their grasp more than actually standing.

"However did I miss this?" The clerk was messing with something on his screen. He frowned. "It looks like you passed your psych eval."

"How the hell did he pass a psych eval?" one of the guards asked. "Didn't he murder a guy?"

Well actually, I didn't, Kaiden thought, *that's probably why I passed.*

Both the guard and the clerk stared at Kaiden incredulously.

"What does this mean?" Kaiden asked.

"It means," the clerk said, speaking slowly, "that your psychological profile suggests you have a higher chance of rehabilitation than almost every criminal in here. You've qualified to shave some time off your sentence. "

"Yay?" Kaiden said, unsure what was happening.

"Yay, indeed, Mr. Moore." The clerk threw another object and Kaiden reacted on instinct this time, plucking something small and metal from the air. Opening his hand, he found it was a small brass pin. A sigil of sorts, consisting of a shield with two war hammers crossed in front of it. It must have been recently polished as the metal positively glowed in the sterile light of the prison.

"Congratulations," the clerk said, then looked to his guards. "Take him to the Warden program."

Chapter Two

Kaiden's first tour of the prison was a blur of sterile, white-tiled hallways and silent, crisp-uniformed workers. But he soon learned that was just the administrative wing as he was drag-carried through a security terminal and into the prison proper.

Ding.

A green check mark popped up on the screen as he passed.

"Welcome Kaiden Moore, inmate number 1041293," a robotic voice droned in something approaching a cheery tone.

"A pleasure to be here," Kaiden fired back in a mockery of its cheeriness.

One of his guards laughed.

"That's right. Welcome home," the other said with all the tenderness of a taser.

Kaiden opened his mouth to say something sarcastic, but a glass door slid open and a tidal wave of voices slammed into him. Kaiden swallowed hard as they walked in, trying to rid himself of the taste of the injustice being done to him.

The cylinder-shaped room they now stood in was, simply put, massive. Presumably there was a ceiling, but as far and high as Kaiden could see, there were only cells. Level upon level of them lining all sides of the room, filled with prisoners and rising ever higher. No bars kept the prisoners in; instead, each cell was fronted by near-clear glass tinged with a metallic sheen.

Kaiden recognized the unforgiving material – palladium glass. Light as aluminum but stronger than steel, and clear enough to purge any semblance of privacy from one's cell. A fact made all the more apparent by the tower rising through the center of the room.

All reinforced concrete and mirror glass, it looked like an aircraft control tower, and allowed the guards – presumably within – to watch each prisoner's every move. This was to be his home for the rest of his life.

Surely the prison was loaded with cameras and sensors and all manner of security measures. There was hardly a need for such a dramatic display, yet Kaiden couldn't deny the tower dominated the space. A constant reminder of where he was.

I don't belong here, he reminded himself, fighting the sensation of drowning as he stood in the shadow of the tower with cells and cells and cells rising on all sides. He felt his eyes well up with tears, and he quickly wiped them away with his sleeve. It would do to show weakness in this place.

"This is general lockup," a guard shouted above the clamor and nodded toward the wall. Kaiden followed his gaze to where man-sized letters were laser printed on the concrete. "Cell Block G-1." It was impossible to miss the next words. "Blocks G-2 through G-9 this way."

There were eight more cell blocks just like this one? The thought bounced around Kaiden's head as he tried to calculate exactly how many prisoners that was. He finally settled on "a lot".

"The Warden program briefing room is this way," the guard on his right shouted, then pulled him toward an offshoot corridor.

Just before they left cell block G-1, one of the inmates took notice of Kaiden. He slammed himself into the glass of his cell and screamed, an ear-piercing howl like some sort of animal. Kaiden recoiled without thinking, stumbling to the side as the inmate smiled. It would almost have looked friendly, if not for the display of apparent insanity moments before.

"*Another* one for the Wardens?" The tattooed and scar-covered inmate's smile fell into a scowl as he pressed his face up hard against the glass, distorting his features. "Think you lot are better than us, don't you? Comin' in here with your special privileges and your shiny badges." His tongue emerged from his mouth to leave a long stream of saliva along the glass.

"But don't worry. You'll soon learn the truth." And with that, he gave a wink and fell back from the glass, retreating to his bunk.

"He, uh, seems friendly," Kaiden said as the guards led him away from cell block G-1 and down the corridor.

"Oh, we're all friendly here," one guard said.

"For sure," the other chimed in. "One big, happy family. You'll fit right in."

~

With how fast everything had occurred – it'd been mere days since he'd found Bernstein's body – Kaiden hadn't exactly had time to prepare for his new life as a prisoner of the state. His plan thus far had consisted of two points: don't cause any trouble and lay low. Apparently, his acceptance into the Warden program had already violated both of those. Not that he had any idea what the program was, or why he'd been accepted into it, for that matter.

Seated in the briefing room where the guards had left him, all he did know was that twenty-three other male inmates had been selected for the program, and of those twenty-three, the biggest and meanest brute had been seated directly next to him.

All muscles and bulging veins, the man looked to be made more of iron than flesh. Kaiden did his best to look at the man without actually doing so. Crew cut black hair, five o'clock shadow on his chin and cheeks, and deep blue eyes that, if one were inclined to be rude, could be described as beady.

The man seemed to notice he was being side-eyed and Kaiden suddenly found a spot on the far wall terribly interesting. He also scooted sideways in his chair a bit, giving the man a smidge more space. Not that he had much choice. Shoulders wide as a doorway meant the brute next to him took up about two and a half chairs.

The man kept looking at Kaiden, brows ever so slightly furrowed.

"Uh, how's it going?" Kaiden finally asked, unsure why he'd even said anything as his voice spilled out to fill the awkward silence that had settled over the room. The big man took a long, slow look down at the white jumpsuits they were required to wear, then the armed guards lining the walls, then, finally, after a painfully long time, at Kaiden.

"How do you think it's going?" he growled, voice as gentle as sandpaper dragged through a gravel pit.

"Yeah, uh, fair enough," Kaiden said, mentally reprimanding himself. *How's it going? Really? That's your icebreaker? Why not ask him what he's in for too, huh?*

"Gentlemen, gentlemen!" a voice shouted. A man entered the room, clapping as if to quiet them down. He wore a blue-and-gray camouflage military uniform, not unlike those of the guards, except with long, buttoned sleeves and a series of gold chevrons adorning the shoulders.

"Why, it's like a hospital waiting room in here," he said, shaking his head. "Positively dour, wouldn't you say, Franks?" He nodded to one of the guards.

"Dour indeed, sir."

Sir? So that meant this was someone important. Considering the way he'd strode into the room, commanding everyone's attention, Kaiden found that unsurprising.

"Gentlemen, the world outside of this humble facility can be a dangerous place. One of temptation and deeds most foul." The man waved his hand as if gesturing for a word on the tip of his tongue. "A storm-tossed sea, let us say. Now, I know how easy it is to lose one's way in that chaos. Surely you do too, considering where you're sitting now," he said, adding a chuckle to the end as if the thought amused him. "But fear not! You may have been blown off course by the ferocious storm that is the world without; you may have been drowning, but now, you've found salvation." He paused, as if thinking. "Well, a chance at salvation, at least."

The air of despair that had pervaded the room moments before was gone now, replaced by one of downright confusion.

"The choices you've made in life may have led you astray, but I'm here to offer you a chance to fix that. Call me your navigator. Call me your captain. Or simply call me 'The Governor.' Either way, I'm here to lead you through the storm. Calmer waters await, gentlemen. Now, who'd like me to show them the way?"

The Governor paused as if waiting for applause, or cheers, or something. Up front, one man gave a slow, awkward clap. It was quickly silenced when the man next to him slapped him upside the head.

"Well, well, don't get too excited," The Governor said. "I'm only offering you a chance at a new life, you know." He turned to Franks again. "Ungrateful lot, aren't they?"

"Terribly ungrateful, sir."

"Don't appreciate the chance they're being given," another guard interjected.

"Too true, Himmel. Too true." The Governor turned back to face them, then took a long, deep breath. "Ah, well. On to the main event, then. The Warden program." He pulled a prisoner in the front row to his feet, then turned him toward the audience.

"As you'll have no doubt noticed, during processing you were all awarded a badge for passing our special psychological evaluation." He pointed to the badge pinned to the collar of the prisoner. "This means you have been accepted into the Warden program. Congratulations!" He burst into a wide, toothy smile and clapped wildly, then gestured for the guards to join him. Soon, the entire room was filled with the sound of applause while the prisoners watched. Kaiden felt his own brow scrunch in confusion and noticed he wasn't alone. Even the brute sitting next to him seemed thoroughly lost by the display.

OK, they had been accepted into the Warden program. He'd been told this multiple times already. Seemed like a big deal.

Problem is, no one's telling me what that actually means.

"Stop clapping!" The Governor silenced the room with a shout. "The Warden program is your chance at salvation. Perform well in it and you'll be eligible to shave time off your sentence." Some heads perked up at that. Kaiden couldn't blame them. A shorter sentence? Why would they offer them that?

"You're all very lucky to have been accepted into this program," The Governor continued. "But you'll need more than luck if you want to *remain* in it." He wagged a finger and winked knowingly at them.

Ah. A catch.

"The Warden program, you see, is the product of two unique situations. The first is the government's trust in my ability to rehabilitate you into functioning members of society. Research has shown that criminals are generally isolated individuals, without any stake in society or reason to conform to the Party's new order."

He smiled broadly and straightened his uniform.

"The Warden program," he went on, "has been our answer to this in recent years and we have successfully managed to reintegrate over five thousand inmates back into American society. We have found that becoming part of a regimented chain of command, with heavy focus on teamwork and group based goals can serve to give law breakers the discipline they need to change their ways."

He took a deep breath as if knowing his next words would rouse the inmates. He'd clearly given this same speech many times before.

"The second is the need for an in game force to represent the Party in Nova Online." The Governor waved his hands as if calming down a series of excited cheers from the crowd, though there were none.

"I know, I know," he continued. "Nova Online. Most played video game in history. Largest in-game universe in history. Best...well, everything in history, really. Just the name inspires awe, does it not? And now you're being offered the opportunity not just to play this game, but to become an integral part of it! Please, please, do contain your enthusiasm."

Nova Online? A force to represent the Party? Kaiden thought that a bit rich seeing as the Party's system had just wrongfully thrown him in jail. He wasn't sure what to think of this news. He'd heard of Nova Online, of course – who hadn't heard of the fully immersive sci-fi MMORPG that dominated the headlines? – but he'd never played it.

He loved gaming. Had been something of an addict while growing up, but his father's sudden death had forced him to drop out of his first semester of college and support himself. It had been a devastating blow, since he had no other family. His mother had died during the Great Test, when the world had fallen into chaos and war, before the Party had won and stabilised the region.

Since his father's death, he hadn't had anything close to spare time; the lack of an education meant the only jobs he was eligible for were data entry roles, which forced him to work inhuman amounts of overtime just to make rent each month. As far as Kaiden had been concerned, videos games were a luxury of the past. A remnant of happier days. Until now, it seemed.

"Now, does anyone here know anything about what wardens do?" The Governor asked, snapping Kaiden's attention back to the present. "No one? Truly?" He shook his head. "Well, buckle up, then. It's story time."

The Governor smirked as the two dozen men stared at him with rapt attention.

"In-game credits in Nova have a real-world value. As such, any transactions that occur are taxable. Now, you've lived outside this prison. You know the great lengths our government goes to, the great lengths the *Party* goes to, in order to maintain this utopia of ours. Free social programs, basic income assistance, a home for every family – oh, and protection. Protection from fear-mongering terrorists, from chaos-loving rebels, and, of course, from lowly criminals."

He chuckled.

"No offense, but criminals such as, well, yourselves. As you can imagine, it takes a good deal of money to support all of this. Seeing as Nova Online represents the world's fourth largest GDP each year, you can imagine that's a lot of money. That's where the Warden program comes in." He smiled from ear to ear, looking positively giddy.

Probably just excited to hear himself talk some more.

"The job of a warden is to keep Nova a safe place for players to game and trade. When the players trade, money changes hands. When money changes hands, taxes are paid. When taxes are paid, the Party gets funded. When the Party gets funded, our utopia stays strong and everyone is better off for it. And, lucky day, you all now have the chance to become an essential part of this cycle. You get the chance to be wardens."

At the last line there were some grumbles from the guards stationed around the room.

"Now, now," The Governor said, gesturing for quiet. "The Warden program was originally only for government employees. Only for good, hardworking folks like your guards here. But – and you'd all best thank your lucky stars for this – there's simply too much work these days. The Party needs help. It has enough staff to fill the upper ranks – the officers, the commanders, the essential staff – but there's a growing need for fodder. For worker drones. Simply put, for you."

It was beginning to make sense. Kaiden's heart quickened at the thought of it. It sounded like work, sure, but...better than being in an empty box all day.

"The other inmates here will have spare time to reminisce about their crimes. You lot, on the other hand, will be working. Hard and long. Day in and day out, you will be serving the general populace of Nova Online as a warden, and ensuring the players enjoy themselves and money keeps changing hands. In return, you all will learn how to become functioning members of society again, and you will significantly shorten your stay at my humble facility." The Governor paused, then smiled at them. "How does that sound, gentlemen?"

There was silence for a moment, then one man mumbled his approval. Then another, and another, until the room echoed with a half-hearted cacophony of "okays" and "why nots?" Not an inspiring chorus, by any means, but a 'yes' all the same.

Kaiden didn't join them. Not because he wasn't excited – the thrumming of his heart slamming into the back of his ribcage was all too clear an indication that he was – but because he'd finally seen an opportunity to earn his freedom. Perhaps this Warden program was finally a way for him to get the guys in charge to listen to him. As a warden, it sounded like he'd be working below real government employees. People who could help. Kaiden would bide his time, earn a name for himself, impress his superiors and gain their trust. Then maybe they would listen to him, and consider re-opening his case.

It was barely a glimmer of hope, but it was enough. Perhaps he'd somehow be able to prove his innocence. He hadn't killed Bernstein. Now, maybe, he had a way to show the Party they'd made a mistake. Maybe that wasn't much, but staring down fifty years in state lockup, it was enough.

"It warms my heart to hear you're all excited to join my little program," The Governor said, waving the room back to quiet. "There's just one little catch."

Kaiden swallowed hard, along with several others.

"You've passed the psychological evaluation, qualifying you for the Warden program. But if you want to stay in the program, you have to earn your spot. You have to prove you're good enough."

Silence followed The Governor's declaration. As if relishing the drama, he let slip a small smile.

"The test will be first thing tomorrow morning, gentlemen. Sleep well."

Chapter Three

As it happened, Kaiden did not sleep well.

A guard's voice had come across the loudspeaker announcing quiet hours, and shortly after, the roaring clamor of cell block G-1 had fallen silent. Moments later, the lights throughout the facility had faded, one by one, dimming until all that remained of them was a spectral image on Kaiden's eyelids when he blinked.

Inmates were one to a cell, which made sense considering there was hardly room for more than Kaiden, his cot set into the wall, and a hole-in-the-floor toilet. Alone in his cell, in the quiet dark, he'd been left with only his thoughts. Not a happy fact, that.

The past few days had been...hectic, to put it lightly. In all actuality they'd been a complete and utter mess.

The whole ordeal had begun innocently enough. On his way home from work Kaiden had stopped to pick up groceries for Bernstein, as he did one or two times a week. Nothing exceptional about that. That was, until he'd found Bernstein's front door broken and shattered and, a few steps inside, his body in the same state.

Kaiden would have vomited right then and there, but his adrenaline had kicked in. He had rushed to his fallen friend and cradled him in his arms, but it was too late.

He didn't know how long he sat there, holding his friend, thoughts swirling in his head as he tried to figure out what to do. Not that it mattered. The decision was made for him when the police stormed the house. A baton had slammed across Kaiden's skull, and the next thing he'd known, he was in a holding cell and the world thought him a murderer.

Not that that made any sort of sense. He'd had no reason to kill anyone, least of all Bernstein. From a logical standpoint, Bernstein paid Kaiden to run errands for him throughout the week. That was money Kaiden sorely needed. But beyond logic, from a purely emotional standpoint, killing Bernstein made even less sense. After all, he'd been his friend. Or the closest thing to a friend he'd had time for.

Kaiden's coworkers had always ignored him, angry that he made them look bad by working so hard. Meanwhile, management refused to promote him based on his less than exemplary first semester departure from college. He'd needed a degree to be promoted, but money to get a degree. It'd been a vicious cycle. One Kaiden had seen few ways out of. Bernstein had been a way out of the cycle.

The money he'd paid Kaiden – far too much for the services rendered, certainly – meant that soon Kaiden would have saved enough to take online classes. He could have started working toward a degree again, and one day, a better job. That was the future Kaiden had imagined for himself. It wasn't much, but it was a start. A step in the right direction. Instead, he lay in his cot, tossing and turning and all too aware that his future had been thoroughly flushed down the drain.

For the life of him, he couldn't imagine who had killed Bernstein, or why. He'd been a quiet, peculiar old man. He didn't bother anyone, or really leave his house, for that matter. He'd stayed inside, working away on his computer. Despite his age, Kaiden had shared a love of gaming with the old man.

Kaiden's past as a gamer had appealed to Bernstein and the two of them had spent many a late night reminiscing about games whose servers had long been shut down. Or working on mind puzzles. Aside from gaming, that had seemed to be Bernstein's favorite hobby. Loved a good puzzle, did that man. And he'd rope Kaiden into them, too, when he was stuck on one or needed a fresh perspective.

Considering his lack of any sort of life outside of work, Kaiden had appreciated his time with the old man. It was, at the very least, social interaction that didn't revolve around the monotony of his data entry day – and night – job. And he was good at the puzzles, too. A trait that Bernstein had encouraged. "The obvious answer is often a distraction," he'd loved to say when they were tackling a particularly challenging puzzle. "True answers are found when one digs deeper."

Kaiden didn't know who had murdered Bernstein, or why, but alone in the dark of his cell, he resolved to find out. To do justice by the old man, first and foremost, but to clear his own name as well.

It would be a long and difficult process, he didn't doubt. First, he'd have to gather the evidence to prove his innocence. Then he'd have to convince someone, anyone, to believe him. And then, with any luck, the courts would reevaluate his case. It would all start the next morning with passing The Governor's test.

After a restless night, breakfast in prison had been...interesting. A hot, home-cooked meal of bacon and eggs, with a side dish of toast. Or that's what Kaiden had pretended as he'd forced down an alarmingly warm glass of EazyMealz brand "nutrient-filled, low-fat" Cup-o'-Breakfast™.

Even now, a solid forty-five minutes later, the taste stuck to his tongue, hardening like concrete left to set. Kaiden did his best to swallow the remnants of 'breakfast' while The Governor introduced them to the Warden program wing of the prison.

"This is the warden ward," he said with a chuckle. "The warden *ward*. It's a play on...see what we did...never mind." He waved irritably. "All Warden program business will be conducted in this facility."

Whatever funding the government had set aside for the Warden program was obviously considerable. Everything in this wing of the prison was brand new, or darn near it. Kaiden was waved through a security scanner and even it must have been new, as the infuriating *ding* of its green check mark played in a slightly different tone.

"And here," The Governor said, leading the group into a darkened space. "is what we like to call the pod farm."

An army of egg-shaped full immersion virtual reality pods

spanned the length and width of the room, which, as Kaiden realized, was an unknown distance. As far as he could see it was all low, red overhead lights and the silhouettes of VR pods. Air conditioning poured into the room from above with a constant whooshing, while the pods themselves vented hot air, no doubt from the strain of running the graphic powerhouse that was Nova Online.

These are powerful machines, Kaiden thought, admiring the technology. No lag or technical limitations to ruin their experience. Kaiden had seen Bernstein's pod once, though it had been a much older model. Truly, these ones were top of the line.

"As you can see, some of the pods are already occupied. We keep wardens in-game and on watch all day, every day here." Kaiden looked closer and noticed many of the pods were dimly lit from within. Just enough light trickled through the tinted glass of the pods to reveal the form of each occupant. They lay still, as if asleep.

"So we're taking the test in the pods, then?" one of the inmates asked.

"Taking the test in the pods? Of course you are!" The Governor gestured to a section of unoccupied pods off to one side. "This batch is yours." Silence followed his words as they stared at him. He stared right back.

"Well, what are you waiting for? Get in. The test has already started."

Kaiden and the others burst into movement at that, rushing toward open pods and lying down inside.

"Last one to log in fails on general principle," The Governor taunted, watching their panic.

Kaiden found an unoccupied pod and pulled himself into it. A shadow momentarily blocked out the lights above, and he noticed the brute from yesterday had selected the next pod over. He wasn't getting in it, however. Instead, he stood fidgeting with his hands and staring at the pod. He was clearly nervous, and from his positioning, unclear how to enter the VR pod.

Kaiden felt himself frown. What, had the big man never seen a pod before? They'd been common now for years. Even non-gamers were somewhat familiar with them. Who was so out of touch they didn't even know how to get into a VR pod?

His loss, Kaiden thought to himself. One less person in the

test meant one less person to compete against. If he was going to prove his innocence, he needed all the advantages he could get. It was logical to let the big man flounder. It made sense. The reasoning was flawless. And yet, he couldn't do it. Before he could stop himself, the words had left his mouth.

"You get in from the other side."

The big man turned to look at him.

"Don't look at me. Get into the pod!" Kaiden could hear the other pods closing now, could imagine the inmates logging in to the game. Every moment he spent helping this stranger was a moment more that he risked being the last to log in.

Now in the pod, the big man looked as confused as ever.

"Flip the switch by your right hand," Kaiden shouted more than said, feeling himself drawing closer and closer to flunking out of the program.

"I'm not as dumb as I look," the big man growled. Kaiden's heart caught in his throat as the man shot him a glare that could have melted steel. "Sorry I didn't waste my life playing games." And with that, he flipped the switch and the glass casing of his pod slipped over to cover him.

Maybe I came on a bit too strong, Kaiden thought, mentally facepalming as he leaned back into his own pod. He'd just been trying to help – against his own better logic – and now he'd insulted the man. Great. Just what he needed.

His thoughts flashed back to the tattooed maniac who'd screamed at him the day before. Two enemies in just as many days. Things here were off to a great start.

"Tick tock." The Governor's voice echoed through the darkened room. Kaiden flicked the ignition switch for his pod. It closed around him and then the NextGen Games logo filled his vision. A moment later, it faded and was replaced by a line of text.

Welcome to Nova Online

The title screen faded out to white and then Kaiden found himself staring at a character creation screen. An image of himself, reproduced in the realistic graphics of Nova Online stood before him, looking around idly and shifting its weight from one foot to the other every couple of seconds.

My favorite part, Kaiden thought, taking in all the customization options. There were sliders for avatar height, weight, age, musculature, on and on. He took them all in, but even as he looked, the list just kept going. He even saw 'Left and right nostril width' at one point. Say one thing for Nova Online, say its character creation was robust. The choices seemed limitless. Except, Kaiden realized, they were all grayed out.

He tried to move the slider for character height. Nothing happened.

What gives?

Even his avatar name was already set to 'Kaiden.'

So much for 'Wrongly Accused Warden 67,' he thought, trying to make light of the situation.

The character creation screen grayed out and a popup message appeared.

Character creation locked to warden account guidelines. Continue to game?

Well, that's no fun. Kaiden clicked the 'no' option and the character creation screen reappeared.

It can't be that easy, can it?

It wasn't.

A moment later, the popup returned.

Character creation locked to warden account guidelines. Continue to game?

Kaiden almost clicked 'no' again simply out of spite, but he didn't want to be the last into the game. Failing out of the program for being late seemed about the worst way to go.

Mumbling to himself, he clicked the 'yes' option.

The screen went white once more and Kaiden Moore entered Nova Online.

Chapter Four

It was safe to say NextGen Games had gone the extra mile in designing a fully immersive virtual reality experience for Nova Online. Some would say it was a mile too far. Kaiden couldn't help but think there was some merit to that argument, considering he was currently wiping a drill sergeant's spit off his face. It was a strange nuance to include in the game's design.

"Do you know what a line is, Private?"

Kaiden barely had a chance to take in the vast, metal-walled space surrounding him before the man had jumped down his throat. His ears were still ringing and the sergeant showed no sign of stopping. Seemed the man took his role-playing seriously. Perhaps he was an NPC.

"I said do you know what a line is, Private?"

"Yes, I know what a line is—"

"Then fall in before I fail you for wasting my time!" The sergeant cuffed him on the side of the head and Kaiden took off at a sprint toward a rapidly forming line of new recruits. Lucky for him, the pain setting in the game seemed to be at its lowest point, so there was no pain, only a feeling of impact. *One less thing to worry about, I guess.*

"Run! Run! Run! Move those legs!" The drill sergeant dogged him every step of the way, screaming loudly as Kaiden simultaneously marveled at the realism of Nova Online and shook the ringing from his ears. As he reached the line, a light flared to his left and the silhouette of a freshly spawning player materialized inside of it. The drill sergeant's head snapped toward the sight like a wolfhound catching a scent, and then he was off, already inhaling for another round of head-splitting screaming.

As soon as he was gone, a line popped up into Kaiden's view.

Location discovered: WCSS *Anakoni*
Class: Carrier
Current Assignment: Greater Spiral Arm System
Commanding Officer: Captain Ava Thorne
Faction Alignment: Warden Corps

Quick facts: The Greater Spiral Arm System is designated as a 'Starting Zone'. The threat level of this system is low and overall challenge rating is reduced. Level cap is in effect; current level cap is 25. To progress further, seek out more difficult zones - or don't, you might live longer.

So I'm on a ship? A big ship, from the looks of it.

Standing in formation, back straight and hands at his sides, Kaiden finally had a moment to think. NextGen Games was all about immersive minimalism, he knew, and looking at his heads-up display, it showed. 'Less menu, more game,' as they put it.

Focusing on the edges of his vision, Kaiden could see two small bars – one green, the other blue, denoting his health and stamina, respectively. In green text, numbers over his health bar showed he was at one hundred percent, but his stamina bar was depleted a bit. From running into formation, probably. There were also two icons. The first was labeled "settings", while the second, a power button, needed no label. That was clearly the logout button. Minimalist, indeed, Kaiden thought.

Out of curiosity, he clicked the settings icon, focusing with his eyes. A menu appeared showcasing many of the options he'd expect to find in a game. He ignored most of them, however, opting to open the one he found most interesting: his character sheet.

Character
Name: Kaiden
Race: Human
Level: 1

Class: Warden
Attributes:
Strength: 10 *Intelligence:* 10
Endurance: 10 *Perception:* 10
Dexterity: 10 *Unassigned:* 0
Abilities:
None
Perks:
None

Well, I'm looking awfully neutral. Not that that wasn't to be expected on his first login to the game. *Hopefully I can find an opportunity soon to earn some experience and start building my character.*

He closed out the character sheet, and his eyes were drawn to the last feature of his heads-up display. It was a minimap. Pretty run of the mill, it was a small circle in the bottom of his screen. A dot in the middle of it no doubt denoted him, while the yellow blips moving around on the map must've been his fellow recruits and the drill sergeants. At the very edge of the map Kaiden could just make out the far wall of the hangar they were in.

That could come in handy.

Looking back to the center of his vision, Kaiden's eyes drifted over a distant drill sergeant screaming at a recruit. Unintentionally, he left his eyes on the man for a moment. Faint wording appeared above him.

Dawson
Warden Drill Sergeant
Class: Power Warden
Faction: Warden Corps
Level: 15

Quick facts: Wardens are often described as the in-game police force for the Nova Universe. Whether collecting trade tariffs or rescuing stranded or endangered players, the Warden Corps is near universally respected.

Interesting. So I can learn more about a person by focusing on them for a moment?

As the drill sergeant continued to sprint and scream, wrangling new players into formation, Kaiden took a moment to study the inside of the ship. The game already told him he'd spawned on the starship WCSS *Anakoni*, but apparently they'd spawned specifically in its hangar. Not a hundred paces away the vast, empty expanse of space loomed before them. Easily forty feet high and twice as wide, two massive hangar doors lay open to the stars.

Except 'open' might not have been the right word for it. A faint, glowing field covered the doors. Some sort of magnetized barrier, Kaiden assumed. He and the other recruits were still breathing, which meant whatever the field was, it was doing a fine job of keeping the air in.

Inside the hangar, everything was metal. The floors, the walls, even the roof, far above. Various lines and lanes had been painted across the floor in colors ranging from white to bright yellow. Denoting flight lines, Kaiden assumed, eyes turning to a small fleet of what looked to be shuttles and attack craft aligned on the far side of the hangar.

As he watched, a pilot climbed into the cockpit of one of the more aggressive looking ships.

WCSS Skirmisher N-38
Class: Skirmisher
Faction Alignment: Warden Corps

With a whirring whine its engines fired up, then lifted the ship straight up into the air. A moment later and it had slipped forward, straight through the glowing field and out into the void beyond. The ship tilted next, directing its engine away from the hangar doors, then launched forward in a flash of light. For a moment Kaiden was blinded, his vision seared to pure white. When he could see again, the ship was nothing more than a gray speck and a dissipating thruster plume as it dwindled into the distance.

Kaiden had to stop himself from smiling. Sure, he was in the middle of having his eardrums blown out by screaming drill sergeants, and sure, he was playing this game from a state penitentiary, but he had to admit, seeing that ship explode away to some distant destination had been downright cool.

Nova Online was going to be his gateway to freedom, and he

had some serious work to do, but that didn't mean he couldn't also enjoy himself a little bit, right?

"You are not here for fun and games. Do you understand me?"

Kaiden was dragged back to the present by Sergeant Dawson. The biggest and loudest of the drill sergeants, he was standing and shouting at the recruits. He bared his teeth, the pearly whites stark against his dark skin.

"I said do you understand me?"

An unsure chorus of 'yes, sirs' trickled out from the recruits.

"Louder!"

"Yes, sir!"

More of a shout this time.

"Louder!"

"Yes, sir!"

Kaiden joined in now, if only to get the sergeant to stop yelling. His ears were ringing again.

"Very good, recruits." He lowered his voice a smidgeon. On a scale of one to ten he was still somewhere around a twelve, but it was an improvement. Kaiden figured he'd only suffer partial hearing loss now.

"My name is Gunnery Sergeant Dawson, but you will refer to me as sergeant, sir, or gracious overlord. Your choice." He paced the deck in front of them, hands behind his back. "Now, Captain Thorne is the commanding officer on this carrier. She's an outstanding leader, straight-laced, loyal, and clever as they come. She's one heck of a battle-hardened veteran, too. Both in-game, and without. But Captain Thorne isn't your direct commanding officer; you're way, way, *way* too low down the food chain for that. No, no, no." He smiled long and wide.

"No, recruits, you've been lucky enough to have me assigned to you. I hope you will find my hospitality most agreeable. If not—" He paused, leaning toward one recruit close enough to touch him. "You're welcome to leave." He gestured toward the gaping hangar doors and the void beyond. "There's the door. Don't let me stop you."

Sergeant Dawson waited, staring at them as if personally offended by what he saw. Kaiden took those few blissful moments of silence to stare back at the man. He wore a suit of the most hi-tech armor Kaiden had ever seen. Overlapping gray metal plates fit his form perfectly, covering most of his body, but still bending and moving freely as needed. There were no visible wires, but a series of lights on the chest plate and wrist clearly indicated some sort of control mechanism. A sleek helmet fit snugly on the sergeant's head, and could presumably become airtight in an emergency.

Or for spacewalking. When do we get to do that part?

All in all, the gray-on-slightly-lighter-gray camo almost made the sergeant blend entirely in with the matte metal covering every inch of the hangar. The more Kaiden thought about it, the more he realized that was probably exactly the idea.

There was one part of the uniform that stood out, however. The shoulders bore light gray markings, emblazoned with the sigil of the wardens, the same crossed hammers on a shield as the pin Kaiden had been given on his first day.

He looked down at his own shoulder. He'd spawned in armor similar to the sergeant's, but now that he paid attention, he found it lacked the sigil of the wardens.

Basic Warden Armor
Durability: 100%
Stimulant Chamber Cooling Slots: 2 (Locked)

"Seeing as you all are wardens, or aspire to be, you've spawned in your armor. Accustom yourselves to it, as it will save your life many times in the coming days and months."

Basic warden armor. That made sense, he figured. It was made from some sort of advanced metal.

The police had been using body armor similar to it in the real world for ages now. The technology in Nova Online was loosely based on predictions of the far future, but that didn't mean it actually had to make sense. That was the benefit of being in a video game. Some things just worked because the game said so.

His armor also came with a helmet, just like the sergeant's. It fit so comfortably on his head it'd taken a moment to realize he was even wearing it.

"You may have noticed," Sergeant Dawson said, still shouting, "your armor comes with a stimulant cooling chamber in the wrist. This chamber is capable of holding two stimpacks that, when activated, will instantly heal twenty-five percent of your health. Then a two-minute cooldown will kick in before you can use another stimpack. But you recruits don't need to worry about all this. Your stimulant chambers are empty, and will remain so until you've earned the right to carry a stimpack."

Another sergeant stepped in front of Kaiden, and then something solid thudded into his chest, nearly knocking him over. He didn't so much catch it as bend around it, but he did stop it from falling to the floor. Straightening up and unfurling his arms, he found he was holding a hammer.

Warden Battle Hammer
One-Handed
Base Damage: 5 bludgeoning, 7 smashing

Quick facts: Warden hammers may expend charge to attack with special abilities. Warden shields will build charge by absorbing damage. Your warden class implants will store charge, depleting at a rate of 5 every 30 seconds.

Now *that* was useful information. Things were starting to make a bit more sense now. Kaiden had heard Bernstein mention wardens in Nova Online before, but he'd never explained how the class worked. Now that Kaiden was beginning to understand, he felt a bit more grounded. Nova Online was a revolutionary MMORPG, but it was still an MMORPG. And when it came to those, well, Kaiden boasted his fair share of experience. Feeling a renewed confidence, Kaiden looked down at his hammer, this time studying the weapon and not looking for additional information.

The name 'hammer' hardly seemed to do it justice. It was as much a weapon as it was a work of art. The handle, just long enough to fit two hands, rose to meet the two-headed business end of the weapon. Made of some sort of light but clearly sturdy metal, the heads were positioned back to back. Each was roughly cylindrical in shape, though they narrowed slightly as they approached the ends meant for smashing. To better channel the force of the impact, Kaiden figured. Less surface area striking the enemy meant more force driven into a concentrated area. It was simple physics.

Between the two opposite-facing heads of the hammer rested a smooth circle of fine metal. Thin in construction, it was hollow, and almost looked like a chamber meant to hold something. Or maybe to channel something, Kaiden realized, remembering what he'd just read about the hammer expending charge for special attacks.

He wrapped a hand around the hammer's handle – seemingly coated in some sort of semi-solid gel – and it molded to fit his grip. All told, the weapon was as long as his forearm and, despite its size, weighed surprisingly little. Made of some futuristic alloy, no doubt.

"These," Sergeant Dawson shouted as the others tossed more hammers at the recruits. "Are your battle hammers. They're good for hitting things." Next, a series of what appeared to be bracers were thrown at the recruits.

"And these are your shields. They're good for stopping things from hitting you."

Kaiden slid it onto his left wrist. It locked into place via a series of small clamps, then contracted until it fit comfortably.

Warden Shield
Damage: +10 resistance to melee attacks, +10 resistance to energy attacks
Current charge: 0/100 units (Locked)

Quick facts: When too much damage is absorbed, this shield will overload and shut down for 30 seconds.

Not much of a shield, Kaiden thought, staring at the device. How was he supposed to block any attacks with this? It was far too small.

"When your shield is equipped, you simply have to think 'on' and it will turn on. Think you can handle that?"

On. Kaiden thought the word and sure enough, his bracer sparked to life. A glowing light poured from it, then spread out in front of him in waves of crackling, fizzing energy. It grew and stretched until it had formed into the distinct shape of a rounded shield. Next, the energy seemed to solidify. If Kaiden didn't look too closely, he could almost mistake it for blue-tinged glass. Every so often a little crackle of electricity jolted through it with a faint hiss.

The bracer felt no heavier with the shield turned on.

Impressive.

Next, he had an idea. If the shield turned on with a thought, could it...? Yup. Kaiden merely had to think the word *'off'* and the shield flickered once, then disappeared, returning his bracer to a dormant state. Okay, he had to admit that was cool. And useful, too. No buttons or switches required. All he had to do was think.

"Your shield and hammer work together," Sergeant Dawson said when everyone had stopped flicking their shields on and off. "There's virtually no limit to the creative ways they can be used. But, considering the look of you lot, I'll keeps things simple. When you block an attack with your shield, it will absorb some of the blocked energy. You can then use that energy to perform special moves – abilities you'll learn as you level up."

Kaiden's mind was already filled with ideas on how that could be utilized. The first of them was too good to be true, but he had to try.

Flicking his shield back on, he held it in front of him, then gave it a good knock with his hammer. The energy that made up the shield flared at the hammer's impact, then thrust the weapon away, almost like two magnets repelling each other.

"You cannot charge energy by hitting your own shield," the sergeant said, eyeing Kaiden with a smirk. "Though if you want to go on hitting yourself, don't let me stop you, recruit."

Well, sorry, Kaiden thought, feeling his cheeks burning as the others turned to stare at him. *I got lost in all the oh-so-detailed instructions you've given.*

"Why don't you try hitting each other's shields next?" Based on Sergeant Dawson's expression, it didn't take a genius to tell there was some reason that wouldn't work either. "Only players, NPCs or other mobs marked as neutral or hostile toward you can charge your shield. No dice with allies or party members, I'm afraid. You'll have to build charge by getting into the thick of the action.

"Today will be your first taste of some action, and for many of you, your last. For this test, you'll be given no abilities or warden class variations. If you want either of those, you'll have to level up and earn them. In the meantime, I suggest you get awfully familiar with your hammers and shields. Along with your fellow recruits."

Sergeant Dawson pointed to a waiting shuttle, a loading ramp extending from its rear.

"It's time to see who's worthy of joining my beloved Warden Corps," he said, his ever-present scowl replaced briefly with a smile. "Load up, recruits."

Chapter Five

_____

Achievement Unlocked!
Novice Voyager - 50 EXP gained!
You've begun your first voyage out into the universe.
Here's to many more! Just watch out for asteroids. And
pirates. And...well, you'll figure it out.

At any other time, Kaiden would have found the surprise achievement pretty cool. But currently, he had a more pressing issue.

"Your weapons and your fellow recruits will be the only
things not trying to kill you today." Sergeant Dawson had said
something to that effect shortly before their shuttle departed,
but now, huddled in with the other recruits, Kaiden wasn't so
sure that was true. Whoever the woman sitting across from him
was, she clearly wanted him dead. Hadn't stopped scowling at
him since he'd sat down.

He'd boarded the shuttle along with the others to find seven-
teen more recruits already waiting within. Recruits from the
other wing of the prison, he'd realized, as they were all women.

More people I have to beat in this test.

They wore the same uniforms as the men, carried the same
weapons, and for the most part, looked the same degrees of
worried, scared, and confused as did everyone else.

Except for _her_.

Based on her avatar she couldn't have been much older than

himself, with dark hair and eyes to match. A gentle slope to her features gave her an inquisitive look, as if she were studying everything around her.

Kaiden hadn't had a crush on anyone since high school, but in different circumstances – another life, maybe – he might have tried to strike up conversation with her.

But he had a test to pass, and there was no time for distractions. Besides, they were both prisoners of the state with virtually no control over their own lives. Oh, and there was the little fact that she hated him.

Or that was what her expression said, at least.

If eyes could bore holes, Kaiden's head would've been nothing but pulp, drilled through the wall of the shuttle behind him and left floating in the eternal abyss of space. Thankfully, his head remained firmly attached to his shoulders. He took advantage of this fact to focus on her a moment to see what information the game would give him.

Zelda Yoshida
Warden Recruit
Class: None
Faction: None
Level: 1

Thanks for that. Real helpful.

She scowled deeper and cracked her knuckles, eyes never leaving Kaiden. Feeling his cheeks go hot, he swallowed hard, and for the second time in two days found a spot on the far wall to thoroughly study.

"Approaching the SS *Dalcinae*, sir," the pilot said from up front, half-turning to call over his shoulder.

"Well, alright, then." Sergeant Dawson turned to the recruits. "The situation is as follows." He pointed up to the front of the ship, through the cockpit to a distant point of light. As they drew closer, it resolved itself into the wreckage of some sort of ship.

"Earlier today, the merchant vessel *Dalcinae* broadcast an emergency signal reporting a voidspawn incursion within their vessel. Shortly thereafter, the ship experienced a lethal pressure breach. There were no survivors." He spoke in a matter-of-fact manner, hardly even giving pause to those who had been killed.

Kaiden wondered if they were non-player characters, but then a much more disturbing thought took over. The sergeant had said 'voidspawn incursion.' Kaiden didn't know what that meant, but he knew it didn't sound good. He swallowed hard as his mind had far too much fun conjuring up exactly how terrifying a 'voidspawn' could be.

"This sky is under Warden Corps jurisdiction, and I don't know about you, but I don't tolerate voidspawn in my sky. Now, we know those tentacled freaks can survive the vacuum of space, so don't expect the depressurization of the ship to have done anything other than inconvenience them. We slapped a patch on the breach and the *Dalcinae's* systems auto-restored gravity, temperature, and pressure to normal levels." Sergeant Dawson flicked a switch on the wall and the lights in the shuttle faded to a dim red.

"This is where you come in," he said with another slight smile. As he did, the stars outside spun as the pilot rotated the shuttle into docking position.

"The *Dalcinae* was carrying a particularly valuable cargo of vibranium crystals, which was, most unfortunately, scattered all over the place by the pressure breach. You, recruits, will board the *Dalcinae*, exterminate any voidspawn that remain, and then bring me no less than five vibranium crystals each. For every extra crystal you bring, you will be handily rewarded."

Quest: Collect 5 vibranium crystals
Expected difficulty: Novice
Reward: Initiation into the Warden Corps, +200 EXP
Notes: Additional crystals will award bonus EXP

Something large shuddered within the walls of the shuttle and an electric whirring drew Kaiden's eyes out the window to where a long, accordion-style tunnel was extending from their shuttle to the docking bay of the *Dalcinae*.

"Should you fail to personally bring me one, two, three, four, five crystals," he counted the numbers off on his fingers, "you fail this test and will be removed from my corps. Should you die while attempting to complete this mission, you fail this test and will be removed from my corps. Should you do anything other than board that ship, kick some voidspawn rear, and return victorious, you fail. Do you understand me, recruits?"

There was no hesitation this time as they shouted in unison.

"Yes, sir!"

A green light flicked on above Sergeant Dawson's head. He pulled a lever on the wall and at the rear of the shuttle a door slid open to reveal the accordion tunnel, now connected to the *Dalcinae*. Air rushed in to fill the space as the sergeant crossed his arms.

"Well alright, then, recruits. Time to earn your keep."

~

I can do this. It's just a game, Kaiden told himself over and over, gritting his teeth as he crossed the accordion tunnel, each step taking him closer to the *Dalcinae*. Somehow it didn't do much to make him feel better. NextGen had done too fine a job with this game. Sure, he might've been playing it, but it felt like he was *living* it.

The situation was fake; the world around him, fake. Even the voidspawn – whatever horrors they were – were fake. But his terror? His fear? The adrenaline pumping through his veins? That was real. "Best adventure game of the decade", one company had rated Nova Online, but right about now, Kaiden found himself wondering why it hadn't been named "best horror game of the decade".

He'd been sitting at the rear of the shuttle, which meant he was first across the tunnel. The other recruits followed him in silence and even Sergeant Dawson, usually so boisterous, had fallen quiet, face set in a stern frown.

Kaiden clenched his hammer tight and took another step closer to the *Dalcinae*. The ship's docking port was still closed, but he'd been instructed to cross over to it. A few more steps and he was there, breath caught in his throat. This was insanity. What kind of test was this, anyway?

It's just a game, he reminded himself, and once again, it did little to help.

The rest of the recruits were in the tunnel behind him now, the sergeant watching from the shuttle. He gave a curt nod, then the door in front of him slipped closed with a hiss of air. They were sealed in.

Sergeant Dawson's voice came over the speakers.

"When that door opens, I want you to put the fear of humanity in those tentacled abominations, you got that?"

Tentacled abominations, Kaiden thought. *That's...inspiring*. He shivered, imagining what the voidspawn looked like.

"Door opening in ten...nine..."

Kaiden shook out his arm, readying himself to charge in, and thought '*on*.' His shield flickered into existence.

"Eight...seven..."

I can do this, I can do this.

"Six...five..."

I have to do this. For Bernstein. For my freedom.

"Four...three – oh, and recruits? This is a novice-level mission. Try not to embarrass yourselves, huh?"

A hiss of air shot through the airlock and the *Dalcinae's* door stuttered into movement, groaning slow and tired as it raised into the ceiling. The sound echoed out and away down the halls of the *Dalcinae*, fading into the distance like the howl of some celestial giant.

Fighting the chill of ice in his veins, Kaiden huddled down behind his shield, hammer at the ready. Virtual reality didn't make his fear any less real.

I can do this.

The door was open a good six inches now, moving slow and sure. As it did, Kaiden squinted into the darkness beyond, sure a horde of voidspawn would come pouring out. From the ceiling a light flicked on – briefly illuminating the docking bay – then right back off. In the moment, Kaiden took in a metal floor covered in debris. Remnants from the pressure breach, he figured.

Finally, when the door stuttered to a stop in the ceiling, a passageway leading deeper into the ship was revealed at the back of the room.

Location discovered: SS *Dalcinae*
Class: Medium Transport (Hauler)
Faction Alignment: Neutral

The lights flicked off again and the docking bay fell into darkness. It felt like some giant mouth, opening and waiting for Kaiden to step in. Foul air escaped from within, mingling with the cold, sterile air of their own shuttle, then smothering it entirely.

I can do this. Kaiden steeled his nerves and took a step forward. Then another. As he did, the recruits behind him shuffled forward too. Another step. And one more toward the looming dark ahead.

"What's the button to sneak?" one of the recruits whispered from behind.

"Just crouch, you idiot. Like in real life," another hissed back.

"This game needs to come with an instruction manual..."

Kaiden tuned out the others, then lifted his shield as he neared the end of the tunnel. The glowing light from its energy barrier trickled into the room. Enough light to guide him forward, but hardly enough to do much beside make him a target for whatever was undoubtedly hiding in the dark.

Every inch of his body felt exposed. Vulnerable. He could already imagine tentacles slipping silently through the trash-covered floor, rising up at his ankles, wrapping themselves around his legs and—

Something nudged his shin and Kaiden's heart near burst from his chest. He jumped to one side, then slammed his hammer down. Something crunched beneath the blow, but as Kaiden drew back to strike again, nothing moved.

Just trash. Just debris. He took a deep breath and tried to shake the fear from his thoughts. *I'm scaring myself. Imagining something where there's nothing.*

The lights stayed on for the most part, but were unstable, flickering as if they were strobe lights.

Emboldened by the fact Kaiden had yet to be tackled and strangled by some horror from the abyss, the other recruits began to trickle into the room. In the strobing lights their movements were choppy and quick.

"At least in here we're not getting yelled at," one of the recruits said, laughing. "I forget if I'm in prison, or joined the military. Am I right, boys?"

"Shh!" Kaiden shushed him with a look and a gesture.

Nothing had attacked them yet, but that didn't mean the room was safe.

"It's just a game, bro. Chill out."

"A game that can get us out of prison early. I'd consider that a bit more than a game," Kaiden said as he moved across the space, eyes locked on the passageway at the rear.

His foot hit upon something that rolled a few steps, clattering the whole way. A crystal, he realized, bending to pick it up. Its surface was a vibrant red, smooth as glass and warm to the touch. Kaiden slipped it into his inventory with a smile.

Vibranium crystals collected: 1/5

One down, four to go. Maybe this wouldn't be so difficult after all.

"Was that a crystal?" one of the recruits shouted, rushing over to Kaiden.

"Crystal?" another said, perking up. And just like that, their fear was forgotten as the recruits dropped to the floor, scouring the debris for more. A few found some, too. But in less than a minute there was nothing left but trash.

Kaiden waited for them to finish, then turned his eyes back to the passageway leading deeper into the *Dalcinae*. There was no avoiding it. They had to press on.

Kaiden kept his shield firmly in front of him as he inched closer to the passageway. Emergency lights did their best to cut through the darkness in the hallway, lining the walls a few inches above the floor and glowing a faint yellow.

As best as Kaiden could tell in the low lighting, the hallway had several doors on either side, then an intersection where it split into two directions.

We need to make a plan. Maybe form a wall, move down methodically.

"We're here to pass the test and shave time off our sentences," a recruit said, pushing past Kaiden and lighting the hallway with the blue glow of his shield. "So what are we waiting for?"

"Quiet!" Kaiden hissed, grabbing at the man. "We don't want to attract attention!"

The man shrugged off Kaiden's hand.

"Are you even sure there *are* voidspawn on this ship?" He looked around, then banged his hammer against the wall. It connected with a clang that echoed down the hallway and sent shivers through Kaiden's spine.

Certain an onslaught of voidspawn would come charging toward the sound, Kaiden readied himself in his best approximation of a fighting stance. However, all that came from the hallway was a long silence in which nothing happened, and then, the laughter of several recruits.

"This is just some stupid trick by the sergeant, isn't it?" one of them said, joining the first recruit in the hallway. "They're not going to kill us off on our first mission. They're testing to see if we're ballsy enough to be wardens."

"We should at least stay together," Kaiden said, but the rest of the recruits had apparently turned into fearless battle-hardened veterans and were pushing past him, spreading down the halls.

"So I guess we're doing this..." Kaiden shook his head, sighed, then followed the other recruits deeper into the *Dalcinae*.

Chapter Six

Docking Bay 01, Kaiden read, noting the lettering above the door as he reluctantly followed the other recruits out into the hall. He'd need to find his way back – something the other recruits seemed to have forgotten.

If they weren't going to work together, then he couldn't afford to fall behind and miss out on all the easy crystals. From his previous gaming experience, he figured the quest would have enough crystals for everyone, but some would be more dangerous to retrieve than others. The more 'safe' crystals he could retrieve, the less voidspawn he'd have to encounter.

Between the blue glow of everyone's shields and the yellow of the emergency lights, the surroundings no longer looked like a scene out of a horror film. The darkness was close on them, however, and as the group moved on, Kaiden felt it nipping at his heels. If he fell more than two strides behind it was as if he'd been abandoned entirely.

Safety in numbers, he told himself. *Or maybe we're just making ourselves a bigger target.*

As the hunt for crystals continued, the recruits spread out more and more, branching off down hallways or into side rooms. Despite Kaiden sticking with the largest group, they were soon spread thin. Within minutes, there were only eight of them. Thankfully, Zelda had gone off with another crew.

The big man was still with them, however. Kaiden had given

him a large berth so far. If their prior conversation was any indication, they weren't exactly on good terms.

Kaiden realized he still didn't know the man's name. He
focused on him for a moment.

Titus
Warden Recruit
Class: None
Faction: None
Level: 1

Titus, huh? An appropriately frightening moniker for the big
man. Even in-game he towered over everyone else, his muscles
on muscles all too visible even beneath his armor. Not that they
would help him here. Here, the massive man's strength stat was
the same as everyone else's. It was an oddly comforting thought.

"Well, this might be a problem," someone said from the front
of the group. Kaiden looked up to find the floor ahead of them
buckled and bent. Some sort of hydraulics were visible beneath.

It's not a floor at all, Kaiden realized, creeping closer.

"This is some sort of freight elevator," he said, peering
through its torn and bent surface and into the darkness beneath.
"Odds are it goes straight down to the cargo bay."

"Looks like it's seen better days," Titus said. He stepped
forward and gingerly pressed one foot on the edge of the buckled
floor. It groaned almost immediately. An electric hiss burst into
the air followed by a shower of sparks that tumbled downward,
fizzling from existence as they were swallowed up by the chasm.

"Maybe there's another way down?" he asked, turning back
toward the group. Before Kaiden could respond, a line of text
popped into his vision.

Channel Joined: SS *Dalcinae* general

There was a buzzing in his ears that popped and crackled and
then Sergeant Dawson's voice filled Kaiden's head.

"Seems like you're taking your sweet time in there, recruits."

He's talking through some sort of comms system in the armor, Kaiden
realized as the others reacted to the voice in their ears.

"Now, I'm nice and cozy over here. I can wait all day. But according to our scans, you can't. The *Dalcinae's* core was more damaged than we thought. The ship's power-hungry systems are going to start failing one by one."

A groan broke out through the ship. Rising from the lower decks, it echoed through the halls, then ended in a deep clang. Following the clang, several machines in the floor wound down, a faint humming Kaiden hadn't noticed before slowing, before stopping entirely.

Then the floor was slippery and his feet slid out from under him. But he didn't fall. Instead, he toppled forward, almost in slow motion. And floated.

"Yeah." Sergeant Dawson's voice returned in Kaiden's ear. "Looks like the gravity just gave out – though you probably noticed that."

You think? Kaiden flailed as he continued his slow spin, then bumped into the ceiling. All around him the other recruits were struggling similarly. One pushed off the ceiling and careened down toward the still-stable section of the floor.

"Hah!"

He landed with a cheer that quickly devolved into a groan as he bounced off and floated back up.

With the artificial gravity off, the lights seemed to find enough power to switch back on for a moment. They flickered rapidly on and off, casting the same strobe effect as before.

"How are we supposed to find any crystals like this?" a recruit said, kicking toward the nearest wall and moving basically nowhere.

"How are we supposed to defend ourselves like this?" Kaiden corrected him.

*If we were to be attacked right now...*He shook the thought from his mind.

The whirring in the floor kicked back up into a gentle hum and the lights clicked off.

"The gravity's coming back on!" Kaiden said, even as the gravity kicked back in and he face-planted onto the metal floor.

In the corner of his vision, his health bar flashed and dropped. The numbers above it now read ninety-five percent.

You're kidding me, right? That fall actually did damage?

"It's back? You got it back on?" The drill sergeant's voice

came through the comms distantly, as if he were away from the mic. A moment later it cleared up. "Alright, recruits. We're feeding the *Dalcinae* some of our power to keep it alive. Gravity should be restored."

"Uh, we might have a problem here," Titus said. Kaiden looked up, finding himself near Titus' hulking figure. While the artificial gravity was out, they must have drifted over the elevator because they had landed on the center of its damaged platform. The platform groaned and shook around them but seemed to hold steady.

Right up until it didn't.

The elevator shuddered violently then gave way entirely. It was as if the artificial gravity had gone out again, except much quicker, and in the opposite direction.

Kaiden descended into the darkness below, a brief trip ending in an echoing crash.

The good news was they'd found the cargo bay and it was *loaded* with vibranium crystals. All around, the gleaming red treasures lay scattered and spilled from a debris field of overturned crates.

The bad news was the fall had done a significant amount of damage. His health bar had turned from green to yellow and now read sixty-five percent. Which made sense, considering the hole they'd fallen through was a good distance above them.

The worse news was they'd also found the voidspawn. Or at least Kaiden couldn't imagine what else the monstrous masses of tentacles, teeth and spidery legs surrounding them could be. Sergeant Dawson had been quite clear about the horrors having tentacles, but why hadn't he mentioned the teeth? Kaiden shuddered. So. Many. Teeth.

The voidspawn were everywhere. Curled up on the floor, the shelves, even hanging from the ceiling. He couldn't get too good a look at them in the low yellow of the emergency lights, but what he did see was more than enough. No two looked the same, beyond the fact they all had tentacles, teeth like saw blades, and were variations on pink, gray and black. Some were large as a car, others no bigger than his head. To some degree, they all looked like an abominable mix between octopus and spider.

Kaiden focused on one for a moment and text faded in across his vision.

Voidspawn
Level: 1

Quick facts: While hard to quantify due to their great diversity, most voidspawn boast active abilities including Tentacle Whip and Binding Grasp, and passive abilities that allow them to hibernate to regain health or survive extreme conditions such as the vacuum of space.

The very worst part was that they appeared to be waking up.

One of the recruits' voices echoed down from above.

"Hey, I see crystals down there."

"Crystals?" said another. "Let's get down there!"

"He said crystals!"

"They found crystals!"

"Wait," Kaiden said. "Don't—"

But too late. The first recruit jumped down, hitting the floor with a heavy thump. Then came the others.

"You guys are idiots," Titus' deep voice boomed.

A chittering filled the air as the already waking voidspawn began to stir in haste. Tentacles, previously curled up tight, unfurled as if stretching. Teeth, previously still, gnashed together, preparing for the feast to come. The chittering rose to a fever pitch and all around the room, the voidspawn turned to face them, and opened their eyes.

Eyes.

Eyes on eyes on eyes. Each spawn was covered in random clusters of them. They caught the glowing blue light of the recruits' shields, a thousand pinpoints of light staring, unblinking, from the darkness.

All at once, Kaiden's minimap lit up in a flurry of red dots. Too many to count.

Kaiden's breath caught in his throat and his thoughts rushed in a mad frenzy. Adrenaline surged through him and he lowered his stance, preparing to take as many of the abominations with him as possible.

An inquisitive tentacle slipped along the floor, feeling its way forward through the dark.

"To hell with this," cried a recruit.

The recruit brought his hammer down on it with a wet

squelch and the tentacle was flattened into goo. There was a squeal of pain – and then chaos erupted. The spawn surged forward.

Kaiden ducked behind his shield as the front runners slammed into him. His shield held as combat text began to fill the bottom corner of his vision. Yet he didn't seem to be getting this charge resource he'd read about. Maybe that came later?

Kaiden leaned away as, just on the other side of the energy barrier, slimy flaps of skin retracted from a voidspawn's underside and a stinger as long as his hand plunged into the shield. It struck with a dull thump again and again, striking so fast Kaiden could hardly follow it.

Through his shield, Kaiden could make out a health bar above the voidspawn's head in the form of a thin green line.

Let's put that to the test.

Letting loose a battle cry, he brought his hammer down on the voidspawn.

Quick facts: A warden's basic melee attack can be used with no charge. It deals base damage and has no cooldown.

The notification ticked in his periphery. He continued to whack the creature over and over, draining its health bar; it flashed from green to yellow and then to red. Two messages popped into in the corner of his vision.

Voidspawn killed - 50 EXP gained!

Achievement Unlocked!
First Blood - 50 EXP gained!
You've killed your first opponent. As a warrior, you'll likely have to kill many more – unless they kill you first.

He ignored the text and raised his shield again as another voidspawn threw itself at him. He stepped into this one, bashing his shield into what was probably its face. The creature flattened against it, but its tentacles wrapped around, grabbing Kaiden by the shoulders.

You've been bound! Movement slowed by 50% until freed.

Another stinger plunged into his shield. With each strike the energy barrier wavered a bit, rippling like a pond assaulted by a barrage of stones.

How much longer before the shield overloaded? Kaiden remembered reading something about that when he'd received it, but he couldn't remember the specifics. Not with the voidspawn doing its best to impale him.

Kaiden stretched his shield out away from him and the tentacles were pulled from his shoulder.

Normal movement speed regained.

A few hammer strikes and the spawn's health bar flashed, turning yellow as it emptied a bit beyond halfway. This one was more powerful than Kaiden's last opponent; it was level two. One of its rubbery tentacles caught him across the torso.

His health bar flashed, then drained. It was now in the red, at forty-five percent.

I can't afford to get hit much more.

He slipped on some gore underfoot, falling onto his back. His shield arm stretched out wide, not protecting his body at all. The spawn took its chance, leaping above him. As it dropped, its stinger reared back, aiming for his chest.

This is it, Kaiden thought, fighting to raise his shield to no avail. So *much for my freedom—*

A hammer flashed above him, catching the leaping voidspawn dead center. The creature's health bar fell from yellow to zero as it burst in a spray of slime.

Voidspawn assisted kill - 25 EXP gained!

So I get experience for kills and assisted kills. Nice. Makes teamwork even more important.

His savior grabbed his shoulder and pulled him to his feet. Titus.

"We need a way out of here," the big man shouted, leaning in close. Even as he spoke, Kaiden saw how badly the battle was going. Two recruits already lay face down, their bodies almost entirely buried under a swarm of gray-pink flesh. The others were losing ground quickly, stumbling backward beneath a barrage of stingers, tentacles and teeth.

An idea sparked in Kaiden's mind.

"Gravity!" he shouted, barely holding back the screeching creatures with his shield.

"What about it?" Titus yelled.

"We need less of it!" Kaiden felt himself smile.

This might just be crazy enough to work.

"Sergeant Dawson?" he ventured, hoping he was listening.

"I'm here. What's going on in there?"

"We need you to cut the artificial gravity."

"What?"

"Just do it!"

"I don't take orders from you, recruit," the sergeant growled. Then, after a moment: "The power's cut."

Sure enough, even through the din of battle, Kaiden heard the gravity generators in the floor winding down.

"Aim for the gap left by the elevator," Kaiden shouted, then kicked off the floor with all his might, launching himself into the air. A moment later he soared through the hole and slammed into the ceiling. His health bar drained down to forty percent.

But he was out of the cargo bay!

Looking down, Kaiden watched as Titus followed almost his exact trajectory, then tucked a shoulder in and hit the ceiling. Two more recruits followed them.

"That was close," one said.

Moments later, a many-eyed monstrosity rose from the blackness. And another, clinging to the first. More and more swarmed as a legion of tentacles wrapped around the edge of the hole. The first of them surged out of the cargo bay in a chittering frenzy.

Kaiden guessed that now they'd aggroed the mobs, the spawn would chase them down.

One recruit began scrambling along the wall. "Screw the program. I'm getting out of here!"

Titus tried to do the same, but couldn't get a grip on the

smooth metal wall. A tentacle grasped at him, stretching at his kicking foot.

"We don't have time for this," Kaiden said, pushing off and grabbing Titus in a bear hug. Spinning in the zero gravity, he pulled his knees up to his chest and placed his feet against the big man's back.

"What are you doing?" Titus said, but Kaiden had already made his decision.

"Get back to the shuttle!" he shouted, then pushed off. The force threw Titus back toward the docking bay, and Kaiden deeper into the ship.

"Turn the gravity back on, sergeant!" Kaiden yelled.

A moment later, the generators in the floor hummed back to life. Kaiden fell to the metal floor and slid several feet. He was on the far side of the elevator shaft now and had taken another chunk of damage in the fall.

The gravity caught hold of the voidspawn and pulled them back into the cargo bay. Barely a moment later, however, their tentacles found purchase around the pit and they began to pull themselves up.

"Don't let the shuttle leave without me!" Kaiden called.

"I don't wait for stragglers," Dawson said.

Kaiden cursed. He'd have to find another way back. The hole was too big to jump across, and it was filled with writhing voidspawn anyway.

Kaiden was left with no other option. He turned and ran.

His path was lit only by emergency lights and he had no idea where he was going. But the voidspawn chittering behind him left little time for anything other than a mad, fear-fuelled sprint as he plunged down the darkened corridor.

Chapter Seven

Sergeant Dawson's voice came over the comms again as Kaiden jogged through the darkened hallways of the *Dalcinae*.

"Time's running out, folks. Get back to the shuttle. And you'd better have five crystals with you. Understand?"

Several voices answered him. "Understood, sir."

The comms channel clicked closed and Kaiden was alone.

He slowed to a walk as his stamina bar fell to empty. Even if he wanted to keep running, he couldn't. The game didn't let him. The only good news was that his health appeared to be regenerating. Slowly, but surely.

I have to get four more vibranium crystals and find my way back to the shuttle. And now, I have to do it alone.

Navigating the corridors of the *Dalcinae* wasn't too daunting a concept. He'd already been using the guidance of his minimap and the signs leading him toward the docking bays. But this route was a new one, which meant it hadn't been cleared of voidspawn. Not that their old route was doing much better, he figured. Probably worse, if he was being honest.

Suddenly, a notification appeared.

Achievement Unlocked!
Lucky Escape - 50 EXP gained!
You've survived your first voidspawn swarm. It won't be your last.

Level 2 Achieved!
Max health and stamina increased
+3 stat points

Shield capability unlocked: Charge

Ability unlocked: Hammer Smash

Finally, a level up!
Eagerly, Kaiden opened his character sheet.

Character
Name: Kaiden
Race: Human
Level: 2
Class: Warden
Attributes:
Strength: 11 *Intelligence:* 11
Endurance: 11 *Perception:* 11
Dexterity: 11 *Unassigned:* 3
Abilities:
Hammer Smash
Perks:
None

Hm. My attributes went up by one point each. Safe to assume, then, that they'll go up by one point for each level? Our overall stats will increase as we level, while allowing us the option to boost specific stats through allocating additional unassigned points.

Those would be particularly useful, Kaiden knew. But he didn't have enough information about what to specialize in to use them yet. He could distribute them later. Maybe once he had a better understanding of the warden specialization choices Dawson had mentioned.

Charge and Hammer Smash, he thought next. Now those sounded interesting. Kaiden focused on the text and further clarification appeared.

Charge: Blocking attacks with your shield will grant

**charge in proportion to the damage that would other-
wise have been dealt to you. Your warden class implants
will store charge, depleting at a rate of 5 every 30
seconds.**

**Hammer Smash: The warden pounds the ground with
their hammer, dealing base damage to enemies in a 5-foot
radius. Cost: 10 charge. Cooldown: 15 seconds.**

This is starting to get fun. Kaiden couldn't help but smile. Level
two had brought some very useful abilities, including an area of
effect attack (AOE).

*If only I'd had these in that last fight. I wouldn't have come out half
dead.* But even as he glanced down to his health bar he noticed it
had instantly returned to full.

So leveling replenishes my health? That could be very useful. For the
time being, however, he had vibranium crystals to find,
voidspawn to avoid, and a shuttle to catch.

Focusing back on the corridor, Kaiden stumbled to a stop.
Something lay in the darkness ahead. *Voidspawn*, he thought at
first. But no. Whatever it was, it wasn't moving. Looked rather
limp, actually. He took a few steps closer, then focused on the
dark shape.

Marcel **Deceased**
Warden Recruit
Class: None
Faction: None
Level: 1

The 'deceased' status indicator over the recruit's body sent a
pretty clear message, but the gaping holes punched through his
armor sent an even clearer one. He wasn't the only downed
recruit, either. As Kaiden walked on, more limp forms materialized out of the darkness. Four, five, six...nine of them in total.

Based on the splattered ooze and limp tentacles, they'd taken
more than a few voidspawn with them.

Something red flashed in the corner of Kaiden's eye and he
spotted a crystal on the floor, half-fallen out of one of the
recruit's pockets.

Did they find a cache of vibranium before they were attacked?

As Kaiden approached, a line of text materialized over the recruit's body.

Loot corpse?

Don't mind if I do, he thought.

A window appeared in his vision showing his inventory as well as that of the recruit. The recruit didn't have much, but he had what Kaiden was looking for. Four vibranium crystals.

Smiling, he selected the crystals. As they popped into his own inventory, the game notified him one by one

Vibranium crystals collected: 2/5
Vibranium crystals collected: 3/5
Vibranium crystals collected: 4/5
Vibranium crystals collected: 5/5

Kaiden turned his eyes to the other corpses, then looted those as well. He felt bad for the dead recruits, but he also couldn't help but feel relieved at the same time.

Vibranium crystals collected: 6/5
Vibranium crystals collected: 7/5
Vibranium crystals collected: 8/5

A final line of text flashed in his vision, then faded as the last of the crystals appeared in his inventory.

Now we're talking, he thought, patting his pockets. All he had to do now was get back to the shuttle in one piece.

Achievement Unlocked!
Waste Not, Want Not - 50 EXP gained!
You've looted 5 corpses. How very thrifty of you!

He set his mind to the task with renewed vigor, and his feet even more so. His stamina bar had replenished now and he put it to good use, sprinting through the corridors. With the level up increasing his dexterity, Kaiden was moving more quickly than he ever had before and the increased stamina meant he could run for longer. He was making good time.

Every so often the clangs and screams of battle would echo out from some distant part of the ship, but for the most part, the *Dalcinae* was abandoned as Kaiden made his way ever closer to the docking bay. His minimap showed him as the only blip in a sea of empty hallways.

A nearby clattering sound made him stop. He flicked his shield on and huddled close to the wall. Peering into the room the sound had come from, he saw movement inside. Something was digging around in one corner, tearing at a shelving unit.

Something human, he realized, as a woman's voice echoed through the room.

"Come on. I just need one more."

A box tumbled off the shelf and a vibranium crystal rolled across the floor.

"There you are!" The recruit bent to pick up the crystal and a voidspawn dropped from the ceiling behind her.

It was injured, with several mangled tentacles and a yellow health bar, but the creature reared back nonetheless, stinger at the ready.

"Behind you!" Kaiden shouted, his eyes widening in horror as three more of the monstrosities dropped to the floor. He charged.

The woman spun, shield at the ready, and Kaiden fell into line beside her as the voidspawn surrounded them.

The strength of the voidspawn, Kaiden figured, was in numbers. They were the same as any low-level mob. Like giant rats or slimes in fantasy games, they were weak enough to be a fair fight for new players, but increasingly fearsome in a group such as this.

The closest spawn lashed a tentacle at Kaiden, its suckers sliding across his shield. The blow sent ripples of energy across the face of the force field, and Kaiden saw a white bar appear in the lower right of his vision.

Charge bar activated
Current charge: 10/100

Let's try this new attack, huh?

Just like he flicked his shield on with a thought, Kaiden thought *'Hammer Smash'* as he slammed his hammer into the ground.

Lightning crackled across the floor for five feet in all directions, a glowing wave of light that lit up the room as if it were day. The energy slammed into the four voidspawn and the two previously injured creatures screeched and collapsed.

Voidspawn killed - 50 EXP gained!
Voidspawn killed - 50 EXP gained!

The remaining two spawn recoiled, hissing in pain, but still standing with their health bars in the green. A quick focus told him the pair were level three.

Kaiden brought his shield to the front and reared back with his hammer.

"I'll take the one on the left," he said, backing up shoulder to shoulder with the other recruit. The burst of light from Hammer Smash had ruined his night vision, and in the darkened room he couldn't quite make out her face.

"I don't need your help," she spat, but raised her weapons nonetheless.

Her response made Kaiden furrow his brow, but he had little time to think on it as the voidspawn attacked.

Both launched at his shield together, slamming their bodies against it and pushing him back, inch by inch. The voidspawn were fast, but while they excelled in aggression, they seemed lacking in intelligence. Their fighting style largely consisted of hurling themselves at their enemies which, considering Kaiden had a shield, worked to little effect.

The other recruit lunged with her hammer, but her target dodged aside before lashing at her feet beneath her shield. She yelped in surprise and dropped to her knee, crouching behind her shield to be more fully covered by it. Kaiden did the same, bracing as his shield was slammed into again and again.

He had built twenty-five units of charge, and launched another Hammer Smash. The voidspawn were unable to dodge, and the energy crackled through their bodies as their health dropped into the yellow.

Lunging with his shield, Kaiden pushed his still-twitching

voidspawn opponent back into the other, tangling them together. He raised his hammer for a finishing blow, but was interrupted when the other recruit jumped in front of him.

She crushed one voidspawn's head with a forehand swing, then splattered the other against the wall with a backhand blow. It was a one-two punch that left both creatures limp on the floor.

Voidspawn assisted kill - 25 EXP gained!
Voidspawn assisted kill - 25 EXP gained!

Kaiden shook himself from his thoughts to find the other recruit standing still and staring off into space.

"Level two," she said, no doubt reading the text on her screen. "Hammer Smash unlocked. So that's the attack you've been using." She almost smiled then, but as her eyes fell on Kaiden her face twisted into a scowl.

It was then that he recognized her.

Zelda.

"Oh. Oh, uh..." The words caught in his throat as he panicked over what to say. The recruit he'd just fought with – the recruit he'd just saved, one might say – was the very same one from the shuttle earlier. The one who'd been trying to bore a hole through his head with her gaze alone. Kaiden felt his cheeks flush, then grow even hotter as anger rose in him.

"What's your problem with me?"

"I already said I didn't need your help," she huffed, then turned toward the door.

Before either could speak again, Sergeant Dawson's voice came over the comms.

"Boat's leaving, recruits. If you've managed to live this long, consider me almost impressed. Be a shame to see you fail because you couldn't make it back on time, though. You have five minutes, starting one minute ago." A timer sprang into being in the corner of Kaiden's vision, counting down.

After the sergeant's message, Kaiden looked back to Zelda.

"Look, I don't know what your deal is, but if we don't make it back we're both going to fail this test. We need to–"

She didn't even wait for him to finish before sprinting from the room and down the corridor.

Kaiden sighed, then broke into a run.

Gaming had never been this intense before. Then again, he'd never been playing to earn a chance at freedom. The stakes, as it happened, were just a bit higher here.

Apparently, whoever Zelda was, she knew her way back to the docking bay. Kaiden followed her at a comfortable distance, footfalls clanking and clanging on the metal floor. It wasn't the stealthiest method, but they didn't really have time to worry about attracting attention, as Sergeant Dawson repeatedly reminded them over the comms. The timer continued to tick down.

Turning back into corridors Kaiden recognized, they came across the remains of what had to have been a massive battle. Recruits and voidspawn alike littered the floor, bodies torn and battered. It was all too obvious who'd won, however, as several living voidspawn still lingered among the fallen, feasting on the corpses with macabre jerking motions.

They hissed and reared back as Kaiden and Zelda ran past, but there was hardly time for a fight. Kaiden bobbed and weaved, dodging the creatures' attacks as he sprinted after Zelda.

A chorus of chittering rose up behind him, and after stealing a glance backward, Kaiden ducked his head and sprinted even harder. Apparently, more voidspawn than they'd realized had survived the fight, and now they'd been worked into a frenzy. In a rolling, writhing wave of tentacles and pink-gray flesh, the voidspawn surged after them.

"We've got company," Kaiden yelled up to Zelda. Whether she heard him or not, he couldn't tell.

The horde of voidspawn was mere paces behind him, and only thirty seconds remained on the timer. Kaiden turned one last corner and breathed something resembling a sigh of relief as the docking bay drew into view. His stamina bar was near empty and he couldn't outrun the voidspawn for much longer.

A clattering from an open door to the left caught his attention and he flicked his shield on, expecting more voidspawn to come charging out as he ran past. Instead, Titus leaned his head out and grimaced deeply at the oncoming horde.

"Gotta move," Kaiden yelled as he sprinted past.

"I can't leave yet," Titus' voice trickled back.

"Run or die, up to you!"

Titus stood frozen for another moment, then, with a last look back into the room he'd been searching, sprinted after Kaiden.

Zelda was first into the tunnel, then Kaiden followed moments later.

Another recruit was already in there, banging on the door to the shuttle and shaking wildly.

"I can't handle this shit. I'll wait my time out in a cell. Just get me out of here!"

"That everyone?" Sergeant Dawson asked over the comms.

Titus rounded the corner, a barrage of tentacles lashing after him, and dove into the tunnel.

"We're all here," Kaiden said, pulling Titus to his feet, then backing up against the door to the shuttle.

A hiss of air filled the tunnel and the *Dalcinae's* damaged door began to open. But too slowly. The voidspawn were streaming up to them, tentacles and teeth at the ready.

"One last fight, then," Kaiden said, raising his shield and pressing his back against the door. "You with us?" he said to the shaking recruit.

"The hell I am!" He turned around, trying to help pull the two halves of the sliding door open. Another hiss and the door to the shuttle shot open, and the four of them fell through.

"No time to dawdle, recruits." Sergeant Dawson said, dragging the terrified recruit inside.

As the door snapped shut, one ambitious voidspawn dove through the gap. It pulled itself up and hissed at the recruits.

"This party's invite only," Sergeant Dawson said and picked the voidspawn up by its throat. He shoved it into the trash chute, then closed the latch and pressed a button, ejecting the voidspawn into space.

Sergeant Dawson turned, wiping voidspawn ooze off his hands, and smiled.

"Well done, recruits. Some of you might even pass this test."

Chapter Eight

Fourteen survivors. That was all who'd made it back.

Fourteen 'victors,' as Sergeant Dawson called them, but Kaiden wasn't so sure that term was appropriate. Fourteen recruits had made it back, which meant as many others had died in-game.

In and of itself, it wasn't that bad a punishment. Dying in Nova locked you out of playing for seven days, Kaiden knew. Not fun, certainly, but nothing permanent. These recruits hadn't just died, though. They'd also failed the test. They'd botched their chance at becoming wardens.

They'd all done something wrong to end up in prison – or probably had, considering his own case – but that didn't mean they didn't deserve the chance to make up for their actions.

The Governor might've been a bit odd, and Sergeant Dawson was certainly a bit too dedicated to his job, but spending your time in prison playing the most popular video game in the world didn't sound like such a bad deal.

Looking around the silent shuttle, Kaiden could see several of the survivors weren't long for the program. It was obvious from the dejection in their faces.

The closest to him was Titus, slumped in his seat. Whereas the other recruits simply looked happy to be away from the terror of the voidspawn, Titus was different. Something about him didn't look afraid. No, it was more...disappointment.

He's more afraid of failing the test than he was of the voidspawn.

The realization struck Kaiden like a hammer blow. As he processed it, he noticed what Titus was holding. In his loosely closed fist were two vibranium crystals.

What an unfair system, he thought. *We fought together in that mess. Titus proved mastery of the basic elements of the game, held his own in combat, and saved my life. Why should he fail just because he didn't stop to collect some useless crystals?*

Kaiden patted his own pockets where he'd stored a total of eight crystals. Three more than he actually needed to pass the test. But the bonus experience from them would probably be helpful, right?

And then an idea crept into his head. It wasn't a good idea, not by any means, but it was the right thing to do. Once again, he found himself acting without thinking, moving from his seat to plop down next to Titus.

"That was a rough first mission, huh?" Kaiden said, realizing just how bad he was at small talk.

"You like to state the obvious, don't you?"

"Well, you know, it's one of my favorite pastimes," Kaiden said, not making much sense, but not caring either. He was too distracted watching the rest of the shuttle, trying to see if anyone was looking their way.

"I'm going to have plenty of time to waste on useless conversations while I serve out the rest of my sentence," Titus said. "So why don't you give me these last few moments of peace before they kick me out of the program?"

"Fair enough, fair enough," Kaiden said, then patted him on the shoulder. As he did, he let three crystals fall from his hand and into the man's lap.

"What're you doing?"

"I have no clue what you're talking about," Kaiden whispered as he stood to head back to his seat.

Titus opened his mouth as if to say something, then stopped, eyes darting around to the other occupants of the shuttle. Kaiden did the same. No one seemed to be paying any attention. After another moment, the big man nodded, then took the crystals.

"Thank you, Kaiden."

"My friends call me Kai," he lied. No one called him that, and the only friend he'd had had been murdered. But he'd always wanted someone to call him Kai.

"Thank you, Kai."

"It was a pleasure killing voidspawn with you, Titus."

Kaiden headed back to his seat, fighting a smile. Who needed the bonus experience points from extra crystals anyway? He'd done what was fair, and that had been in short supply in his life lately. Better yet, he'd pulled it off without anyone noticing. Or so he hoped – he was pretty sure if he'd been caught, both he and Titus would be kicked out of the program.

Guess I'm just that smooth, Kaiden thought, until he noticed Zelda staring at him.

He felt his smile give way as the shuttle seemed to instantly rise in temperature. A bead of sweat ran down his forehead. Had she seen him give Titus the crystals? Would she report them to the sergeant?

A dozen questions raced through his mind, but as the shuttle continued its journey back, the only answer he found was silence.

~

It was lucky Kaiden had passed the crystals on in the shuttle. As soon as the shuttle returned to the WCSS *Anakoni*'s hangar, Sergeant Dawson had them all turn their crystals in. Thankfully, Zelda didn't rat him and Titus out. Maybe she hadn't seen the exchange after all. Or maybe she just hadn't cared. But with the looks she'd been giving him, Kaiden was sure she would have jumped at the chance to get rid of him. Perhaps he'd earned some goodwill when they fought together? He doubted it.

All in all, he was thoroughly confused. But he didn't get reported for sharing crystals, and just then, that was enough.

He and Titus, Zelda, and most of the others passed the test. Two of the fourteen survivors were short on crystals, however.

"Close," the sergeant said. "But close doesn't cut it in the Warden Corps. Turn in your hammers and shields, and log off."

"This is a load of crap!" one of them protested.

"Turn in your gear and log off," the sergeant said. "I won't ask again."

The recruit reared his hammer back instead. A bad choice, as it happened. He never stood a chance.

Sergeant Dawson punched his chest, then swept his feet out from under him. The surprised recruit slammed to the floor, his hammer clattering away. The two strikes had almost entirely emptied his health bar.

In the span of a heartbeat Sergeant Dawson stripped the recruit's shield bracer from his forearm, then hefted him by the shoulder. He dragged the man to the edge of the hangar, stopping just where the glowing energy barrier separated them from the frozen abyss of space.

"Last chance to willingly log off," he said with a growl.

"Screw you," the recruit spat and reached for a latch on the wall labelled "decompression alarm."

Sergeant Dawson jerked him away before he got near it.

"Pull that alarm and you'll be locked in this hangar with me for an hour or more until the gearheads get it deactivated. For your sake, this is a much preferable alternative," he said, and tossed the recruit through the energy barrier.

For the first few seconds he flailed, arms moving as if he were swimming back toward the hangar, but his momentum carried him further and further away. What little was left of his health bar ticked away in a matter of moments. Soon he'd fallen still but for a slight rotation as he spun slowly into the void. It didn't take long before his darkened form was indistinguishable from the blackness beyond.

Sergeant Dawson placed his hands on his hips and gave a firm nod.

"Been too long since I got to do that."

He turned back to the other recruit who'd failed.

The man yelped, then logged off. One moment he was there, the next he was gone.

"Well now, I believe congratulations are in order, recruits," the sergeant said, dusting off his hands and walking back to them. "Though 'recruits' is no longer an appropriate title. You proved yourselves today. Welcome to the Warden Corps."

Quest complete: Collect 5 vibranium crystals
Rewards: +200 EXP
Initiation into the Warden Corps

"You've earned the honor of wearing our sigil." As the

sergeant spoke, a light glowed to life on each of their shoulders and then the crossed hammers and shield of the Warden Corps materialized on their armor.

Faction Alignment Update
Alignment: Warden Corps
Rank: Ensign

As the notification appeared, Kaiden felt another addition to his uniform snap into place. A small metal band now sat just below the base of his helmet. It ran the whole way around his neck like a strange piece of sci-fi jewellery.

"I see a few of you are admiring your shiny new collars," Sergeant Dawson said with a smirk. "You, my fortunate little ensigns, are now the exclusive property of the Warden Corps." His smirk became a grin as he continued. "From this day forward, until your release from service, that collar signifies your duty to the corps and all it stands for. While you are wearing that collar, we will always know where you are, and you will be bound to this station as your one and only spawn point." His expression made it clear that he considered this a wonderful prospect.

"Those of you who manage to make it to retirement will have your collars personally removed by Captain Thorne and become veterans, retaining all of your levels, gear and abilities but without any formal affiliation to the corps. Though why anyone would want to leave my beautiful *Anakoni* is, personally, beyond my understanding."

Kaiden fingered the collar. It was a not so subtle reminder that even in this virtual world his situation was the same. He was a prisoner. Pushing the collar from his mind, he tried to focus on the game.

"You'll now enjoy many of the benefits of my beloved corps," the sergeant explained, pacing in front of them. "Equipment repairs, shuttle refueling, and other necessities will all be taken care of here free of charge. Next, you'll be grouped into squads of three, then paired with a handler. This handler will relay your orders from command, give you quests, and travel with you on said quests to ensure you do the Warden Corps proud." He squinted as he delivered the next part of his speech, leaning in close to their formation.

"Don't expect your handler to assist you on your quests. They are there to observe and report. Bravery, honor, and quest completion will be rewarded with experience, better equipment, and eventually, rank ups. Anything else – acting outside of quest parameters, attacking non-hostiles, failing to complete quests – will be met with punitive action." He straightened up. "You're part of the Warden Corps now, and that means you help protect the players of Nova Online and enforce the rule of law. Do so with honor and you will be rewarded beyond just in-game. Understand?"

"Yes, sir!" they shouted in unison.

"Very well, then. Log off, ensigns. It's chow time in the real world."

As Sergeant Dawson gave the orders, Kaiden realized he hadn't even considered eating. How long had he been in-game? Hours, at least. But how many exactly, he had no idea. Not that it mattered. Every moment he spent in-game was a moment not spent in prison. At least, not really. His body was there, sure, but his mind? His mind was here.

And that meant he could use the resources of Nova to clear his name, to earn his freedom. He made a mental note find out how to access the internet in-game when next he logged in, then looked down to the logout icon on the bottom right of his vision.

Just before he clicked it, Zelda stepped forward.

"Sergeant Dawson, I–"

"Log off, ensign."

"Sir, I need to talk to you."

Kaiden's heart jumped into his throat.

She's going to tell him about the crystals!

He darted forward, but stopped a moment later as the sergeant spoke.

"What you need to do is log off."

"But, sir, I–"

"Log. Off." With that, he turned on his heel and strode across the hangar. As he drew away, heading toward the exit, Zelda turned toward Kaiden. He balled one hand into a fist.

"You were going to rat me out, weren't you?

She glared at him, anger burning in her eyes. Kaiden expected her to lash out. Verbally, for sure. But maybe physically, too. Instead, she looked down at the floor, then shook her head and sighed.

"We need to talk," she said. "Next time we log on."

"Yeah, we do. About why you're so determined to–" Kaiden began, but found she'd disappeared. Already logged off.

What was her deal? Kaiden shook his head, equal parts angry and confused.

"Log off before you find yourself tumbling out of an airlock!" Sergeant Dawson's voice carried from across the hangar.

"Yes, sir," he said, then clicked the icon.

The world went black.

Chapter Nine

Dinner, just like breakfast, consisted of another delicious prison meal. Roast beef, steamed vegetables, and a side of pudding.

Yup. That's what this is.

Kaiden forced his mind to stop wondering – and his nose to stop smelling – what the kitchen staff had actually dumped onto his tray and took a seat at the far end of the cafeteria. The room echoed with the constant low roar of a hundred conversations happening all at once, and every other table was occupied by one group or another.

Loosely organized by gang affiliation, no doubt.

Kaiden had heard of the gangs that prowled the lower levels of the cities, of course. The media always maintained that crime was at an all-time low, but everyone knew which areas to avoid and what times it was dangerous to be out at night. The country was still rife with their illegal, and often violent, activities. Still, from the looks of things, it appeared the Party had done a good job of catching a lot of them. Too good a job, perhaps, considering Kaiden was now trapped in here with all of them. Just about every other prisoner was marked with tattoos showing loyalty to their gang.

One group had tattoos depicting gambling dice rolled to snake eyes, caught in a spiderweb. Kaiden hadn't a clue what gang they belonged to, but they obviously had a problem with the men sitting at the table beside them, who were marked by tattoos of a crown with a five-pointed star above it.

Behind Kaiden sat a group with tattoos of brass knuckles across the back of their necks. They shared their table with prisoners boasting crossed tridents inked onto their forearms.

Were the two gangs allied? Kaiden wasn't really sure. All he was sure of was that he didn't belong here. And not just because he was innocent, but because he seemed the only prisoner in the room without some sort of gang affiliation.

The only affiliation he had, by any stretch of the word, was with the wardens. Right about now, that felt as useless as a soup sandwich.

As soon as he'd logged off Nova and exited his VR pod, The Governor had strode past with a hurried "congrats" and tossed a new pin at him.

Where his old warden pin had been small and made of brass, the new one was larger and made of some sort of gleaming silver steel. It was almost the exact color of the shoulder patches worn by Sergeant Dawson and the other wardens in-game. But right now, he wasn't in-game, and in the cafeteria, surrounded by tattooed men, all the pin did was make him stand out. Make him a target.

Forcing another mouthful of delicious, delicious roast beef down his throat, Kaiden moved to inconspicuously take the warden pin off his collar. Maybe if he didn't wear it outside of the warden ward he would draw less attention to himself. Not that anyone seemed to be noticing him now, anyway.

A few moments later, he'd removed the pin and slipped it into his pocket.

"Oh, no, no, no! There's no need to be ashamed. Don't hide that fancy badge of yours."

Kaiden's heart dropped into his stomach as he recognized the voice. His thoughts flashed back to the screaming maniac licking the glass of his cell, a smiling face above a tattoo- and scar-covered body.

"Oh, come now. It's only polite to face someone when they're talking to you. Didn't your mother teach you that?" A hand latched onto Kaiden's shoulder then spun him around.

Not a step away, the same prisoner who'd screamed at him on day one stood, arms crossed. Two thugs stood behind him, scowling from behind broken noses and scarred faces. Each of their biceps looked as thick as Kaiden's head.

The prisoner Kaiden recognized stood eerily still in front of them all, looking like a storm ready to break. Then he moved, and Kaiden winced. But the man was just extending a hand.

"Manson Roxbury. It's an absolute delight to meet you." He drew his lips back in something approaching a smile but with far too many teeth. "And you are?"

"Kaiden...uh, Kaiden Moore," he said before he could stop himself.

Manson grabbed his hand in a crushing grip and shook it, slow and deliberate.

"Oh, it's simply wonderful to properly meet you, Kaiden. It's just so nice to have a...conversation without that pesky glass and those meddlesome guards between us. Wouldn't you agree?"

No, actually, I preferred the guards. The guards were good. And the glass, too.

"He don't look like much to me," one of Manson's thugs grunted.

Manson backhanded the man across the face, so quick Kaiden would have missed it if he'd blinked.

"I'll tolerate no disrespect of our new friend Kaiden," he shouted, eyes ablaze with anger. Then, in a flash, his anger was gone. But no, not gone. Kaiden looked closer and saw it was still there, just disguised. Boiling right beneath the surface.

This man is straight unstable.

About that, there was no doubt. But Kaiden was at a loss for how to handle the situation. He was outnumbered and outmuscled.

"No, we won't disrespect Kaiden the warden," Manson said, drawing him from his thoughts. "In fact, we should all be so lucky as to learn from him. Follow his example, even."

Or just pretend like I'm not here. That would be good.

"After all, you're one of the Party's little experiments, aren't you?" He sat down at the table and pushed Kaiden's tray aside. It slid several inches, then clattered to the floor. The noise rang out through the cafeteria and the room fell silent. All eyes were on them now.

"Chosen by the Party for rehabilitation. I bet that feels good, doesn't it?" He leaned in close as he spoke, hot breath washing across Kaiden's face.

He leaned away on instinct, then caught himself.

I can't show fear. Especially not with the whole cafeteria watching. No, I have to stand my ground.

Hadn't he read that somewhere? Fight back hard so he wouldn't be messed with? But how? Actual fighting was out of the question, certainly. And not just because they were all bigger and stronger than him, but because he hadn't been in a single fight in his life.

So I have to bluff. Right? What other option is there?

Kaiden swallowed hard at the thought. He had absolutely no way of backing up anything he said. It was almost enough to make him wish he had some hideous gang tattoo plastered across him. At least then he'd have people to back him up. Well, and he'd be an actual criminal. But criminal or not, right about then all Kaiden was concerned with was not being beaten to a pulp.

"You think you're better than us, don't you, *warden?*"

Think, Kaiden. Think! Say something intimidating.

"Uh, uh..."

Insult their appearance! No, that's not enough.

Kaiden's blood was turning to ice, spreading through his body and freezing him in place.

Talk smack about their love lives?

Why was he so bad at this? He would've thought all those years watching people flame each other back and forth in various games would have taught him a thing or two.

Well, say something, at least!

"Uh..." Kaiden's eyes flicked to the gang tattoo on Manson's neck, then below it, a smaller tattoo. 'Mother,' it read, complete with a small heart.

"Your mother was a–" Kaiden began, but before the rest of the sentence was out of his mouth Manson slammed a hand into his throat and bent him backward over the table.

"My mother was an honest-to-God saint, you little maggot," he snarled, the word spraying from his lips in a shower of spittle.

Kaiden gasped as Manson's grip squeezed his airway shut. He pried and clawed at the man's hand, fingernails digging into it, but to no avail. The grip only tightened.

"That was your last mistake, warden." Somehow, he squeezed tighter still. The thugs surrounding them were hooting and hollering now, hands cupped around their mouths as they egged Manson on.

Kaiden could barely hear them for his own pulse pounding in his head and some sort of sad, wheezing noise leaking from his near-closed throat. Blooms of darkness began to form at the edges of his vision and his head fell to one side.

And then a hand clapped down on Manson's shoulder. He snarled, turning to look down at it. A series of tattoos covered the knuckles. Four little Xs with a long, bold line running beneath all of them.

At the sight of the tattoos, Manson froze, then released his grip. A rush of air filled Kaiden's lungs and he rolled to the side, coughing and breathing heavily. His vision was still black at the edges, but with each breath it faded some.

"My apologies, friend."

Kaiden rolled back over to find Manson with his hands retracted in front of his chest.

"We don't want any trouble with the King Street Gang," he said to a figure towering over him. "Nor with you, my friend. Especially not with you."

Kaiden blinked once, then twice, steadying his vision.

Titus. The figure was Titus.

"Best you move along, then," he said, as calm as if he were greeting a friend.

"Right you are," Manson said, backing away. "Uh, enjoy your meal." And with that, he turned and fled across the cafeteria with his thugs in tow.

Titus picked Kaiden up and sat him back in his seat. Then, as if nothing had happened, sat down and started eating his meal. As he did, all those who had been watching turned back to their meals and the buzz of conversation resumed.

Still in shock, it was several moments before Kaiden managed to respond.

"Thank you," he said, voice still hoarse from nearly being choked to death.

Titus shrugged.

"This isn't your world. You don't belong here." Then, after a long moment: "Video games aren't my world." He swallowed another mouthful of dinner, then turned to face Kaiden, meeting his eyes directly. "You get my back in-game. I get your back out here. Fair?"

"Uh, yeah," Kaiden nodded enthusiastically while rubbing at his throat. "Sounds very fair."

It didn't take a genius to tell Titus wasn't a gamer. Likewise, Kaiden knew it was obvious he didn't belong in this prison. Whether he hid his warden pin or not, it wouldn't make a difference. But with Titus by his side? Well, there was a chance he might just live long enough to prove his innocence. And in the process, he could help Titus in Nova. Yeah, that sounded good. That sounded very good.

"You going to eat that?" Titus asked, nodding to a portion of spilled slop from Kaiden's tray.

"Uh, no. All yours."

"Cool."

Titus scooped the mush onto his tray and dug in.

Chapter Ten

Welcome to Nova Online.

The title screen dissolved to a blank field of white, then faded to reveal the hangar of the WCSS *Anakoni*.

Day two at the new job. Hopefully fewer of us will die today, huh?

After the rigors of the test the day prior, Kaiden had slept like a dead man. Exhausting himself in Nova Online seemed to carry over somewhat to the real world. Whatever the reason, the night had passed in a blur followed by an even quicker breakfast and then right back into the pod farm. He was a warden now, after all.

"So you made it to day two of your service in the Warden Corps," Sergeant Dawson said, striding through the freshly ranked up ensigns as they logged in. "I bet you're feeling awful proud of yourselves right now, aren't you?" He stopped alongside Mara, one of the women who'd come in with Zelda's batch of recruits.

"You feeling proud of yourself today?"

"Sir, I am feeling proud, sir."

"I'll tell you when you're allowed to feel proud, ensign. Give me a lap around the hangar. Go, go, go!"

Mara took off at a sprint and everyone else averted their gaze as Sergeant Dawson searched for his next target. Kaiden kept himself turned slightly away, which was evidently a mistake.

"Ensign Kaiden!"

"Yes, sir," he said, snapping to attention as the sergeant stalked over.

"You feeling proud of yourself today?"

Kaiden glanced over to the running Mara, then back to the sergeant.

"Sir, I'm not feeling proud today, sir."

"You're not proud to be an ensign in my Warden Corps? Unacceptable! Give me a lap."

"Yes, sir." Kaiden suppressed a sigh as he leaned forward into a jog and followed Mara's path around the hangar.

"As a matter of fact, you all look a bit too smug for my taste this morning. Get to running."

Mara led the fourteen of them in a lap around the hangar, which, considering the size of the place, was a considerable distance. By the time they got back to the sergeant, Kaiden's stamina bar was completely empty.

Achievement Unlocked!
Ground Pounder - 25 EXP gained!
You've completed your first physical training exercise. In the service of the Warden Corps you'll complete many, many more.

"You're wardens now, ensigns. You're not allowed to be low level. But don't you worry, I've got just the thing to fix that." He paused, then smiled. "You know what grinding is?"

A few mumbled 'yes, sirs,' trickled out from the winded recruits. Kaiden joined in. Of course he knew what grinding was. Virtually every game required some form of it. Most of the time it just involved killing endless amounts of weak mobs until you leveled high enough to move on to bigger and better things.

"Bullcrap. You don't know what grinding is. Not yet, at least. By the time I get through with–"

An alarm blared through the hangar, rising and falling in pitch like an air raid siren. Orange lights on the walls began to flash on and off. A moment later, a woman's voice came over the ship's intercom.

"This is a priority two alert. I repeat, priority two alert. All crew to staging areas."

The intercom clicked off and the siren followed. The lights continued flashing, however.

"Priority two?" Zelda asked, turning toward the sergeant.

"Developing situation," he said, eyes distant. A moment later they snapped back down.

"Grab your gear and get to your staging area in the canteen. Double time, ensigns! Go, go, go!"

"What do we do once we get there, sir?" a recruit asked.

"You wait," Sergeant Dawson yelled, already jogging toward the hangar's exit.

"Wait?"

"Hurrying up and then waiting are traditional warden pastimes. Get used to it." He paused at the doors leading out of the hangar. "Canteen's to the left. Now move!"

Kaiden forced himself into a jog along with the other ensigns as Sergeant Dawson disappeared to another part of the ship.

Mara led the way as the ensigns left the hangar then turned down a hallway. Here, the ship was flooded with activity. Wardens of all ranks rushed about, calling out to one another and hurrying to destinations unknown.

The hallways of the *Anakoni* were similar to those of the *Dalcinae,* except bigger in every way and in tip-top shape. Rows of pipes covered the ceiling, while matte gray walls lined the hall. Every so often, they passed thick-framed doors leading into other passages or rooms.

The route to the canteen was simple, but highlighted on their minimaps anyway, and by the time it drew into view the activity in the hallway had slowed to a trickle. Apparently the crew had reached their various staging areas.

Mara led the ensigns into the canteen. Kaiden made to follow, before a hand grabbed him from behind and yanked him back. Before he could get his feet under him he was shoved into an empty room. The door slammed shut.

Kaiden stumbled to a stop, then spun around, flicking on his shield and raising his hammer. Zelda stood near the door, facing him.

"What the hell is your problem?" he shouted, lowering his hammer but keeping his shield at the ready.

"I don't much like hired killers."

Okay? Who does?

Kaiden felt his brow furrow.

"Thanks for sharing?" he said, unsure what she was on about. "Care to explain why you dragged me in here?"

"Why try to hide it?" She advanced forward a step. "You know what you did." Another step. "You know why you're in prison." One more step and she was right up in his face, scowling. "You murdered my friend. You murdered Fred Bernstein."

Kaiden sighed.

This again? It's going to take a long time to prove my innocence if literally everyone thinks I'm guilty.

But the media had made sure of that, hadn't they? His trial had been blasted across the networks, plastered in the headlines. He hadn't had the best access to the outside world while imprisoned before his trial, but from what limited information he'd had, the court of public opinion had ruled him guilty pretty swiftly. Kaiden didn't know what he'd done to so royally tick off the news networks, but it seemed as far as they were concerned his case had been an open and shut one. Apparently, Zelda believed that too.

"Who told you to kill Bernstein?" she demanded.

"I didn't kill him," Kaiden said, trying to keep the frustration from his voice. The world had all been sold a great fat lie about him and there was nothing he could do about it. Not yet, anyway.

"I saw you with Titus. Saw you help him when we were on the shuttle. Are you working for his gang?"

"I didn't kill him," Kaiden repeated, voice growing louder.

"Someone ordered you to kill Bernstein, and you're going to tell me who it was."

"I didn't kill Bernstein!" Kaiden shouted it this time, then slammed his hammer into the table next to him, leaving a deep dent in its surface. "I'm tired of this. I'm tired of you. I'm tired of the whole damn world saying I'm some sort of criminal!" It was his turn to get angry now. "First, I get back from work to find the tortured and murdered body of my only friend. Then I get arrested and the world says I'm the one who did it."

He strode forward, jabbing with his finger to hammer home each point. "Then I get thrown in prison and some tattooed psycho wants to kill me on general principle. And now—" He took a deep breath and felt the anger ruling his every thought.

"And now I help a person out when they need it and you accuse me of being a gangster for it? I've never committed a crime in my life, much less murder. And hell, I saved you yesterday when I had no incentive to whatsoever. All I've done is be a decent person, and all I've gotten for it is punished."

He paused and let out a long breath.

Zelda stared at him, as defiant as ever.

She still thinks I'm the guilty one. Just like everyone else.

He sighed.

"If you think I'm the one who killed Bernstein, you need to think again." He paused, then said one last thing as Bernstein's favorite phrase popped into his mind. "The obvious answer is often a distraction, you know. True answers are found when one digs deeper."

Silence greeted his words, but the anger drained from Zelda's eyes.

"Wait, who told you that?"

"Bernstein did. Said it all the time." Kaiden shook his head, anger fading as he thought back to happy memories of solving complex puzzles and thought games with the old man. "He never was one for obvious answers. Always suspected something more."

"Oh my god," Zelda said, eyebrows scrunched as a look of realization dawned across her features. "You really did know him."

"Yeah. Pretty sure I mentioned that before."

"You didn't kill him."

"Definitely sure I mentioned that."

"So, who did?"

Kaiden crossed his arms.

"And there's the million-dollar question that, until right now, no one else but me was asking."

"You have to tell me everything about what you saw. Did you notice anything when you found him? Did something seem out of place? Did it look like his murderer had broken in?" She leaned in as she talked, speaking more quickly with each question.

Kaiden paused before answering.

As good as it feels to have someone believe me, something doesn't add up. Why is she so interested in all the minuscule details?

"Why do you care? Up until now, no one's believed me. No one's even wanted to hear my side of the story. But you come in here, spitting mad and demanding answers. What, did you get yourself thrown in prison then press-ganged into the Warden program just to ask me why I killed Bernstein?"

For the first time since Kaiden had known her, Zelda gave something approaching a smile, then followed it with a little laugh.

"Well, pretty much. I pre-tested myself with a copy of the psych eval to make sure I was eligible for the program and I made sure to get arrested in the same jurisdiction as you."

Wait, what? Surely she was kidding.

"You're messing with me, right? This is some sort of elaborate joke?"

"We knew Bernstein was working on something big. Something so important he wouldn't tell anyone what it was. But someone killed him for it. I've been assigned to find out who it was, and what they did with his project."

This doesn't make any sense. Who 'assigned' her to this? What project?

That couldn't be right. Kaiden had known the man for years. Had never known exactly what he did for work, but there was no way it was something worth killing over. Was it? He'd been a smart man, sure, but mostly he'd just minded his own business and gamed. Rarely left his apartment, in fact.

And yet, he was dead. Was this really the reason why?

"Wait a minute. You said '*we*.'" Kaiden's mind was a mess of possibilities and swirling thoughts. "Who's 'we'?"

Zelda shook her head.

"I'm not allowed to tell you that."

"Oh, okay. No worries."

She balked at that.

"Wait, really?"

"Oh yeah, I've always been a trusting per– no! Of course not. If you want me to believe some organization told you to put yourself in prison and track down Bernstein's murderer, you're going to have to give me more than an ambiguous 'we.'"

Zelda sighed.

"What if I told you Bernstein was not just a friend, but a former colleague of mine?"

"That'd be a start."

"Look, Kaiden, I–"

"My friends call me Kai."

"Kaiden, Kai, whatever." She shook her head. "I'm kind of on my own in here and I don't know much about you, but I believe you were friends with Bernstein. If he trusted you, then that's good enough for me. But if you truly were his friend, then you'd help me find his murderer. Not to mention clear your own name in the process."

A spark of hope sprung to life in his heart.

"You have evidence that can help me?"

"Well, not yet."

Just like that, it spluttered out.

"But I do have leads." She nodded earnestly. "What I need is help pursuing those leads."

"And what happens when you get your evidence? You just get to waltz out of prison?"

Zelda shrugged.

"Yeah, something like that."

"Somehow, that's the craziest thing you've said so far."

"Look, I really can't say much, but that 'we' I was talking about can get things done. They hacked a copy of psych eval out of the government database, and arranged for me to be here. Trust me, they'll get me out of here."

Kaiden shrugged, disbelieving.

"I can promise that if you help me find Bernstein's murderer and whatever it was he stole, your name will be cleared. You can have your life back." She gave him a hard stare, a fierce stare, then held out her hand. "What do you say, Kai?"

Either this is legit and I'm going to help track down Bernstein's murderer, or I'm being suckered into something I don't understand.

She'd been nothing but cold to him since they first made eye contact, and at one point he was sure she'd been bent on seeing him dead, but for some reason, right then, Kaiden felt he could trust her. Couldn't explain why, exactly. Maybe it was the conviction in her voice. Maybe it was simply the fact that she didn't think he was a ruthless murderer. Whatever it was, it worked.

"Alright, I'll play along for now."

She smiled.

"This could be a good thing, Kai. We can prove your innocence and discover what someone was willing to kill our friend over." Her smile faded after she spoke. "Though there's just one problem."

Kaiden felt his heart fall. Now that the high of someone finally believing him was fading, there were several problems. Starting with the little issue of how they were going to conduct an entire criminal investigation, in a video game, from inside a prison. Maybe this hadn't been the best idea.

"We have to find a third person to help us," she said.

Or a private army of detectives...

He raised an eyebrow. "Aside from the obvious reason – that we have no idea what we're doing – why do we need a third?"

"The squad system."

"The what?"

She sighed.

"Honestly, did you even research this game? Never mind. Don't answer that. Wardens are broken into squads of three to maximize their effectiveness. I expected they would have already done it by now. You and I can be in the same squad, but we'll need a third."

Kaiden didn't even hesitate.

"Titus."

"Who?"

"The guy that's pretty much a walking wall of muscle?"

Zelda frowned.

"You've seen his tattoos, right? He's a member of the King Street Gang."

"I'm good at reading people," Kaiden said.

He wasn't.

"And I trust Titus. Gangster or not."

He sort of did.

"He's a criminal."

"According to the rest of the world, we're all criminals in here."

"That's not the point."

Kaiden crossed his arms.

"The point is I won't help you unless Titus is our third. He saved my life yesterday. A maniac would have wrung my neck thin as a straw if not for him. We can trust Titus, and right about now, that means a lot."

Zelda crossed her arms as well, then bit her lower lip, thinking. Finally, she cursed and shook her head.

"Have it your way, Kai. But if this goes belly up, I'm blaming everything on you."

"Fair enough. Now let's go solve a murder. What do you say?" He extended a hand.

"I really hope we don't regret this decision," she said, giving him a firm handshake.

"We won't."

At least, he hoped they wouldn't.

Chapter Eleven

"This is no longer a priority two developing situation," Sergeant Dawson said, pacing before the assembled recruits. "We've got ourselves a bona fide priority one. To put it plainly, ensigns, the you-know-what has hit the fan."

They'd been waiting in the canteen for what felt like hours with no news of what was happening until Sergeant Dawson hurried in moments ago. Now, the canteen was filled with the thrum of anxious conversation and shouted questions as every ensign tried to shout louder than those next to him.

Kaiden didn't mind the noise, however. It provided great cover for the conversation he'd been negotiating between Titus and Zelda. She hadn't wanted to trust Titus with all their information, but Kaiden wasn't in the habit of keeping secrets from his friends. He had so few of each he couldn't afford to do anything other than make full use of them.

"So you want to find whoever murdered this Bernstein guy—"

"And what they stole from him," Zelda added.

"...and what she says they stole from him, and in the process, clear Kai's name?" He emphasized the 'she' with a nod toward Zelda. She hadn't exactly been friendly to him since Kaiden had introduced them. Titus had been more than happy to return the favor.

"That's about the gist of it," Kaiden said, making sure to keep his voice down.

"Hm." Titus nodded slightly, then looked at Kaiden. "And you want me to help you?"

"We need a third we can trust."

"Fine. I'll be your third."

Kaiden breathed a sigh of relief at that. He'd been legitimately concerned Titus would turn the offer down. The big man didn't really have any incentive to go out of his way to help them.

"On one condition."

Oh. Well, here comes the incentive...

"When we clear your name, Kai, and you get back out into the world, you have to take a message to my brother."

"Yeah, sure. That's no problem at all. What's the message?"

"I need to word it right. Give me some time and I'll get back to you. I just need you to promise you'll get it to him."

"I promise."

"Then I'm in."

"Glad to hear it!" Kaiden slapped him on the shoulder.

Party formed!
Ensigns Zelda & Titus have agreed to join your party.
Party members will appear green on your minimap. A party comms channel has been created.

Achievement Unlocked!
Party Time - 25 EXP gained!
You've created your first party. Congratulations, it appears you have friends.

Having a party comms channel would be useful for situations like back on the Dalcinae when he got split up from Titus. For now, he didn't open it as the three of them were close enough to speak normally.

"Tell him what you told me about the leads, Zelda," Kaiden said. He shot a glance to the front of the room to make sure Sergeant Dawson was still being barraged with questions. "Might need to make it quick."

Zelda hesitated a moment, still clearly unhappy with bringing Titus fully into the fold, then cleared her throat.

"We believe whoever killed Bernstein did it to take what he was working on. Odds are they're looking to blackmail the Party with it. Whatever it is, though, it's not a physical item." She rapped her knuckles on the table next to them. "We think it's an in-game item."

Titus frowned at that.

"Why would you kill someone for a virtual item?"

"Because," Zelda said, exasperation in her voice, "just because the item is in-game doesn't mean it started there. This item, this *file*, was uploaded into Nova by Bernstein. As backward as it sounds, Nova is one of the safest places to store important files. NextGen Games has entire departments dedicated to making sure no one hacks them, and they're such a big corporation the Party rarely challenges them."

Now that was saying something, Kaiden knew. Ever since the war – or 'the great test,' as it was supposed to be called now – the Party had been the single most powerful force in the nation. No one opposed them because no one could, or had a good reason to.

The war had been caused by the worst of humanity. It'd been a civil war of zealots, terrorists, cult leaders, separationists and wannabe dictators. It had culled the weak and left only the strong, until the Party came out on top and brought peace. In the new world the aftermath had created, there wasn't room for the sins of the past. There was only room for the Party, and the bright new future it guaranteed for everyone. That was the truth, plain and simple.

In recent years, NextGen Games had been growing in power, enough that they could make their own rules to a certain extent. But, like the Party, NextGen wielded its power responsibly. For the time being, that was enough to keep the status quo.

"So he uploaded this file to keep it safe from the Party?" Titus asked, drawing Kaiden's attention back to the conversation at hand.

"Yes," Zelda said, nodding. "And more. Before Bernstein was killed, he was tortured. Likely to force him to move his Nova Online character into a PVP zone so that when he died, he could be looted."

"PVP?" Titus asked.

Wow. He really knows nothing about gaming.

"Player versus player," Zelda said in a hurry. "It's any area where you can kill players. This represents nearly all areas of the game. There are only a few select areas where PVP is not enabled – major trading hubs and early starting zones, mostly. When a player dies in a PVP zone, you can loot their inventories. PVP is allowed in most of Nova, but there are safe zones for noobs, traders, casual players. Bernstein would have been careful with this item, hiding his character in a safe zone where he couldn't be attacked. He wouldn't enter a PVP zone of his own free will."

"But if this happened in-game, couldn't NextGen just look up who killed him? They have circuitheads that can do that stuff."

"That's what I thought at first, too," Zelda said, shaking her head. "But NextGen Games strictly adheres to a no interference policy. Players are anonymous unless they choose not to be. Not even the Party can make NextGen break that promise."

Titus shook his head at that.

"The King Street boys really need to get in on this gaming stuff. Nobody can catch you in here."

"Anyway," Zelda continued, frowning only slightly at the mention of Titus' livelihood. "The leads we have tell us the in-game assassin who killed Bernstein's character and looted it had two distinguishing features: a nose ring, and a red streak of hair. I need to question him. He might be able to lead us to the real-world murderers, too. But even if I catch the assassin, he'd just be able to log out. That's why I had to become a warden. With the warden-only ability 'Shackle,' I can–"

She stopped as a shadow fell over her face. Her eyes widened and Kaiden turned to find Sergeant Dawson standing over them.

"If I could just bother you three for a moment," he said, voice way too calm. "We are in the middle of a system-wide priority one alert that could end with the annihilation of a planet. Now, I don't want to intrude, but I'd appreciate it if you could find it in your hearts to *pay attention!*"

He screamed the last words so loud it left Kaiden's ears ringing.

"That sound alright to you all?"

"Yes, sir," Kaiden joined Zelda and Titus in saying, feeling his cheeks flush as he realized the rest of the room was staring at them.

"Well, thank you. That's very kind," Dawson said, then stomped back to the front of the room.

"We'll talk more later," Zelda whispered.

"As I was saying," Sergeant Dawson continued. "Normally, you'd get a more in-depth overview of all this, but right about now, there's really not time. So you get the quick and dirty." He clapped his hands together and drew in a deep breath.

"If you read your in-game lore guide, you would know voidspawn originally came through tears in space called 'rifts.' These rifts were left over after humanity's earliest attempts at using jump drives."

"Is this guy for real?" Titus asked, leaning over to whisper to Kaiden. "He takes the game too seriously."

"It's called role-playing," Kaiden said, pretty sure Titus had never heard of the concept. "Some people enjoy a game so much they pretend it's real while they're playing."

Sergeant Dawson's eyes flicked over and Kaiden straightened in his seat as quick as he could.

"Talk later," he muttered.

"Ahem." Sergeant Dawson let a long pause hang in the air before continuing. "Our modern drives don't create rifts when used anymore, but these rifts from the old days remain open, and voidspawn have started coming in greater numbers and with increasing frequency. Which is a roundabout way of explaining why there's a starship-sized mass of organic matter swarming with voidspawn hurtling toward Nassau."

Dawson ran his hand over his close-cropped scalp.

"Now, I know Nassau isn't exactly a shining beacon of civilization, but it's a planet in the Greater Spiral Arm, and that means it's under our protection. Like it or not, we're the ones who get to deal with this 'Leviathan,' as Command is calling it. But this fight's too hot for ensigns. I'm not letting you all walk in there and get an easy week's vacation."

Kaiden shuddered at the thought. Dying in-game meant he'd be locked out of his character for seven days. That'd be seven long days to spend in prison with the general population. Seven days looking over his shoulder, waiting for Manson to make good on his threats.

"No, you're all sitting this one out. But that doesn't mean you don't have a job to do. Whenever something big like this goes down, the local pirates have a field day. If you don't think they're going to capitalize on us being distracted, you're wrong. Those scum never pass up an opportunity to prey on new players." He cracked his knuckles and shook out his shoulders.

"That's where you all come in. Command wants you on standby as a quick reaction force. When any piratical scum show their faces, well, I think you know what to do. That sound good?"

"Yes, sir!" A few of the more zealous recruits looked disappointed at the news, while others seemed relieved not to be heading into the fight with the Leviathan. Personally, Kaiden wasn't sure which option was better. If they were in the main battle, they'd have the support of virtually every other warden in the system.

Chasing down pirates, they'd likely have little support, if any at all. But they could expect lower level opponents, as well. Or so he hoped. He was still only level two. Focusing on the others, he could see some of them had reached that level too, but for the most part, they were all level ones. Not a fearsome force by any means.

"I mentioned before you would be divided into squads and assigned a handler. Normally, this would be an official process, but again, there's no time." As he spoke he looked to the still-flashing orange lights on the walls. As if on cue, the ship-wide intercom clicked on.

"Leviathan task force to hangar two. Leviathan task force to hangar two. Shuttle scramble in T-minus five minutes."

"Ensigns!" Sergeant Dawson shouted, drawing their attention as he moved to the door. "Divvy up into groups of three and report to hangar bay one. There, you'll be assigned a handler and a shuttle. From now on, you report directly to your handler." He moved to leave the room, then paused. "Fight well, ensigns"

And then he was gone, sprinting down the hallway as the orange emergency lights flashed around him.

In his absence, there was silence. Everyone lingered, looking back and forth between one another. On Kaiden's display, the suggestion to assign their party into a warden squad flashed across his vision.

Kaiden turned to Titus.

"Might as well make the team official, huh?"

He shrugged as if to say, "Why not?"

Kaiden looked to Zelda.

"What do you say? Should we squad up and go make the Warden Corps proud?"

She laughed.

"Yeah, something like that."

Achievement Unlocked!
Better Together - 25 EXP gained!
You've joined a warden squad. At least now you won't die alone, eh?

Chapter Twelve

Down in hangar bay one, a sergeant pointed to the first ensign squad ahead of Kaiden, Zelda and Titus.

"The *Tempel* with Lieutenant Pleasant." The squad was sent off with a gesture. As they hurried past, Kaiden peered into the hangar bay, then focused on one of the four waiting shuttles.

WCSS *Halley*
Class: Light Transport (Shuttle)
Faction Alignment: Warden Corps

It was a long, streamlined ship made of a non-reflective metal and a basic design. It didn't have much more than a round-edged rectangle for a body with a cockpit upfront, a front-side door, a few porthole windows along the hull, and a loading ramp at the rear. Wings jutted from the hull at the front and rear, but they weren't so much wings as they were engine support struts.

All in all, it was much the same as the shuttle they'd used on their mission to the *Dalcinae,* except scaled down. From the looks of it, there was only space inside for a small crew of five or six.

"The *Halley* with Lieutenant Turjic." The final squad in front of their own was sent off, and Kaiden stepped up to the sergeant.

"Fairly obvious, ain't it?" The sergeant nodded to the last available ship. "It's the *Borrelly* with Lieutenant Ellenton for you three."

Zelda led the way over to their new shuttle. 'WCSS *Borrelly*' was clearly laser-painted on the side of the hull.

The other squads had met their handlers outside their shuttles, but as the three of them arrived beside their shuttle they found their lieutenant was decidedly absent.

The loading ramp was down, leaving the rear of the *Borrelly* open.

"Permission to come aboard granted, if that's what you're waiting for," a woman's tired voice called from within.

"Lieutenant Ellenton?" Kaiden called back, caught off guard by her lax tone.

"Yup."

Kaiden felt himself frown.

"Uh, Ensigns Kaiden, Zelda, and Titus reporting for duty, ma'am."

"If you must."

Kaiden felt himself frown deeper.

"Ensign reserves load up and prepare to scramble as necessary," the *Anakoni's* intercom echoed through the hangar.

"You heard the intercom lady," Ellenton called from somewhere in the ship. "Get up in here and grab a seat. Pray we're not needed today and maybe we can all catch a nap or something, ya know?"

Still adjusting to the apparent radical attitude shift between Sergeant Dawson and their new commanding officer, Kaiden waved the others over, then hesitantly started up the ramp.

The inside of the *Borrelly* was the same dark matte metal as the exterior. It was punctuated here and there with storage lockers, supply crates, and seats strapped into the wall.

As Kaiden moved further in, an equipment locker on the left gave way to a rack of bunk beds set into the wall, stacked four high. When he reached the cockpit he found the pilot and co-pilot seats were empty.

Where was their lieutenant?

He turned back to Zelda and Titus and shrugged.

"Excuse me for asking, Lieutenant," Kaiden said, still trying to figure out where her voice had come from. "But where are you?"

"Ah, right." A ceiling panel popped down an inch, then slid to the side on a near-hidden trackway to reveal a cargo net holding some sort of bundle of equipment. The net lowered out of the ceiling and Kaiden realized it wasn't holding equipment at all.

Lieutenant Ellenton gave them a lazy salute.

Ellenton
Warden Lieutenant
Class: Blast Warden
Faction: Warden Corps
Level: 15

"Closest thing I can get to a captain's quarters on this space-faring shoebox. Makes for a mighty fine hammock, though."

"Uh, right," Kaiden said for lack of any better reply. He wasn't exactly sure what he'd been expecting their lieutenant to look like, but whatever it was, Ellenton wasn't it. Her uniform was ruffled and baggy – an impressive feat considering clothing in-game seemed resilient to wrinkles – and she wore a short-billed military cap on her head, tilted back such that the bill was almost straight up in the air.

Her avatar placed her somewhere in her thirties with shoulder length blond hair that was buzz-cut short above her right ear. Her eyes were hidden behind a thick-rimmed pair of reflective sunglasses. Kaiden wasn't sure what made the glasses more unnecessary: the fact that she was in space, or that she'd just been apparently napping in the *Borrelly's* hold.

Reaching a hand to her face, she tipped her sunglasses down a touch and gave Kaiden and the others a quick once-over.

"You three are far too tense. Grab a bunk, take a load off." She flicked a hand at the impossibly cramped bunk beds across the ship, then replaced her sunglasses in front of her eyes.

Kaiden looked at Titus.

The big man shrugged.

"Oh," Ellenton said, as if just remembering. "I'm supposed to brief you on..." She dug around in the cargo net, searching for something.

"On..." She continued searching. "One minute. I just had it." Considerably longer than a minute passed as she dug around in her cargo net-hammock.

"Aw. Oh well. I'm sure it wasn't important."

Zelda frowned at that.

"Actually, are you sure you don't have it somewhere? We might need—"

A blaring alarm went off in the hangar outside and the orange flashing lights on the walls changed to blue.

"Shoot," Lieutenant Ellenton said, then cursed as she rolled out of her hammock. She dropped to the floor with a thunk, then ambled up to the cockpit and flopped into the pilot's chair.

"Best strap in," she called back to them. "Looks like someone in the system is misbehaving."

"That alarm is for us?" Kaiden asked, looking to the blue lights, then back to the lieutenant. "We're heading out?"

Her only response was to fire up the *Borrelly's* engine, then launch the ship into the air. Kaiden stumbled to one side and slammed his shoulder against a bulkhead.

"Into the cold, lifeless vacuum of space," Ellenton called from the front. Through the cockpit's transparent screen, Kaiden could see the energy barrier at the end of the hangar approaching quickly.

"Best you all hold on. This might get bumpy," she said, then launched them into space.

In the minutes that followed, Kaiden learned the lieutenant's definition of 'bumpy' was decidedly more terrifying than his own.

~

"Right. Uh, attention to the cockpit, or whatever," Lieutenant Ellenton called from the front of the shuttle as she removed her headset and half-turned to face them. "See that speck we're headed toward?" She pointed to a series of flickering lights through the windshield. "That's the *Mochinki Station*."

Kaiden followed her finger and could just make out the shape of a distant starship. Their trajectory had them aimed right at it and closing at a startling speed.

"It's damaged," he said, squinting toward the *Mochinki* as it rapidly grew larger. "Badly." He stared a moment longer and the game gave him some more details.

Mochinki **Station **Crippled****
Class: Mobile Space Station
Faction Alignment: Neutral

A hole had been blown through one side of the hull and a field of debris was radiating out from it, spinning away into space.

"Yeah, so that's why we're here," Lieutenant Ellenton said, then launched into an explanation, waving her hand as if the whole thing was tiresome.

"The *Mochinki* is a prime location for some easy side quests, which means it's often loaded with noobs collecting computer chips or whatever other useless task they're assigning these days. The long and short of it is, with most of the wardens in the system busy with that whole Leviathan mess," she rolled her eyes at that, "the local pirates are having a party. And, oh joy, it's our job to do something about it. Or yours, actually."

Without looking where they were going she nudged a joystick on her control panel and the *Borrelly* altered course, hurtling just a bit more precisely toward the center of the floundering transport freighter.

"We're coming in kind of fast, aren't we?" Zelda asked, knuckles white as she held on to a handrail.

"Some first-time players were on the *Mochinki* when the pirates put a nice big hole in its side," continued Ellenton, ignoring Zelda's words completely. "Now they're trapped there, whining for help and interrupting what was otherwise going to be a pretty sweet nap for me.

"Command wants you and the other reserve ensigns to board the *Mochinki*. A couple veteran squads are already dealing with the pirates, so all you have to do is find the noobs and get them out safe."

Quest: Rescue trapped players on the *Mochinki* Station
Part 1: Reach the players
Expected difficulty: Novice
Reward: +400 EXP, +2 faction prestige

"Now, I know what you're thinking. 'But Ellenton, why do we have to go babysit the noobs?' Well, it's simple, really. One, you lot are noobs yourselves. Two, and more importantly, if you keep the players happy, you keep them playing, which means trading, which means more taxable income for the Party. Thirdly, helping players is one of the conditions of the deal the creators of Nova

Online made with the Party when the Warden program was first agreed…lucky us." She paused, as if realizing she'd gone off on a tangent, then shook her head.

"Anyway, I'll keep the engines running here," Lieutenant Ellenton said. "You get in, find the new players, then we skedaddle. Cool?" She still hadn't turned back to the controls.

Kaiden dismissed the quest prompt and found the massive hull of the *Mochinki* looming before them, far too close.

"Lieutenant!" he shouted, pointing forward.

"Hmm?" She turned to face the front. "Oh, right."

She thumbed her flight control joystick hard and the *Borrelly* swerved sharply to the right. The *Mochinki's* hull was the only thing visible in front of the shuttle as the lieutenant held the turn.

Just as it looked as if they were going to crash into the freighter like a bug, they cleared the edge of it and spilled back out into open space.

"Whew. That was close," the lieutenant said as she guided the *Borrelly* into position behind another warden shuttle. "Why didn't you say something sooner?"

Before Kaiden could answer, a distinctly torpedo-shaped blur zipped past their cockpit and slammed into the shuttle in front of them. The explosion rocked their ship and a barrage of metal clacked and clattered against their hull in a shower of debris.

A warden corpse floated by the window, the face behind the smashed visor frozen in surprise.

"Pirates don't normally shoot at warden ships." The lieutenant frowned. "Must have a feisty group here today." She clicked a button on her console and a laser fired from their ship, exploding an incoming torpedo Kaiden hadn't even noticed.

"I really wasn't planning on trying too hard during this mission," Lieutenant Ellenton growled. "Stop making me do my job!"

She clicked another button and the *Borrelly* shook back and forth as a salvo of missiles launched from under its nose, swarming toward a target Kaiden still couldn't even see.

"That'll buy us a moment," the lieutenant said, pulling the shuttle around toward the *Mochinki*. "Looks like the hangar's open. I'll drop you in there." She leaned against the cockpit glass, muttering at their unseen attackers. "And then I'm coming back to turn you into scrap!"

The shuttle hurtled toward the *Mochinki*, ducked under its belly, then banked hard. Their momentum carried them right through a glowing energy barrier and into the freighter's hangar.

"This is your stop," the lieutenant said, then hovered the shuttle in place above the ground and lowered the loading ramp at the rear. "Go rescue some noobs."

Chapter Thirteen

Location discovered: *Mochinki Station*
Class: Mobile Space Station
Faction Alignment: Neutral

The message flashed across Kaiden's screen as he jumped down from the loading ramp to the metal floor of the hangar. Zelda and Titus followed, clanking down one after the other. The space looked very much like the hangar on the *Anakoni,* except only about a sixth as large. There was enough room to fit one other shuttle aside from the *Borrelly,* and that was it.

Achievement Unlocked!
Nosy Novice - 25 EXP gained!
Congratulations, you've explored 3 medium or large class ships. Don't stop now!

"Here are the trapped players' names and statuses," Lieutenant Ellenton's voice came through their comms. "Last we heard, they were holed up in the *Mochinki's* galley. Don't let them die, huh?" As she spoke, ten health bars faded into view on the right side of Kaiden's vision.

If he didn't look directly at them they stayed mostly transparent, but when he focused on them they would solidify so that he could read each individual name and their hit points. As he did, he noticed six of the health bars were already empty. The remaining four players reorganized to the top of the list.

Clutchtime - 90%
gtrain_737 - 33%
MadKilla - 20%
Tomari9 - 82%

"Command says that for each player who dies you'll lose fifty percent of your reward EXP. Being realistic, though, if you get two out alive, I'll consider it a success. Sound good?" Lieutenant Ellenton said, inspiring as ever.

"I've sent you the layout of the *Mochinki,* so your minimaps will guide you to relevant destinations. Right now, that's the galley. If you need me, holler. In the meantime, I've some pirate scum to scrap."

With that, the *Borrelly* exploded out of the hangar with a roar and a flash of light.

The backblast from its engines slammed into Kaiden and the others, nearly throwing them to the ground. Kaiden stumbled several steps, struggling to catch his balance as crates and shelves toppled to the floor.

"That was an...enthusiastic exit," Zelda said, straightening after bracing against the shockwave.

"So, about those noobies we're supposed to rescue?" Titus said, drawing everyone's attention back to the job at hand.

"Noobs," Zelda corrected him. "No one says 'noobies'."

"Sure, whatever." Titus turned toward the door leading out of the hangar.

"Stay ready for any pirates," Kaiden cautioned them. *No need to be reckless.* But at the same time, he was kind of hoping they'd run into a fight. He had work to do in uncovering Bernstein's murderer, but he also had to admit, playing Nova was fun.

Maybe that was why the thought of facing battle again wasn't anywhere near as frightening as it had been on the *Dalcinae.* It probably helped that they weren't here to fight a swarm of tentacled, many-toothed, stinger-wielding voidspawn. Compared to that, simple pirates were considerably less frightening.

"Lieutenant Ellenton said she'd marked the route to the *noobs* on our tiny maps?" Titus said.

"*Minimaps*," Zelda corrected him.

"Yeah, those." Titus looked annoyed at being corrected again. "So what are we waiting for? Let's get to it."

"Let's," Zelda agreed. "And hurry. I want to be the first squad to reach the trapped players. It'll make us look good to Captain Thorne and Command."

They followed their minimaps along a predetermined route and left the hangar with shields on and hammers raised.

A fight had obviously already taken place in the hallways. The walls were scorched and gouged, the metal still molten and glowing in some areas. And then there were the bodies.

Everywhere. Face down, face up, and some torn apart, though Kaiden tried not to pay special attention to those.

Does this game have a gore filter? There's no way they can legally let kids see this kind of stuff...

"I've seen gang wars that caused less mess than this," Titus said, taking in the chaos with raised eyebrows. "Except for when the Southside Boys get involved." He paused at that. "You don't think they're playing this game, do you?"

"Uh, probably not," Kaiden said, keeping his eyes on their surroundings as they progressed through the halls.

Static blared in Kaiden's ears and then a message appeared in his vision.

Local area comms detected
Join channel?

"Are you seeing this message?" he asked the others.

"Yeah. Should we tune in?" Titus asked.

"Oh god. That's not good." Zelda's eyes were distant, staring at nothing in particular. A moment later she blinked, then looked at them. "Join the channel. You need to hear this."

Kaiden focused on the 'yes' option of the message.

Channel joined: *Mochinki* Station general

The static hissed louder, then resolved itself into voices. Panicked voices, set to a backdrop of the sounds of battle.

"They got one of the squads over at the docking port. Ganked them as soon as they left their shuttle, then took down the shuttle too. They didn't stand a chance," a man said. Something exploded near him and he grunted. "They're on us now. Where are you, Sola?"

"We're headed your way, Terrel. Hold tight," a woman's voice – presumably Sola – replied with a steely calm that was somehow reassuring.

"Our enhanced is KIA and the other squad's shielder and blaster are below twenty percent."

"We're coming."

"It's not looking—"

His mic fell silent.

"Terrel? Talk to me. What's happening?"

Kaiden looked to Zelda and Titus. Both stood with wide eyes and deep frowns.

"Should we say something?" he whispered to them, hoping his mic didn't pick it up.

"Say again. I could barely hear you."

Crap. She heard me.

"Not Terrel. This is, uh, Ensign Kaiden. Reporting in?"

"Ensign? Stars above, you shouldn't be here." Sola's calm tone changed to a more admonishing one. "Command needs to get their heads on straight. This isn't a mission suitable for ensigns. You're going to get torn to pieces."

"Ensign Zelda here. What are we dealing with? We were told there were pirates."

"Pirates?" she laughed. But it wasn't a happy laugh. It was more of a 'there's no hope, why are we even trying?' sort of sad chuckle. "No, not just any pirates. Raged."

Raged? Why is that name familiar? Kaiden swallowed hard as he read the text that faded into view.

Update – Parameters Changed
Quest: Rescue trapped players on *Mochinki* Station
Part 1: Reach the players
Expected difficulty increased: Veteran
Rewards increased: +900 EXP, +4 faction prestige

From novice difficulty to veteran. That can't be good.

"Raged?" Zelda asked.

"Yes, raged. You know, cannibalistic pirates driven insane

from contact with voidspawn? Bloodthirsty berserkers some twisted dev at NextGen decided should be virtually immune to pain."

"I didn't know," Kaiden said. "But now that I do, I kind of wish I didn't."

"Wait until you meet one."

"Ensign Titus here. The raged are human, right?"

"Barely."

"A scruffy-looking bunch? Carrying big weapons? Covered in blood and sweat?"

"Yeah," Sola said. "Spot on. How did you know?"

"We'll call you back," Titus said, then tapped Kaiden on the shoulder and pointed down a hallway. "I've finally found someone messier than the Southside Boys."

Kaiden turned to look, then froze.

"You know, maybe the voidspawn weren't so bad after all. Can we have those back, please?"

Ahead of them, a hulking figure broke into a trot, then snarled and kicked its pace up into a wild sprint. It was a monster of a man, and all out of proportion, too. As if someone had taken a picture of a normal person, then stretched it a bit too much in every direction.

Too-long arms were coated in bulging muscles. A broad chest was clothed in scars and painted with dried blood.

A scream echoed down the hallway as the figure raised an axe with what appeared to be electricity crackling down the blade. Clutched in its other hand was a warden hammer, perhaps freshly looted from a recent kill.

"Ensigns? What's happening?" Sola's voice crackled through the general comms, but was ignored.

Kaiden focused on the approaching figure, desperate for any information the game would tell him.

Raged Berserker
Level: 6

Quick facts: Raged will attack on sight. They almost exclusively prefer close-range combat. Their active abilities reflect this through devastating melee attacks and grapples, while their passive ability reduces damage

received while in combat by 50%. Their attacks have a small chance to apply the 'Touched by the Raged' debuff.

A health bar above the berserker's head was yellow, but verging on the red.

He's badly injured. That's something, at least.

"Fight together. If we all attack him at once, we can do this. I'm sure of it!" Kaiden said, lying through his teeth. Staring at the man-beast charging down the hallway, he wasn't sure of much except that this fight looked like it was about to go south, and fast. Even injured as it was, the berserker was four levels above him. Not that Kaiden had time to worry about that, because even as he raised his weapon, the raged was on them.

The giant spun, whipping its hammer at Titus, who blocked the blow with a resounding crack against his shield. A second blow from the axe followed, then another and another.

Kaiden watched in horror as Titus' shield flickered...and died.

Before Titus had regained his balance, the raged kicked him in the chest and sent him to the ground. A health bar appeared above Titus' head, then drained to yellow as he fell away.

So I can see my squadmates' health bars now? Is that a perk of being in a party?

Zelda charged in with a hammer strike at the berserker. He slapped her attack aside with the flat of his axe, then swung his axe into her shield. Her shield flickered, but remained on.

While the berserker was distracted with Zelda, Kaiden rushed forward to attack it from the side. He scored a solid hit on its body, drawing its attention onto him.

The raged swung its axe and Kaiden managed to jump aside at the last moment.

Attack dodged!

Note to self: dodging works.

Despite his attack, the brute's health bar had hardly moved at all.

This...could be bad.

The raged took a swing at his head next. Kaiden blocked it

with his shield and saw the white of his charge bar fill nearly to the max. One more and the charge bar maxed out.

Shield overloaded. Shutting down.
Reboot in 30 seconds.

It blinked rapidly, then disappeared.

Crap.

The berserker was already swinging again. Desperate, Kaiden leaned backward, turning his head. The axe blade missed, if only by a millimeter, then embedded itself in the wall.

The raged pulled back, trying to rip the axe from the wall. For a moment his arm was stretched taut, muscles straining.

Zelda took her chance, whacking the raged on its torso just like Kaiden had. Its health moved a smidgeon down.

Hitting this thing in the easy spots doesn't do much. But what about the head? Does Nova have a critical hit system? Only one way to find out.

Before the berserker could pull his axe free, Kaiden straightened and brought his hammer down on the raged's head with a sickening crunch.

Critical hit!
+50% damage (Headshot)

Quick facts: The chance of a critical hit is determined by dexterity and location of the strike. Striking points of weakness, such as strikes from behind and to skeletal joints, will result in a higher critical hit chance. Strikes to the head will always result in a critical hit.

Finally, the raged's health bar slid a noticeable chunk.

"Well done," Titus called. He was on his feet and advancing slowly, wary of attacking without his shield.

"Headshots are guaranteed crits, guys," Kaiden said. "Hit it now while it's stuck."

Zelda wasted no time.

"What's a crit?" Titus asked.

"A big boost to your damage," Kaiden said, taking another swing.

Critical hit!
+50% damage (Headshot)

"Just hit it."

"That I can do," Titus said. The big guy rolled up just as the raged pulled its weapon free. Zelda and Kaiden got in one more hit each, and Titus managed to smash his hammer into the raged's face before it had a chance to react.

That finished the job.

Raged Berserker assisted kill - 150 EXP gained!

Achievement Unlocked!
Indiscriminate Killer - 50 EXP gained!
First it was voidspawn, now you've killed a raged. How very diverse of you. Think of all the other things you can kill next!

Level 3 achieved!
Max health and stamina increased
+3 stat points

Ability unlocked: Shield Bash

Wow, Kaiden thought as he scrolled through the text. *Taking that raged down earned me enough experience to hit level three, though I guess the achievement helped as well.*

He hadn't yet allocated the stat points he'd earned from his first mission, and while he was tempted to use all six of them now, he needed to learn more about which warden specialization he wanted to pursue. As with most MMOs, he suspected different specializations worked best with different stats. Until he knew more, it didn't make sense to spend stat points. The ability, on the other hand, he could use right away.

He focused on it and more details faded into view.

Shield Bash: The warden strikes out with their shield, dealing no damage but stunning the target for 2 seconds. Cost: 15 charge. Cooldown: 2 minutes.

A stun effect? Now that's interesting. This could be a game changer. Kaiden almost wished another raged would show up so he could try it out. Almost.

Speaking of shields, his came back online. With his new move, there was even more incentive to not overload his shield. If it was offline, then he couldn't use Shield Bash.

As Kaiden returned his attention to the others he noticed Zelda was staring off into space.

"Leveled up?" he asked her.

Her eyes were still moving side to side, reading text he couldn't see, but she responded with a nod. He looked to Titus next and found the big guy's face screwed up in confusion.

"'Shield Bash?'" Titus said. "And some more of these stat points. What do I do with them?"

From their lack of a proper introduction to the game, Kaiden had figured Nova Online assumed its players came in with some basic MMO experience. In Titus' case, they had apparently assumed wrong.

"Nova's like most role-playing games, and has stats," Kaiden explained. "It's a system which you use to increase the general power of your character. In Nova, it's perception, endurance, dexterity, strength, and intelligence. Which stats you choose to improve can synergize with your class's playstyle and make you exponentially more powerful. I don't know much about the warden specializations, so for now I'm saving my stat points."

"Right," Zelda chimed in. "But if you knew what spec you wanted to be, you could start using your points right away."

"So," Titus began slowly, "it's like how if you were going to be a thief with the King Street Gang, you'd want to burn your fingerprints and learn how to hack door codes."

"Er, yeah," Kaiden said. "Something like that."

He noticed a line of text hovering in the air nearby. It was above the raged's body.

Loot corpse?

"Can you guys loot this?" he asked.

"Yep," Zelda said. "Seems like that hammer it has is a warden one. Maybe it picked it up during a battle with one of the other squads. One of us could use it."

"Let's see," Kaiden said, eager to see if it was better than the weapon he currently had. He wasn't disappointed.

Strategic Warden Battle Hammer
One-Handed
Base Damage: 9 bludgeoning, 12 smashing
+20% damage inflicted on critical hits

"Wow," Kaiden said. "That extra crit damage looks pretty powerful."

Decimating the raged's health with critical hits had given them a fighting chance. *Maybe there's something to maximizing its output? Probably increasing my dexterity would improve my crit chance like in most other games.*

"So how do we decide who gets it?" Zelda said.

"I say Kaiden gets it," Titus said. "He's the one who figured out the crit thingy and all."

"It wasn't exactly difficult," Kaiden began, then stopped himself. He *really* wanted that upgrade. "But, y'know. If you guys insist?"

Zelda harrumphed.

"You want it?" Kaiden asked.

"No, go on, Kai. You seem most excited about it."

"Awesome," Kaiden said. He looted the new hammer and immediately equipped it.

"Hey, looking good," Titus said.

Kaiden looked down to the weapon and had to agree with the sentiment. It didn't have the same design as a standard battle hammer. Its handle was about one and a half times longer, and instead of a completely flat surface, its two smashing heads rose to slight points such that they looked like a pair of low, flat pyramids.

His old hammer was just sitting in his inventory. Checking on it, the game gave him another option.

Would you like to dual wield weapons?

Note: dual wielding will disable any equipped shields.
Note: weapons cannot be switched during combat.

An interesting idea, but losing my shield is too great a price. Building charge is core to the class design.

Kaiden selected the 'no' option and his old hammer remained in his inventory.

"I have one last question," Titus said, sounding annoyed, though more at himself. "How come my shield turned off?"

"It overloaded," Zelda said, a touch wearily. "When they absorb too much damage too quickly, they shut down. It takes thirty seconds for it to reboot."

Titus look at Zelda.

"Didn't you listen to what Dawson told us?" Zelda said. "Or read your notifications?"

"There's a lot going on," Titus said. "Lay off, alright?" He crossed his arms, then turned very deliberately to Kaiden. "Is there anything else I need to know about this game?"

Zelda snorted.

"Anything else? How about *everything* else?"

"Actually, never mind." Titus stormed off down the hallway. "I'm following my *tiny map* towards the *noobies* we have to rescue. You coming or what?"

Chapter Fourteen

Titus led the way through the corridors of the *Mochinki*, keeping his shield on and at the ready. Zelda was in the middle, head turning side to side as she scanned for signs of more raged. Kaiden watched their rear, but also couldn't stop his eyes from drifting to the health bars on the edge of his vision.

Clutchtime - 90%
gtrain_737 - 33%
MadKilla - 20%
Tomari9 - 82%

Kaiden found it strange that their health bars weren't regenerating. If they were in a safe location, then surely they would be out of combat and would be regaining their health. Maybe the raged were still close to them, or had been regularly raiding the area. But they hadn't been outright killed yet, and that was something.

Four out of four still alive, Kaiden thought to himself, glancing at his minimap. They were getting close now.

"They're all still alive," Zelda said for the thousandth time. "But we have to hurry. Captain Thorne won't consider this a success unless we get all of them out of here."

"Why are you so concerned with impressing the captain all of a sudden?" Kaiden asked. She'd been going on and on about it since they'd left the shuttle. "What's the point if we're planning on, you know—" He lowered his voice. "If we're going to find the assassin who killed Bernstein, we're likely going to have to go off script a little bi—"

"That's one heck of a mess," Titus said, cutting him off as he stared at something down the hall.

"That might qualify for understatement of the century." Kaiden swallowed hard as he too took in the sight.

This must be what's left of Terrel and his group, the ones Sola was trying to rescue. Clearly, she and her squad hadn't made it in time.

The remains before them had been wardens, but beyond that, there wasn't much information to be gained. There was too little left. Kaiden focused on the closest of the corpses.

Cencar Ollo **Deceased**
Warden Private
Class: Power Warden
Faction: Warden Corps
Level: 12

Level twelve? That's really high, relatively speaking. We just barely managed to survive a fight with an injured level six berserker. I can't imagine what seeing a level twelve in combat would look like. It could probably kill us with a look.

Kaiden checked the other corpses for more information. Finally, he came to Terrel.

Terrel **Deceased**
Warden Private
Class: Blast Warden
Faction: Warden Corps
Level: 11

"These Wardens were all at least level eleven," he said, feeling himself frown. The way his shield had overloaded in the recent fight weighed heavily on his mind. One raged had taken down both his and Titus' shield. Against multiple berserkers they wouldn't last more than ten seconds.

"You mean they were all nearly twice as strong as that raged we fought back there? And they *still* died?" The normally rock-steady confidence in Titus' eyes faltered a moment, interrupted by a look of concern. "I need to find some more of those little spawn things and kill a bunch of them until I level up about a dozen times."

"That's called 'grinding,'" Zelda said, but only halfheartedly. The realization of just how far they were in over their heads was a daunting one.

"Um, guys? Are you seeing this?"

Kaiden had looked back down to his minimap, and what he saw there was less than comforting.

Aside from the fight with the raged, thus far his map had shown only their green dots weaving through a maze of hallways. Now, however, several other signatures were being picked up. These were red dots. Enemies. More appeared, a good ten or so, until the dots turned the corner at the end of the hall and stepped into physical view.

Kaiden focused on the first of the newcomers.

Raged Berserker
Level: 10

He focused on the next.

Raged Berserker
Level: 12

He focused on another, then one more for good measure. Both were berserkers. It was a safe bet all the rest were, too.

"Back!" Zelda hissed, yanking them back toward the corner they'd just turned. A scream silenced her efforts, however, as the raged spotted them and broke into a sprint.

Kaiden glanced down to his minimap. They were nearly to the galley, nearly to the new players they were here to rescue in the first place. All that stood between them was the pack of raged. Which, all things considered, might as well have been an army for all the difference it made. There was no way they could hope to fight their way through.

"We can't fight them. We won't stand a chance," Zelda said.

"We have to run," Kaiden said. "Maybe we can lose them and double back?"

The raged were halfway down the hallway now, a screaming,

frenzied mass of flesh and weapons and, as the smell assaulted his nostrils, stink.

"Guys, if we're going to go, we need to do it now..." She trailed off, staring at something behind Kaiden. He turned and found a wall of shields rushing toward him.

The general comms channel crackled to life. "Ensigns, stay behind us!"

It was Sola! The lieutenant they'd heard earlier.

Four wardens with large rectangular shields rushed past. They spread out as they passed Kaiden and the others, then bunched back up, side to side so that their shields formed a near complete wall, protecting them from shin to shoulder.

Kaiden stared in awe, bringing up the additional details screen on one of them.

Gareth Marleon
Warden Private
Class: Shield Warden
Faction: Warden Corps
Level: 11

Quick facts: Shield Wardens are the tanks of the Warden Corps. Boasting shields increased in size and charge capacity, they fight on the front lines, drawing enemy attention and protecting weaker allies.

Tanks in the front; that makes sense, Kaiden though, entirely forgetting his fear as he studied the new arrivals.

The raged howled with renewed anger and excitement at the sight of the reinforcements, then threw themselves at the shield wardens. Several berserkers launched into the air, weapons held high above their heads, all slamming against the shield wall. The shield wardens were driven back a pace, but dug their feet in and held their ground.

"Ensigns!" A hand grabbed Kaiden's shoulder and pulled him to the side. A warden he could only assume was Sola stood over him. He focused on her to be sure.

Sola
Warden Lieutenant

Class: Enhanced Warden
Faction: Warden Corps
Level: 13

**Quick facts: Enhanced wardens are a unique support
class able to quickly process strategic information, using
speed to scout ahead, deliver vital intel and escape deadly
situations. Powerful visors allow them to analyze additional information.**

It was Sola, all right. She wore some sort of advanced combat
armor which included the aforementioned visor over her eyes. It
wasn't much more than a thin, sleek strip of glass, but numbers
and images flashed on it, detailing a vast amount of information.

Zelda and Titus were still staring in awe at the shield
wardens, but she grabbed them too and pulled them back to
stand beside Kaiden.

"Stay here and stay alive." With that, she turned toward the
fighting.

"Shielders ready?" she called out.

"Ready!" the wardens on the front line called back.

"Blasters on three, then. One, two, three!" Sola shouted the
command, then ducked to one side. As she did, the shield
wardens in front parted, spinning to the sides of the hallway. For
a moment the raged were left staring, confused by the unex-
pected move, perhaps. They weren't left confused for long,
however, as a second line of wardens stepped up, leveled their
hammers as if they were guns, and fired.

A barrage of spears made of crackling, glowing light exploded
forward. All the berserkers were hit at least once, and those hit
more than once fell backward, clearly severely injured.

"And again!"

Another barrage, this one of smaller blasts that looked more
like laser-bullets and far less powerful, though it killed several of
the weakened raged.

Kaiden focused on one of the hammer-gun-toting wardens to
get more information.

Terhan
Warden Private

Class: Blast Warden
Faction: Warden Corps
Level: 11

Quick facts: Blast wardens are the ranged fighters of the Warden Corps. Wielding modified hammers that sacrifice melee attacks for the ability to fire a variety of laser-based projectiles, blast wardens engage from a distance and are particularly strong when front line fighters distract the enemy.

"Now that's a sensible way to fight," Zelda said, jaw near hanging to the floor as she watched the 'blasters,' as Sola had called them.

Just as the shield wardens had larger, shoulder-to-shin shields, so too had the blast warden shields changed based on their specialization. They had become thinner, with half-circles cut into either side so their bodies could still be relatively covered while their hammer-guns fired through the slots.

The hammer-gun itself was long and thin, with the weapon's handle turned into a gunstock. A trigger protruded along its bottom and the laser blasts emerged from the adapted head of the hammer.

The ranks of the raged were considerably thinned by the one-two punch of the shield wardens followed by the blast wardens. But the remaining raged charged through the short corridor left by the parted shield wardens, screaming bloody murder.

"Powereds," Sola yelled, turning to the last few wardens not engaged in the fight. "Have at 'em."

There was no need to say anything else. Like bizarre, angry grasshoppers, the remaining four wardens launched into the air. Their behemoth-sized hammers near struck the ceiling before they slammed down into the raged. Each blow sent a roiling, shimmering shockwave out in a small radius. One, two, three, four shockwaves in total that battered the raged.

When the air cleared, only two were left standing. A quick glance told Kaiden their health bars were in the red, but he might as well not have bothered looking because one moment and several hammer strikes later they fell to the floor, dead.

Achievement Unlocked!
Impossible Odds - 100 EXP gained!
**Somehow, you survived a near-impossible fight. You're
not hacking, are you?**

In the wake of the battle, Kaiden focused on one of the
grasshopper-like wardens who had gone blow for blow with the
raged and come out just fine.

Marsin
Warden Private
Class: Power Warden
Faction: Warden Corps
Level: 11

**Quick facts: Power wardens are the warriors of the
Warden Corps. All offense, all the time, they have a
much-reduced size of shield, but also gain some charge
by hitting with their hammers. An appropriate ability,
considering how charge-hungry their onslaught of
attacks can be.**

"Well done, wardens," Sola said, nodding at the results of the
incredibly quick skirmish. "Good thing we had some charge left
over from the last fight. Now, reform ranks. Those players aren't
going to rescue themselves, eh?"

The shielders took the front, followed by two of the power
wardens, then the blasters, then the remaining two power
wardens. The whole formation locked together tightly, then
awaited further orders.

"Ensigns," Sola said, turning to them. "You came in on the
Borrelly, right? I'm afraid we lost contact a while back. Have you
heard anything from Lieutenant Ellenton?"

"No, we haven't," Kaiden said, feeling more concern for their
laid-back handler than he'd expected to. "Is she okay?"

"Well," Sola chuckled, "I'm not sure she was ever *okay*. Last I
heard from her she was merrily dogfighting a bunch of pirate
ships, then she cut off. The long and short of it is, you're stuck
with us until we can hail another warden ship to give us a ride."

"Our mission was to rescue the new players holed up in the

galley," Zelda said. "We have to get them out of here. Even if we could, we can't just leave."

"Command had a mix-up, or bad intel," Sola said. "Either way, you shouldn't be anywhere near this fight. But, since you are stuck here, you're my responsibility, and I won't have you dying on my watch. Stay with the group and stay out of the fighting." Without missing a beat, she turned to the wardens under her command. "Move it out, you lot. Those players aren't going to rescue themselves."

Chapter Fifteen

The noobs had barricaded themselves in the galley. Toppled freezer units made something approximating a wall. Power wardens and shield wardens made short work clearing the debris and Sola strode into the galley, Kaiden following in her wake.

"Someone called for a rescue party?" Sola said.

Four sets of eyes peered over the top of an overturned table.

"Wardens," a relieved whisper ran through the group.

"Well, it's about dang time!" One of the noobs stood up with an aggravated gesture. The game revealed his name was 'Mad-Killa' as Kaiden focused on him. It also showed his health was still low in the red. "We called for you more than half an hour ago. What, did you stop for lunch on the way over?"

"Ran into a spot of trouble." Sola rested her bloody hammer across her shoulders. "Nothing we couldn't handle."

"Fine, whatever," MadKilla said. He held out a hand expectantly. "I need some health stims."

Sola shook her head. "No can do, kid. We had to use them all ourselves fighting the raged. Sorry."

MadKilla looked aghast. "What? We all got cleaved by some attack and got a crappy debuff called 'Touched by the Raged' which is preventing our health regening for like a whole hour. Ridiculous."

Sola shrugged. "Bad luck, I guess. That's why we're here."

"Well, maybe next time you should do a better job," MadKilla said. "With how much this game costs each month you'd think we'd be able to get some decent protection."

"You know," Sola said, approaching him. "I don't expect gratitude for doing my job, but a bit of civility would be nice."

"Maybe you shouldn't have gotten yourself thrown in prison if you wanted *civility*."

This, apparently, was the last straw. Sola touched MadKilla with her hammer – gently, no more than a tap – and there was a flash of light. The light shrank, then solidified into a mess of chains. They coiled around MadKilla's wrists, arms, legs, and ankles, then with a snap, tightened all at once. The noob balked, then gasped as he fell to the floor, securely bound.

"What did you do?" he shouted.

"I've Shackled you, you little twerp," Sola said. "And if you don't apologise, I'm gonna just leave you here for the raged."

"That's it," Zelda hissed in Kaiden's ear. "That's the ability I was trying to tell you about during Sergeant Dawson's briefing. It's the wardens' most valuable ability."

"What does it do?" Kaiden whispered back.

"So, it chains players up, like you see there," Zelda explained. "They can't physically move in-game from it. More importantly, it prevents them logging off."

"That seems a bit...broken."

"It was a sticking point for NexGen, but they capitulated in the end," Zelda said. "If wardens are catching players who've committed fineable offences in-game, or have to question them about something, they can't have the player just log off or fight to the death. This is partly why not every warden gets the move as a standard ability. You have to earn it from the higher-ups."

Kaiden now better understood Zelda's plan. "So, if we have Shackle, when we find this assassin we can use it on him and get him talking."

"That's the idea," Zelda said.

Further conversation was interrupted by MadKilla's sobbing.

"Let me out of this, please. I'm sorry."

"Oh, be quiet for a moment, will you?" Sola said. "I'm trying to check if we can get a shuttle out of here." She began to pace the galley, speaking over another comms channel. "This is Lieutenant Sola to all craft near *Mochinki Station*. Looking for evac. Over."

From behind their table, the other players in peril trotted out to stand near their shackled friend. Tomari9 looked down on him with a withering look. Clutchtime was smirking to himself.

Now Kaiden was close enough to all the players, quest notifications started popping up.

Quest Complete: Rescue trapped players on *Mochinki* Station
Part 1: Reach the players
Rewards: +900 EXP, + 4 faction prestige

Level 4 achieved!
Max health and stamina increased
+3 stat points

Ability unlocked: Hammer Toss

One whole level jump, just like that? And another new move as well! I guess the quest difficulty changed to veteran, so it makes sense. We weren't supposed to be on a mission this hard.

He focused on his new ability.

Hammer Toss: The warden throws their hammer, dealing x 2 base damage if they successfully hit the target. The hammer will return itself to the warden's hand. While disarmed, the warden is unable to use other abilities that require a hammer. Minimum range: 10 feet. Maximum range: 30 feet. Cost: 20 charge. Cooldown: 30 seconds.

Kaiden felt himself smile as he finished reading the specifics of Hammer Toss. The ability to hit a target without getting close enough to be hit back would be very useful.

"These new abilities we've been unlocking are a huge step forward," Zelda said. "Hammer Toss, particularly. After fighting that raged, I'd quite like to put a bit of distance between myself and enemies."

Titus groaned. "Another thing? I'm just getting used to

swinging my hammer, never mind tossing it. Might ignore it. I prefer things up and personal, anyway."

"Ignore it?" Zelda said, clearly appalled. "Why would you not want to use a perfectly good—"

Kaiden placed a hand on her shoulder to stop her, gently shaking his head. She got the message.

"I mean," she recovered, "whatever playstyle suits you, Titus. Go for it."

Titus hefted his hammer onto his shoulder with a grunt of satisfaction. "That's mighty kind of you."

Sola finished pacing and rounded on her wardens and the noob players with purpose.

"Alright. Here's the deal. I can't reach any other warden vessels. I suspect most craft have been re-routed to deal with the Leviathan. In which case, I say we head for the hangar and see if—"

"Hello in there!" A voice boomed through the room, ringing up and down the hallways of the *Mochinki.*

Lieutenant Ellenton?

"Can you hear me? The *Borrelly*'s comm array is currently floating away in about a dozen pieces, so I had to hack into the *Mochinki*'s systems. I can see you through a security cam. Nod if you can hear me." Wardens and noobs alike nodded toward the ship's speakers embedded in the ceiling.

"Cool. Alright, so here's the skinny. I've got good news, bad news, more good news, and then some *really* bad news. The good news is all the pirates out here have been scrapped. And boy, you should have seen it. Heck of a battle. But they had it coming to 'em. No one shoots at the *Borrelly.* No one shoots at my baby!" She paused, as if remembering they were on a mission. "Ahem, uh, anyway, the bad news is I'm the last warden ship out here. The others took an involuntary week-long vacation."

"Just glad you're alright," Sola said.

"Sola, I see your mouth moving, but I don't have any sound. The system wasn't really meant for this, so it's kind of a one-way deal."

Sola gestured as if to say, "Out with it, already."

"Right, right. So, the other good news is I'm en route to the *Mochinki*'s hangar now. Might be a bit cramped in my little shuttle, but we'll make it work. That just leaves the really bad news."

Lieutenant Ellenton paused, then sucked in a breath. "From what I'm seeing on the *Mochinki's* cams, the raged took the bridge. They'll have control of the ship any minute now."

Yeah, Kaiden had to agree, *that's some really bad news.*

A rumble growled through the floor, then traveled up the walls, shaking its way into the ceiling and to the decks above.

"That was the engines," Sola said, frowning. "They're trying to commandeer the station."

"Then we'd better move quick," Sola said. "Ready up, everyone."

"Huh, that's not good," Lieutenant Ellenton said. The room waited in agonizing silence for her to speak again. "Um, the berserkers are moving toward your location now. Why would they be...how did they know...oh. Oh, crap."

A scream ripped through the corridor outside. Then another. A moment later, a third.

When Lieutenant Ellenton spoke again, her words came quick, urgent.

"They hear me. They hear me talking to you through the speakers. I can see them on the cams. They're heading your way. All of them."

Even as she spoke, the room erupted. Sola shouted commands, her wardens shouted back acknowledgements, and the noobs just shouted.

In the midst of the chaos, Kaiden watched as red blips appeared on his minimap. They were filling the nearby corridors, heading for the galley.

"Meet me in the hangar," Ellenton urged. "We gotta blow this joint. Oh, and Sola? Looks like you're flying with me again after all, eh?"

Kaiden stepped toward the noobs. "We'll need to keep them alive."

"I'm not carrying the mouthy one," Titus said, nodding toward MadKilla.

"No one's carrying anyone," Sola said. She tapped her hammer and the chains binding MadKilla blinked out of existence. "Don't complain, and do as I say if you want to get out of this. You players stay close to the ensigns. My wardens and I will cover you all. Hopefully you don't have to engage in too much direct combat. Sound good?"

Update
Quest: Rescue trapped players on *Mochinki Station*
Part 2: You found them. Good for you. Now get them out of there.
Expected difficulty: Veteran
Rewards: +1,500 EXP, +4 faction prestige

"This game sure likes to poke fun," Titus said. He flicked his wrist and his shield blinked on. "Still, sounds good to me."

Zelda bit her lower lip, but her eyes were determined.

"Sounds like a chance to impress Command."

Kaiden nodded at them, then turned back to Sola.

"Sounds like the best plan we've got."

"Sounds like we're all going to die," MadKilla said.

Sola rolled her eyes.

Kaiden ignored him, turning to the rest of the noobs.

"Alright, guys. You've all had a pretty rough day, I know. But stick with us and we'll get you out of here." He slapped the nearest one on the back, hoping his false confidence might instill some of the real thing in them. "Now, who's up for a run?"

~

Chaos. Kaiden had once thought he'd known the definition of the word. He'd been wrong.

After pelting through the melee of raged and Sola's wardens, draining their stamina bars, the sounds of battle were beginning to fade. Kaiden, Zelda, and Titus directed the players toward the hangar.

"Ah, there's my squad," Ellenton's voice blared above their heads. "You're close now, but be careful. The bulk of the raged are dealing with Sola but there are a couple just outside the hangar."

Kaiden checked his minimap again and, sure enough, red dots sprang to life.

The bulkhead door at the end of the corridor had the words 'hangar bay' emblazoned above it. In front of the door were two raged berserkers, both level six and at full health. The raged caught sight of them and began running straight for them.

Their own small group stopped dead.

"Now what?" MadKilla sneered.

"We fight them, that's what," Kaiden said.

"Not many other options," Titus said, raising his shield.

They had all blocked some damage during the rush here, so they had some charge. The single raged they'd fought before had been hellish, but they'd levelled up twice since and gained new abilities. They could handle two raged.

Kaiden turned to Zelda. "Hit them from ranged?"

She nodded, raising her hammer, preparing to throw it.

"You too, big guy," Kaiden said. "Help us out here. Hit that one on the right."

He used Hammer Toss, launching his hammer toward the raged, and managed to hit it squarely in the chest.

Hammer Toss hit!
+100% damage

Zelda's hammer thudded into it next, bringing the raged to half health. Titus', however, veered to the side, missing the creature completely.

"So not my style," Titus bellowed. "I'm on this one." He pointed to the raged on the left then charged off without his hammer.

"Okay, we'll finish this one off," Kaiden said. Not wanting the raged to get too close to the noobs, he surged forward as well, Zelda at his side. Their hammers flew back to their hands, ready to meet the enemy.

It took a swipe at Zelda first. She skidded, nearly lost her balance, then backed away.

"I really don't like being so close to them," she said. "Maybe I'll back away and use Hammer Toss again.

The raged let her run, turning on Kaiden instead.

"It's got a thirty-second cooldown," he shouted at her back. "Help me here."

An axe swing forced him to drop into a squat as it sliced the air overhead. Down low, he took the chance to aim for its knees.

Critical Hit!
+20% damage (Kneecapped)

Combined with the extra crit damage from his new hammer, his attack had more of an impact than before. The raged's health flashed and fell by a nice chunk into the red. It screamed in annoyance, raining putrid spittle upon Kaiden. A heavy hammer strike to its face silenced it.

Raged Berserker assisted kill - 150 EXP gained!

Zelda stood behind the collapsing raged. "Headshots are always crits, right?"

"Mind hitting this one a bit?" Titus called.

Kaiden scrambled to his feet, concerned to see Titus' health in the yellow, though his shield was still up.

"Try Shield Bash," Kaiden said, already running over to help

Titus' shield crackled and sparked, energy surging within it. He rammed his shield into the raged and it stood still, looking dazed.

Kaiden scored an easy headshot on the stunned mob.

Critical Hit!
+50% damage (Headshot)

He was beginning to see a nice strategy forming around getting crits, and stunned mobs were far easier to hit in the right places.

The raged was emerging from Titus' stun, so Kaiden tried his own. He used Shield Bash, lashing out at the raged's back.

Warning! Using consecutive stunning abilities on a single target reduces their effect.

Raged Berserker stunned for 1.5 seconds

Kaiden took what time he had to fit in another critical hit, but only just. As the reduced stun wore off, the raged turned on him. He supposed it was only fair. Chain-stunning enemies would have been overpowered, and most games did have a system of diminishing returns.

He tried to dodge the raged's next attack but failed

horribly, losing a third of his health in the process. Titus cracked the mob in the back, but it wasn't enough to kill it.

A hammer slamming into it did.

Raged Berserker assisted kill – 150 EXP gained!

"Yes!" Zelda cheered.

"Nice shot," Titus called, proffering a hand to Kaiden to help him up.

"Good work, guys," Kaiden said. He looked to MadKilla and gave a mock bow. "Does that satisfy you, sir?"

MadKilla scowled. "Let's just get out of here."

They all ran up to the bulkhead door to the hangar bay.

"It's not opening," MadKilla said. "Make it open, or we won't escape in time."

"Thanks for the tip," Titus said, pulling on one of the manual handles with all his might. "You know, we have a special way to deal with guys like you out on the streets. First, you find a nice big dumpster—"

The speaker overhead blared into life. "It's sealed, big fella," Ellenton said. "Don't waste your time. The raged on the bridge locked me out but I should be able to take back control of the door. Give me two minutes."

"Not sure we have two minutes," Zelda said. She was pointing back to the far end of the corridor where four more raged had appeared. Each one was level seven and in various states of lowered health from some recent battle.

"Sola and her crew aren't all dead, are they?" Titus asked.

The raged howled and broke into a run. One spun two axes as it ran, kicking up sparks as their blades screeched against the metal floor.

Kaiden reopened his general comms. Sounds of battle echoed over the channel.

"Sola? Sola, are you still there?"

"Just about," Sola said. "You?"

"Four raged are on us. We're stuck outside the hangar."

"On my way."

The raged were nearly on them.

"Is she coming?" MadKilla demanded. "They're getting close.

Do something!"

Kaiden faced him. "You really are the worst. You know that, right?" Then he raised his hammer and shield and stepped forward. His Hammer Toss was off cooldown so he could use that in a pinch, but Shield Bash would be on cooldown for over a minute still. Hammer Smash wasn't a game changer here.

He felt stuck.

Zelda and Titus came to stand by his side. They'd put up a good fight, at least.

And then Sola was there.

She was running incredibly fast, some sort of ability obviously enhancing her speed. She flashed behind the raged, striking mercilessly fast at their backs and heads, polishing off the three weaker ones before facing the fourth. As it turned on her, her form began to flicker, blurring almost, and she dodged its attacks with ease.

Kaiden and the others ran forward to help, using Hammer Toss and adding their blows to Sola's own.

"Thank you, Lieutenant," Kaiden said once it was over.

Sola waved a hand as if it were nothing. "I remember my early days in the program. Pay it forward by helping others out sometime."

A whoop of joy echoed up the entire corridor. "The hangar door is open, guys," Ellenton said. "Can my training wheel squad and the players they are rescuing hop aboard? Time to leave this hell hole."

Everyone turned and bolted for the hangar.

All except Kaiden. He hung back.

"Aren't you coming?" he asked Sola.

She shook her head. "There's no way we're all fitting on that one shuttle."

"But the quest to rescue the players—"

"Is your quest," Sola said. "Mine was to bring a company of wardens and clear out the raged from this corner of the system. Like I said, Command screwed this one up for you guys."

"So you're staying to fight them?"

"Sort of. There are too many on this station, though, I think. Too many for a fair fight and I'm losing wardens with each battle. But just a few decks below us is the *Mochinki*'s reactor room. Destabilize the core on a station this big and there won't even be a debris field by the time it's done imploding on itself. I'll do it myself."

Kaiden opened his mouth to respond, then paused. He looked toward the distant *Borrelly* sitting inside the hangar for him. Even if Lieutenant Ellenton was flying, it suddenly seemed far safer.

"Hurry up, Kaiden Moore," Sola said. "We're not really going to die, remember? My company has worked hard today. The way I see it, we're owed some time off. Nothing wrong with a little vacation."

"Thanks for saving us," Kaiden said. Then he made for the *Borrelly*.

Sola called after him. "And make sure you tell Ellenton I chose death by implosion rather than fly with her again."

Chapter Sixteen

To Kaiden, the word 'implosion' had seemed to imply that when the *Mochinki*'s core was destabilized the station would disappear into itself. Maybe in a flash of blinding light. Or maybe with a great, void-shaking roar. Or maybe even with a terrible silence. What he hadn't expected was that it would be all of those things, one after the other.

Oh, and then there was rapidly approaching shockwave.

Alarms beeped and sirens blared throughout the cockpit as seemingly every one of the shuttle's systems warned them about the incoming blast.

"This might be a bit bumpier than usual," Lieutenant Ellenton said, pushing the *Borrelly* to max thrust.

"Considering how bumpy her usual is, that's a thoroughly worrying prospect," Zelda said, bracing herself against one wall.

"Hold on back there!" Titus shouted to the noobs. "Strap in if you can."

"She really chose implosion?" Lieutenant Ellenton seemed completely calm despite the chaos around them. "I mean, we *barely* crashed last time." She paused. "Oh, but there was that time when–"

The shockwave hit them and the *Borrelly* near shook itself apart. Somehow, it made it through in one piece. Or in enough of one piece to make it back to the *Anakoni*. When the hulking carrier class ship appeared in front of them, silhouetted by a thousand, thousand stars, an audible sigh of relief swept through their shuttle.

～

"The medbay's not that far," Kaiden said, leading the noobs they'd rescued down the *Borrelly*'s ramp and into the hangar. "We'll show you the way, then you can get that debuff removed and be on your way."

All four had miraculously survived.

"I'll take them from here, ensigns," Lieutenant Ellenton said, striding down the ramp.

"Really?" Kaiden asked, pausing a moment. He hadn't known her long, but volunteering for a job she didn't have to do seemed pretty contrary to her usual priorities.

Ellenton smiled.

"Before the *Mochinki* went...whatever the opposite of 'boom' is, Sola forwarded the details of what happened on your mission." She shook her head. "It made me tired just thinking about it, but for ensigns tossed into an impossible situation, well, you did alright." She shrugged. "So I forwarded a report along to Command. Way I see it, maybe your hard work can earn us all a little time off, eh? Ava – er, Captain Thorne wants to see you." She pointed to an officer striding across the hangar toward them. "Personally."

Kaiden's breath caught in his throat. He looked to Zelda and found the same expression on her face that he imagined was on his own.

"Captain Thorne," she said, excitement building in her eyes.

"Looks like we impressed Command, alright." Titus said.

"We're still dealing with the Leviathan," Captain Thorne said, head turned slightly to one side as she spoke into her comms. "Yes. I know it has to be killed soon." She paused. "Understood, sir." With that, she turned to face them.

"Ensigns Zelda, Titus, and Kaiden. You did good work out there today. Made the Warden Corps proud."

Thorne
Warden Captain
Class: Power Warden

Faction: Warden Corps
Level: 25

Quick facts: Captain Thorne, one of the most decorated officers in the Warden Corps, is also the captain of the WCSS *Anakoni*. A famous power warden on the fast track to admiralship, her exploits in combat are as well-known as her effectiveness as a peacekeeping agent.

A shiny captain's badge was pinned to her chest, and her well-muscled physique was apparent even through her armor. Considering character creation was locked to default for wardens, a physique like hers meant she actually was that muscular in the real world. That seemed fitting, considering the steely ambition Kaiden saw in her eyes. She looked far too young to be a captain, but here she was.

Her nondescript brown hair was trimmed short in a military cut, and despite the determination in her eyes, she greeted them with an easy smile. The behemoth hammer of a power warden was strapped to her back; a thing of beauty, ornate and elegant, with the color of shining silver.

Some sort of high level, epic weapon, most likely. I bet it has awesome stats.

"We knew some heroes would emerge out of this whole Leviathan crisis, but I don't think anyone expected to find them down at the rank of ensign. I reviewed the report from Lieutenant Ellenton, and I have to say I'm impressed. You never should have been on the *Mochinki* in the first place; that one's on us." She sighed and gave them a guilty smile. "Reports said to expect pirates in the area, but we'd heard nothing about raged. Though that didn't stop you from completing your mission, did it?" She nodded at the backs of the noobs as Lieutenant Ellenton led them from the hangar. "Well done, ensigns."

"Thank you, ma'am." Zelda gave a half-nod.

"We can't take credit for everything, though," Kaiden said. "Lieutenant Sola and her wardens helped us immensely. We never would have made it without them."

Thorne nodded at that.

"Lieutenant Sola and her unit did a fine job, as well. They'll be rewarded for it once they're back online. In the meantime, I'm giving you three a commendation."

As she said the word, a barrage of system text filled Kaiden's screen.

Quest Completed: Rescue trapped players on *Mochinki Station*
Part 2: You found them. Good for you. Now get them out of there.
Rewards: +1,500 EXP, +4 faction prestige

Commendation
Impressed by your actions, a superior officer has awarded you an EXP and faction prestige bonus for this mission.
+3,000 EXP, +2 faction prestige

Level 5 achieved!
Max health and stamina increased
+3 stat points

Class specialization unlocked!

Level 6 achieved!
Max health and stamina increased
+3 stat points

Armour capability unlocked: Stimpacks

Achievement unlocked!
A for Effort - 100 EXP gained!
You've impressed the higher-ups in your chosen faction and received a commendation. Well done! 2 more commendations and you'll unlock the optional player title: Teacher's Pet!

"Holy cow, that's a lot of text," Titus said, eyes wide as he took it all in. "Level five and six at the same time? Ha!"

Captain Thorne laughed.

"Ah, to be a newbie again and earn levels so easily." She shook her head. "Anyway, if I can fill your screen with one last message, I have another reward for you. I think you've earned it."

Kaiden felt himself smile as one more system message faded into view.

Restricted ability unlocked: Shackle
Allows a warden to touch a player with their hammer, creating restraints made of pure energy. Restricts all movement and use of abilities or items. Prevents players from logging out until removed. Can only be applied when a character is at critical health.

He tried to keep his enthusiasm contained, but the harder he fought, the more he felt his smile grow.

Yes! This is a huge step forward!

For the first time since he'd been thrown in prison, he felt like he was making progress toward freedom. Felt like maybe he could actually clear his name.

We can do this. We can actually do this.

He reined his excitement in for a moment. He still needed to look professional in front of the captain, after all.

"You three have made great strides today," she said, giving them a slight smile. "Whatever happened in the real world, whatever happened outside of Nova, is history. There's no changing it. But that doesn't matter. In here, you can make up for your mistakes. You're not there yet, but keep it up and you might just earn yourselves a fresh start in the real world. If you didn't already know, I'm the one who decides how much time gets shaved off your sentence."

"Thank you, Captain," Zelda said, and Kaiden and Titus repeated her words.

"I'll be watching your future exploits with interest, ensigns. There's not much time left in the day, so I'd use it to pick your specs, if I were you." She turned to leave. "And get some rest tonight. I've got a big mission for you tomorrow."

"Yes, Captain," they said in unison as she walked away. When she was out of earshot Zelda gave a fist pump and an excited cheer.

"Yes! We actually did it. I mean, I figured we could, but so soon?" She shook her head. "I have to say, I'm kind of impressed."

"You could say we make a good team," Kaiden said, smiling at her excitement.

Zelda hesitated, then looked to Titus. He met her gaze and held it for a long moment.

"Yeah," she finally said. "I guess you could."

"Not half bad," Titus agreed. "Not half bad at all."

"It's good to see you two finally agreeing on something," Kaiden said, laughing.

Titus gave a low, gravelly chuckle.

"Let's not make a habit of it."

"Let's not."

Chapter Seventeen

Kaiden's settings menu showed it was approaching dinnertime in the real world, which meant they'd be forced to log out soon. As such, they hurried to the canteen to discuss their class specializations. Not that they needed to sit down – standing didn't use any stamina — but waiting in the middle of the hangar to discuss their choices felt somehow wrong. Nova was a game, but it was a realistic game, and old habits died hard.

"Zelda, you care to go first?" Kaiden said to kick off the conversation.

"Sure thing."

There was a long moment of silence as he and Titus waited for her to speak. Instead, her eyes went distant. Then there was a flash of light and her hammer and bracer began to glow. They became so bright Kaiden had to avert his eyes, blinded by the burning light.

"And...done," Zelda said cheerfully as the light faded.

Kaiden turned his eyes back to find her hammer had changed, matching the hammer-guns he had seen on the *Mochinki*. The handle was now a gunstock, complete with a trigger on the underside and the hammerhead on the end forming the barrel.

An ally has chosen their class!
Ensign Zelda has chosen the blast warden class.

Blast wardens are all about the long game. Their shield is now circular and transparent with twin hollows on each side to fire through. Their hammer is now a hammer-gun. Melee attacks are disabled. Laser blasts fire from their weapon as a new basic attack. Their hammer-gun has also gained the 'Atmospheric Charge' ability.

Atmospheric Charge: Allows you access to an alternate source of charge, drawing energy from your surroundings at a rate of 5 charge every 1 second in combat.

"Oh," Kaiden said, hesitating. "I thought we were going to talk about it first. Maybe pick specs that work well together."

"No need." She waved his suggestion away. "From the moment I saw Lieutenant Sola's blast wardens doing their thing, I started dumping my stat points into perception and intelligence – the primary attributes needed for blast wardens. Perception increases my accuracy and intelligence increases damage instead of strength. Ranged fighting is the only way to do it, in my opinion." She paused a moment. "Uh, you two should pick what works best for you, too."

"Well, alright," Kaiden said. "That's one down, I suppose."

Kind of wish we could have talked that out first. Whatever. On to Titus.

"What were you thinking? Did any specs catch your eye?"

The big man shrugged.

"To be honest, I wasn't paying much attention. To busy trying to keep everyone alive. Not to mention myself."

Kaiden nodded. Couldn't blame him there. It had been one crazy mission they'd just finished.

"There are four warden specializations," Zelda explained like an excitable teacher. "Blast wardens, power wardens, shield wardens and enhanced wardens."

Kaiden recalled watching each of the classes battle back on the *Mochinki*. Each one looked like it had its own distinct advantages. He wouldn't pick blast warden, since now their squad already had a ranged damage dealer. He wished he could speak to some other wardens about the choice – he really didn't want to make a specialization decision without complete information.

I'll figure it out later. Let's get Titus settled first.

"You know," Kaiden said to him. "Power warden might be a good choice. A big man like you would be an intimidating opponent."

"Not that size has any correlation to strength in this game," Zelda added.

"Oh yeah." Kaiden nodded, half-lost in his own thoughts.

The more he thought about it, the more it made sense. Titus was already intimidating of his own accord. Give him the movement abilities, massive damage, and the huge hammer of a power warden and he'd be a walking terror to his enemies.

"I'll pass on that one."

Huh?

That was far from the answer he'd expected. Maybe Titus just wasn't seeing the advantages.

"Really? Power wardens are like the front-line fighters of the corps. They have a lot of offensive abilities. You could deal massive amounts of damage."

"I'm not interested."

"Why not?"

"I...uh..." Titus sighed, then shook his head. When he spoke again, his eyes were distant and sad. "I've killed before. For real. Not by choice," he added quickly. "Or so I tell myself. But there's no way around the fact that I killed a man." He breathed deeply, then continued, as if he had been wanting to get it off his chest.

"Back in the day, before the King Street Gang and all that, I was a bare-knuckle boxer, and a darn good one. Maybe too good. I was in a title fight with big money on the line. Enough to pay my family's bills for a year. We weren't well off, not in any sense, so for us that was life-changing kind of money, you know?" Titus sighed, but soldiered on with his story.

"I had the better of my opponent from the first round. Knocked him silly, but he stayed up. Punch after punch, he stayed up. Now, this was street rules boxing. You don't just go twelve rounds then pick a winner. No, if both fighters are still standing after that final round, no one wins." Titus cracked his knuckles and frowned at the memory.

"He knew I had him beat. Everyone did. But he wouldn't go down. Wanted me to lose with him, I guess. But my family *needed* that money. I had to put him down. So I hit harder. And then next time he stumbled, I hit him harder than that. Somehow, though, he made it to the end of the twelfth round. Made it until the bell rang, then collapsed. The doctors later said he was dead before he hit the mat."

The big man sat in silence a moment as Kaiden reeled from the story. He managed a glance at Zelda and found her looking similarly shaken.

"I didn't mean to kill him," Titus said. "But that's irrelevant, because I did kill him. And my family didn't get the money, either. And then my brother..." he trailed off. "That doesn't matter right now. All I'm trying to say is, if I can avoid being a killer, I'd like to. I know we're just in a game, but I don't do aggression anymore. I'm done with that path."

Kaiden found himself at a loss for words.

What do I say to follow that? What does anyone say?

"I...uh, I'm sorry about all that, Titus. I had no idea."

Titus shrugged. And then, to Kaiden's surprise, he chuckled. Not in a happy way. It was a sad sort of chuckle.

"That's why I believed you, Kai. I've spent my life around thieves and murderers, and worse. I know what those kinds of people look like. I know the darkness in their eyes. The lack of feeling, of kindness, inside them. I know the look, and you don't have it. You didn't kill Bernstein, but you didn't have to tell me that, I could tell from the moment I met you."

"Thank you, Titus. For believing me. And for trusting me enough to say all of that."

"For trusting *us*," Zelda said with a gentle smile. Then she clapped, snapping them out of the moment. "Though if I'm being honest, things are getting a bit too chummy around here for my taste. I liked it better when you were just a big dumb brute Kai had decided to drag along." Her tone was jovial, and she elbowed Titus in the ribs for good measure.

"Well, maybe I liked you better as the snarky know-it-all with a reckless plan that's going to get us all sentenced to life in prison. Again."

"We're agreeing on things," Zelda said. "We have to stop doing that."

Titus smirked. "Agreed."

Zelda sighed.

Kaiden laughed at the two of them.

"Alright. Back to business. Titus, I have another idea. Power warden is off the table. But what about shield warden? Based on what you told me, you'd make a great tank."

"Tank?"

"Yeah. A tank is a character that draws the enemy's attention and takes damage for the rest of the team. They protect the squishier classes – those not designed for taking punishment – so the rest of the group can focus on dealing damage."

Titus rubbed his chin, considering. "Like how Sola's shield wardens held the front line while the blast wardens attacked from a distance?"

"Exactly!" Kaiden said. "And, as it happens, we already have a blast warden."

"I wouldn't mind having someone up front to keep the enemy distracted," Zelda said. "Makes my job that much easier."

Titus smiled, the dark mood his memories had brought on seemingly forgotten.

"You know, that sounds pretty good." He slapped a hand on the table. "How do I do it?"

Kaiden took a few moments for himself as Zelda walked Titus through the process of selecting his specialization. First, he pulled up his character sheet to see how it'd changed since the last time he'd checked it.

Character
Name: Kaiden
Race: Human
Level: 6
Class: Warden
Attributes
Strength: 15 *Intelligence:* 15
Endurance: 15 *Perception:* 15
Dexterity: 15 *Unassigned:* 15
Abilities:
Hammer Smash, Shield Bash, Hammer Toss, Shackle
Perks:
None

Class specialization unlocked! Choose now?

That's a lot of unassigned stat points.

He was tempted to assign them all now. The flashing final line of his "abilities" section appeared to want the same.

Part of him wanted to do it, but another part knew it was a foolish decision. He needed to pick his spec with intention and purpose. He needed to pick whatever spec would best help them complete their mission and reveal the truth about Bernstein's murder.

And he did need to consider his own playstyle, too. Fun was a part of it, but being stuck in a class that didn't mesh with his playstyle would be detrimental to the team. So what spec to pick?

On one hand, Zelda's choice of fighting from a range made a lot of sense. But the argument against that was that having two blast wardens in the group would leave them vulnerable in close combat. So blast warden was out.

Going for shield warden was likely out, too, as that would cripple their damage output. He and Titus would likely be able to tank for an extended amount of time, but that would leave Zelda to deal all the damage. And if anything happened to her, they'd be crippled. So not that, either.

That left power warden and enhanced warden. From what he'd seen of the power wardens, they were experts at close combat. If he were being honest, going that route would round out the group quite well. Maybe that was the correct choice. But would he be good at it? Would the class mesh with his playstyle?

In the past, he'd enjoyed both high damage-per-second (DPS) classes and support classes. But he'd never played a game as advanced as Nova. Even a support class like enhanced warden seemed able to fight decently well. Lieutenant Sola had been right in the thick of it with the rest of her wardens.

He assumed that as a power warden he would be stacking strength and trying to deal as much damage as possible. But he wasn't even sure what an enhanced build would look like. The quick facts had said enhanced were some kind of scout-type class, so perhaps they focused on speed? Kaiden didn't know much about how the mechanics worked in Nova, so he wasn't sure how an agile class would work in battle.

Opening his character sheet for more information, he

focused on the 'dexterity' stat, which he assumed was used to improve speed.

Attribute: Dexterity
Higher dexterity increases a character's base movement speed and also gives them a higher chance of dodging attacks and landing critical hits.

So dexterity was linked to speed and critical hits. He had already seen the power of critical hits against the raged, so clearly stacking dexterity for DPS was another valid option.

Power warden or enhanced warden? There were arguments for both, and despite the fifteen unassigned stat points waiting to be used, Kaiden just wasn't sure. He didn't feel he had enough information to make the best decision. He was saved from having to choose just then, however, by a flash of light from Titus.

When the light faded, the big man rose from the table with a smile and flicked his shield on. It had grown. A lot. Stretching all the way from his shoulders to his shin, Kaiden couldn't deny that the new shield was an impressive sight.

An ally has chosen their class!
Ensign Titus has chosen the shield warden class.

Becoming a shield warden shows a true commitment to defending those weaker than yourself. Your shield is permanently expanded in size to make absorbing enemy attacks, and covering a fellow warden or ally, easier. Absorption capacity increased by 25%

Titus lowered himself into a fighting stance and locked his shield in place in front of him. Virtually all his body was protected behind it, and combined with the hammer in his other hand, he struck an imposing figure.

"This, I could get used to," he said with a smile.

"Shield warden looks good on you," Kaiden agreed. "I kind of want to get into our next fight already."

"First, you'll need to assign your stats," Zelda said, continuing

Titus' lesson. "If you're going to be our party's tank, you'll need to be able to take a lot of hits. Increasing endurance increases your hit points, so that's helpful. You already said you don't want to focus on damage dealing, so I'd recommend a min-max strategy focusing on endurance."

Titus frowned. "Which in English means...?"

"Put all your points into endurance," Zelda said.

"Could've just said that," Titus grumbled.

Zelda then turned to Kaiden.

"So, have you made a decision? What spec are you taking?"

"I'm going to wait and surprise you. Figure it'll be more fun that way."

"What you mean is, you haven't decided yet," Zelda said, astute as ever.

"I'll figure it out. Just let me sleep on it."

Zelda crossed her arms.

"As long as you make a decision at some point. Preferably before the captain sends us off on whatever mission she has planned tomorrow."

"Sounds good," Kaiden said with a smile, his mind no more made up than it'd been before.

Chapter Eighteen

Kaiden was thankful the bulk of his days were spent in Nova Online. Unfortunately, they were forced to log out every day to join the general populace for dinner. For Kaiden, that meant Manson.

The sneering maniac hadn't tried anything just yet, but he'd been watching, waiting. Ready for a moment in which Titus was gone.

Kaiden met Titus in the morning as soon as the cells were unlocked. The other prisoners ignored him, but Manson seemed to have made a game out of the whole ordeal. He almost looked to be enjoying himself.

It had only been a couple of days, but sooner or later, Kaiden knew Manson would find his opportunity. All the more reason to redouble his focus on the investigation and earn his freedom.

"Kai." Zelda's voice called to him, distant at first. "Kai. You in there?"

He snapped away from the bad dream that was the prison and back to the reality of Nova.

"I said we're here. You coming in, or what?"

Zelda stood in a doorway a few steps behind him. They were on the *Anakoni*.

"Oh, the armory. Right." He must have walked right past it, too lost in thoughts of the prison to stop. He shook himself from his daze and followed her in.

The room was smaller than Kaiden had expected, and far

cleaner. When he'd heard 'armory,' he'd imagined something, well...dirtier, for starters. The room was pristine, and even though suits of armor hung from ceiling hooks in various state of disassembly and racks of tools adorned the walls, everything seemed perfectly organized.

"Ah, you must be the new ensigns I've been hearing about!" A man in a mechanic's uniform stood behind a sparkling-clean workbench, a smile plastered across his face. "I wondered when you'd show up. Figured it wouldn't be too long, the beating you've all been taking."

Marlo (NPC)
Civilian Armorer
Faction: Warden Corps
Level: 10

An NPC has heard of us? That has to be something he says to every player, right? Make them feel special?

"I'm sorry," Kaiden said, frowning. "You've heard of us?"

"'Course I have!" He crossed his arms and snorted. "Everyone's talking about the ensigns who survived the *Mochinki*, then imploded that horde of berserkers along with it."

"To be fair, Lieutenant Sola did most of the imploding."

"Ah, nonsense. You should stick with the other version of the story. More interesting, that one is."

Either this is very realistic dialogue, or NextGen has some powerful AI running their NPCs. In fact, now he thought about it, he'd read somewhere that they definitely did.

"So, you here to chat all day, or do you want your armor repaired?" Marlo leaned forward on his workbench and tapped his fingers expectantly.

"Yes, please." Zelda must've unequipped her armor because one moment she was wearing it, then the next it was in her outstretched hand. Without her armor she wore only the basic warden uniform. About as utilitarian and un-stylish an outfit as one could find, and yet...

Kaiden felt his cheeks grow hot as he noticed her athletic frame. Good thing characters in Nova couldn't blush. Or could they? Kaiden turned away as a spontaneous coughing fit overtook him.

Zelda placed her armor on the workbench.

"Here you are. It's looking pretty rough. Durability down to eighteen out of a hundred."

Marlo raised some multi-headed tool. It looked like a screwdriver, hammer, drill, and welding torch had all been thrown into a blender. He touched one of the many heads of the tool to Zelda's armor as she began to speak.

"So how long will it take you to fix—"

"Done."

She frowned.

"Done?"

He nodded.

"Done."

Her mouth fell open and Kaiden felt his own do the same.

"Did you even do anything to it?"

"Durability one hundred out of one hundred. It's good as new."

Zelda took her armor back and examined it with a scrutinizing gaze.

"You're not lying." She shrugged and the armor popped back onto her body.

"Oh, and the system cleared you for stimpack usage, so I filled up your stimulant chamber as well. You've two fresh stimpacks ready to go."

"Nice!" Zelda grinned. "What did Sergeant Dawson say about these? Twenty-five percent healing on use, with a two-minute cooldown? That could come in handy."

Marlo nodded, then gave them a stern look.

"Just make sure you only use stimpacks that have been stored in a stimulant chamber. You can't just go using any ol' stim, you know. They have to be kept at near-freezing temperatures, otherwise they go bad. Use a stimpack what's gone bad and you'll take twenty-five percent damage instead."

"That *would* be bad," Titus said with a small frown.

"Bad's putting it mildly. Odds are it'd kill you. But if you did survive, well, we'd just throw you in a medpod over there." He nodded to a series of pods – similar to the VR pods in real life – in the corner. "Fix you right up, that will. We used them on those noobs you brought in, took that nasty raged debuff right off them."

Armory, stimpak depot, medbay. Is there anything this room doesn't do?

"Alright, then." Marlo clapped. "I see two sets of damaged armor in here what need fixing. Let's get to it, huh?"

Titus handed his over first.

As Marlo touched his multi-tool to it, a voice crackled through the comms.

"Ensigns, you there?"

Lieutenant Ellenton.

"I hear you," Kaiden said.

His armor gone, Titus frowned, unable to hear the lieutenant.

"Yeah, I'm gonna need you back at the shuttle. Command's breathing down my neck about some errand we have to go run. Some big hullabaloo down on Nassau. Waste of time if you ask me, but this came direct from the captain."

"Be right there," Kaiden said. By the time he'd finished speaking, Titus had his armor reequipped.

"Going to have to make this quick, Marlo. We've just been given our next mission."

He flipped his tool into the air, then caught it and smiled.

"Quick is the only speed I work at."

Chapter Nineteen

"You know, most planets' seedy underbellies have the decency to stay hidden in the shadows and back alleys. Not here." Lieutenant Ellenton initiated the *Borrelly's* auto-landing sequence and spun the pilot's seat around to face them. "Welcome to the festering wound of a rock they call Nassau."

"Doesn't look that bad to me," Titus said, peering through the windshield.

"*That,*" Lieutenant Ellenton said, nodding to the landscape out of the windshield, "is the sulfur wastes. Boyd City is behind us." She flipped a switch and the rear loading ramp whirred to life and began descending.

"Oh, don't get me wrong, it's a nice enough place. As long as you don't get off the ship. Speaking of..." She gestured to the ramp, now fully lowered and inviting them to the world beyond. "That's your cue."

Kaiden looked at the ramp, then at Titus and Zelda, then back to the lieutenant.

"You still haven't briefed us on our mission?"

"Oh, right." She shook her head. "So this is gonna be a basic tax run. In-game credits, as you know, have an exchange value with real-world currencies. The Party taxes all in-game transactions, just like real-world transactions. As such, it's in their best interest to make sure things are safe enough for those transactions to happen. So, the Party sends us to provide security for bigger trade deals." She waved her hand tiredly. "Blah, blah, blah.

Basically, you go to the location I've marked on your minimaps, stand there, look imposing, and let the merchants haggle out their deal. Oh – and, you know, if anything goes bad, take care of it." With that, she waved them off the shuttle.

Quest: Provide security for the trade deal between Hyperion Mercantile and the Vega Trading Alliance
Expected difficulty: Novice
Reward: +800 EXP, +1 faction prestige

Kaiden read through the quest specifics as he descended the ramp out of the shuttle.

Novice difficulty again, huh? That's inspiring. How many surprise berserkers can we expect to show up and ruin this party?

Location discovered: Boyd City, Planet of Nassau
Faction Alignment: Government of Nassau, Coalition of the Greater Spiral Arm

The 'location discovered' message distracted Kaiden from his thoughts and brought his attention to the scene around them. As he stared, the loading ramp retracted and the *Borrelly* blasted off, near bowling them over again.

"Make sure nothing exciting happens down there, you three." Lieutenant Ellenton's voice came over the comms. "I'll keep an eye on things from above."

Kaiden heard her words, but barely processed them. He was too distracted by the view.

It rose like a mountain before them. Towering into the dirty orange sky, the city was a massive, sprawling mess of skyscrapers, smokestacks, and skyscrapers that doubled as smokestacks.

To call it unattractive would be an insult to the word. Boyd City was as beautiful as a shattered slab of concrete, rebar rising from inside like the ribs of some long-dead industrial golem. Metal, stone, and rust seemed to be the preferred building materials, complemented everywhere with a generous share of ash. All in all, the city appeared nothing more than a mountain of manufacturing districts piled on top of each other, up and up, and belching thick, black smoke into the atmosphere.

The lieutenant had set them down on a landing pad on one of

the city's outer districts, at ground level. The majority of the smog-filled towers and ash-coated streets were still ahead of them.

Kaiden looked down to his minimap. Their path led them directly into the thick of it.

"Boyd City, here we come."

~

A "tax run," as the lieutenant had called it, hadn't sounded particularly fun. By some measure of impossibility, it turned out to be even more boring than Kaiden had dared to imagine.

"The terms of the contract shall be amended to reflect that any shipments from the Vega Trading Alliance will be received at trading station 0138, located in the Greater Spiral Arm at the aforementioned coordinates." The representative from Hyperion had a monotonous drone so dull that Kaiden could only assume it'd been practiced and perfected.

"Unacceptable," the representative from the Vega Trading Alliance said, preparing a return volley of lifeless droning. "The additional fuel our ships would require to travel the increased distance to trading station 0138 would render the profits from each shipment negligible. I propose the terms of the contract remain unaltered. Hyperion will take delivery of all shipments at trading station 0137."

The two had been conducting a form of verbal combat back and forth for the last hour or so. From what Kaiden could tell, the argument was less about convincing the opponent of your position, and more about boring them to death until they conceded, or lost the will to live. Whichever came first.

The meeting destination hadn't been particularly far from where the lieutenant had dropped them off, and even now she was hovering somewhere in the ash clouds above, monitoring the surroundings for signs of trouble. Or so she said. Kaiden could've sworn he'd heard snores through his comms half an hour ago. Ellenton clearly wasn't worried.

Apparently, the Warden Corps often attended deals such as these. Many trade guilds had their headquarters in 'starting zone' systems like the Greater Spiral Arm as it allowed them to conduct business in a low-risk environment without worrying about god-like high level players.

Trade deals were frequent in this system, although this was supposed to be quite a major one. That was why the Warden Corps were primarily located in starting zones. It enabled close proximity to their two main functions: facilitating trade and assisting low-level players.

"Zelda, Titus, you two still awake?" Kaiden asked, glancing toward the pair.

"Present," Zelda whispered as she adjusted how she'd been standing, shifting her weight to the other foot.

"Wishing I wasn't here," Titus said a moment later and crossed his arms.

"Think they'll finish any time soon?"

"In this situation, I think the 'soonest' we can hope for would be sometime next week," Zelda said with a yawn.

The meeting had been arranged on a vacant landing platform a little way inside Boyd City. A table and two chairs had been set in the middle of the platform – currently occupied by the representatives from the respective guilds – while the north and south edges were occupied by each representative's retinue. Though 'retinue' seemed too gentle a word for the heavily armed and armored soldiers each had brought.

Kaiden had led Zelda and Titus to the east side of the platform, along the edge, approximately midway between the two groups of soldiers. He didn't like the idea of being in the middle of the two groups if things went south, but if they were here to provide security, the soldiers looked to be the most likely threat. Thankfully, they appeared about as bored as everyone else.

That was, until a laser bolt cut through the head of Hyperion's representative. He slumped forward onto the table, dead. The sound of a single shot echoed from the nearest skyscraper.

That's not good.

For a moment, silence.

The Hyperion soldiers stared at their slain kinsman, then slowly, slowly, raised their heads to the Vega representative.

The man frowned.

"Obviously, negotiations will have to resume at a later–"

A volley of lasers from the Hyperion soldiers cut him off. Then it was all-out war.

The Vega soldiers returned fire, while those with melee weapons charged across the platform. The two sides met in a resounding clash of noise as offensive and defensive abilities were all unleashed at once. Explosions, blasts of light and AOE shockwave attacks rocked the platform.

Kaiden barely had time to flick his shield on and duck behind it before splash damage from a half-dozen attacks flared close by him. Combat text filled the side of his screen.

"What do we do?" Titus yelled through the comms, stepping in front of Kaiden and Zelda and putting his newly enlarged shield to good use.

"I...uh..." Kaiden stumbled to come up with any sort of plan. Everywhere he looked, it was chaos. He could hardly see for all the particle bloom effects from special attacks, not to mention the countless lasers ricocheting every which way.

Achievement Unlocked!
Warmonger - 100 EXP gained!
Your actions, or lack thereof, have kicked off a guild war!
Congratulations!

Zelda took up position beside Titus, hammer barrel forward. She aimed at one target, a Hyperion soldier, then switched to another in a Vega uniform, then lowered her weapon.

"Who do we target? We can't subdue them all."

"We can't stop this." Kaiden stared at the mess of fighting. So far, no one was attacking them, but if one side – or both – decided to, there wouldn't be much they could do.

"My scanners picked up the shot. It came from that skyscraper that's under construction." Lieutenant Ellenton's voice came through the comms, and then the *Borrelly* burst through the clouds above. "Let these thugs fight it out. Command will want the assassin more. Get in."

The shuttle pulled a hard turn, then drifted to the edge of the platform. The wrong side of the platform, as it happened.

"We can't get through," Kaiden said, eyes locked on the mosh pit of combat separating them from the shuttle.

"I got this." Titus stepped forward without warning. "Been wanting to try this bad boy out."

"Wait, what're you–"

"No time," Zelda said, dragging Kaiden along with her as she followed Titus.

"Shield Charge!" Titus bellowed a battle cry and plunged forward. As he did, his shield flared a bright white and his legs began to pump at a furious pace.

He slammed into the thick of the fighting like a wrecking ball through a building. Soldiers were bowled over or tossed aside as Titus pushed through like they weren't even there. The wake of his charge left just enough of a gap for Kaiden and Zelda to follow.

Titus only stopped running when he slammed into the side of the *Borrelly* with a resounding *thunk*.

"Get in!" Lieutenant Ellenton swung the ship around, the ramp already extended.

Titus leapt first, followed by Zelda, and then Kaiden.

Kaiden had just enough time to grab a handrail before the shuttle blasted off, leaving them with a shrinking view of the battle below.

Chapter Twenty

"He's moving deeper into the building. Probably knows we're tracking him," Lieutenant Ellenton said as the shuttle covered the distance to the assassin's skyscraper in a matter of seconds. "If he gets out of range, the shuttle will lose him."

"Can you drop us off near him?" Kaiden said, working his way to the cockpit and talking through the comms.

"No need if I can take him down first."

The entirety of the *Borrelly* vibrated as the lieutenant opened up with a barrage of laser fire. The rounds streaked into the assassin's half-built skyscraper and exploded in a fiery storm of sparks and scrap. A glowing red dot projected onto the windshield tracked the movement of the assassin inside the building. When the smoke cleared from the lasers, he was still moving.

The lieutenant cursed, then unleashed another barrage.

Metal crumbled and blew apart, fires burst to life, and great chunks of the building's exterior were blasted away. The dot kept moving.

It manifested into a figure as a man leapt from the empty skyscraper, clearing an impossibly long jump, and landed in the neighboring tower. He ran along a balcony for a dozen steps or more.

"There's your shot!" Kaiden leaned forward, expecting at any moment to see the assassin caught in another burst of lasers. None was forthcoming.

"What are you waiting for?"

"Civilians," the lieutenant said, and even as she spoke, near a hundred blue and white dots appeared on the windshield as the shuttle's scanners located them inside the skyscraper.

"The last building was mostly abandoned, still under construction. This one is full of players and NPCs. Even on Nassau, I can't fire on civilians. NextGen would have a fit."

She dogged the assassin's movements as she spoke, trailing him along the outside of the building.

Zelda's voice spoke softly in his ear over the party comms line. "Did you get a good look at the assassin as he jumped?" she asked.

"No, why?" Kaiden whispered back.

"I'm pretty sure I saw a red streak of hair."

"And?"

"The assassin that killed Bernstein—"

"Had a red streak of hair!" Kaiden said. "You don't think this is the same guy?"

"Only one way to find out."

Luckily, Ellenton hadn't noticed their exchange. She was still lamenting her inability to continuing firing. "So heavy artillery won't work. We're going to have to try something else."

"Lieutenant! Will my Burst Arrow ability penetrate through the building?" Zelda shouted into the channel as she pulled herself onto the still-extended rear loading ramp.

"Probably not?"

"Good enough for me."

She opened fire and an energy spear burst from the barrel of her hammer. It struck the balcony right next to the assassin, staggering him to one side.

She fired again, but he dodged it, rolling beneath.

Kaiden was wondering how Zelda had charge to use this new ability, then he remembered she could now generate charge passively while in combat. A useful trick. Perhaps having two blast wardens wouldn't be such a bad thing.

The assassin turned hard, then disappeared into the building through an open doorway. His figure faded back into the red dot as the shuttle tracked him through the walls.

"I'll put you down here," Ellenton said. "Follow him in while I cover the exits."

She maneuvered the shuttle closer to the building, slowing to let them out. As she did, the assassin reappeared from the doorway and flung a disc-shaped piece of metal.

"Hold on!" The lieutenant slammed her joystick hard to the side and the *Borrelly* rolled to the left, attempting to dodge whatever the assassin had thrown. She pulled away, but even as Kaiden watched, the object followed them. Whatever it was bounced from the forward-starboard wing, then slapped down and stuck fast.

Clunk.

For a moment, nothing happened.

"Did it bounce off?" Titus asked from the back, moving to peer out a side window.

"Magnetic EMP mine," Lieutenant Ellenton said, dread in her voice. "This is going to hurt."

A blast of light and electricity tore through the shuttle. The energy snapped and crackled across the hull, filling the windshield and side windows with a burning light.

The control console hissed and popped, then started spewing smoke into the cabin. They dropped several feet as the engines stuttered before fighting their way back online.

"We're going to lose power any moment. I'll put her down on the balcony," Lieutenant Ellenton growled through gritted teeth. "Just make sure you get this punk."

Console still smoking, she punched the throttle and the *Borrelly* plunged forward, directly into the skyscraper.

They slammed down onto the balcony and slid several feet. Kaiden just had time to see the outer wall of the building rush up before the windshield buckled in a spiderweb of cracks.

The shuttle jerked to a stop, throwing everyone to the floor, and the electric hum of the *Borrelly*'s systems wound down to silence.

"I'll work on getting the shuttle flying again. Might be able to force a system reboot once the cooldown wears off." She turned her eyes to the building ahead of them. "I updated your maps with the tracking data from the shuttle's computer. Go get him."

Kaiden jumped from the shuttle's ramp, hitting the balcony with a heavy thud. A heavier thud followed: Titus. Then Zelda landed too. His map recalibrated, white lines reforming to show the environment of the skyscraper they'd crashed into, and a red dot appeared, already on the move. The assassin. A quick nod to each other and they were running.

The building appeared to be the corporate office for some sort of manufacturing firm. NPCs walked the halls here and there, no doubt programmed to look busy.

Nonetheless, they reacted to the wardens bursting through their hallways. Some even wanted to help, pointing after the assassin or shouting encouragement.

But from the looks of his minimap, it didn't look like they would catch him. He had a huge head start.

They burst through a set of double doors and out into what appeared to be the main atrium, a massive open space with glass windows rising for stories and stories on either side. Ahead, Kaiden caught the first glimpse of their quarry. It wasn't a promising one.

"He's getting away," Kaiden shouted, trying to run faster as the assassin reached a spiral staircase on the far side of the central fountain.

Zelda was right behind him, almost stepping on his heels as they ran, but Titus' green dot was far behind them.

"These NPC guys won't get out of my way," he shouted through the party comms. "Just go on without me."

We need to be faster somehow, or we'll never catch him.

And then a thought struck Kaiden.

Can I pick a spec right now?

Still running, he brought up his character sheet. The option to pick a spec was still flashing at the bottom.

Lieutenant Sola had seemed supernaturally fast back on *Mochinki Station. That might just be what I need to catch this guy. But I'll be locking myself into the enhanced warden specialization. There's no going back.*

An energy arrow zipped past Kaiden and exploded against the staircase, sending the assassin sprawling. For a moment, Kaiden thought the man might not get back up. But no such luck.

Two more smaller beams followed as Zelda used her normal attack. They went wide, and the assassin rounded the corner out of sight. The red dot denoting him on Kaiden's minimap disappeared. He'd run out of range.

"We'll never catch him like this" Zelda said.

"I have an idea!" Kaiden shouted back. "Double back and help Titus. I got this."

Chapter Twenty-One

As soon as Kaiden selected the enhanced specialization, his shield morphed from its original round shape to that of a medieval kite shield. Its pointed lower half stretched past his waist, while the top half was broader, covering his chest.

The edges of his vision glowed as a visor materialized in front of his eyes. He couldn't get a good look at it while running, but it looked to be a band of slim glass that curved in front of his eyes. A compact blue circle formed on the inside of the visor, not unlike a scope on a ranged weapon in many shooter games he'd played. The blue circle moved as his eyes did, and Kaiden assumed it was some sort of lock-on or tracking feature.

A flood of text poured into his vision.

Enhanced warden specialization chosen!

Enhanced wardens are a unique support class able to quickly process strategic information, using speed to scout ahead, deliver vital intel and escape deadly situations. Your new enhanced visor now allows you to focus on players, NPCs and items to learn additional information about them and their abilities. Increased sensory knowledge has doubled the area size of your minimap.

Still running, Kaiden saw his minimap zoom out, expanding the area shown to him, and the red dot of the assassin blinked back onto it. His quarry was still ahead of him, but at least Kaiden could keep track of him better. What's more, a blocky yellow arrow appeared beside the assassin's red dot, indicating what direction he was travelling in. It must have been a new feature from his improved visor and it was certainly handy.

Yet all the extra intel in the world didn't change the fact that the assassin was simply faster than him.

But there was a stat for that.

Remembering the description from his stats page, the dexterity stat would increase his base movement speed. Kaiden doubted it was a one-to-one ratio, but surely fifteen points would make a difference. Plus, with the hammer he'd looted and his new class, a dexterity-focused build made sense.

Kaiden mentally added all his available points into dexterity.

The effect was immediate. Suddenly, his legs began to push a little harder, his body seemed a touch lighter. Kaiden felt more balanced, more in control of his movements, able to more easily dodge the NPCs that occasionally blocked his path. He was definitely faster, but it still wasn't enough; the red dot that was the assassin continued to move closer to the edge of Kaiden's expanded minimap. Soon he'd escape entirely.

I need more speed! I thought enhanced were supposed to be fast.

Then he noticed one last notification.

Ability Unlocked!
Burst of Speed: Energy is channeled to your leg implants, increasing current movement speed by 100% for 10 seconds. Cost: 30 charge. Cooldown: 1 minute.

Now, that's what I'm talking about! Except...

Kaiden's eyes flicked down to his charge bar. The assassin hadn't given him any chance to build charge. Throwing an EMP mine at the *Borrelly* hadn't exactly been an attack he'd had any chance of blocking.

Kaiden rounded another flight of stairs and found himself on the top floor of the building. The red dot halted on his minimap, losing the directional arrow. The assassin had stopped – but why? Kaiden ran on through the sliding door in front of him and emerged into a glass-ceilinged cafe.

Patrons were on their feet, looking to a commotion at the far side of the room, steaming mugs and plates of cakes forgotten.

The assassin was being held up by a security officer for the building. Kaiden used his new visor to get some info on the guard, locking the blue circle reticle onto him.

Marsten (NPC)
Security Officer
Status: Neutral
Level: 5

Even as Kaiden made to catch up, the assassin knocked Marsten in the forehead with the butt of his rifle. He stumbled backward, apparently stunned. The assassin threw a glance over his shoulder, saw Kaiden approaching, and started to run again, heading for a set of stairs marked 'Shuttle pads this way'.

An idea struck Kaiden then. He needed charge. But he didn't need the *assassin* to attack him. He just needed *somebody* to attack him.

"Officer, shoot my shield!"

The stun effect wore off and Marsten turned, a look of confusion on his face.

"What?" he said, then his eyes went wide as he took in Kaiden's warden armor. "I mean, yes, sir!"

He drew his blaster with a sharp, practiced movement, and fired. The laser washed over Kaiden's raised shield in a burst of light and his charge bar filled by twelve units.

"Two more!" Kaiden angled his shield as he passed Marsten, still sprinting.

The shots hit and Kaiden's charge bar filled to thirty-six percent.

"Much obliged!" Kaiden yelled. Ahead, the assassin disappeared up the staircase to the shuttle pads.

Now things get interesting.

Kaiden activated Burst of Speed. At once, he felt the muscles in his legs twinge as though shocked with electricity. It was like an adrenaline rush, only doubly so. He lurched forward, almost toppling over at the sudden acceleration. The room flew past in a blur. He was practically flying up the stairs.

He whooped. "Now *this* is fun!"

The distance between him and the assassin on the minimap was quickly closing. A neon-lit doorway indicated the shuttle pad area was just ahead, its sliding door still closing from the last person to run through. But just as Kaiden slid through the gap in the closing doors out onto the roof of the complex, the red dot on his minimap blinked off.

"What the—"

Kaiden skidded to a halt. A countdown timer in the corner of his screen informed him Burst of Speed had four seconds of time. Plenty to reach the assassin, if he was still there.

Only...the rooftop was empty, save for a couple of transit shuttles and one slender black craft.

No! Where did he go? He can't have just died or vanished!

Yes, he probably could, now Kaiden thought on it. This was an assassin, after all, and he likely had a cloaking ability. From his experience in games, such things usually meant that an ambush was about to—

His minimap flashed as the red dot reappeared, this time behind him.

Kaiden spun, crouching low, shield raised. A laser bolt slammed into the upper portion of his shield, sending painful vibrations up his arm. His charge bar rushed to fill to eighty out of one hundred. Clearly, that shot had been very powerful. It might even have killed him if it had hit his body.

Looking up, Kaiden saw the flickering outline of a man as the assassin finished decloaking. The red streak in his hair stood out sharply against his otherwise black combat gear and he held a long-barreled sniper rifle. Now close enough to focus on the player, Kaiden finally got a name.

Jax
Class: Assassin
Faction: Unknown
Level: 15

Kaiden balked at the level. Jax was nine levels higher than he was. How on earth was he ever going to bring his health down low enough to use the Shackle ability?

Smoke trailed from Jax's rifle, but for some reason he

remained there, unmoving. Kaiden moved his reticle onto Jax to see if he could figure out why.

Player has recently used Kill Shot.
Kill Shot: You carefully take aim for a precision attack with your equipped ranged weapon. Successful hits will be guaranteed critical damage and headshots deal quadruple base damage. Recoil from the weapon will stun you for 3.5 seconds. Cast time: 5 seconds.

So, Jax was stunned, but not for long. Certainly not long enough for him to win this fight alone.

"Zelda, Titus, where are you guys?" Kaiden asked over their party comms.

"Ellenton got the *Borelly* back online," Zelda answered. "We're tracking your position. Keep him busy."

"Right," Kaiden said, not entirely sure how.

Jax had recovered from his recoil debuff and was taking aim again.

With nothing else for it, Kaiden stood and used Hammer Toss, flinging his hammer toward Jax. As his weapon flew forward, Kaiden began to run, following behind it. The attack missed, clattering against the door he'd just run through, but it did force Jax to sidestep, his shot going wide.

Kaiden made it into melee range as his hammer returned to his hand. Still with sixty charge left, he thrust forward using Shield Bash, hoping to stun Jax again.

But Jax was far too nimble. Kaiden looked positively clumsy as the assassin slipped around the oncoming shield. His dexterity and dodge chance were probably of a comically high value compared to Kaiden's own.

Then he felt a cold jab at his neck, like an icy needle. Something hissed and Kaiden's health bar flashed, then drained down by two percent. Hardly anything at all, really. But the true effect became apparent as combat text flashed in the corner of his vision.

Poisoned! You've been injected with a dose of intermediate level crippling serum. Your speed and base damage are halved for 1 minute.

Kaiden turned, trying to swing his hammer, but his arm felt sluggish, the hammer travelling lazily through the air. Jax stepped aside with a wink, then backpedaled so Kaiden had no hope of catching him. Burst of Speed was still on cooldown.

"Haven't dealt with an enhanced warden for a long time," Jax said in a snide voice. He lowered his rifle, aiming for Kaiden's head. "So, lowbie, why are you chasing me?"

Kaiden's stomach squirmed. Saying the unofficial reason would likely result in his head getting blown off.

"You just messed up a huge trade deal. Pretty darn illegal stuff. You're under arrest," he added jovially.

But Jax did not laugh. "Yeah? That the only reason? Tell the truth and I might give you a – what do your lot call it? – 'week's vacation'."

Kaiden gulped. "Why else would we have been down there? It's our job to protect in-game trade. Why assassinate the Hyperion rep, anyway? They were just doing business."

Jax chuckled this time. "They're doing their business, and I'm doing mine." He reached up with one finger to tap the scope of his sniper, specifically the symbol plastered there. It showed a smiling skull, fire in its eyes, against the backdrop of a biohazard symbol.

A guild symbol, maybe? A personal calling card? Kaiden wasn't sure.

Jax brought his finger back down to the trigger. "Alright then, do-gooder. I'll send your level six ass back to relax in your cell. Better luck next tim—"

The sound of a shuttle's engines roared from below the lip of the rooftop's western edge. Jax snapped his head in its direction, giving Kaiden just enough time to crouch behind his shield. Jax frowned, shook his head, then turned, running toward the slender, obsidian-colored ship.

Green dots appeared on Kaiden's minimap and Titus' voice crackled over the comms.

"Nearly with you, kid. Can't quite see you on our maps yet, though. You still with us?"

"Just," Kaiden said, unable to hide his relief. "But he's getting away. I'm poisoned and can't catch him."

"Not if I can help it," Ellenton said.

But Jax was already hopping into the cockpit of his own craft.

Kaiden realized the crippling serum would lose its effect soon, but there was no way he would catch Jax now. The least he could do was get some further intel on him, though, so he moved the reticle on his visor over, locking onto Jax even as his ship began to lift off the concrete.

Jax
Class: Assassin
Faction: Unknown
Level: 15
Assassins are high in dexterity and intelligence, and low in endurance and strength. Though powerful when attacking from stealth and ranged, they are weak when caught in close combat.
Key Abilities: Kill Shot, Cloaking, Smoke Bomb, Assassinate, Venomous Strike

That's a lot of good information, Kaiden thought. One key phrase stuck out to him. *'Weak in direct combat'. With some more levels, I might be able to take this guy.*

Jax's ship angled upward as the *Borrelly* emerged into view.

"That'd be him, then?" Ellenton's voice blared loudly in Kaiden's ear. "Priming weapons, targeting his engines and —"

A boom shook the air as Jax's ship blasted off into the sky.

"Ah, come on," Ellenton shouted. A sound of fists hitting a control console followed.

"We need to go after him," Zelda said.

"No can do, Ensign," Ellenton said. "That was a Tychios Model F Blazar. On a good day, we'd have trouble keeping up with it. With the damage sustained to the *Borrelly,* we don't have a chance." She turned the Borrelly to face Kaiden up on the roof and began a landing procedure. "Gonna have to call this chase here. He's gone."

Chapter Twenty-Two

It was a long, tense flight back to the *Anakoni*, in which Kaiden relayed how he'd lost the assassin. The failure stung doubly so considering there was now no doubt the assassin matched the description of the one who'd killed Bernstein in-game.

Kaiden had almost had him – had been *that* close – and had let him get away.

Now, they were back at square one. Or square one and a half. The only saving grace was the symbol he'd seen on the assassin's rifle. A fiery-eyed skull against the backdrop of a biohazard symbol. They could at least follow that lead. Maybe it belonged to some known criminal group? Some guild of assassins? Was that even a thing in Nova? Kaiden didn't know, but it was the only hope he had as they returned to base.

The other silver lining was Kaiden now had a class. He opened his character sheet to view his new stats.

Character
Name: Kaiden
Race: Human
Level: 6
Class: Enhanced Warden
Attributes:
Strength: 15 *Intelligence:* 15
Endurance: 15 *Perception:* 15

Dexterity: 30 *Unassigned:* 0
Abilities:
Hammer Smash, Shield Bash, Hammer Toss, Shackle, Burst of Speed
Perks:
None

He was an enhanced warden. The more he thought about it, the more it made sense. Power wardens could hit hard, sure, but they were often a blunt force, smashing down obstacles. As the enhanced class, Kaiden would have more flexibility. His speed would allow him to get around the battlefield quickly, while his higher critical hit chance meant he could still deal serious damage. The high dexterity might even make up for his lack of endurance, allowing him to dodge more blows. It suited his playstyle; allowed him to think, plan his attacks, rather than just smashing away.

Sirens were blaring and emergency lights flashed in the *Anakoni's* hangar when they landed. The *Borrelly,* still smoking, touched down with a series of sharp jerks and shakes amid a rush of wardens and ship staff rushing to and fro.

"Well, safe to say someone noticed the commotion down on Nassau," Lieutenant Ellenton said, shutting the shuttle's systems down.

"I can only imagine." Kaiden's eyes flicked down to the system message at the corner of his vision. It'd been there since they'd left Nassau and he hadn't had the heart to close it out yet.

Quest failed: Provide security for the trade deal between Hyperion Mercantile and the Vega Trading Alliance
Rewards received: 0 EXP, -2 faction prestige

"Something tells me this has to do with that gang war we may have failed to stop" Titus said, frowning at the commotion outside.

"They're not gangs, Titus," Zelda corrected him. "They're guilds. Trading guilds, specifically. Which means they're trying to make a profit. I doubt war is really in their best interests. They'll talk this out, won't they?"

"Oh, I doubt that," Lieutenant Ellenton answered from the front. "Hyperion and Vega have always loved to argue with each other. And, thanks to their enormous wealth, they each own a considerable number of big guns to drive their points home."

Titus nodded at her words.

"Guilds, gangs, same thing, really. I've seen more than a few turf wars kick off. Might be these guys aren't fighting over who owns what street, but it's the same difference."

Zelda sighed, covering her face with her hands.

"Captain Thorne can't take away our Shackle ability, can she?" Kaiden asked.

Zelda parted her fingers to reveal one eye and part of a furrowed brow.

"I don't *think* so. I mean, I've never heard of that happening. But Shackle isn't exactly a normal ability."

"You'll be the last thing on Command's mind right now," Ellenton said, striding past them and toward the now-opening rear loading ramp. "Just keep your heads down, do what you're told, and you'll be fine. Might even find time for a nap or two." She paused, turning back to them. "That's how I made lieutenant, after all. Now log off and get some grub. Things will be crazy when you're back tomorrow."

～

For the first time, Kaiden dreaded returning to Nova Online. Although his fear of Manson outweighed that dread a hundred-fold, so it was still some relief when he finished scarfing down his disgusting breakfast and made his way to his pod.

Welcome to Nova Online.

The message faded to white as Kaiden found himself in the all-too familiar scene of the *Anakoni*'s hangar bay. Before he could look around, another message flashed in his vision.

Priority alert. All wardens are to report to the deck ten assembly hall for an emergency briefing on the Vega-Hyperion trade war at 08:30 Nova time.

Well, that's a pleasant welcome.

Kaiden turned to find Titus and Zelda logging in beside him. As they materialized, they each paused, no doubt reading the message.

"'Vega-Hyperion trade war.' That, uh, doesn't sound promising," Titus said.

Titus flexed his arms, then did a few quick squats, as he always did after logging in. Then he shrugged.

"At the least, it'll be interesting."

"Actually, I was thinking about this last night," Zelda said, leaning in close and whispering conspiratorially. "This could work to our advantage. It could keep Command and the rest of the wardens distracted, which means we'd have the freedom to capture the assassin. If we can find him, then we can Shackle him and get all the information we need about, you know..." She raised her eyebrows. "The murder."

She has a point. But we can't. Not right now. Command is probably pissed at us. Which means they'll either not let us do anything, or they'll be watching our every move to make sure we don't screw up again.

"I'm not sure a system-wide trade war is exactly a good time to go on a manhunt," Kaiden said. "And besides, command will be watch–"

"Command will be watching what, now?"

Kaiden felt the bottom of his stomach fall away as a voice spoke from behind him. There was a bite to the words, a simmering, ever-present anger he could only attribute to one type of person: a drill sergeant. And specifically – he turned to confirm his fears – Sergeant Dawson. Worse, he wasn't alone. Kaiden swallowed hard. Captain Thorne was at the sergeant's side.

The two officers towered over them, faces stern.

Kaiden snapped to attention on instinct.

"Captain. Sergeant," he said, trying to hide the nervousness in his voice.

They're going to take away our Shackle ability. And who knows what other punishment.

"Hello again, ensigns." Thorne gave them each a brief nod in turn.

"You three probably got that priority alert on login, yeah?" Sergeant Dawson said, his tone sounding all the coarser in contrast to the captain.

"Yes, sir," they said in unison.

"Yeah, ignore that."

Oh jeez. That can't be good. Nothing about this can be good.

The sergeant inhaled, as if preparing to launch into a long explanation, then paused and frowned.

"Shield warden, Ensign Titus?" He gestured to the big man's hammer. "I mean, I expected a support class from Ensign Kaiden. He's a little odd like that. And a ranged class from her." He nodded to Zelda. "Sure, nothing wrong with killing from a distance. But you? A shielder? Thought for sure I'd see you smashing skulls in with the other power wardens."

Titus seemed flustered, but after a moment, his face hardened and he spoke.

"I'd rather protect people than, uh, smash skulls, sir."

"Nonsense!" Dawson barked. "Powereds do plenty of protecting. A player does a bad thing, you smash his head in. Then he doesn't do any more bad things. Not for a week, at least. That's protection at its finest, that is."

"I suppose so, sir," Titus said.

"No supposing about it, Ensign." He nodded like he was satisfied with his explanation, then start to speak again. "Anyway, the captain wanted to see you three personally." He extended a hand toward her.

Kaiden sighed.

"This is because we failed to protect the trade deal, isn't it?"

"Failed, yes," Captain Thorne said. Then, in a gentler tone: "But it's easy to fail when the game is rigged."

Huh? What does she mean? Kaiden shot a glance at Zelda and Titus.

"We send wardens to oversee trade deals to keep things civil. But someone wanted to use that deal to start a war. Lieutenant Ellenton's report made that quite clear. The assassin knew where the deal was going to happen, and far enough in advance to set up an ambush. Whatever this plot was, it was in place long before you three arrived. No one could possibly expect you to stop that."

"So we're not being punished?" Titus asked what Kaiden had been wondering.

"No," Captain Thorne laughed. "You're not being punished."

"I don't know, Captain. I'd like to make them run a few laps, if you wouldn't mind." Sergeant Dawson scowled at them.

Truly, the sergeant was a dedicated role-player. Running laps didn't do much more than drain stamina bars – oh, and make everyone mindlessly bored. Maybe that was the point.

"Later, maybe. For now, I think these three need to learn their new mission."

"Ahem. Right." Sergeant Dawson cleared his throat as Kaiden watched on, thoughts buzzing in his head.

New mission? Something feels off.

"Things have been a bit crazy around here lately. We were already spread thin with the whole ongoing Leviathan situation."

The sergeant waved his hand as if it didn't matter.

"What I'm trying to say is, we already had our hands full before these penny-pinching guilds decided to touch off a system-wide trade war. It'll take time for us to settle things down. A third of our forces have already been sent screaming into mandatory vacation, and we're losing more every day. Problem is, if you let a war like this go on too long, the other guilds get worried. Uncertainty kills business. They stop making deals, stop making trades. No trades means no taxes. No taxes means a drop in funds for the Party. You don't need me to tell you that's hardly acceptable."

Captain Thorne nodded along as the sergeant spoke, then jumped in herself.

"Long story short, we're all going to have our hands doubly full finishing up with the Leviathan and calming this trade war. In the meantime, we're putting all the ensign squads on pirate patrol duty. Except for you three.

"You had an up-close and personal look at the assassin who started this war. Lieutenant Ellenton's report gave us a clear description of him – red streak of hair, nose ring – but it's not enough to positively identify him. Does he have a guild affiliation? Who is this guy and where did he come from? Normally, we'd send a veteran squad out to bring him in and answer all these questions, but all of our vets are busy."

"I wasn't too happy sending low-level wardens on such a crucial mission," Sergeant Dawson growled. "But Captain Thorne has seen something in you. Be grateful to her."

"Now, we know who hired this assassin," Thorne said,

shaking her head at the gruff sergeant with a smile. "One of Hyperion's rival trade guilds, and they'll be punished properly for breach of system laws, disturbing the peace, and a dozen other things. But we need you three to find the assassin himself. We need you to Shackle him, then bring him back here. I want to question him personally. Only then will we be able to scan him and send the data to the Party. They'll track him down and make sure the law and him get acquainted nice and well in the real world." Thorne crossed her arms before continuing.

"Assassins, as you know, are a very legal and playable class in Nova. Assassinations are a mechanic of the game, after all. But assassinations that interfere this greatly with government taxes are off limits. Everyone knows that and most players respect that. Those who don't, well, you don't hear too much about them, and that's for good reason. If we don't come down hard and fast on assassins who take contracts that interfere with trade, things will get very ugly, very quickly. That's why we need you to get this guy."

It took Kaiden a good ten seconds after Thorne had stopped speaking to process everything she'd said. Apparently, the others were having the same problem. After a long silence, Kaiden was the first to say something.

"My visor showed the assassin was level fifteen. Are you sure we can take him down? That's quite the level gap."

Thorne smiled at that and gave an encouraging nod.

"You three have shown great promise so far. There's no doubt in my mind that you'll bring this guy in."

"This sounds far better than pulling pirate patrol duty. It almost..." Kaiden smiled. "It almost sounds like a reward."

"You could think of it as such," Captain Thorne said. "After our veteran squads, you three are our best bet at catching this assassin."

"Now, don't go getting their egos all inflated, Captain," Dawson said. "I just spent the last few days deflating them."

She laughed at that.

"Give them the rest of the news, Sergeant."

He gestured for them to follow, then led them across the hangar to where the *Borrelly* was sitting. Repairs had been made to the shuttle overnight and it looked good as new.

"We'll need every pilot we have for this, and Lieutenant

Ellenton is one of our best. Until this war is all wrapped up, command's putting her in a combat class transport. She'll make scrap of those cheap merc pilots the traders have hired. While she does that, you three will need a way to freely travel to pursue your investigation. That's why we're assigning you the *Borrelly* here."

"And the lieutenant is okay with this?" Kaiden asked.

It'd take a direct order from an admiral, or someone even higher up the chain of command, to get her to part from her shuttle.

"She seemed fine enough. Though she did have a message for you." He paused as if thinking. "Said if you wreck her baby, she's going to get your accounts...what was the wording? Oh, right. 'Perma-banned.'"

"That does sound like the lieutenant," Zelda said.

"I don't know about you, but I for sure don't know how to fly that thing," Titus said, frowning at the shuttle.

"Not much to know." Sergeant Dawson shrugged. "Use the autopilot function. It'll get you where you need to go. If you get into a firefight it even knows some basic maneuvers. Should be enough to outrun your average pilot. If you get into a firefight with a talented pilot, however..." He trailed off, then nodded. "Yeah, don't do that."

"So that's it?" Zelda asked, disbelief still evident in her eyes. "We're being given the freedom to find this assassin on our own, in our own shuttle?"

Captain Thorne nodded.

"Yes you are, Zelda. Think of it as your big chance. Another trial. Pass this and I foresee promotions for all three of you. Not to mention I'm sure I can get a word in with the governor of your facility – Verloren, is it? – and arrange some significant reductions on your sentences." She patted the side of the *Borrelly*. "So how about it? Sound good?"

"Sounds real good," Titus said, nodding. Zelda joined him.

"Uh, yeah. I guess it does, ma'am."

Kaiden thought for a moment, but couldn't come to any other conclusion. This didn't just sound good. It sounded perfect. This was their second chance to capture the assassin and learn the truth about Bernstein's murderer. And if they did that, they could find out what he'd stolen. Somehow, they'd been handed defeat, but it'd grown overnight into victory. It was a miracle.

"Mission accepted," Kaiden said.

Quest: Capture the assassin Jax
Part 1: Investigate the symbol on Jax's gun
Expected difficulty: Veteran
Reward: 2,000 EXP, +3 faction prestige

"Well alright, then." Sergeant Dawson hiked a thumb at the *Borrelly*. "Best be about it. We'll handle the war back here."

"Best of luck, ensigns. I have absolute faith in you. I'm sure you'll be back with that assassin in no time at all. Dismissed."

The two officers turned to leave.

"You're doing that thing with their egos again," Sergeant Dawson grunted.

Thorne laughed in reply as the two of them left the hangar.

When they were gone, Kaiden turned to the others.

"That actually just happened, didn't it?" He was still dumbstruck.

"Yes, it did," Zelda said, smiling. "Yes, it did."

Chapter Twenty-Three

"I'm still in shock," Zelda said, looking every bit the part as the ramp of the *Borrelly* closed behind them. "We failed to stop a war, and we got...rewarded for it?"

"When fortune falls in your favor, it's best to say 'thanks' and move on, rather than wait for things to go bad again," Titus said. He nodded to the all-too-noticeably vacant pilot seat. "Now, where do we fly this thing? The mission just said 'learn more about the assassin.'"

"First things first, how do we fly this thing?" Zelda frowned at the various controls and blank screens at the front of the shuttle. "Finding out where Jax is won't be much use if we can't get to him."

"Sergeant Dawson mentioned the autopilot," Kaiden said, easing himself into the seat. "I bet we can let that do most of the work."

Start shuttle?

Kaiden selected the 'yes' option and the *Borrelly* came to life. All around the cockpit computers booted up, screens blinking on, while outside the engines spun up with a whirring hum.

"That wasn't so bad," Kaiden said, trying to bolster his confidence in the face of the half-dozen screens now waiting for his command.

"Ah, so you think you're going to take my baby out for a joyride, huh?" Lieutenant Ellenton's voice filled the shuttle.

Kaiden spun around, expecting to see her walking up the rear loading ramp – except the ramp was closed. No one was there.

"Which one of you took the pilot's seat, I wonder? My bet's on Zelda."

"Lieutenant?" Zelda said, walking a few steps forward to look at a control console. The screen, normally a status overview of the shuttle, now showed the lieutenant. Or rather, a video of her, Kaiden realized.

"Anyway." The recording of the lieutenant waved her hand. "I'm sure Dawson and Thorne briefed you on the situation, and I don't have long anyway – gotta go bust some mercenary heads – so I'm just going to give you the quick and dirty. The autopilot on the *Borrelly* is as simple as they come. Basically, you type in the destination you want and it'll plot a couple routes. Pick one, and off you go. Simple enough, yeah?"

"You mean she could have been flying with autopilot the entire time?" Zelda looked aghast.

"Where to go, though, that's the question, isn't it?" The recorded Lieutenant Ellenton seemed to ponder a moment. "I did some digging in the warden archives, but we don't have anything on that symbol you saw on the assassin's gun, Kaiden. But the Turen Geniocracy might. Their archives are much more complete than ours."

"The Turen Geniocracy?" Titus' brow furrowed. "Is that another guild?"

"I've already plotted you a course for Jonduu, the nearest turen planet. Luckily, the planet is still in the Greater Spiral Arm, so it's within the shuttle's range. Any further out and you'd need something bigger to get there. But for now, all you have to do is tell the *Borrelly* to follow the course, and off you go."

"Ellenton! Orders just came in. We have to move out." Someone else's voice shouted in the message and the lieutenant turned toward it.

"Yeah, yeah. Give me a minute."

"We don't have a minute."

She frowned, looking annoyed.

"Everything's always life or death with these people." She

shook her head. "Anyway, good luck, you three. And please don't wreck my shuttle."

She tapped a button on her armor and the video cut to black.

"So, I guess we're headed to Jonduu?" Zelda made her way to the cockpit, but Kaiden was already interfacing with the controls. Sure enough, just as the lieutenant had said, the main control console was showing some sort of star map and a dotted line weaving through it.

Course plotted to Jonduu. Begin?

"The course is already set. Should I tell the shuttle to begin?" Zelda strapped into a seat just behind the cockpit.

"Absolutely."

Titus jumped up to the co-pilot's seat.

"Always wanted to sit here." He smirked. "Punch it."

Kaiden did.

The *Borrelly* lifted into the air and eased itself out of the hangar. As soon as they were in space, the thrusters turned, angling themselves away from the *Anakoni*, then launched them forward in a burst of light.

~

Fifteen minutes later, the autopilot system wound down the faster than light drive and brought them into the orbit of a small blue planet. The shuttle spun around, facing the engines toward their destination, then thrusted hard, slowing them down in a decelerating burn.

The flight to Jonduu had been thoroughly unexciting. Considering the repeated near-death experiences of flying with the lieutenant, however, unexciting was just fine by Kaiden.

"The Turen Geniocracy," Zelda said, reading from an in-game menu as Kaiden and Titus pressed up against the glass, watching their approach to Jonduu, "are an alien species that have been exploring the stars long before humanity. How long exactly is unknown."

"Aliens, huh? Like the voidspawn?" Titus reached absently for his hammer.

"Not like the voidspawn." Zelda continued reading, eyes distant. "Their physical attributes are listed as 'humanoid, bipedal, and tall, with bluish skin and four eyes.' Their nature is listed as 'serene, calm to a fault, strictly religious, and highly intelligent.'"

"Hopefully that means they'll give us a better greeting than the voidspawn," Kaiden said.

Or the raged, for that matter. Come to think of it, we haven't been given many warm greetings in Nova so far. Seems pretty much everything just wants to kill us. Or eat us. Or both.

"I don't know if 'warm greeting' would be the right term for it." Zelda said. "It says their current political relationship with mankind is 'guarded neutral.' What does that even mean?"

An alarm rang from the control panel and a warning flashed across the screen.

Foreign ships approaching. Scans show weapons armed to fire. Engage evasive maneuvers?

Kaiden was ready to select 'yes' when a voice crackled through their comms. It spoke slow and calm, and soft. Comforting, almost. Or it would have been, were it not threatening to blow them out of the sky.

"Unannounced shuttle WCSS *Borrelly*, you are entering Turen Geniocracy space on an approach course to Jonduu. Turn over your shuttle controls, then state your business, or you will be fired upon."

"How's that for a greeting?" Titus said, frowning down at the console showing three turen craft surrounding them.

Remote command request from unknown turen craft. Accepting will allow remote control of the shuttle. Accept?

"If we want to use their archives, it'll help to be on their good side," Zelda suggested.

"Agreed. Let's not make these guys angry." Kaiden accepted the request. The consoles in the cockpit switched off and the cabin lighting faded to a low red.

Remote access granted.

"Now state your business," the turen voice spoke again.

"Warden Ensigns Kaiden, Zelda, and Titus requesting, uh, use of your archives? We've been sent to..." He paused. Was there any harm in revealing their mission?

I already gave them control of the shuttle. Might as well be as transparent as possible.

"We've been sent to locate the assassin that started the Vega-Hyperion trade war."

"There are no assassins on Jonduu. The Turen Geniocracy does not abide assassination as morally acceptable. Furthermore, the Geniocracy would not interfere in human affairs to cause such an unacceptable outcome as a war."

"No, no." Kaiden cursed himself for not being clear. "Sorry. I didn't mean to imply the assassin was a turen. He wasn't. He was human. I saw him. He was definitely human. I didn't mean to cause offense. I, uh—"

"We've been sent to formally request to use your archives," Zelda said, cutting off Kaiden's stumbling explanation. "To learn the identity of the assassin."

For several seconds there was no reply.

"That doesn't seem good," Titus said. "Can we take back control if we need to?"

Still no reply over the comms.

"I don't know how all this works," Kaiden said, tapping one of the blank consoles. No response. A moment later, however, the comms crackled back to life.

"Though it is highly irregular for humans to visit turen space, the council of Jonduu wishes to state our archives are open to all who seek to better themselves through knowledge. When you catch this assassin, you will attempt to reform him, yes?"

"Yes...?" Kaiden shrugged. Punishment was a type of reform, right?

"Your request is acceptable. We will guide you to a landing platform near the archives. Welcome to Jonduu, Kaiden, Zelda, and Titus."

Chapter Twenty-Four

Jonduu, as it happened, was blue for good reason. Ice covered its surface from pole to pole. The turen escort didn't fly them to the surface, however, but below it.

At first it looked like they were going to slam head-on into the ice coating the planet, but their escorts expertly guided them into a large tunnel that had been near invisible from above. They followed the winding, smooth-walled ice tunnel down for a good minute or so before the landing pads appeared, along with the rest of a settlement.

"Good thing this is just a game. Otherwise I'm pretty sure we'd just freeze to death out here," Zelda said as they stepped off the loading ramp and onto the icy metal of the landing pad.

Location discovered: Archival Facility, Planet of Jonduu
Faction Alignment: Turen Geniocracy

Achievement Unlocked!
Tourin' the Turen - 50 EXP!
You've expanded your horizons and journeyed to a planet controlled by the Turen Geniocracy. Well done! Whatever you do, while you're here, don't eat the flabberwock soup.

One of the turen ships landed next to them. It was a sleek, silver-bodied craft that bore a striking resemblance to a flying submarine with its long body and lack of any apparent windows or openings.

A beam of light descended in front of the ship, and as Kaiden watched, a figure materialized inside it, appearing no more than a few feet away from them. A turen.

Orias (NPC)
Turen Pilot
Faction: Turen Geniocracy
Level: 14

Quick facts: Turen are exceptionally high in intelligence and below average in all other stats. They are very strategic in combat, excelling in ranged combat, but are exceptionally weak to direct physical attacks.

Well, 'humanoid, bipedal and tall, with bluish skin and four eyes' pretty much sums it up.

Clothed in a flowing, long-sleeved shirt and what looked like the futuristic version of sweat pants, it was a lanky creature. To Kaiden, the figure looked to be mostly arms and legs, topped by a narrow head and scrunched-up face. Two sets of eerily human eyes rose above the thin vertical slits of what he presumed was the nose, and a horizontal slit that must have been the mouth.

"Welcome to the Jonduu Archival Facility, Kaiden, Zelda, and Titus."

Yup, definitely the mouth.

"Thank you for having us," Zelda said, then after a moment, bowed awkwardly.

Titus frowned, then did the same.

"While your display of respect is noted, it is not necessary." Orias, who Kaiden assumed to be male, gestured for them to follow.

He led them off the platform toward a cluster of buildings.

As they walked, Kaiden took in his surroundings. The ice cave they'd followed on the way in had expanded into a vast dome now. At its height it must have been several hundred feet high, and all around the walls arched down, stretching further and further away as they drew closer to the ground. Where they touched exactly, Kaiden couldn't tell. Far away, apparently.

Other turen were moving about between the buildings, reading from handheld consoles as they walked, or discussing with one another in hushed tones. None stopped to look at the humans, or even spare a glance. Titus, on the other hand, couldn't stop staring.

Zelda elbowed him in the ribs.

"I know, I know," he said. "It's just a game. But this...this is incredible."

"Aliens are a lot more interesting when they're not voidspawn and trying to eat us, huh?" Kaiden said, whispering so he wasn't overheard.

"To us, you are the aliens," Orias said, his words slow and soft.

Zelda elbowed Kaiden in the ribs this time.

"But do not worry. We will not eat you. Our mouths are far too small."

Wait, was that a joke?

They worked their way into the cluster of buildings. Each was a slightly different variation on a domed circle, with smooth surfaces that reflected the brilliant white of the ice surrounding them. They almost looked like giant igloos. Giant, incredibly advanced igloos.

Orias stopped before the biggest of the buildings.

"I have brought three human visitors eager to better themselves through knowledge."

Uh, yeah. Something like that.

A light just like the one that had projected from the front of Orias' ship flashed on, blindingly bright. A moment later, it switched off and they were inside the building.

Bookshelves with dots of glowing lights in place of books stretched into infinity in front of them. The rows and rows of bright dots lit the room with a faint blue glow. If there was a roof overhead, it was lost in darkness.

"Hold up, what?" Titus spun around but found only a wall behind him. "That's crazy!"

"Of all the technology to improve on in the future, doors would not have been my first guess," Kaiden said, also staring at the blank wall. "Or my second or third, for that matter."

"When such great knowledge is laid before you, as it has been for us, your perspective is likely to change, young ensign." A voice spoke from behind, soft and slow in what was clearly the turen fashion.

Kaiden turned back around to find a second turen before them now. He, or she – or it? – looked similar to Orias, but for a few differences in their features. Slightly larger nose slits, a wisp of hair curled at the crown of the head, and a set of glasses with four lenses, one for each eye.

"Thank you for bringing them, Orias," the new turen said to their guard. "They are your burden no longer."

Orias waved one hand in a half-circle by way of farewell, then disappeared in the beam of light once more.

In his absence, the other turen turned to look at them. Lifting one blue hand slowly, he reached to his glasses and adjusted them.

"Given you are still collared, I can assume this is official warden business?"

"That's right," Kaiden said. "Captain Thorne send us herself."

The turen bowed his head.

"Welcome to the main archives. I am Elistar, an archive secretary." Every so often, one of his eyes would blink, followed shortly after by another, then another, then another until all four had blinked, one by one.

"It's a pleasure to meet you, Elistar. I am Warden Ensign Zelda."

Elistar blinked slowly, then his nose slits opened wide as he inhaled deep.

"Rank supposes an alleged categorical hierarchy based on merit, yet our research has found it to be largely corrupted by wealth, societal status, and nepotism. As such, we have deemed it superficial and do not recognize it as an effective system for titles." Elistar delivered the statement as if it were a long, slow, and gentle soliloquy.

"Umm, okay. Fair enough." Zelda was clearly taken aback. "You can just call me Zelda, then."

"So it shall be. And your companions are?"

Kaiden stepped up and waved.

"Ensi– er, Kaiden. Though my friends call me Kai."

"This information has been noted, though I am not your friend, Kaiden."

"Titus," the big man said, and stepped up to shake hands.

Elistar stared at the outstretched hand. He leaned forward, getting a closer look, then straightened back up.

"This is a human hand," he declared. "I presume you are offering it in a form of greeting?"

"It's a handshake," Titus said. "A typical, uh, human way of saying hello."

"I have read of 'handshakes.'" They tend to facilitate the spread of infectious illness, yes?"

"I suppose..."

"Noted. It is pleasant to meet you, Titus." Elistar kept his hands firmly at his side, then turned to address all three of them. "I have been told you come in search of knowledge."

"We have," Kaiden said, nodding. "But not just, like, knowledge in general. Specific knowledge."

"You seek information about an assassin, yes?"

"We do."

"What information?"

"Well, we know his name is Jax, and he's a human assassin. We want to know where to find him."

"A name is hardly sufficient to locate on person in the vast expanse of a universe."

"His gun was marked with a symbol. It was a fiery-eyed skull on the backdrop of a biohazard symbol."

"I see." Elistar folded his hands in front of him, one clasping the other. "This should be enough information. I will search the archives for the knowledge you desire."

Wow, that was easy. We should come here more often!

"When you find this assassin, will you fight him?" asked Elistar.

Zelda stepped forward.

"We don't necessarily want to, but it's likely he will attack us."

"It is a shame, the violent ways in which you humans conduct yourselves. Alas, until you have achieved enlightenment, as have we, you will not know a better way. If you are to fight this assassin, I fear you will not prevail."

Kaiden frowned at that.

"And why not?"

"Your shields are interesting, but I fear they will easily overload if you fight such a powerful assassin," Elistar said, gesturing to their bracers. "Although I must admit they are a clever technology, especially for humans. In exchange for the knowledge you seek, I propose a trade. My colleagues would be interested to study your shield technology, and see if it can be improved upon. While they are of human origin, there may be something we can learn from them."

"You want to study our shields?" Titus said, latching one hand around his bracer and stepping back.

"This is what I have said."

Kaiden looked down at his own, then back up at Elistar.

"Will we get them back?"

"Of course. Your shields will be returned to you before your departure."

"Well, I don't see why not." Kaiden turned to the others. "I don't plan on getting into any fights while we're here, so we probably don't need them."

"I don't like it." Titus frowned. "We'd be defenseless."

"We'd still have our hammers."

"Violence is not condoned on Jonduu. You will not come under attack while here, unless it is between each other."

"We need this information, guys," Zelda said. "Hand over your shields." She took hers off and handed it to Elistar. Instead of reaching for it, he merely blinked all four eyes at once and the bracer was lifted into the air. It floated, tumbling slowly end over end in front of him.

Telekinesis. How about that?

"She's right," Kaiden said, and held out his as well.

Titus grumbled, but did the same. A moment later, Elistar blinked and the bracers floated into the air.

"Thank you, Kaiden, Zelda, and Titus. I will return with your shields, and your information, in one human hour."

Light suddenly flooded the space around Kaiden. He looked to see the same light around Zelda and Titus.

"I am sending you to the facility's shop," Elistar said. "Perhaps while you wait, you may enjoy some of our famous turen flabberwock soup."

Chapter Twenty-Five

The dazzling light of the transporter faded and they found themselves in another room – the shop Elistar had mentioned, from the looks of it. A counter lined one side of the space, with a few turen seated at it, eating from steaming bowls. They did so without touching anything, however, the food rising and floating into their mouths with each bite.

The rest of the room was full of an assortment of junk, advanced technology, and items that looked somewhere in between.

"Ooh, the humans Kaiden, Zelda, and Titus have come. Welcome, welcome!" A voice greeted them, but this one was unlike the others. Its words were quick and energetic, almost more human than turen.

Kaiden turned to find the source of the voice, only to find a turen standing there.

"Miloter Litlal, pleased to be greeting you," the turen said, then extended a hand.

On instinct, Kaiden took it and gave it a shake. Miloter's grasp was light and gentle; it was almost like shaking hands with a small child. When Kaiden released it, Miloter laughed and raised his hand to stare at it.

"Oh, I've ever so wanted to perform the human greeting ritual called a 'handshake.'" He smiled at them with the turen approximation of a smile, which was to draw his mouth slit back across his face, bending it up ever so slightly at the edges. "Such an interesting manner in which to say hello. So physical, so rough. Ah, it's just so exciting!"

He clapped his hands together, then hurried over to some sort of sink. A laser flashed over his hands and they steamed for a moment.

"Well, then, humans. Your exploits so far have been quite exhilarating. I imagine you're here to sell some very interesting loot. That's why you've come to my shop, yes?"

"Our exploits?" Titus frowned. "You've heard of us before?"

"Heard of you?" Miloter laughed again. "Of course not. We don't keep tabs on humans – there's far too many of you for that. But we did scan your ship when you entered our space. The scan told us all about your history with the Warden Corps."

"What you mean to say is you hacked the *Borrelly* and read about us?" Zelda didn't look too happy about that.

"The *Borrelly*! Ah, and you name your ships. Truly, you are a curious species." Miloter sat down at his counter and crossed his legs. "But yes, you could say our scan hacked your ship. Or you could also say it was so advanced that reading your data was almost unavoidable. Really, you humans should work on your security measures." He waved a hand. "But no matter. You've brought me interesting loot from across the system, haven't you?"

I haven't looted anything but my new hammer since the Dalcinae.

The more Kaiden thought about it, though, the more he realized he probably should have been looting constantly. It was a good idea to loot your enemies in most games. Maybe they'd drop valuable stuff, but even if they didn't, you could offload mostly worthless items in large amounts to shops – very much like this one – for a decent amount of money.

"I...haven't got anything, really," Kaiden said sheepishly.

"I've got some stuff," Zelda said. "Been carrying it in my inventory for a while and looking to get rid of it, actually."

"I have some, too," Titus said. "Got a fair bit of junk off those raged."

"I'll take the lot of it."

Zelda balked.

"But you haven't even seen what you're buying."

"Actually, our scans of your ship also provided a full inventory for each of you."

"Right." She sighed. "Of course they did."

"So, what do you say? Your inventories for something special from my shop?"

Kaiden shrugged.

"I've nothing to trade. This is up to you two."

"Well, what will you give us for 'the lot?'" Zelda asked.

"Why, nothing less than this incredibly rare galvanized skull of a Jonduu wooly mammoth!"

A huge, metal-covered skull levitated up from one corner of the room, knocking aside a dozen small piles of scrap. "Very beautiful, as you can see. And very rare."

"And rather useless," Kaiden said, analyzing the object with his enhanced visor. It apparently served no purpose beyond decoration.

"Uh...we really don't need that," Zelda said, frowning.

"Could we even fit that on the *Borrelly?*" Titus asked, staring with a doubtful gaze.

"Fine, fine." Miloter waved the skull away and it slammed back to the floor. "Then what about...a well-used but still completely operational suit of CrySec Elite-Tier Power Armor?"

This time, several pieces of what appeared to be scrap flew from across the shop, then assembled themselves into a rusted and clearly damaged suit of armor that stood at least ten feet tall.

Kaiden focused on it. The stats were unimpressive, to say the least. Its low durability had significantly reduced its usefulness. In fact, when he considered the large decrease in movement speed against its reasonable boost to attack power, well, the suit actually seemed detrimental. Plus, the description said it couldn't be used by humans.

As if to show the armor still worked, Miloter gestured at it. Lights blinked to life and the armor snapped into action, raising one hand, a six-barreled machine gun embedded in its wrist.

"Now we're talking!" Titus said, striding forward. "That's a mean-looking piece of machinery—"

"*No,*" Zelda said, cutting him off. "We don't need that, either."

"We can't actually use it. It's race-specific gear," Kaiden noted.

Miloter snapped his fingers and the armor turned toward Titus, one hand reaching out as if begging him to trade for it.

"I said no." Zelda stepped between the big man and the armor.

"She's right, Titus," Kaiden chimed in. "Besides, even if you could use it, I'm pretty sure the Warden Corps wouldn't let you keep it."

"Fine," Titus grumbled.

The armor collapsed back into a pile.

"You're a tough crowd," Miloter said, frowning. "I didn't want to do this, but I might have just the thing." He paused a moment, as if thinking, and then a cabinet across the room started rattling. Its door burst open and three tiny metal spheres shot across the room. They stopped just in front of Miloter, hovering in place.

"These are turen personal defense shields. Older models, to be sure, but I couldn't legally give you the current generation of them. They'll work just fine, though."

Kaiden focused on one of the spheres and a detailed description appeared.

Turen Personal Defense Force Field
When active, this force field will negate all damage dealt to the wearer, including debuffs and stunning attacks, for a duration of 5 seconds. Good for single use only.

"Now that sounds like something we could use." Kaiden said.

"I can see how something like that might be useful in a pinch." Zelda rubbed her chin while Miloter floated one of the spheres in front of her.

"They look a lot less awesome than a full suit of power armor," Titus said, half-frowning at the spheres. "But I suppose they could be cool."

"I'll even throw in the third for free," Miloter said. "Then you can each have one."

Zelda deliberated for another moment, then shrugged.

"I guess we do it. I don't see why not."

"Yeah, I agree," Titus chimed in.

"Joyous news!" Miloter clapped his hands together. "Now, if you two will just accept my trade request...and... perfect."

A rain of items popped into existence beside them, then clattered to the floor as Titus and Zelda emptied their collected inventories. Kaiden recognized body parts from voidspawn, several of the bent and broken weapons the raged had carried, and a vibranium crystal.

"You had an extra crystal?" Kaiden said, turning to Zelda. Surely it hadn't come from Titus; he'd barely had enough to pass the test. "You could have given it to someone, or turned it in for extra experience."

"Experience isn't hard to get. You can grind for it. But the crystal was rare. I thought it might come in handy someday."

"She was right," Miloter said, levitating the crystal over to him. "The vibranium crystal was the only item of any real value between your combined inventories."

Zelda flashed Kaiden a look as if to say, "See?"

Sometimes, I wish she wasn't always right. Just once in a while.

"Anyway, now that our business is concluded, may I offer you a bowl of our famous flabberwock soup while you wait?" Miloter gestured to the bar where the other patrons were chowing down.

"Why not?" Titus took a step toward the bar. Before he could take another, however, the teleportation light – or whatever it was – flashed on.

"Ah. Well, maybe next time," Miloter managed to say before they were transported back to the archives.

"I have the knowledge you seek," Elistar said by way of greeting.

Kaiden was still blinking, trying to adjust his eyes from the brightly lit shop to the soft darkness of the archives.

"And our shields?" Titus asked.

"Those as well. We did not learn as much as we had hoped from them, but my colleagues couldn't help themselves and tinkered with their energy conversion processors."

"You messed with our shields?" Kaiden said, taking a step forward. He did not like the sound of that.

"'Improved' is a more accurate word. We improved your shields."

Their bracers hovered over. Kaiden slipped his back on and the others did the same.

Perk acquired: Turen Tinkering!
Your shield has received a 10% increase to base charge capacity.

"Huh, you're not kidding."

"Turen do not 'kid'. We speak only the truth."

"Well, thanks for that," Zelda said, tightening her bracer. "So, about the assassin?"

Elistar inhaled deeply, preparing to speak.

"The symbol you described accurately aligns with that of the Oneshot Assassins' Guild. Our research indicates they are a small group of human assassins and spies who have a reputation as discreet but effective killers."

Quest Complete: Capture the assassin Jax
Part 1: Investigate the symbol on Jax's gun
Rewards received: +2,000 EXP, +4 faction prestige

Update
Quest: Capture the assassin Jax
Part 2: Confirm Jax is a member of Oneshot
Expected Difficulty: Veteran
Rewards: +3,500 EXP, +5 faction prestige

"Oneshot..." Zelda said, rolling the name around on her tongue. "I haven't heard of them."

"As I said, discreet." Elistar nodded. "Hardly discreet enough to avoid our attention, however. Their current headquarters can be found on Kal Reya, the third moon of Jalpurn."

"Kal Reya. Kal Reya," Kaiden said, memorizing the name. "Third moon of Jalpurn. Perfect. Thank you!" He turned to the others and smiled. "We've got him. Let's rest up tonight and stake it out in the morning."

"Jalpurn, the second largest celestial object in its system, is what you humans refer to as

a chthonian planet. Its close proximity to neighboring binary stars..."

Kaiden smiled at Elistar "Oh, you've told us all we need to know."

"...has stripped away the once thick hydrogen and helium atmosphere of the planet, resulting in..."

"Maybe we should just go?" Titus suggested, backing away from the rambling turen.

"...a rocky, metallic core that resembles a terrestrial, telluric, or 'rocky' planet in many respects, namely..."

"Yeah, that sounds good. Uh, thanks again, Elistar." Kaiden waved at him, then backed away with the others.

"How do we work this thing?" Zelda shook her hand in front of a small sensor on the wall. A moment later, a light flashed on–

"...a central metallic core comprised primarily of iron, with a surrounding silicate mantle..."

–and then they were gone.

Chapter Twenty-Six

Viewed from orbit, Kal Reya had been something of a mystery. Thick clouds filled its atmosphere, obscuring any hint of what Kaiden could expect below. An elite guild of assassins? Evidence that he was innocent? Or maybe even nothing at all. There was only one way to find out.

The *Borrelly*'s sensor showed the ground was still far below them, but hurtling downward through the thick clouds of Kal Reya was still an unsettling experience. All it'd take would be for one mountaintop to escape their instruments' notice, and they'd end up as nothing more than an impact crater on the mysterious moon's surface.

Thankfully, the clouds broke to reveal no impending mountaintops. Only a constant drizzling rain and a clear flight path ahead of them. The reason for the moon's green color, however, was immediately clear.

"Trees," Titus said, pressed up against a window. "And a heck of a lot of them."

"Not just trees," Zelda said, eyes distant as she read from an unseen menu. "Jungle. Very thick, very dangerous jungle. At least according to what other players have written about this place."

Location discovered: Kal Reya
Faction Alignment: Unclaimed

"What makes it so dangerous?" Kaiden asked. He'd been

sitting in the pilot's seat, monitoring the shuttle's flight path. He didn't understand too much of the information the consoles showed him, but from what he did, it looked like the *Borrelly* was scanning the ground for anything of interest. Lifeforms, artificial structures, and areas large enough to land in.

"The animals, for one," Zelda answered his question with raised eyebrows. "There isn't too much information about this place – probably another reason Oneshot decided to set up camp here – but some players have left notes about their time here. They all mention the wildlife being high level – compared to us – aggressive, and particularly difficult to kill."

"That's encouraging." Kaiden frowned down at the seemingly impenetrable canopy of the jungle. "Here's hoping we can avoid anything that wants to eat us."

Ding.

Kaiden's eyes were pulled back to the console in front of him.

Ding.

Two messages filled its screen. He read the first of them.

Lifeform search complete
View results?

Kaiden selected 'yes' and the results of the scan were projected onto the *Borrelly's* windshield. What must've been tens of thousands of glowing white dots – each signifying a detected life form – appeared, overlaid onto the landscape below.

"So... what were you saying about avoiding things that want to eat us?" Titus said, mouth agape as he took in the results.

"Hold up a minute." Zelda squeezed past to the front of the shuttle, the cockpit now too full with all three of them in it, and accessed the console.

"Filter out life forms under forty pounds in weight." The console ran a few calculations. Zelda whispered as it did. "Right now, it's showing results for every living thing it found down there. Insects, birds, rodents – harmless things like that."

The console finished its calculations and a good seventy or eighty percent of the dots faded away.

Well, that's better. Still not preferable.

"Filter out life forms under level three."

Half of the remaining dots disappeared.

"And filter out life forms with a known non-hostile nature."

Once again, half of the remaining dots faded.

"That's a bit better, eh?" Zelda stood up, and rested her hands on her hips with a smirk.

"Much better, actually," Kaiden had to admit.

"Okay," Titus said, nodding. "So we can worry a bit less about being eaten by some jungle monster. Now what about actually finding the assassin guild base?"

"Actually..." Kaiden said, looking back down to the console. "Hold on."

The *Borrelly* had conducted two scans as they'd arrived. He'd yet to view the results for the second one.

"Ah, here we go." Kaiden brought up the results of the second scan for all to see. "The shuttle found four artificial structures within range, which, considering how small a moon this is, is about forty percent of the surface."

"Structures one, three, and four don't show any signs of power," Zelda said, reading the results. "The shuttle says they're likely ancient ruins. Points of interest with some cool loot, no doubt, but unrelated to our mission."

Kaiden nodded at that.

"Right, but structure two is showing some low-level power usage." He squinted at the screen, reading the specific wording. "Likely 'seepage from a shielded power core.'"

"Sounds like someone's trying to hide the fact that they're here." Titus leaned back in his seat. "I think we just found our assassin guild."

"I think we did." Kaiden smiled as he looked down at the console. "Take us to structure two."

The *Borrelly*'s engines switched from the idle speed they'd been coasting at to half thrust and the shuttle launched forward.

"And land us somewhere far enough away from the structure to avoid detection," Zelda added. "Let's not tip off Jax that we're here, yeah?"

～

The rear loading ramp touched down to the ground with a wet squelch. Wisps of thick, slow-moving mist swirled away from it as it did. The rain still fell, constant and seemingly unending. It cut down visibility to virtually nothing, the shape of the jungle beyond nothing more than hazy shadows.

Still underneath the tail of the shuttle, instinctively staying out of the rain even though it made no difference in a video game, Kaiden came to the end of the ramp. His boots sunk into the ground a half inch as he stepped onto the rain-soaked surface of Kal Reya.

Achievement Unlocked!
Far Out - 50 EXP gained!
You've journeyed to an uninhabited system. Looking to become an explorer, eh? Maybe you'll discover a new species! Or, maybe you'll just get eaten by one.

Level 7 achieved!
Max health and stamina increased
+3 stat points

Ability unlocked: Enhanced Senses

"Hold up..." Kaiden said, reading the text. Behind him, the others froze, still on the loading ramp.

"What's wrong?" Titus asked, hefting his shield.

"I just reached level seven from an achievement. That's crazy. All the experience it takes to advance in level now and setting foot on this moon is what puts me over the edge."

"I hit seven back on Jonduu," Titus said, following him off the ramp.

"Only on Jonduu? I made seven when we handed those noobs back," Zelda smirked.

Nothing seemed to be set on eating them just yet, so Kaiden took a moment to read his new ability.

Enhanced Senses: Amplifies visual sensory data for a duration of 8 seconds. Nearby players and NPCs will be detectable through walls via heat signatures and sound. Cost: 10 charge. Cooldown: 1 minute.

Nice! Kaiden envisioned more than a few ways the ability could be useful.

Next, he pulled up his character sheet.

Character
Name: Kaiden
Race: Human
Level: 7
Class: Enhanced Warden
Attributes:
Strength: 16 *Intelligence:* 16
Endurance: 16 *Perception:* 16
Dexterity: 31 *Unassigned:* 3
Abilities:
Hammer Smash, Shield Bash, Hammer Toss, Shackle, Burst of Speed, Enhanced Senses
Perks:
Turen Tinkering

Kaiden dumped his unassigned points into dexterity. He was committed now; he might as well stick to the plan and continue his dexterity build. He closed out his character sheet and returned to the world around them.

They'd landed in a clearing some distance from the suspected base. The *Borrelly*'s calculations predicted it'd be a thirty-five-minute hike through the jungle to reach the overlook they'd marked as a good observation point.

"Everyone ready to get moving?" Kaiden asked, turning to the others. "The sooner we start walking, the sooner we get there."

"Never much cared for hiking," Titus said, stepping off the ramp. "Or nature, for that matter."

"A bit of fresh air will do you good," Zelda said, following him. "Or the virtual version of fresh air, at least."

"At this rate, we're going to need gills," Kaiden said, following his minimap toward the suspected base they'd marked. He stepped out from beneath the tail of the *Borrelly* and rain splattered against his helmet, then ran down his face mask in winding rivulets. Ahead, the jungle waited at the edge of the clearing, all shifting mists and looming shadows. Somewhere in there,

Kaiden hoped, they'd find Jax, and the truth about Bernstein's murder.

~

"Hold up," Kaiden said as he came to a stop in the mud. Something had moved just ahead. It wasn't a shape so much as a disturbance in the mist. As if something had darted past. And, based on the amount of displaced mist, it'd been something large.

"Shields at the ready, guys," he said.

"Again?" Titus grumbled from behind.

They'd been hiking for near thirty-five minutes now, which meant, with any luck, they were moments from arriving at the overlook they'd marked.

As soon as they'd left the clearing, the jungle had closed in tight around them. Combined with the ever-present rain and the steam-like mist rising from the very soil, it was safe to say visibility was essentially zero. But Kaiden had seen something ahead of them. He was certain.

They stood in silence for several moments, shields and hammers ready, the patter of rain the only sound.

Nothing.

If I had any sort of charge, now would be the perfect time to use my new Enhanced Sense ability. Keyword there being "if."

"Another false alarm," Titus said, then stepped forward. "I swear, this place is playing tricks on our minds—"

The beast hit him from the side, striking his shield in a flash of light. Titus was there one moment, then flung backward the next, tearing a path through the mist as he tumbled down the slope of the forest and disappeared from sight.

"Titus!" Kaiden lunged after him, then stopped as the beast growled and turned toward him. As long as Kaiden was tall, it looked like someone had mixed the DNA of a gorilla with that of a jaguar. The beast stood on its knuckles, with thick, muscular front legs rising to an even more muscular chest. The fur was colored a muted gray and white, a combination that blended all too well into the mists around them.

Even staring at it from mere strides away, Kaiden had to focus to differentiate it from the dense brush around them. The eyes gave it away, however. Small and beady, they glimmered in the light trickling down from the stormy skies above.

Zelda moved to flank the creature, but its head – vaguely gorilla-esque but for a jutting snout filled with teeth – snapped to follow her.

Kaiden focused for a second and his visor began to display detailed information about the animal.

Baboulian Manhunter **Elite**
Level: 11
Baboulian Manhunters are the supreme predators of Kay Reya, able to sneak up on prey using Camouflage. Their incredibly thick hides repel most attacks.

The manhunter spun with a growl. Kaiden ducked behind his shield as a muscular arm swiped in his direction. The beast's fist reared back to reveal a set of four blade-like claws, then the blow reverberated through Kaiden's shield, driving him backward several steps. His charge bar filled to sixteen percent.

Even as the beast advanced on him again, a spear of light cut through the mist, leaving a steaming patch of burned fur. Zelda had fired a Burst Arrow.

The beast growled as it spun to face her.

"Watch out for its claws!" Kaiden shouted.

Zelda fired again, a basic shot, catching the manhunter in the shoulder. The wound barely registered as it thundered toward her. Zelda dove to the side at the last moment, but a reaching arm caught her and pinned her to the ground.

Kaiden was already moving, his hammer raised.

Sixteen units of charge was hardly enough to use any special abilities, so his only option was to strike a critical spot on the manhunter.

He slid into range and brought the hammer down on the beast's back. No crit. It hardly seemed to notice his measly damage, grunting as it began to slash at the prone Zelda. She got her shield between its claws and her chest just in time. Kaiden struck again and again, but there were no critical hits; just a slow, fractional chipping away at the green health bar above it.

The beast roared in frustration as its claws slipped on the

shield, then unleashed a great bellow that shook the ground. It spun, lowered its head, and bit down on Zelda's calf.

She cried out in panic as Kaiden watched her health bar flash, then drop to sixty-five percent. Shaking its head side to side, the beast tossed Zelda back and forth like a rag doll.

Sixty-one percent. Fifty-five percent.

Kaiden hardly had time to think, and no miraculous solutions came to him. All he could do was strike the manhunter's back again and again. Each blow seemed about as effective as the others, which was to say, not at all.

The beast widened its stance as it continued to savage Zelda, lowering itself closer to the ground to compensate for the weight of slinging her around. Somehow, during the chaos, she managed to aim her hammer-gun and fired a Blast Arrow into the creature's face. It howled at that, then turned and slung her to the side. She fell and rolled several feet away, health bar dropping down to red.

"Use a stimpack!" Kaiden shouted at her, then backpedaled as the manhunter unleashed a fury of slashes at him.

Each blow drove him backward, slamming into his shield, but also filling his charge bar.

Keep it coming, big guy, he thought, losing ground quickly, but now able to use his abilities. But which ones? Zelda's attacks had done little but agitate the beast, and his hammer strikes had done even less. The thing was four levels above him, which meant there was no way he was winning this fight head-on. He needed to get some critical hits.

Then, as if by magic, the beast disappeared. No...a shimmer in the air, barely perceptible to the naked eye. Camouflage.

Instinctively, he ducked beneath his shield, but a slash knocked his feet from under him, sending his health plummeting to just over half.

Kaiden dropped to his knees, the blurred air in front of him like a desert heat haze. The next attack slammed into his shield a moment later, pushing him back as his feet struggled for purchase on the slippery leaves and fungi.

His charge bar was nearing full now, at eighty percent. He needed to use an ability. Needed to do something.

Burst of Speed activated. Current movement speed increased by 100% for 10 seconds.

Kaiden immediately turned and leapt away from the invisible beast so quickly it didn't have time to react. He heard it scrambling through the undergrowth after him. Kaiden was moving so fast he cut a swath through the mist, buying himself a moment to think. In the corner of his screen, a timer counted down until Burst of Speed's effect would wear off.

08...

I need more critical hits, but there's nothing to aim at! There was a growl from behind as the creature gained on him, but Kaiden slipped out of range again, too fast to catch. The jungle foliage shifted for a moment, outlining the invisible monster as he lured it further from Zelda, noticing her health bar has risen from the stimpack.

05...

You can't hit what you can't see. But maybe that new ability can help me?

04...

Kaiden activated Enhanced Senses.

His charge bar dropped by ten units, but his visor kicked into high gear. The dense brush around him faded from solid and choking to a faint gray haze and every living thing around him lit up in a dull red: Zelda, waiting on the sidelines to take a shot. A flock of birds, wheeling above the canopy. The now-clear manhunter, rearing to pounce about twelve feet behind. While still camouflaged, only Kaiden could see it.

01...

With his last second of Burst of Speed, Kaiden used Hammer Toss. His hammer hurtled through the air, crashing into the manhunter's muscled chest. Even with the ability's double damage for a successful hit, the damage done was minimal. However, hitting the creature had brought it out of stealth.

00…

Burst of Speed ends.

No longer fast, the beast was upon Kaiden quickly. He raised his shield, praying it would hold.

A scream from the side caused the manhunter to turn. It was Titus, charging at a speed he shouldn't have, shield held out before him like a battering ram.

Kaiden checked on the ability.

Ability: Shield Charge
Charge at double your speed for 3 seconds. Direct impacts deal 50% of base damage. Cost: 40 charge. Cooldown: 2 minutes.

Titus slammed into the manhunter, bowling it onto its side, then slid to a stop.

"Miss me?" Titus said, flashing Kaiden a smile.

"Missed my tank," Kaiden jibed.

"Any plan for taking this thing out?" Zelda called from further back.

A timer was still flashing in Kaiden's vision, this one for Enhanced Senses. It had a few seconds left. And as Kaiden watched the beast on its side, he noticed something.

Most of the beast was glowing a dull red — its heat signature, no doubt — but its stomach was bright orange.

Because the hide is thinner there, Kaiden realized. *Could that be a weak spot? It has to be, right?*

"The stomach!" Kaiden shouted, pointing at the prone beast. "That's its weak point!"

The manhunter scrambled back up, then rose up on its hind legs, beating its chest and roaring. Its glowing belly was almost like a target.

"Hit it right in the middle," Kaiden said. Hammer Toss

would have been perfect if it hadn't been on cooldown. Zelda sent a precise Burst Arrow and even Titus was up to something, stepping backward.

"Been wanting to try this 'Shield of Fury' thing out anyway," he said, then whipped his arm forward in the beast's direction. Titus' shield flew from his arm and slammed into the manhunter's belly before glancing away. The manhunter made to charge at them, but its attack was interrupted as Titus' shield knocked off a nearby tree and flew back, slamming into its head.

What? Kaiden stared in disbelief as, in a way only possible in a video game, Titus caught his shield. Kaiden locked onto Titus with his reticle.

Ability: Shield of Fury
Launch your shield against an enemy to ricochet to up to 3 times. Deals +50% base damage, reducing by half with each successive hit. This replaces Hammer Toss.
Minimum range 10 feet. Maximum range: 30 feet. Cost: 20 charge. Cooldown: 30 seconds.

Both the attacks on the manhunter's stomach had been enough to put its health in the yellow.

"Hitting that spot gave a massive critical damage multiplier," Zelda said.

"We'll need to get it to expose its stomach again," Kaiden said, watching as the manhunter rolled to its feet, but kept its belly low to the ground.

"Distract it for me!" Zelda said. "I have an idea."

"Over here, big ugly!" Titus banged his hammer against a tree trunk and his shield upon the undergrowth. The manhunter eyed him, then Zelda, apparently unsure which was the bigger threat. A moment later, it turned to face Zelda.

She backed up a pace.

Kaiden bellowed and threw himself at the manhunter. He slammed into it shield first, bouncing off its shoulder and doing virtually no damage, but definitely getting the beast's attention.

The manhunter turned with a slash that caught Kaiden across the chest and knocked him on his rear, dropping his health into the yellow.

Seeing his weakness, the manhunter growled and rushed forward.

Zelda was quicker. As soon as the beast had turned away from her, she sprinted forward. Looking every bit a professional baseball player, she fell into a slide and slipped right underneath the creature's stomach.

Zelda pulled the trigger on her hammer-gun.

A new attack Kaiden hadn't seen before – something she must have unlocked at level seven – exploded upward. It looked like a shotgun blast of lasers, and considering the force with which it hit the manhunter, it dealt damage like one, too.

Ability: Scatter Shot
Fires an expanding spray of 10 energy blasts each dealing 30% of base damage. Cost: 35 charge. Cooldown: 1 minute.

Every one of those blasts hit the beast squarely in its weakened belly, meaning her attack essentially hit the thing for triple damage. And if she got a crit, too...

The beast yelped as it was blasted up and to the side. When it collapsed back to the ground, its health bar was empty.

Baboulian Manhunter assisted kill - 1,500 EXP gained!

"Note to self," Zelda said, standing up from the mud she'd slid through. "Scatter Shot does a lot of damage in close quarters."

"You can say that again." Titus stared in awe at the dead beast as the jungle returned to quiet but for the pitter patter of rain on the leaves.

"Hopefully we didn't attract too much attention with that fight," Kaiden said, looking around. As far as he could see, they were still boxed in by dense foliage. Except...was that...?

He moved forward several steps. The fight with the manhunter had led them some distance from the route they'd been following, and now he could just make out a gap in between two trees.

He came to a squelching stop in the mud as the brush gave

way. The world before him was all open air. He was standing right on the edge of a vast cliff.

But not just any cliff. It was the overlook they'd been trekking to. And sure enough, as Kaiden turned his eyes down to the valley floor below, he spotted what they'd come for.

The base was housed in the crumbling frame of an ancient temple, but the massive power cables running along the ground, the ships berthed beneath the surrounding trees, and most importantly, the flag hung on the side of the temple, told Kaiden all he needed to know.

Zelda stepped up beside him. Titus did the same. The big man whistled low.

"Looks like we found our assassin guild."

Chapter Twenty-Seven

Waiting. It was perhaps the single worst thing to have to do in a game, and it was still morning in the real world. It was going to be a long day.

No one gamed so they could waste their precious free time sitting around waiting for something to happen. It was just objectively not fun. But Kaiden wasn't playing Nova Online for fun. Neither were Zelda or Titus. And so, from their vantage point above the Oneshot guild headquarters, they waited, and they watched.

And nothing happened.

Night fell, and still nothing. Except for more rain. Kaiden had pretty much given up all hope of that ever stopping. The sound of it had beat an unending rhythm into his mind. A symphony of drizzles and drips and light splashes, performed along with a chorus of crickets, frogs, chirping birds, and the occasional long, deep moan of something else. Something big. Hopefully not another Baboulian manhunter.

"I've never camped before," Titus said, lying prone on his stomach between Kaiden and Zelda as they all peered over the cliff's edge and down to the valley below. "Aren't we supposed to, I don't know, make a fire or something?" He adjusted his position for what seemed the thousandth time. "I mean, I know we don't feel overly cold or hot in this game, but I'd at least like to be able to see something. It's so dark I might as well have my eyes closed."

"No fire," Zelda said, eyes focused on the base below. She hadn't moved in what seemed like hours. It'd likely only been an hour, even though Kal Reya had gone from daylight to the deep dark of night.

In-game day and night cycles moved faster than in real life. It helped players experience the full effect of the game without having to actually spend entire days online. There was also the fact that Kaiden had no idea how long a day was on Kal Reya. Space was funny like that. And Nova, the hyper-realistic, physics engine-driven game that it was, was sure to emulate it accurately.

"No fire," Zelda said again. "It'll give away our position. If anyone down there is paying even a bit of attention, they'll instantly spot us. We're too close to finding Jax to make a mistake like that now."

"You're right, as usual," Titus said, sounding none too happy about it. "I just wish I could see."

"It's not that I don't also want some light," Zelda said, her usually sharp tone softening somewhat. "It's just that the stakes are high now. Think of how hard we've worked to get here. Think of everything we've overcome. And we're so close now. If we catch this assassin, we can prove Kaiden's innocence. We can get justice for Bernstein's murder, and we'll finally be able to expose..." She trailed off suddenly.

Kaiden felt himself frown at that. He pulled his eyes from the dark valley below to look at her.

"Finally be able to expose what?"

"The truth about Bernstein's murder," she said, hesitant at first, then with more confidence. "The criminals who killed him framed you for it, Kai. That's why the Party found it so easy to convict you. The evidence was stacked against you – too obvious to be true, but the Party took it at face value. Or didn't care to dig deeper."

Framed? Kaiden mulled over the word. That was quite the illogical jump. Someone had definitely murdered Bernstein; of that there was no doubt. But that he had stumbled upon the scene right before the police had arrived, that'd just been sheer bad luck, right? As bad as it was, it'd been a case of wrong place, wrong time. Hadn't it?

"Bernstein's killer likely tripped some sort of security measure, which made an emergency call to the police, who arrived right after I did. Look, I'm not happy about it, not by any means, but I can understand how it looked."

"Planted evidence and bribes are a powerful combo, Kai," Zelda said. "How could the crime scene investigators, the detectives on your case, even the judge, get the facts so wrong? All it takes is a sixty-second conversation with you and it's obvious you're no murderer."

"When we first met, you were convinced I killed Bernstein."

"Because that's how they wanted it to look. Whatever criminal organization killed him needed someone to take the fall so they could lie low. At least until they ransom the information they took from him back to the Party."

"You think the Party would make a deal with criminals?" Kaiden felt himself frown at that.

"They do it more than you'd think. *They* do a lot of things most people don't know about."

A shuffling in the darkness signified Titus was moving. In the dim light, Kaiden could just make out his form, crouched now and staring at Zelda.

"The only people who say 'they' like that are a dangerous kind to be associated with," Titus said. "Dissidents don't have a long shelf life, if you know what I mean."

Zelda sighed, then crawled back from the lip of the cliff herself.

"Look, I'm not trying to go all conspiracy theorist on you. But you have to look at the facts."

Kaiden joined them now, edging back from the overlook of the valley. Zelda turned to him.

"The obvious answer is often a distraction. True answers are found when one digs deeper."

Bernstein's words. The same ones I used to convince her I wasn't his murderer.

"Dig deeper into something like this, and all you're going to end up is dead," Titus said, stepping over to him. "Look, Kai. There are factions even the gangs steer clear of. I'm starting to think *she* might be involved with one."

Factions even the gangs steer clear of? What was he talking about?

"Oh, that's rich," Zelda scoffed. "Coming from a gangster like yourself."

"Guys," Kaiden said, stepping between the two of them. "Calm down."

"We made a mistake getting involved with her."

"Well, at least we agree on that," Zelda said. "It was Kai's idea to bring you in, anyway. I warned him we couldn't trust someone like you."

"Guys!" Kaiden near shouted. "Stop it!"

"Oh, someone like me, huh? You see these tattoos and you think you know me. Think you know my story." Titus took one stomping step forward, his voice boiling into anger. "You want to know why I joined the King Street Gang, Zelda?"

"Oh, this'll be good." She was yelling now, too. "Here, let me take a guess. Money? Greed? For the thrill of it?"

"To protect my family."

It was spoken soft. Slow. Gentle, almost. Silence followed for many moments.

"To protect my family." He finally said it again, with a sigh this time, all anger gone from his voice. "After I retired from boxing, I worked a regular job. Made terrible money, but it was honest work. Problem was, the people who ran the gym I used to box at? They were powerful people on the streets. The kind of people I kept far away from." He paused, taking a long breath.

"But my little brother, he always had a nose for trouble. A nose that led him to owing these people a whole lot of money. Now, I'm all for paying for your mistakes – every man has to own up to his actions – but the people my brother owed money to, well, when you don't pay, they don't come after you. They come after your family – all of them. You want to know why I joined the King Street Gang? It was to work off my brother's debt. To keep my family from being abducted and murdered, or worse."

He finished with a shake of his head, his lower lip quivering in rage.

"And now I'm in here, playing a ridiculous video game, and hoping for the sake of my family that my brother can keep making his payments."

He inhaled deeply, and when he spoke again, there was a renewed resolve in his voice.

"I don't want to see anyone else walk the road I have. Getting involved with people who go against the Party sounds like an even more dangerous path." He turned to Zelda as he finished, giving her a long, hard look.

"Jeez, Titus," Kaiden said. "I'm...I'm sorry. I had no idea."

Behind the tattoos and wall of muscle, Titus was a gentler person than his outward appearance would suggest. But that didn't mean he was a big ball of fluff. Didn't mean Kaiden could just make things better with a hug or an apology. Instead, he was left standing a step away, wanting to comfort the big man, but not knowing how. Emotions weren't exactly either of their strong points.

"Titus," Zelda said, breaking the awkward silence. Her voice was sincere as she spoke. There wasn't even a hint of its usual cutting edge. "I'm sorry. I shouldn't have said those things about you. And worse, I shouldn't have let my prejudice influence my opinion of you."

"Yeah, well. That's the way of the world, isn't it?"

From his tone, he wasn't too interested in apologies.

"Maybe we can work on that," Zelda said softly. "I'll do better."

Kaiden breathed a sigh of relief that the two weren't at each other's throats anymore. Hopefully, this would be a turning point.

But there were still some lingering questions about Zelda. Questions that really needed to be asked.

No better time than the present, huh? Might as well air all the dirty laundry at once.

"Zelda," Kaiden said, drawing her attention. "You're interested in Bernstein's murder because he was your friend. I get that. But there's more to it, isn't there? Something you're not telling me. Something Titus is obviously concerned with."

"Yeah." She sighed. "You weren't supposed to find out this way. It's a...delicate topic. Most people react like, well, about how Titus did. Which isn't to put any blame on him. Most people just don't know. But that's part of my job. I want to help people see."

"Help them see what?" Kaiden asked. He fought to keep the annoyance from his tone. She was dodging the question better than a politician.

"Help them see that the Party isn't as in control as it likes to appear, which makes them dangerous. They're covering up the fact there are criminal elements in the world that they've been thoroughly unable to control."

Hold up. What? Kaiden felt his face scrunch up in confusion.

"Are we thinking of the same Party? The one that led us through the chaos of the great test? That ended the war and united us back into an actual, functioning society?"

"I'm not denying they've done good."

"So what *are* you saying, then?"

She turned to Titus for a moment, speaking quickly. "Titus, you might not like the path I walk, but you can back up what I'm saying. Working in and around the gangs, I know you've heard things. Things the average citizen wouldn't have."

He was silent for a long time before finally speaking.

"Yeah," he grunted. "I've heard some stuff. Nasty stuff. The kind that encourages even us to stay far clear of associating with...dissidents."

"You don't have to use the Party-approved language. You can call us what we are."

"Extremists?"

"*Rebels.*"

Was there a touch of pride as she said the word? Kaiden wasn't sure. He wasn't even sure what she meant.

"Rebels?" Kaiden said. "Against what? Against the Party? That's insane."

"I don't blame you for thinking that. But, Kai, listen to me for a moment." There was a sincerity in her voice, backed by a passion that caught him off guard. This was important to her.

"I'm a journalist. Or I used to be. Bernstein was, too. We worked together at the Broadstreet Herald."

"Never heard of it."

"What about Metagamer Weekly?"

"Yeah, they're an eSports publication covering the competitive gaming scene."

Zelda laughed at that.

"That wasn't always the case. When Bernstein and I worked there, it was the Broadstreet Herald. We were investigative journalists, and our first few truly groundbreaking stories were done on the gangs. We dug deep, deeper than anyone before us, and our work resulted in a public outcry. The Party was forced to act – and they did, arresting dozens of gangsters. For our 'service to the people and the Party,' Bernstein and I were awarded medals of Special Merit. And then summarily told to close any further investigations."

"Something tells me you didn't do that."

"Of course not. Our digging uncovered more than just gang activity. It led us to believe the Party was not only aware of the gangs, but actively allowing many of them to operate in exchange for a portion of their profits. They were taking bribes to look the other way."

That's not good, but it's nothing groundbreaking.

Kaiden shrugged. "So there were one or two bad officials. Power is a corrupting force; we've all been taught that. That's why the process to get into politics is so rigorous. You have to truly have the interests of the people at heart."

"And line the right pockets. This corruption didn't stop at one or two lowly officials. We were following a trail that led all the way to the top."

"So why didn't I ever hear about this? Why wasn't it all over the news networks?"

"Because when we didn't stop our investigation, the Broadstreet Herald was purchased by an anonymous business magnate. It was time for a change, they higher-ups told us. Time to get into the eSports game. The entire publication rebranded to 'Metagamer Weekly.' All staff were told to refocus on eSports and competitive gaming. Those who refused were fired."

Kaiden hardly had to ask the question.

"I take it you refused?"

"And Bernstein, too."

"You got lucky," Titus chimed in. "You should have let things lie and moved on."

"I couldn't," Zelda said. "I can't. The gang stuff was just the tip of the iceberg." She took a steadying breath. "We took our investigation to a new paper. We made some headway, then guess what happened? The paper was bought out. Decided to pivot to a new subject. All staff who complained were fired. Rinse and repeat. Are you starting to see the trend?"

Kaiden pursed his lips. An uneasy feeling was rising in his stomach.

"Do you want to know why the Party's repressive activities are news to you, Kai?" Zelda went on, her words tumbling like a waterfall now, rushing past one after another with no sign of stopping. "Do you want to know why none of the media questioned the circumstances of your trial? Because there are no independent papers anymore. No independent media. No real journalism. It's all controlled by the Party. It, and so, so much more."

In the wake of her words, there was silence. Silence so deep it seemed even the rain itself lessened – for a few moments, at least – as if waiting to hear what was coming next.

"This is a lot to hear all at once," Kaiden finally said. "Which isn't me saying I believe you. I've come to trust you since we teamed up, and you were Bernstein's friend. Those are the main reasons I'm even entertaining the idea that what you're saying is legit."

"That's a start, I suppose."

"But let's say, just for a moment, that I do believe you. You really think some criminal element framed me for Bernstein's murder?"

"The information Bernstein had was valuable to the Party – they wouldn't want it to get out. It happens all the time, you know. Some gang gets hold of footage of some official misbehaving, that sort of thing. And the Party pays up every time; money, favors, whatever it takes."

"Favors?" Kaiden asked.

"Remember the O'Reilly trial a few years back?"

Kaiden shook his head, but Titus chuckled.

"The King Street boys had a laugh watching that go down."

"Back when there was still real news, we covered this big crime boss getting arrested," Zelda explained. "Then suddenly some last-minute evidence comes in and he walks free?"

"Yeah, lucky git," Titus said.

"The Party leaned on the judge, some files were doctored...all because a low-level official got filmed in a drug den and O'Reilly's gang got their hands on it."

"That was why? Titus said, shaking his head. "Figures."

"So anyone who has the information, and the balls to hold it for ransom, stands to make a lot of money," Zelda said. "But they still needed someone to take the fall."

This is crazy. Kaiden's thoughts were swirling and spiraling in a mad, disjointed rhythm. *I'm not sold on what Zelda is saying, but there's no denying I'm wrapped up in something big here. Something I had no intention of getting involved in. I just want to prove my innocence.*

"I'm not saying I agree or disagree," Titus said, speaking for the first time in a while. "I've heard of officials getting blackmailed for cash, it's true, but nothing on the level you're talking about. But if one of the gangs wanted to cover something up, that's pretty much how they'd go about it. Feed the authorities, and the public, a scapegoat to distract from what's really happening."

"So what is really happening, then? What information did Bernstein have that's worth enough to kill for?"

Zelda swallowed hard at Kaiden's question.

"I don't know. He just told me it was something big. Enough to bring down the top brass."

"I thought you were working with him? I thought you both gathered all this evidence?"

"We did," Zelda said, defensive now. "At the beginning, anyway. But Bernstein didn't want to act on it. Not until it was perfect. Not until we had everything just right. I, uh, well. I disagreed. I sought out the rebels and told them what we were working on. Against Bernstein's wishes. That was when we parted ways.

"He didn't like the rebels, you see. Thought they were too extreme. And he was right, to a degree. There are some extremists, people willing to harm civilians to prove their point. But I didn't go to them. I went to the moderates. To those aiming to act with dignity and reason. Those who wanted to expose the Party, not for the purpose of gaining power, or on some quest for vengeance, but because it's the right thing to do."

She sighed.

"But Bernstein didn't trust them – thought they'd use it to start a bloody civil war, take power for themselves. It wouldn't be the people's revolution he envisioned. He went underground, and took our work with him. After that, he only contacted me through Nova. Sent me updates through the secure file transfer system built into the game. And then, the day after he told me he'd got hold of something big...he just stopped."

Jeez. This rabbit hole just goes deeper and deeper.

Kaiden could feel the comfort of the world he'd known, of what was truth and what was fiction, slipping away. He still wasn't sold on the Party's corruption, but now there was doubt in his mind. A seed, perhaps, but it was there.

"So, you're telling me the information Bernstein was killed for would expose earth-shattering revelations about the Party. Evidence that would shake our society to the very core?"

"I couldn't have said it better myself."

"And that's what we're chasing? What we're trying to recapture before it's auctioned back to the party by whoever took it? That's what this assassin is involved with?" Kaiden nodded down toward the valley. "That's what – hold up." He paused. "Is that a light?"

They all turned toward the valley as one, and sure enough, there was a light down there. The front door of the base had opened, casting a long beam across the field in front of it. A shadow moved in the light; a person, walking out from within the base.

Surrounded by darkness, but illuminated by the brilliant light pouring from inside the base, there was no denying the assassin was Jax. Even from this far away the streak of red through his hair stood out like a beacon. Not to mention the rifle slung across his back.

Just to be sure, however, Kaiden focused on him, able to zoom in closer with his enhanced visor. Sure enough, the assassin's name came up along with the other relevant information. That was Jax. That was their man.

Quest Complete: Capture the assassin Jax
Part 2: Confirm Jax is a member of Oneshot
Rewards received: +3,500 EXP, +5 faction prestige

Update
Quest: Capture the assassin Jax
Part 3: Find a way to capture the assassin
Expected Difficulty: Veteran
Rewards: +7,000 EXP, +5 faction prestige

Level 8 achieved!
Max health and stamina increased
+3 stat points

Kaiden wanted to be excited about the level up, but instead he dumped his new stat points into dexterity immediately, then looked back to Jax.

The assassin strode across the field and up to a ship – the same ship they'd seen leave Nassau – and hopped in. The engines fired to life, casting a burning new light into the night.

"I'm not the only one who saw that red hair, right?" Zelda asked, watching the ship.

"That's our man," Titus said.

"Yeah. The only problem is, he's leaving." Zelda turned and ran into the trees, back the way they came earlier. Even as she did, Jax's ship lifted into the air and turned its nose toward the stars.

"Oh no."

Kaiden cursed. They'd found their assassin. Had found his guild base. But now, he was leaving. And with how far away they'd left the *Borrelly,* he was going to have one heck of a head start.

"Anyone have a flashlight?" he asked, turning to follow Zelda.

It was going to be a long run without one.

Chapter Twenty-Eight

We lost the assassin. We lost him.

Kaiden couldn't stop thinking about last night. And Jax. How they'd lost him.

Inside his shower stall – one among the two or three dozen in the bathroom – he cranked the water temperature up and sighed.

They'd confirmed Jax was a part of Oneshot, at least, and that Oneshot's headquarters were in fact on Kal Reya, but when it came to actually catching the assassin, that all counted for very little. Staking out the moon until Jax returned could take a day, or a month. Maybe more. They'd no way of knowing. No, they needed to find him. Which was far easier said than done, considering he was, apparently, quite good at not being found.

More worryingly, Kaiden's understanding of the real world was now in flux. If only Zelda hadn't dropped that rebel nonsense on them. How much of it was true? All he knew was proving his innocence was the best way out of prison, and to do that they needed to catch Jax.

"Everyone out!" The command came from somewhere near the door, echoing through the tiled floor and walls of the bathroom.

One of the guards?

Kaiden stepped out from under the showerhead and peeked through the mostly opaque plastic curtain that separated his stall from the rest of the bathroom.

The far wall was loaded with sinks, the mirrors above each

fogged up, with water dripping down the tiled walls between them.

"I said everyone get out!"

Kaiden leaned through the shower curtains and looked to his right, toward the entrance. Other inmates were joining him now, a dozen or so heads poking out between him and the entrance.

At the end of the room, five or six fully clothed inmates had rushed in. They were ripping open curtains and searching the shower stalls one at a time, pulling still-dripping men out and removing them from the room.

This isn't good. Something's up. Kaiden leaned back into his stall to get his clothing. Just before he did, another inmate entered the bathroom. Kaiden recognized the scowling, tattooed man immediately: Manson.

He's here for me. Oh, crap.

Kaiden yanked his curtain closed as Manson continued to draw closer. Shadows passed outside his stall: apparently, other showering inmates had realized what was up and were eager not to be involved.

I need to get out of here. Now.

Staying near Titus had kept him safe thus far, but they'd been assigned different shower groups. Kaiden had always felt exposed in the shower, but it hadn't been a problem yet. Apparently, his luck had run out.

"Kaiden! Oh, Kaiden!" Manson called out, his too-happy voice echoing through the room. "I just want to talk to you. Can we talk?"

How about no?

For a moment, Kaiden's instincts told him to activate Burst of Speed and make a run for it. But of course, he wasn't in-game. He'd spent so much time there recently that even the real world was starting to feel like Nova.

I need another plan.

He grabbed the divider separating his stall from the next and pulled his head up above the top to peer toward the back of the room.

No exit there.

He looked back toward the entrance. Manson and his thugs were halfway to him now.

"Hey! Eyes to yourself!"

Kaiden looked down to find the occupant of a nearby stall glaring up at him, a shirt half-pulled over his head.

"Sorry," Kaiden said, dropping back down.

As soon as his feet hit the floor he made a move to grab his clothes, but slipped and whacked his knee on the tiles.

Cursing, he pulled himself to his feet and reached for his clothing again. As he scrambled into his underwear, an idea struck him.

The bathroom was wet from water and steam. Which made it slippery. That meant any sort of physical struggle, if things came to that, would be difficult. Why not make it even more difficult?

Step one...

He turned back to his showerhead and cranked it on to max heat. The water began to steam even more than it already had been, clouding the air.

And step two...

Next, he loaded his hands up with soap and rubbed it all over himself, careful to stay out of the path of the water lest it wash the suds off.

"No sign of him yet, boss," someone shouted.

"Keep looking."

When Kaiden was covered from head to toe in soap, he dropped to the floor and looked under the knee-high dividers to the stalls neighboring his. Their occupants had abandoned them.

Here goes step three.

Slipping along the floor, any traction he'd had completely gone because of the suds, he squirmed his way into the neighboring stall. Once he was there, he turned the shower on and turned the lever all the way to max heat.

"You can't hide forever, Kaiden!"

Kaiden dropped to the tile floor again and scrambled to the next stall, turned the water on and the heat as high as it would go, then repeated the process in the next stall as well.

There were three stalls on max heat now, pouring steam into the air. The already saturated walls began to run with streams of water. Outside his stall, someone slipped and fell with a curse.

"I see you in there."

Kaiden froze as Manson's voice came from right outside his stall. Through the mostly opaque curtain he could see a silhouette, hand raised and reaching for the edge of the curtain. Some-thing shiny and thin was gripped in Manson's other hand.

A knife? A shiv?

Whatever it was, Kaiden didn't relish the idea of finding out.

There was the crackling of plastic as the curtain was ripped back.

"Aha!" Manson smiled, then took a step into the stall. "Found you."

"This stall's occupied," Kaiden said, then pointed the shower-head at the maniac. Steaming hot water sprayed across Manson's face and he yelped, ducking behind his forearms and stumbling backwards.

"You little—"

Kaiden didn't wait to hear what he was going to say. He darted out, slipping past Manson's reaching arms, and sprinted toward the exit.

"Get him!"

There were three thugs between Kaiden and the door out of the bathroom. The first lunged forward, slipped on the wet tile and collapsed face first.

One down.

Kaiden jumped over him. His feet slid forward as he landed, throwing his balance off and sending his arms waving. The second thug launched toward him, and in that split second, reflexes Kaiden had never had before clicked into place. He found his balance just in time to spin to the side, dodging the thug's barging shoulder. His would-be assailant bounced off the wall, crumpling to the floor.

Wow. Maybe I've picked up more from playing my warden than I thought.

"You're mine, you little rat!" Manson shouted from behind.

No time to think.

Kaiden sprinted forward, right at the last of Manson's goons.

The man set his feet wide and spread his arms, preparing to wrap him up in what Kaiden was sure would be the least friendly hug of his life.

The only way out is through.

Kaiden threw himself at the thug. They both tumbled to the floor, knees and elbows going every which way. Something bony caught Kaiden in the chin and his head snapped back. His vision shook and his ears were ringing, but he had to escape.

He clawed at the floor, slipped in the suds, and made no headway. His hands shoved at the meat of the thug's chest, finding purchase there and pushing off to rise to his knees. He was almost free. Just a few more steps and–

A hand like a vise wrapped around his elbow and squeezed tight. Too tight, as it happened. Kaiden pulled his arm away and the hand slipped right off. The sound of someone falling slapped behind him. Manson howled, but Kaiden was free. And he wasn't stopping now.

He slid and scrambled through the exit and out into the hallway.

A crowd of other inmates, in various stages of undress, was huddled there, watching with expressions ranging from disinterest to pure excitement.

Some cheered as Kaiden ran past, others laughed.

Kaiden hardly cared.

His heart was pounding in his chest, adrenaline surging through his veins. But he wasn't safe yet.

Bare feet slapping on the floor, Kaiden sprinted through the hall, slid around a corner, and didn't stop running until he was back at his cell.

Ducking inside, he forced the door shut, then collapsed onto his bed, breathing heavily.

He was locked in now, and had abandoned one of his two sets of clothing in the bathroom, but he was alive. Considering how things could have gone, that wasn't so bad.

Chapter Twenty-Nine

Boyd City again. Except this time we've managed to work our way into an even seedier underbelly. The under-underbelly? Kaiden chuckled at his own bad joke. *Something like that.*

They were in what the game had referred to as a 'high threat area' due to the increased levels of criminal activity. Not the best locale for wardens to be, but the only place where they could put their plan into action.

It was a plan days in the making, having spent their last few sessions fruitlessly searching the labyrinthine back alleys of Nassau. Now, finally, they were sure they'd found it.

"You sure you're okay with this, Titus?" Zelda asked for about the thousandth time. "If this goes badly, there's a worryingly high chance you end up on a week's forced vacation, while we get assigned a new partner."

"It's a good plan."

"It's a risky plan."

He shrugged.

"We have to catch this assassin one way or another, but I'd much prefer taking a gamble on this than waiting for him back on Kal Reya."

Kaiden slapped the big man on the back.

"We've been looking for this place for ages. I'm not backing out now," Kaiden said, smiling. "Don't worry. I've a good feeling about it."

Zelda turned to him next.

"You're confident with your part? Know what you have to do?"

"For the fifth time, yes," Kaiden said, then smirked. "Wish me luck?" With that, he broke from the shadows of the alley they'd been hiding in and strode across the street.

The establishment loomed before him, a damaged strip of tube light lettering flickering on and off. 'Finest Theatre on Nassau' it read, when all of the letters were on, at least.

The front door slid open with a hiss and Kaiden stepped inside.

It took a moment for his eyes to adjust to the darkness within. As they did, there was a commotion in front of him, rushed curses and footsteps as someone fled the room.

"What's a warden doing here—"

Kaiden's eyes adjusted in time to see the speaker get slapped by the suited man next to him. An NPC by the name of Marty, Kaiden's visor told him. From behind a chipped and scarred counter, Marty smiled, his eyes wandering to the collar around Kaiden's neck.

"Officer. So good to have you stop by. Is there something I can help you with?"

"Actually, there is," Kaiden said, stepping up to the counter and doing his best to look like he belonged.

The establishment called itself a theater. The interior almost made that lie look believable. Plush red cushions and lounge sofas adorned the lobby, their grandeur only spoiled slightly by the suspicious stains coating most of them. Hidden lights in the ceiling projected a flickering slideshow of theater posters. The same two on a loop.

Not much variety in this theater. But then again, Kaiden hadn't come here to appreciate the fine arts. The warden archives said this was home to the upper crust of Boyd City's criminals, the preferred playground of the best of the worst.

"I think you'll find we're all paid up this month, boss," Marty said with a gracious smile.

"I'm sure you are," Kaiden said, pretending like he knew what that meant. "But that's not why I'm here."

"Oh?" Marty leaned across the counter and somehow managed to smile even wider. "Marty Macmara," he said and extended a hand. "At your service, then. How can I help?"

"I'd like to place a hit on someone."

The shorter man next to Marty – Lou, the game said his name was – burst out laughing.

"'Place a hit,' he says?"

Marty patted him on the shoulder and his laugh dried up to a slight chuckle.

"My sincerest apologies, officer, but I'm sure I don't know what you mean. You're still working for the corps by the looks of your collar, and that's definitely not something they'd approve of."

Marty's eyes lingered on Kaiden's collar a little longer.

"The only 'hits' we deal in here are of the theatrical variety." He gestured to the posters advertising the venue's whopping two plays.

"The warden archives say otherwise." Kaiden had to look authoritative. Like he had done this before.

Marty frowned at that.

"The archives must be wrong."

"They're not." Kaiden leaned on the counter and smiled at Marty, big and wide like the man had done before. "Now, who should I speak to about having a warden killed? A shield warden, specifically, by the name of Titus."

The suited man leaned away, frowning deeper, and crossed his arms.

"Assuming I had any idea what you're talking about – which I don't – *and* knew someone who could help – which I decidedly do not – why would I even consider something like that? You're a warden. In uniform. If this were some sort of undercover sting on my perfectly legal establishment, it's the worst I've seen. Not that I've ever seen any, mind you."

"Besides, no one would take that job–" Lou said, before stopping himself.

Kaiden looked down at the shorter man and gave him his best intense gaze.

"I thought this was Nassau's finest theatre? Surely you know someone...talented enough? I've heard Jax is a particularly good 'actor' who frequents your establishment."

"You're serious, aren't you?" Lou's brow furrowed, then he turned to Marty. "I think he's actually serious."

"Maybe he is..." Marty was stroking his chin. "And Jax has so much heat on him already, a warden target wouldn't make a difference."

Kaiden wasn't sure what Marty was thinking, but he seemed to be considering the offer. From a criminal's perspective, having a dirty warden on your side could be a huge advantage, he didn't doubt. Hopefully Marty was thinking the same thing.

"Alright, kid. Let's talk business."

"About time."

"I'd like to offer you a role in one of our little productions. A starring role, as it happens. One night only."

Kaiden balked at that.

"I didn't come here to be an actor."

"No, you came here to place a hit on another warden. Which, frankly speaking, is incredibly illegal. If you and I are to talk business – not related to hiring an assassin, of course – you need to prove to me that you're...into the same hobbies as us. A fan of the theatrical arts, you could say."

"You want me to act in one of your plays?"

"Well, not a play, exactly. More of a spectacle. And you won't be acting. You'll be fighting to the death."

Well, that escalated quickly. Though I am literally trying to send an assassin after a fellow warden...

"You want me to fight for you?"

"For me? No, no. Of course not. You'll be fighting for the fans. In my arena. Tonight."

"Tonight?"

"You say you want to kill another warden? Then prove to me this isn't some ruse. Prove you're actually here to talk business. My arena's never hosted a warden before. You'll draw massive crowds. And I'll even sweeten the deal. Survive a few rounds – say, three? –give the crowd a good show, and I'll pay for the hit myself." Marty extended a hand. "How's that sound?"

Well, what other choice do I have? Kaiden wanted to hesitate, wanted to buy time to think things through. But a dirty warden wouldn't balk at this, he didn't think.

I have to play my role, he thought, already tiring of theatre puns.

He grabbed Marty's hand and gave it a firm shake.

Quest: Survive 3 rounds in Marty's arena

Expected difficulty: Veteran
Rewards: +3,000 EXP, +5 faction prestige with Nassau's
criminal underground, -15 faction prestige with the
Warden Corps (if they find out, that is).
Bonus reward: Access to the services of Nassau's finest
'theatre'.

Marty smiled.

"The performance starts at sundown. Don't be late."

"Fair enough." Kaiden nodded, then turned to leave.

How am I going to explain this to the others? How am I going to tell them—

"Oh, and officer?"

Kaiden turned.

"Make sure you've memorized your lines. This is an audition you don't want to screw up."

~

"Ladies and gents, this is the moment you've waited for." Marty's voice boomed out across his 'theatre.' It was of minimalist design, which is to say it was a dirt-floored ring surrounded by electrified metal walls and rows and rows of cheering fans.

Kaiden had hoped news of his 'role' in the performance tonight wouldn't spread too far. The completely packed house around him proved his hopes had been for naught. At least they were NPCs by the looks of it.

"We've a very special performance for you tonight, headlined by a very special actor. But I'm sure you're all already aware. So, without further ado, allow me to introduce your star for the evening!"

The spotlights on the ceiling illuminated Kaiden, bathing him in blinding light, and a hand pushed him from behind. He stumbled forward and into the arena.

This was a terrible idea, he thought as the crowd erupted into a renewed round of roaring. He almost wished he'd let Zelda talk him out of it. Almost. They needed to catch Jax, and if this was what he had to do, then so be it.

Just three rounds. I just have to survive three rounds, then I can place the hit and meet back up with the others on the Borrelly.

The others. The thought hit him like a punch and he swallowed hard. This would be his first fight without them. Here, he was truly alone.

Maybe enhanced warden wasn't the greatest specialization to pick? It's a great support class, but maybe not so good for solo combat.

"As usual, folks, I'm not going to draw things out. Let's get right to it, shall we?" From his booth in the stands, Marty twirled his hand in a flourish. "Let the show begin." He pulled hard on a lever. "Release the gobbers!"

At the far side of the arena, a door in the wall slid open. And about a dozen...somethings poured out.

They spilled into the arena like angry bees – if bees were bipedal, stout, and ugly as sin. Their skin was an orange-brown reminiscent of rusted metal, their faces were smashed and flat like they'd all been dropped face down at birth, and their short arms ended in grasping, clawed hands.

Kaiden gripped his hammer tighter and activated his shield. As it flicked on, the crowd went wild again. Ignoring the noise, he analyzed the closest of the creatures.

Gobber
Level: 3

Quick facts: Gobbers are a simplistic race of beings found on most low-level planets, usually in their primitive, underground warrens. These scavengers breed prolifically, though their low intellect means they have no classes or abilities of their own.

Okay, so they're low-level mobs. There's just a lot of them. I can handle this, Kaiden told himself.

The first of the creatures rushed him, snarling as it did so. Kaiden stepped up to it and swung his hammer. The blow caught the creature square in its smashed-up face, knocking it down and leaving its face considerably more smashed. Its health bar flashed from green to yellow to red, then to an empty black.

Critical Hit!
+50% damage (Headshot)

Gobber killed - 50 EXP gained!

One down. That wasn't so bad.

Seeing their downed companion, the remaining eleven gobbers rushed him. The first of them launched into a leap, one arm reared back with a knife in hand. Kaiden leaned forward with his shield and the creature jabbed its knife into it, then bounced off to one side.

Kaiden's charge bar filled by two percent.

If they don't hit any harder than that it'll take forever to build any charge.

As it happened, they didn't hit harder than that.

Without activating his abilities, Kaiden swung three times and crushed three more gobbers with headshots.

Eight left. And to think level one voidspawn used to terrify me, he thought, obliterating the smashed-faced creatures around him with impunity.

A gobber rushed him on the right, and Kaiden swung at it. He only hit its stomach this time, and far from killed it. It took at least three more regular attacks to achieve what one headshot crit could.

Gobber killed - 50 EXP gained!

Seven left.

A bolder specimen lunged at him with a taser-tipped spear, the sizzling point coming within an inch of Kaiden's visor as he ducked. As ineffectual as the gobbers appeared, the taser-spear looked deadly. He raised his shield, then dove aside as a laser blast from another gobber nearly took him in the chest. So, Marty had thrown a few ranged weapons into the mix.

The taser-tipped spear jabbed at him again, and Kaiden bent like a bow to avoid it. As his assailant's momentum sent it stumbling past, Kaiden brought his hammer down, bowling the creature backward in a tumble of limbs. Its health dropped substantially more than before. Kaiden wasn't sure why; he hadn't used any special ability. He glanced down to the combat text at the corner of his screen.

+25% damage (Riposte x 1)

Riposte? What's that about? Kaiden thought to himself, ducking behind his shield as the rifle-wielding gobber took aim again. Its weak attacks hit him for a few seconds as he investigated a new notification.

Natural Ability Unlocked!
As a level 8 enhanced warden, your instincts are honing. Riposte: After successfully dodging a melee attack, your next attack deals +25% damage. Dodging 2 attacks in a row stacks to +50% increased damage. Can only stack twice. Taking damage will remove Riposte. This ability is passive.

Natural ability? That's new.
The gobber with the rifle stopped firing, its weapon smoking from overheating. Yet another mob came at Kaiden, a small hammer in hand – an actual hammer, not even a futuristic version of one – and swung it two-handed at him. Kaiden ducked the attack, dodging it.

Riposte x 1 gained

The gobber raised its weapon for another attack. Kaiden risked evading it again to try stacking Riposte, but his gamble didn't pay off. The gobber caught him on the arm, knocking a few percent off his health.

Riposte lost

So, I can try stacking it twice for more damage, but I risk losing the first stack altogether if I take a hit or block with my shield rather than dodging.
It left the decision up to the player, and meant those more skilled could pull off better damage more regularly. An outrageous dodge chance would help too, of course, but that just played right into the design of the enhanced class. Kaiden was beginning to see the extra depth to his spec emerging now.

With fresh focus, Kaiden returned to the fight. With easier opponents before him, he could take a few extra risks and learn a little.

Both the spear-wielding and hammer-wielding gobber were close to him, one on either side. The spear struck out and Kaiden swerved – gaining one stack of Riposte – and then spun as the hammer came for his hip, gaining him a second stack. He finished turning from his spin to find the spear-carrying gobber's back to him. Kaiden struck it on the shoulder.

+50% damage (Riposte x 2)
Gobber killed - 50 EXP gained!

I like this ability, Kaiden thought, then turned to the remaining gobbers. He took the chance to practice building Riposte stacks, though he lost the double stack quite often. He supposed it wasn't meant to be easy.

When the last gobber fell dead, Marty's voice rang across the arena.

"We have a victor!"

It was only then that Kaiden noticed everyone cheering for him.

Have they been doing that the whole time? He'd been so focused on the fight, easy as it was, that he'd forgotten the noise.

"What do you think of our new lead performer?" Marty asked the audience. They responded with more riotous cheering. "Well, don't get too attached. He still has to survive act two!" He pulled another lever and a second door opened in the wall.

Kaiden set his feet in a fighting stance and raised his shield to the ready position.

This time, a human walked out of the door. Then another, and a third.

Kaiden focused on each of them in turn.

Human mercenary (NPC), level five. Human mercenary (NPC), level five. And...human mercenary (NPC), level six. This could actually be a challenge, he thought, then glanced down to his charge bar. It was still too low to do anything.

The mercenaries fanned out and fired a volley of laser blasts.

Kaiden ducked behind his shield, catching two of the blasts, but a third slammed into his leg and near knocked him off his feet.

His health flickered and fell to eighty-five percent. These guys had some serious firepower. Luckily for Kaiden, his charge bar had surged to thirty percent.

Now we're talking!

"Keep hitting him, before his shield charges!" one of the mercenaries shouted. "He can't block them all."

Too late, my man.

Kaiden activated Burst of Speed and surged forward. A timer began counting down in the corner of his screen.

08...

The mercenary who'd called out just had time to blink before Kaiden was on him. The first hammer strike caught him in the chin and sent his health into the yellow.

Critical Hit!
+50% damage (Headshot)

Kaiden pivoted, rounding on the merc and sending a flurry of quick attacks while in Burst of Speed. A last hit on the NPC's forehead finished him off.

Human mercenary killed - 200 EXP gained!

05...

"Stay close!" the level six mercenary yelled, stepping next to her last remaining teammate, then taking aim with her blaster.

It would've taken Kaiden two steps to dodge to one side and avoid the oncoming shots, but he chose to stay in place and catch them on his shield. Except the mercenary never fired. Instead, she simply kept the laser pointed at him.

04...

She's killing time, he realized. *Waiting for Burst of Speed to run out.*

He charged, and she unleashed hell from her blaster. Kaiden skirted to the right, the volley hissing past him in a scattergun of blue flares. She kept her finger on the trigger and swung the barrel around, following his trajectory.

02...

Kaiden leaned into his shield as the laser-fire converged on him. The energy field shook and glowed as the barrage hit it square, then he was within striking distance. She lunged forward with the stock of her blaster, using it like a club. Milking the final second of Burst of Speed, Kaiden dodged the attack —

Riposte x 1 gained

And swung over her rifle, bringing his hammer down onto her elbow.

Critical Hit!
+25% damage (Shattered Elbow)
+25% damage (Riposte x 1)

The blow sent her spinning aside, until she collapsed in a heap.

Human mercenary killed - 200 EXP gained!

00...

Burst of Speed ran out. Kaiden spun to face the third opponent, who wasn't wasting any time.

The merc charged, slicing a glowing energy blade at Kaiden's chest. It passed straight through his shield before cutting deep into Kaiden's chest armor, dropping his health to fifty-six percent. Stumbling backward, Kaiden focused his reticle onto his opponent's weapon.

Electro-blade
Ultrasonic attachments create pulsing vibrations along

the metal help bypass fluctuating shield frequencies. Requires expensive micro-fuel cells to power.

Alright, I better finish this quick.

His shield couldn't help him, so Kaiden couldn't afford to make mistakes.

The merc was on him again, thrusting forward. Kaiden twisted as the first stab cut past his stomach, then bent backward to avoid the next, grateful for dumping so many points into his dexterity. He saw a stack of Riposte tick once, twice. He spun, aiming a blow to the man's torso.

But it seemed his foe had a decent dexterity score as well.

The merc danced to the side, Kaiden missed his swing and saw the stacks of Riposte fade away. He received a slash across his shoulder for his trouble and his health dropped alarmingly to forty-one percent.

Damn it.

He backpedaled, putting distance between himself and that deadly sword.

The mercenary smiled. "That's a nice shield you got there. Too bad my sword isn't affected by it."

Kaiden realized he was a good distance away now, and had just enough charge left for—

Hammer Toss.

Kaiden launched his hammer at the smiling mercenary. It conked him on the head.

Critical Hit!
+50% damage (Headshot)
Hammer Toss hit!
+100% damage

The mercenary fell back and his health dropped all the way to red, no longer smiling.

Kaiden's hammer flew magnetically back to his hand as he sprinted to the fallen merc. He swung down with a final blow.

Human mercenary killed - 250 EXP gained!

The crowd went wild. Marty's voice boomed out once more, encouraging them further.

"Calm down, superstar. You're supposed to be challenged by these fights. At least make it look like you're trying, huh?"

Kaiden turned to the man and shrugged.

I'm here to survive three rounds, not make a good show out of it.

"No matter, though." Marty reached for a third lever. "We've reached the final act of our performance. And folks, it's sure to be a wild one."

Chapter Thirty

Kaiden did a double take as the third door opened and his new adversaries came out. The last thing he'd expected to see were turen.

Ealis (NPC)
Turen Marksman
Faction: Turen Geniocracy
Level: 9

He focused on the second of the two turen that had emerged from the tunnel.

Silae (NPC)
Turen Marksman
Faction: Turen Geniocracy
Level: 9

Each turen warrior held a strange-looking blaster, with thin, translucent tubes spiraling around the barrel.

"Presenting your home field favorites! Your reigning arena champions!" Marty called out to cheers from the crowd. "The Twin Turen Terrors, Ealis and Silae!"

The crowd's response was deafening. The turen ignored it, however, opting to spread out to either side, guns raised as they maneuvered around Kaiden.

Kaiden countered their movements, backing toward the wall behind him. If they got on either side of him, he couldn't stop their shots with his shield. No matter which way he blocked, one side of him would always be exposed.

From what I've learned about the turen, I need to get in close to get the upper hand; even if they are each a level above me.

"Luck is a widespread human misconception," Ealis said. "Nonetheless, we understand it is customary to wish one's opponent 'good luck' before engaging in combat. Good luck, human warden."

"Huh. That's awful polite of you," Kaiden said. "Good luck to you, as we—"

Silae's blast slammed into his shoulder, sending him to the ground.

His health, already lowered from the last round of fighting, dropped to twenty-three percent.

Another blast from that and I'll just about be finishe—

A piercing bright light flared on his right and the translucent coils around Ealis' gun began to glow. A moment later, she fired. Kaiden rolled to the side as an unseen force exploded a wide patch of ground beside him in a blast of steaming dirt.

Jeez, that's bright, Kaiden thought, squinting and turning his eyes from Ealis' blaster as she revved it to fire again. A humming from behind betrayed the fact that Silae was charging his gun as well.

I can't get hit, Kaiden thought, then remembered his stimpack. He activated it.

-1 Stimpack

The healing serum was injected into him through his armor. His health bar filled to forty-eight percent, putting him just back in the yellow.

He had just enough time to be disappointed about that fact before both siblings fired. The first blast came from the right. Kaiden spun away from it.

He leaned into the second shot with his shield, expecting to absorb the blow and fill his charge bar. His charge bar filled, but as the blast detonated on his shield, he was thrown backward, stumbling to catch his balance. Before he did, he slammed into the wall of the arena. Electricity jolted through him and his health bar flashed in warning.

"Gahhh!" Kaiden pulled himself off the wall before it did too much damage.

"I just regained that health!" he shouted, scowling at Silae.

"Our objective is to win this fight. Your lost health brings us closer to this goal. I do not regret my actions."

"Regret this, four-eyes!" Kaiden used Hammer Toss and flung his weapon at Silae.

The turen blinked all four eyes at once. Kaiden's hammer stopped mid-flight, then shot back to his hand.

Hammer Toss blocked by Telekinetic Pulse.

Right, they're minorly telekinetic. Apparently, that means my ranged attacks are going to be entirely ineffective.

The siblings were charging their weapons now and maintaining their angle on him, one on either side.

Kaiden charged the nearest one, Silae, shield held in front of him. He got about halfway to his target before Ealis' blaster fired from behind. Kaiden sidestepped and the shot whirred past him. Silae fired next, before Kaiden could ready himself to dodge again. The blast hit him square on his shield, filling his charge bar to near-max and knocking him on his rear.

"Argh..." he groaned. His plan so far – block their shots, build charge, and get in close – was getting him nowhere. He needed a new strategy. But what?

Burst of Speed is still on cooldown, so that's no good. Hammer Toss is useless. Enhanced Senses...I doubt that's going to do much. And Riposte isn't good for anything if I can't get close to them. What do I do?

For a moment, Kaiden considered trying to get them to shoot each other. If he dodged at the last minute, maybe they'd miss him and hit one another?

Rising to his feet, he lined up with Silae such that if Ealis missed, the blast would hit her sibling. Silae moved with Kaiden, however, keeping himself out of a direct line with his counterpart as both of them charged their weapons for another volley.

The piercing light burst out again, forcing Kaiden to look away.

And then an idea struck him. What if he tried funneling

charge out of his shield, in the same way that he did with his hammer when performing attacks? Maybe it would emit enough light to throw off the turens' aim, giving him a better dodge chance. He had a near-full charge bar and nothing to do with it.

Worth a shot.

Praying his plan would work, or do something, at least, Kaiden funneled charge out of his shield as he ran at Silae. It wasn't something he'd done before, or even realized that he knew how to do. But when he tried, it worked. His charge bar drained by a fifth, and as it did, his shield began to glow.

Kaiden pointed it at Silae as he neared him. The turen frowned for a moment, then raised his blaster to take aim. Kaiden's shield went off first.

The glowing reached peak brightness, then exploded outward in a burst of white-hot light. Even from behind his shield, Kaiden was forced to look away.

Silae flinched, startled from the explosion, and his shot went high, blasting into the air to detonate against an invisible energy barrier over the arena.

"That's new," Ealis said, then fired.

Kaiden dropped to the ground, narrowly avoiding her shot.

"I can't see!"

He turned to find Silae stumbling backward, a hand reaching out as if feeling for the wall. He found it, then yelped as it sent an electric jolt through his system.

"Brother?" Ealis called, concern in her voice. "What has happened?"

"He has blinded me!"

Natural Ability Unlocked!
Flash Bang: Discharge an intense light from your shield that blinds opponents within 10 feet for 5 seconds. Has a 3-second cast time. Cost: 25 charge. Cooldown: 5 minutes.

Now that's useful!

Wasting no time, Kaiden rushed at Silae, hammer raised. Still blinded, the turen couldn't evade him. He hit Silae right between his four eyes, cracking his head back and sending him stumbling into the electric wall once more.

Critical Hit!
+50% damage (Headshot)

This dropped Silae's health into the red – turen really were weak to physical damage, weren't they? – and the wall promptly finished him off.

In the span of a heartbeat, Silae collapsed to the ground, health bar empty as steam rose from his burned skin.

Turen warrior killed - 400 EXP gained!

"Brother!" Ealis fired a shot from her blaster, but Kaiden was already moving. He dodged the attack and charged.

Ealis' eyes were wide as he drew closer, fear clear in her expression. She charged her blaster again, aiming dead center at Kaiden's chest.

This is going to be close.

Kaiden raised his hammer and shield, praying he made it to his opponent before she fired again. He was so close now she was highly unlikely to miss, and he wasn't sure if his shield would overload on impact. He was committed now. It was all or nothing.

Ealis jabbed the barrel toward him, the weapon glowing with a taser charge, and Kaiden dodged aside, gaining a stack of Riposte. Kaiden turned and swung, as did Ealis. They hit each other at the same time.

Kaiden felt a shock from the taser and his health fell to ten percent.

That was too close.

Ealis was quick, lunging again with her taser. Kaiden met her using Shield Bash, and his shield left her stunned. An easy headshot ended the fight.

Turen warrior killed - 400 EXP gained!

Quest Complete: Survive 3 rounds in Marty's arena
Rewards received: + 3,000 EXP, + 5 faction prestige with Nassau's criminal underground, - 15 faction prestige with the Warden Corps (if they find out, that is).

Bonus reward: Access granted to the services of Nassau's finest 'theatre'.

Level 9 achieved!
Max health and stamina increased
+3 stat points

Ability Unlocked!
Blur: You discharge a small energy field so that your movements appear to blur, increasing your dodge chance by 25%. Does not affect the chances of AOE effects to hit you. Cost: 5 charge per second for 10 seconds. Cooldown: 2 minutes.

Relief flooded through Kaiden as the level up restored his health.

"That's...that's unbelievable." Marty's voice boomed through the arena, for the first time sounding unsure. "Our champions, the Twin Turen Terrors, have been...dethroned!"

For a moment, there was stunned silence. Then someone in the back started clapping. It grew like a wave, rising through the arena until the sound was all Kaiden could hear.

He couldn't help but feel a rush of pride as the applause washed over him. He'd done it. The others had been worried, Titus had even offered to take his place, but Kaiden had won. It felt good.

He quickly made his way over to Marty, looking up at the theatre owner's booth with his arms crossed.

"Can we talk business now?"

Clapping along with the rest of his arena, Marty broke into a smile.

"Can we ever, officer. Can we ever."

Chapter Thirty-One

It was thirty minutes later when Kaiden returned to the others, waiting in the *Borrelly* on the far side of the district.

"You did it?" Titus said.

"You won?" Zelda asked at almost the same time.

Kaiden smiled as he walked up the rear loading ramp of the shuttle, then clapped Titus on the shoulder.

"Good news, my friend. I've successfully hired Jax to kill you."

A quest prompt appeared on his screen.

Quest Complete: Capture the assassin Jax, part 3 complete!
Part 3: Find a way to capture the assassin
Rewards received: +7,000 EXP, +5 faction prestige

Update
Quest: Capture the assassin Jax
Part 4: Capture the assassin
Expected Difficulty: Master
Rewards: +8,000 EXP, +10 faction prestige

Level 10 achieved!
Max health and stamina increased
+3 stat points

Ability Choice Unlocked!
You may choose 1 of 2 abilities

Onslaught: Following 6 consecutive critical strikes,
Onslaught mode is triggered for 5 seconds. While in
Onslaught mode you deal double base damage and have
double current movement speed. Cooldown: 3 minutes.

OR

Disengage: Endurance and speed are doubled for the
duration of 20 seconds, but you are unable to perform
attacks during this time period. Cost: 20 charge.
Cooldown: 3 minutes.

A choice! That was new.

Kaiden slumped into his seat in the cockpit and considered his decision. Disengage would be useful to...well, disengage if he was taking hits, particularly if his shield overcharged and he needed to get away.

At the same time, though, Burst of Speed was already a similar, albeit more costly, squishier version of it, and Kaiden had found dodging and riposting had served him well against the mercs. Who needed defense when you were too fast and nimble to hit, anyway?

Meanwhile, Onslaught could come in very useful, especially if he ever had to take on a big opponent. Stacked with Riposte, Kaiden could do some serious damage.

He selected Onslaught, feeling no regrets. Then it was on to the stat points.

Kaiden accessed his character sheet and for a moment his finger hovered over dexterity once again, but then he paused. Did he *need* to be faster, or continue to help improve dodge and critical hit chance? It couldn't hurt, but he wasn't so sure it was what he needed most right now.

He remembered his critical hit against the blinded Silae. It hadn't even finished the turen off – that had been the electrified wall - and turen were notoriously weak against melee damage. A little more strength and Kaiden could have killed it in one shot.

Then there was the near miss with Ealis; ten percent of

health was too close for comfort. He could do with a bit more of a buffer there.

Kaiden decided and assigned three points to strength, three to endurance.

Character
Name: Kaiden
Race: Human
Level: 10
Class: Enhanced Warden
Attributes:
Strength: 22 *Intelligence:* 19
Endurance: 22 *Perception:* 19
Dexterity: 40 *Unassigned:* 0
Abilities:
Hammer Smash, Shield Bash, Hammer Toss, Shackle, Burst of Speed, Enhanced Senses, Riposte, Flash Bang, Blur, Onslaught
Perks:
Turen Tinkering

Perfect! Two level ups almost back to back, four new abilities, and a trap laid for our assassin. It's about time things started going our way.

He noticed Titus and Zelda seemed to be finishing up allocating their own new stat points too.

"All good guys?" Kaiden asked.

They nodded.

"Great," Kaiden said, slipping into the pilot seat of the *Borrelly*. "I gave Marty, the owner of the 'theatre,' enough information that Jax should have no problem tracking Titus to the warehouse we scoped out. Now we just need to get there, set the trap and give Marty a call when we're ready."

"Good thing our bait won't be hard to spot," Zelda added with a nod toward Titus. The big man laughed, then hefted his hammer.

"Might be Jax finds this bait has a bit of fight in him."

"He was a pretty powerful player," Kaiden said, thinking back to his encounter with Jax. "We shouldn't take any chances. He was level fifteen, and we're each level ten or thereabouts. Three on one means we have a better chance of winning, but it'll still be tough."

"We will win," Zelda said, her voice firm. "This is too important."

Kaiden nodded. A lot was riding on them shackling Jax and getting the information on Bernstein's true killers. He turned his attention to the navigation console, selecting the warehouse from their list of recently visited locations, and the shuttle plotted a course back to it.

It was across Boyd City, deep in an industrial district. With any luck, it'd be removed enough to give them some privacy to capture, then – if luck was with them – interrogate the assassin.

"Alright. Course plotted. Let's get to it." Kaiden hit the ignition switch and the *Borrelly* hummed to life. Then a siren started blaring and red lights flooded the shuttle's interior.

"What happened? What's wrong?" Zelda asked, rushing to the cockpit.

"Nothing, as far as I can tell!" Kaiden scanned the panels, searching for a sign of what caused the alert.

"Uh oh," Titus laughed, "Lieutenant Ellenton won't be thrilled. Whatever you've done, it sounds bad."

All the consoles in the cockpit flashed as one, then cut to a video screen. Captain Thorne stood on the bridge of the *Anakoni*, a grim expression stretched across her face.

"Calling all wardens in the Greater Spiral Arm system. This is a priority one alert. I repeat, we have a priority one alert."

That can't be good, Kaiden thought, frowning at the video.

"Fifteen minutes ago, our outpost on Andros' scanners picked up a voidspawn Leviathan emerging from a rift at the edge of the system. Be advised, this is not the Leviathan we engaged en route to Nassau. This is a new one."

"A new Leviathan?" Even from a pace away, Kaiden heard Zelda swallow hard. "They only finished off the first one a few days ago."

"Apparently the voidspawn are back for round two." Titus grabbed a seat and strapped in.

"The Leviathan will arrive at Andros any moment now. I've ordered our outpost there to fortify and hold out for reinforcements. They cannot win this fight on their own." She frowned deeper. "All wardens are hereby re-assigned to Andros, effective immediately. Rallying coordinates on the planet have been sent along with this message."

Quest: Defend the Warden Corps Outpost on Andros
Expected difficulty: Master
Rewards: +12,000 EXP, +6 faction prestige

"Everyone was already stretched so thin," Kaiden said, thinking back to the state of disarray the corps had been in. It was, after all, what had provided them the opportunity to personally pursue Jax. "This is not good."

"You will be updated with specific orders once you arrive on Andros." Captain Thorne was walking now, the camera gliding along with her as she moved through the hallways of her ship. "The *Anakoni* is currently on the far side of the system, suppressing hostilities in the Hyperion-Vega trade war, and will be unable to provide orbital support. However, I'll be taking a shuttle to personally join the fight for Andros."

"If the Captain herself is coming, this battle is going to be brutal," Zelda said, following Titus' lead and strapping herself into a seat.

"All wardens, unless otherwise instructed, are to fire engines to full burn toward Andros.

Let's show these bugs what happens when they set foot in our system." She arrived at the hangar of the *Anakoni* and paused, looking into the camera. "Godspeed, everyone. I'll see you on the battlefield." And with that, the consoles flickered back to displaying the status readouts for the *Borrelly*. A line of text was displayed above the rest of the information.

Plot course for Andros?

"We can't disobey direct orders," Kaiden said. "Not if we want to avoid suspicion. Looks like our assassin friend is going to have to wait. We've a date with the voidspawn first." He selected 'yes' and the *Borrelly* lifted off the ground, turned its nose toward a faint point of light in the night sky above Nassau, and lurched forward.

Chapter Thirty-Two

Even from orbit, Andros looked like a war zone. A great plume of ash and smoke rose from the sphere, thrown all the way into space from, apparently, the collision of the voidspawn Leviathan with the planet.

The *Borrelly* dove down through the atmosphere, through the clouds, then through a wall of ash until finally the surface of Andros was visible to them. The planet's surface — where it wasn't obscured by the swarming voidspawn — was barren and rocky, all black volcanic soil and jutting gray boulders. Steam vents lay open in several places, spewing acrid fumes into the air.

In the distance, Kaiden could see the impact site of the Leviathan, a smoldering crater delving deep into the ground. At its center lay the Leviathan's smashed and broken corpse. What it once looked like was all but a mystery now. The impact with Andros had reduced it to a great steaming heap of flesh and slime. Its cargo, however, appeared just fine.

A legion of voidspawn were pouring out of the Leviathan's mangled body, surging over the rim of the crater in a sea of tentacles, eyes, and teeth, heading toward the warden outpost. The base itself was a simple construction: a communications tower and barracks surrounded by four walls. Not exactly built for an all-out war. While the defenders were holding for now, the bulk of the horde appeared to be massing on the southern side for a massive push.

Achievement Unlocked!
Baptism by Fire - 500 EXP!
You've joined your first World Raid event! These occur a few times a month within the universe of Nova Online and reward massive EXP for the survivors. Assuming there are any.

Kaiden disregarded the achievement's less than encouraging message as the shuttle's targeted landing zone was projected onto the cockpit's screen.

"We're going into the thick of it, landing right inside the outpost."

"In there?" Zelda balked. "It's chaos."

"I don't know, it looks fun," Titus said from the back.

"You have a twisted idea of fun."

There came a flash from the wall below, then an explosion of crackling blue energy. Inside the *Borelly* they could only hear a faint echo of the bang. Voidspawn swarmed up the walls, crawling over each other in a terrible race to crest the parapets. Atop the walls, wardens fought them back, clearing great swaths of the creatures with their explosive AOE abilities. Yet the enemy were so numerous, a never-ending writhing mass of pink-black terrors. Even as Kaiden watched, one of the voidspawn waves reached the top of the south wall, overrunning the defenders there.

Other shuttles were arriving around them, diving on the outpost. Most of them touched down for a moment, unloaded several squads of wardens, then headed back into the relative safety of the sky. A few others stayed, however, no pilots left inside to fly them. Without Lieutenant Ellenton here, Kaiden knew the *Borrelly* would do the same.

Landing sequence engaged.

"Here we go," Kaiden said, heading to the rear of the shuttle.

The volcanic plains of the planet around them disappeared as they sunk behind the walls of the outpost, and then, with a thunk, they were on the ground. The rear ramp hissed, then opened.

A cacophony of noise rushed in; booming explosions, crackling laser blasts, screeches of voidspawn, and the thudding hammer blows of wardens fighting for their lives.

"Sounds like hell," Zelda said.

"That the *Borrelly*, I see?" an all-too-familiar voice shouted over their comms. "About time the heroes of *Mochinki Station* showed up."

Exiting down the ramp of their shuttle, Kaiden caught sight of Sergeant Dawson. He was covered in voidspawn blood, and his armor looked cracked and dented. He held a massive two-handed hammer and his shield was more of a small buckler on his left arm, just like Captain Thorne's.

He must be a power warden, too. It had been a while since Kaiden had inspected those power wardens during the rescue mission, and he wanted to see what new information his enhanced warden abilities could provide him. Kaiden locked his visor's reticle onto Dawson and looked at his class details.

Power wardens like it best where the fighting is thickest. Their two-handed hammers deal +25% increased damage, though their shields are greatly reduced in size. A portion of their damage is converted into charge to compensate. They have no ranged attacks.

Interesting. His visor was able to show him the exact damage boost gained by power wardens, as well as their drawbacks - no ranged attacks and a much smaller shield. Useful information.

Something heavy pounded into the ground on Kaiden's right and he returned his attention to the battle. A large egg-shaped pod covered in ooze and spikes had landed nearby. The pod shook powerfully, burst, and a dozen voidspawn scuttled forth, uttering shrill cries.

Kaiden's growing instincts for battle kicked in. He raised his shield, moving lightly on his feet, ready to dodge an attack and build his Riposte damage multiplier. Titus thumped his huge shield into the ground; Zelda angled her hammer-gun through the slot in her own.

They needn't have bothered.

Sergeant Dawson leapt over their heads, bringing his hammer crashing down in the middle of the voidspawn pack. A shock-wave blew out, and Kaiden felt a tremor through his feet as limbs flew through the air. Then the entire group of voidspawn were dead, just like that. Jaw dropping, he placed his reticle back over Dawson to learn what move he had used.

Ability: Jump Smash
Warden will jump 8 feet high before smashing their hammer into the ground, doing base damage with AOE effect of 10 feet. Cost: 20 charge. Cooldown 2 minutes. Replaces Hammer Smash.

"Welcome to the party, ensigns," Dawson said.

"Good to see you, sir," Kaiden said. Around them, other newly arrived squads were dealing with voidspawn from other burst pods. "Quite the party you've thrown."

"It's a bit hectic, sure, but as long as the gates hold, we should be able to last long enough for reinforcements to arrive." The sergeant turned to the south wall. "Though that could be a problem."

Wardens to the south were fleeing a wave of the enemy that had crested the top of the wall and were descending inside the base.

"All new arrivals to me," Dawson called across general comms. "We've some uninvited guests in the house. Why don't we show them the door?"

A resounding chorus of, "Yes, sir!" answered him.

"Care to join us, heroes?" Sergeant Dawson asked, turning back to Kaiden, Titus, and Zelda.

"With pleasure," Titus said, hefting his hammer.

"That's what I like to hear." Dawson turned to direct their troops. "Shielders to the front. I want a nice strong wall."

Titus beat a path to join his fellow shield wardens, slotting in shoulder to shoulder to form a forty-strong line. Their shields flared brightly as energy surged at their edges. Then, with a deci-sive click, they all linked together into one interconnected shield wall. Moments later, voidspawn at the front of the swarm slammed into the conjoined shields, battering at it with their bodies. The wall held steady

That. Is. Awesome.

Kaiden hastily moved his reticle to get a look at this ability.

Ability: Shield Brother
Locking shields with another shield warden boosts
absorption capacity of both your shields by +30%.

Nice! They'll be able to absorb a ton more damage linked together
like that.

"Blasters at max range," Sergeant Dawson yelled. "Powers
behind the wall, catch anything that leaps over. Enhanced to the
sides, weave in as needed. I don't want to see a single spawn
anywhere near our blast wardens!"

"Stay alive, Kai," Zelda said, before darting off to join the
other blasters.

Kaiden's "you too" died in his throat as he dashed to the
flanks of the power wardens as instructed. The swarm on the
other side of the shield wall was growing fast.

"Retaking the south wall is our objective," Dawson bellowed.
"We need to push those buggers back and reactivate the turret
defenses."

**Update – Parameters Changed **
Quest: Defend the Warden Corps Outpost on Andros
Part 1: Join your fellow wardens in retaking the southern
wall and activating the defenses there.
Expected difficulty: Intermediate
Rewards: +3,000 EXP, +2 faction prestige

Dawson raised his hammer high. "For the corps!"

"For the corps!" Kaiden joined in the response, feeling his
heart thunder from nerves and excitement.

He knew it was all just a game, that most of those around
him were likely criminals, but right here, right now, every one of
these wardens felt like brothers and sisters to him. He raised his
hammer.

"Let's soften them up," Dawson said. "Blasters – Kinetic
Grenades, now!"

Kaiden looked to the blast wardens and found Zelda amongst
them. She switched her grip on her hammer, holding it aloft, and
charged a ball of burning energy upon its head. Then, when the
ball fully formed, she swung her hammer like a bat, launching the

grenade high overhead toward the swarm. A score of others followed in its wake.

He couldn't help but investigate it, quickly scanning the emerging text.

Ability: Kinetic Grenade
You throw a ball of energy from your hammer-gun.
Explodes on impact. Radius 15 feet. Deals +250% base
damage to targets within 1 foot and +150% for all others.
Range 30 feet. Cost: 50 charge. Cooldown: 3 minutes.

Kaiden finished reading in time to see twenty pulsating blue orbs drop over the shield wall and explode upon the other side. The noise was incredible, and the raging blue flames felt hot even at a distance. Voidspawn fell in droves, bits of tentacles and teeth raining down around him. The flood of kills filled his combat text, but still so many remained. Already a fresh press began to build against the shield wall.

"Powers at the ready," Dawson called. "Let's ease that pressure again. Shield wall, split!"

At once, the shield wall cleaved in two, opening backward and funneling the voidspawn down the middle. Kaiden saw Titus backpedaling, taking cues from the wardens on either side of him.

"Reform!"

The wall did, closing off the stream of voidspawn. Power wardens surged forward to meet the clustered spawn the shielders had let through, crashing together in a storm of swinging hammers. Voidspawn went flying, and wardens disappeared under a dozen smaller foes. As they gained charge, the power wardens leapt like hulking crickets around the battlefield, using Jump Smash to devastating effect.

Creatures started to break away from the melee. Kaiden clocked the closest one to him; it was a voidspawn like he'd never seen before, erect on two powerful chitinous legs, cleaving the space before it with two blade-like arms. Kaiden's visor told him what it was.

Void Flayer
Level: 6

Flayers are one of the deadliest voidspawn sub-species. They are quick on their feet and their pincers can pierce even the most advanced power armor.

It was fast and heading straight for the blast wardens.

Kaiden sprinted after it, praying his own increased speed would be quick enough. Homing in on the flayer from the side, he lunged the last step, aiming a low swipe at the creature's knee joints. He connected with a rubbery thud, and the flayer collapsed in a mess of tangled limbs – a critical hit. Kaiden put it down with a second hammer strike to the head.

Critical Hit!
+50% damage (Headshot)

Void Flayer killed – 300 EXP gained!

Just like back on the Dalcinae. That feels like a long time ago now.

He hadn't gained charge from the encounter, but no matter. Kaiden turned to face the battle, looking for more flayers, but other enhanced wardens were dealing with them. He wondered if one of them was Sola, but he couldn't tell amidst this chaos. There weren't many of his kind here in the battle; only four fellow enhanced wardens as far as he could see.

I really did pick an unpopular spec.

Dawson was yelling again. "Alright, time for a push. Everyone be ready to mop up the filth left behind."

Kaiden hurried forward to stand amongst the power wardens.

"Push now," Dawson called. "Shield Bash!"

As one, every member of the shield wall used their ability, stepping forward and stunning the front line of voidspawn in a gelatinous smack.

"Run 'em down," Dawson ordered, and together the shielders activated Shield Charge.

They hurtled forward, mowing down voidspawn like laser-cut grass. Spawn were hurled back or trampled underfoot, pressed into the mud by heavy boots. Those enemies left behind the shield wall were blown away by blasters or pummeled by powereds as they followed behind the front line.

As the Shield Charge faded, the shield wall slowed, but it had made significant progress toward the base of the southern wall.

"Flanks, close in," Dawson cried. "Pen those beasts in against the wall."

The shield wardens on the far left and right of the shield wall began to step forward, bending their formation into a giant U shape. The remaining voidspawn were trapped between them and the high wall of the base. Some attempted to scramble back up the wall, others threw themselves with renewed frenzy at the shield wall.

Kaiden approached the front line with the other wardens, ready for any spawn that jumped the shields, or for fresh orders from the sergeant. He was itching for a fight now. The other classes all had their role to play here; wouldn't Dawson give the few enhanced wardens something more to do?

"Blasters," Dawson barked. "Split up and take the spiraling ramps leading to the walls on either side. You'll get clear shots on the swarm. You five powereds." He swept his hammer to indicate the group he meant. "Go with them and keep them safe. There are some scum still up on the wall itself."

Kaiden saw Zelda tear past him in a stream of fellow blasters. He watched her ascend the first turn on her ramp before tearing his gaze away, back toward the shield wall as it began to buckle somewhat under the strain. The compression of voidspawn between them and the southern wall was intense. They might as well have become one enormous mass of tentacles, teeth and terrifying extremities. They piled up so high that many were easily leaping over the shield wall itself.

Kaiden needed no orders. He ran with the remaining power wardens, picking his target. He swung his hammer into the thick of the voidspawn's body and a power warden followed suit.

Voidspawn assisted kill – 75 EXP gained!

Kaiden barely registered the notification, already onto his next foe, another flayer. This time, he blocked its gnashing pincer-like arms on his shield, earning him forty charge. He grinned as he felt the energy flood into his implants.

About time!

He went for a Hammer Smash, injuring the flayer and two

smaller voidspawn around it. He ducked the flayer's sweeping blades – gaining Riposte – side-stepped a lashing tentacle – Riposte stacked – and cracked the next mob he saw in the back. It wasn't a crit, but the extra fifty percent damage sent the little spawn back to the void. Those extra points Kaiden had put into strength might have done the trick.

Now in the thick of the fighting, Kaiden found himself surrounded; a number of voidspawn had managed to encircle him. For a moment he floundered, deep in the fray, but two power wardens hacked their way through to reinforce him. They cut a path with wide swipes of their hammers, leaving crumpled voidspawn in their wake.

Woah, what was that?

Ability: Hammer Sweep
The warden swings their hammer in a wide arc, doing 35% of base damage to enemies directly before them.
Cost: 20 charge. Cooldown: 2 minutes.

Now that's what I call backup.

Kaiden spun, finding the flayer he'd tangled with earlier still at large. It'd brought a friend with it, and both skewered an unlucky enhanced warden between them.

Just three of us left, Kaiden thought, lifting his hammer. He was going to flank the flayers from behind and crit them to hell.

That was until a spray of black acid engulfed his vision.

Kaiden yelled and leapt back, hands clawing at his body to try and wipe the ooze away. A hissing sound rose from his armor, the acid eating through the protective metal at an alarming rate. His health bar fell, through the green and into yellow.

Before him was a more bulbous voidspawn than he'd seen before, its mouth oversized and its cheeks puffing up before his eyes. It almost looked as if the creature was gagging, then it gave a great heave. Kaiden ducked behind his shield as it vomited a spray of black bile at him.

He locked his reticle on this new foe.

Void Spitter
Level: 8
Void spitters are slow but produce a powerful corrosive

acid, able to eat through even capital class ship hulls in enough quantities. Each acid spray takes 3 seconds to cast.

A cast time, huh? I can interrupt that.

The spitter was already revving up for another attack, so Kaiden dashed forward and used Shield Bash, stunning the spawn and cancelling its cast. He followed through with an easy hammer strike to the head.

Critical Hit!
+50% damage (Headshot)

Void Spitter killed - 350 EXP gained!

Even after using two abilities, Kaiden had sixty out of one-ten charge left. The acid that had landed on his shield must have given him quite a lot.

Hoping there would be no more surprises, he searched again for the deadly flayer. His visor helped him sieve the chaos, drawing his eye to the nearest flayer.

Only one remained now, but it stood astride a prone power warden. The warden was Dawson of all people. The flayer raised its pincers and Kaiden threw his weapon in a Hammer Toss, already running after it. His hammer hit the mob square in the back, managing to get a crit and the double damage bonus of the ability. Yet the flayer didn't die.

Kaiden only learned it was an elite mob once he was in range of its blades.

He dodged the first attack and ducked the second, but only just. The left pincer grazed his side and shaved his health down to forty percent. Even worse, the damage he'd taken dropped the stacks of Riposte he'd gained.

Just as he thought to try out that new ability, Blur, the flayer was smashed aside by a brutal swing from Dawson. The sergeant was back on his feet, and his hammer crackled with latent energy.

Ability: Hammer Overload

The warden can charge their hammer with energy and target a single opponent for triple damage. If opponent dies, attack does electrical AOE damage of 25% of base damage to enemies within 5 feet. Cost: 50 charge. Cooldown: 1 minute.

Wow, that's got to pack a punch.

Dawson's empowered hammer fell upon the flayer's head for added punishment.

Elite Void Flayer assisted kill – 500 EXP gained!

"Good job, Ensign," Dawson said. "Seems like you're a hard man to kill."

Kaiden looked around. It seemed the worst of that wave was dead, and the blast wardens were throwing some form of chain-lightning attacks into the horde, peppering them with laser blasts and even the odd Kinetic Grenade, now off cooldown.

He blinked several times, not even having the wits to check on that lightning attack. Dawson was just being flippant, but Kaiden could have 'died' at any point in that brief skirmish. The second acid spray might have melted him, and had Dawson not been there to help at the end he'd almost certainly have died. He'd just run straight at an elite mob without any thought. Pretty stupid of him. One slip up and he'd be back in the prison's general population for a week.

Having to avoid Manson for seven full days...

"Kaiden?" Dawson was yelling at him.

Kaiden snapped out of his reverie, feeling dazed. He was in the middle of a proper war zone, which had felt exhilarating a moment ago, yet now he considered the consequences of dying here...

Dawson shook him. "Snap out of it, boy. Hey, I have a job for you."

"For me, sir?"

"Yeah," Dawson said, as though debating his decision to send Kaiden after all. "Things are easing up down here, but I need at least one of those wall-mounted turrets back online to re-secure this wall. I want you to put those speedy legs of yours to work and do it for me."

Kaiden looked to the wall. He saw the tall, shining metallic turret rising not too far from the top of the closest spiraling ramp, its double barrels hanging limp and inactive. He also saw voidspawn all along the wall, nowhere near the numbers down here on the ground but plenty enough to take him out.

He'd never make it through them all, fast or not. He'd surely get killed.

"I can't, sir."

"This isn't optional."

"Sir, sorry, but I can't. If I die—"

Dawson grunted. "Who cares? You get a nice week off and come back fresh afterward. Lord knows the devs have gone a bit far this past week."

Kaiden couldn't believe the sergeant had just broken immersion. Maybe the pressures of the invasion and the trade war had gotten to him.

"But that's the problem," Kaiden began. "I can't have a week off. Someone's trying to kill me. Some maniac. He tried to shiv me in the showers recently and—" His voice cracked. He felt like a coward before Dawson, but there was nothing for it.

He'd been wrongfully thrown in prison, forcibly placed on a mandatory work scheme, albeit a cool one, and had his life very seriously threatened. He wasn't as strong as the armor he wore, and out in the real world he didn't have it to protect him.

"My health's already low, sir," he began, but Dawson threw up a hand.

"Trying to shiv a kid in the showers." He tutted. "Some spots will never wash out. Look, I don't care what you did to land yourself in a cell to begin with, but while you're in here, you're under my care." He popped the chamber on his left forearm and handed Kaiden a health stim.

"Sir," Kaiden gasped. "I can't. I—"

"That's an order, Ensign." Though it was hard to tell under the gore, Kaiden swore the sergeant smiled. "Now, heal your ass up and go get me that damn turret back online."

Update - Parameters Changed
Quest: Defend the Warden Corps Outpost on Andros
Part 1: You have been personally tasked with re-activating the defenses on the southern wall. Stand within

the turret's perimeter and defend it from enemies until captured.
Expected difficulty increased: Veteran
Rewards increased: +5,500 EXP, +4 faction prestige

Kaiden saluted. "Yes, sir!" He placed the second stim in his cooling chamber and used one of the two, bringing his health back up to sixty-five percent. Being safely in the yellow made him feel a whole lot better. And his charge had only depleted to thirty-five units.

He looked to the turret again and activated Burst of Speed.

Blazing a trail, Kaiden zipped toward the ramp, weaving past blast wardens as he drove himself on. Emerging onto the parapets with four seconds of speed left, he made straight for the turret. A faint blue ring materialized around it - the perimeter he had to occupy to capture it. A pack of six weaker voidspawn awaited him there.

With his last second of speed, he chanced a riskier block against several flailing tentacles than he'd otherwise try. The white of his charge bar rose back up to forty.

Perfect.

Pressing his back up against the tower of the turret, Kaiden crouched behind his shield, protecting most of his body. The spawn closed in, flailing against his shield, building more charge even as he activated Flash Bang.

Flapping tentacles did incremental damage, but three seconds later, the brilliant light from the move burst from Kaiden's shield, blinding the entire pack of enemies.

Kaiden got to work. He opened with a Hammer Smash for some AOE damage, then scored headshot after headshot as he mopped up. When the last of the spawn fell, he noticed a new bar appear in the center of his UI.

Capturing turret – 10%

Great, now I just have to hold here. That really wasn't so bad.

New wave incoming!

Not so great. I should learn not to give Nova's AI an excuse to taunt me.

With his shield raised, Kaiden edged himself around the side of the turret to take a look beyond the walls of the outpost, trying to spot this next wave heading for him. There weren't many voidspawn left beyond the southern wall, in truth. He turned to check on how the shield wall was doing. The horde was much reduced now, the blasters having free rein to unleash every AOE ability they had. Over at the northern wall, things were a different story.

Kaiden saw a turret over there firing like mad, yet still spawn were massing upon the walls. They looked like pinky-grey specks from here, but there weren't many shimmering blue shields left. The gatehouse of the northern wall groaned under the strain of some weighty attack.

Maybe that notification about a new wave wasn't meant for me specifically.

A panicked voice rang over the general comms. "It's a void titan. Repeat, void titan approaching."

Those who understood what this was cried out in horror. Kaiden didn't need to see a creature with that name to know it couldn't be good news. All the more reason they needed this turret back online. He checked his progress.

Capturing turret – 30%

That was when he heard the screeching, far to his right along the wall. He faced the noise and groaned. Two flayers were running at him, their creepily long legs propelling them faster with each second. Kaiden scrambled to analyze them, and, of course, both were elites.

All his fear of dying boiled up again. Then something slapped into his back.

Was that a hand?

"My first day back and everything goes to hell. Typical." Sola's tone was as calm as it had been during the rescue mission on the *Mochinki*.

"Sola." Kaiden's relief was evident. "You have no idea how glad I am to see you."

"Seems you levelled up a bit. Ten already, nice. That was

fast. Just three behind me now. And I approve of the spec choice." She looked to the oncoming flayers. "Dawson said something about stopping you getting shanked. Some girl in my block made my life hell for weeks when I first arrived, so I feel you."

"Can we take both of them?"

"We *can*. Guess we'll see if we *will*. You got your Burst of Speed?"

"It's on cooldown."

"Shame," Sola said, spinning her hammer. "Best to keep abilities on hand to stack them for when you really need them. Use Blur if you can, and don't get hit."

The flayers were nearly upon them, drooling putrid green bile from their thin mouths.

Capturing turret – 60%

We just have to make it through this. Let's see what Blur can do.

Kaiden activated the ability. Blue energy sparked over his body and his hands began flickering in and out of focus. Sola must have done the same, as her entire body became distorted, harder to see, and harder to hit.

Blur activated – dodge chance +25% for 10 seconds.

Not a moment too soon, as a pincer-blade cut at his head. Kaiden slid aside with ease, gaining Riposte. He dodged again, ducking low, and aimed an attack at the creature's pointy knees.

Critical hit!
+20% damage (Kneecapped)
+50% damage (Riposte x 2)

He'd made a dent in the flayer's health bar, but Sola was positively melting it. Not only had she used Blur, she'd also used Burst of Speed at the same time, making the fast-moving flayers look like slugs by comparison. She dodged every pincer, targeting critical weak spots with ease now she had improved movement and attack speed.

Kaiden saw the value in this stacking idea. He dodged another two strikes from the flayer and struck at the same time as Sola did, finishing off the first mob.

That's when Sola went into overdrive. Her whole body flashed, and she began moving faster, if that was even possible. The only way Kaiden could describe it was that she had gone supersonic. Sola was taking on the second flayer single-handed, with no need for Kaiden at all. Despite being an elite, the flayer might have been a level two basic voidspawn the way she was decimating its health.

He had to analyze this.

Player Sola is using Blur, Burst of Speed, and is currently in Onslaught Mode.
Stacking effects: Quadruple movement speed and +100% base damage.

Kaiden stood in awe. He'd only recently unlocked Onslaught from the arena battle but hadn't gained a critical hit streak long enough to trigger it yet. Seeing Sola finish the flayer with three head shots in quick succession, he began to understand the true power of the enhanced warden spec; with careful stacking – and a bit of luck on the crits, too – they could be veritable powerhouses.

"And that," Sola said, "is why I pity anyone who says this spec isn't good in combat."

"Yeah."

It was all Kaiden could say. He was still lost for words when his progress on capturing the turret concluded seconds later.

Capturing turret – 100%
Defenses activated. Auto-lock engaged.

At once, the tower hummed to life. Kaiden looked up to see its twin barrels spin, then the head of the turret swiveled, looking for foes.

Laser bolts punched through the air, shredding dozens of voidspawn in the turret's range.

"Nice work, Ensign," Dawson called over the comms. "I take it Sola is still with us?"

"Here, sir," Sola called.

"Ha!" Dawson barked a laugh. "We might just make it through this yet."

Kaiden stepped to the inner edge of the wall. Below, the voidspawn penned by the shield wall were all but destroyed. The shielders broke apart as wardens raised their hammers in victory, cheering with glee. Kaiden spotted Titus, covered in black gore, but very much still with them.

Quest completed: Defend the Warden Corps Outpost on Andros
Part 1: You have been personally tasked with re-activating the defenses on the southern wall. Stand within the turret's perimeter and defend it from enemies until captured.
Rewards +5,500 EXP, +4 faction prestige

Kaiden couldn't help but grin. It wasn't quite enough experience to level him again, and he reckoned the amount needed would only start getting exponentially higher as he gained in power. Still, they'd done it. He'd done it. Andros had been saved.

I think Captain Thorne might have made too big a deal out of this whole thing. We did just fine in the end. She might be on her way for nothing.

"Hate to rain on your parade back there." The panicked voice from before blared across all channels. "But we still have a god damn void titan—"

The voice cut off. Kaiden snapped his attention back to the northern gatehouse. In his joy, he'd forgotten about this new foe. A tidal wave of black bile rose from somewhere beyond the gates. It arced upward, rising and rising before breaking onto the gatehouse and walls – and the last of the defenders there.

Screaming rang over the comms and Kaiden felt sick. Mercifully, the screams cut out, but the northern turret was a sparking, broken mess, the acid eating away at it.

Kaiden locked his reticle onto the gates themselves.

Durability - 3%

"Oh no," he said aloud.

Even as he spoke, a second wave of black acid crashed against the north wall, leaving the gates nothing more than metallic sludge. Kaiden could see something massive moving. It slammed into the gatehouse, knocking what remained of it aside. An army of small voidspawn began streaming unchecked into the base.

A hush fell over the comms.

Kaiden saw a notification.

Update – Parameters Changed
Quest: Defend the Warden Corps Outpost on Andros
Part 2: Defeat the Void Titan (somehow) and save the Outpost on Andros.
Expected difficulty: Legendary
Rewards: +12,000 EXP, +6 faction prestige

Chapter Thirty-Three

The void titan had to be twenty feet tall, a horrifying amalgamation of all the types of spawn Kaiden had encountered. Like the flayers, it had scorpion-esque pincers at its front, with three chitinous legs on either side.

A gaping maw with endless rows of teeth let loose hoarse, trumpeting battle cries, punctuated by intermittent vomits of acid. Its massive body pulsed like a void spitter with each deluge.

Two huge kraken-like tentacles struck the ground on either side as it walked, crushing wardens or reaching to pull them into a deadly embrace.

The titan's one flaw appeared to be its movement. It lumbered forward ungracefully in short bursts as though it had a hard time figuring out where to go. Kaiden thought he understood why. Unlike its many-eyed counterparts, the titan appeared to have a single enormous eye, protected by a hardened lid. The lid periodically opened and closed like blast doors, the black orb swiveling madly behind it.

With some trepidation, Kaiden hovered his reticle to analyze the beast.

Void Titan **Elite Boss**
Level: 20
With tremendous power, the void titan suffers only from poor mobility. Its vast body is resistant to most attacks;

however, its eye is sensitive. Its acidic deluge has a cast time of 6 seconds.

In the courtyard below, Dawson was waving his hammer madly, trying to rally those wardens who'd just secured the southern wall.

"Regroup! Quickly now."

Sola appeared by Kaiden's side upon the wall. "If we can't get a new shield wall up, we're done for."

Kaiden watched as one of the titan's tentacles fell upon a shuttle and crushed it completely. All around it an army of small voidspawn had free rein on the outpost. Many were chasing down wardens who were trying to make it to the south side to join up with Dawson.

Kaiden gulped. "I'm not sure a shield wall would even help much."

"Better get down there," Sola said. "Remember what I showed you."

"Stack my abilities if I can," Kaiden said. "I got it. And thanks for the help."

Sola took off, but Kaiden remained where he was, checking his minimap for signs of Zelda and Titus. He zoomed in a bit to exclude the useless land around the base, making it easier to pick out two green dots not far from him.

He opened their party comms channel. "Where exactly are you guys?"

"I'm still on the ramp," Zelda said. "Titus is blocking the entrance for me."

"Stay there," Kaiden said. He sprinted off, back across the wall, and back down the ramp. Sure enough, Zelda was there, firing everything she had at the distant voidspawn. He saw one of her Burst Arrows take a basic spawn in the head for a one-hit kill.

Kaiden breathed a sigh of relief to see them both relatively unhurt, their health bars still in the green.

"What are we supposed to do against that thing?" Zelda said.

"It's a boss creature," Kaiden said. "All bosses in games require a specific strategy to kill them." He spoke more for Titus' benefit.

"Right," Titus said wearily. "So what's the lowdown on this one?"

"My visor says its eye is sensitive, probably a weak point."

"Oh, piece of cake, then," Titus said. "I'll just scramble up there and hit it, shall I? What use is that, Kai?"

"Hey," Kaiden snapped. "I'm trying, alright? You know I don't want to end up dead in here. Just let me think."

"Yeah, I know you got good reasons," Titus said. "Sorry, by the way. About the other day."

"That wasn't your fault," Kaiden said. "You're assigned a different shower unit."

"But still," Titus said deeply. "I feel like I let you down."

"Not sure that's possible, big guy," Kaiden said.

"Erm, guys," Zelda interrupted. "Not to spoil your moment, but I think we should move. Like, now."

Kaiden looked to the titan and completely agreed with her. Its body was spasming, indicating an acid spray was coming. And it was aiming south-west, almost right where they were standing.

"Come on." He and Zelda jumped from the ramp, and then all three of them got to running. Most wardens nearby were scrambling to get out of the firing line, but some were not so lucky.

Kaiden saw the dark tide crest and land upon the stragglers, obliterating half a dozen wardens at once.

"Damn it," Dawson called over comms. "Where is that illustrious leader of ours? Damn it all. All survivors rally to me – now!"

A flashing yellow ping went out on the minimap for everyone to see his location, but most wardens still alive were already near the sergeant as far as Kaiden could tell. The titan and the swarm had boxed them into a small quadrant of the inner base.

"We've gone from victory to defeat in about thirty seconds flat," Zelda said.

The titan turned awkwardly, smashing a tentacle into the outpost barracks. Its great eye opened to look upon them, remained exposed for about three seconds, then retreated behind its defenses.

Kaiden made a note of that. The window of opportunity to hit the eye was brief, so anything to make hitting easier would be welcome.

The smaller voidspawn began to line up more effectively, as though the titan were assembling them for a final charge.

"Reform the line," Dawson called, resolve in his voice.

Titus ran to join the new shield wall, but there were only twenty-eight of them left now. Kaiden noticed the power wardens were much depleted, too, though the blasters had mostly survived. *Ranged attacks might help, but it's a three-second window to hit the eye. Barely enough time to aim and shoot, plus it's not an easy target. They'll probably miss more often than they hit, if they hit at all.*

Dawson was still yelling. "We do not surrender. We do not let monsters run our system."

Kaiden tried to ignore the comms for a moment. He'd just noticed something interesting about the voidspawn boss. He'd almost missed it; a flash across his vision. But when he focused in on one of the legs, he noticed it had a health bar. All six supporting legs of the titan had health bars of their own.

That's it!

"Sergeant," Zelda's voice blared over the comms. "How do we take the boss down?"

"Afraid to say I ain't so sure," Dawson said. "It's the captain who's good for this sort of stuff. Ain't seen one of these freaky things before."

"Sir," Kaiden began, "I think I—"

The titan bellowed a cry, drowning out all other sound. As it faded, the army of voidspawn began to charge.

"Aw, to hell with it," Dawson called, pounding his hammer into the ground. "Forward, wardens! And to those about to go on vacation, I salute you. For the corps!"

"For the corps!"

The wardens charged, a chorus of screams of fear, battle lust and excitement driving them on. Kaiden didn't hang back, rushing forward with the rest, shield and hammer at the ready.

He was pretty sure he knew how to take the boss out. He just needed to relay it to Dawson. Maybe once they took down some of this army and things eased up he'd get a chance.

The two forces hurtled toward each other, the gap ever closing, the ground reverberating from the stampede and the lumbering of the titan. Kinetic Grenades arced high, while lightning blasts sizzled into the first of the voidspawn.

A boom sounded above – a shuttle's engine.

Over general comms came a welcome voice. "Holy crap, I'm glad I didn't sleep through this."

"Lieutenant Ellenton!" Zelda called. "Have you brought reinforcements?"

"I brought all the reinforcement you'll need," Ellenton said.

A crisp, commanding voice took over the channel. "This is Captain Ava Thorne. Status report?"

"A whole lot of hell is about to hit," Dawson said. "See you down here, Captain."

"Descending now."

Still running, Kaiden looked up to see a shuttle pass low over the center of the battlefield, and nearly stumbled in shock as he saw a figure leap from its rear doors. Thorne hit the ground, rose, and swung at the voidspawn just as the two armies collided.

If it had been a cinematic cutscene, it still wouldn't have been more perfectly timed.

Kaiden entered the brawl, striking left and right with his hammer, trying as best he could not to be caught in the crush.

"Level twenty?" Thorne growled. "That's double the level of half my corps. NextGen are really pushing my patience. I've fought real battles that were easier than this mess."

Kaiden activated Burst of Speed, ducking and weaving his way toward her. He jumped over the body of a fallen warden, his increased speed making it feel like doing an Olympic long jump. Once close enough, he caught sight of the captain clobbering voidspawn back with her swings. These weren't even abilities. Her attacks were just *that* strong.

"Do we have an enhanced?" Thorne yelled. "I want a read-out on this thing."

Sola didn't answer. Kaiden wondered whether she'd died from the acid or the charge, but thought it best he answer the captain.

"Its eye is the weak point."

"Figured that," Thorne said. She used Hammer Sweep and five spawn fell before her. "Any idea how we get to it?"

"Focus on its legs," Kaiden said. "When it's on its belly, it'll be easier to reach the eye – which opens for three seconds at a time, by the way. Oh, and there's an acid spray that has a large cone of attack, but its movements give away the direction of fire."

"A succinct summary, Ensign Kaiden," Thorne said. "Listen up! All powereds are to make for those legs. Follow my lead and focus on one at a time – do not spread your damage. Blasters maintain range and hit the eye when you can, take out the spawn when you can't."

A particularly fat, elite spitter mob approached her. Thorne activated Hammer Overload and killed the spitter with one clean shot to its face. The electrical AOE effect from killing an opponent with that move sparked outward, severely damaging the small spawn around it.

"Shielders," Thorne went on, as though there had been no interruption. "Defend the blasters. Rotate using Barrier to negate acid spray if necessary. Use your class channels to help coordinate. Understood?"

"Yes, ma'am!"

"Then move out. Powereds, with me."

Kaiden watched Thorne activate her Jump Smash ability, soaring eight feet over the battle, heading for the closest of the titan's legs. All power wardens followed suit, leaping in a deadly hopscotch through the voidspawn ranks.

Swinging pincers from a flayer forced Kaiden to look away. He ducked, but slipped on some slimy discharge underfoot. Luckily for him, the flayer's knees were right there, so he took a shot.

Critical Hit!
+20% (Kneecapped)
+25% (Riposte x 1)

The flayer's health fell halfway. It shrieked, raised its pincers and then took two Burst Arrows to the torso. An assist kill notice flashed and Kaiden struggled back to his feet.

He wondered again why the enhanced wardens had not been given a specific task. Maybe they were mostly needed for understanding how encounters worked, and then one-off missions as required, like bringing the turret back online.

Yet even if that were all, it seemed like the corps ought to ensure they had enough enhanced wardens to analyze powerful foes. Kaiden supposed he should just keep fighting voidspawn. It wasn't as if he could do any more damage to those legs than a dozen power wardens and Thorne combined, nor was he able to hit the eye any easier.

An idea came to him and he opened the enhanced warden specific comms channel.

"Hey, Sola, you there?"

No answer.

"Is anybody there? Come in?"

Nothing.

So, Kaiden was the only enhanced warden left in the battle. Sola must have been taken out. All her abilities would have been on cooldown, so maybe she'd been caught out. Ultimately, it was a balancing act. Become overpowered for a few seconds and weaker for the rest, or have a steady boost to your character's strength. He'd have to start making more active decisions like that.

"That's two legs down," Thorne called over general comms.

The titan groaned and became unsteady on one side, buckling. In the middle of casting an acid spray, this lurch changed the direction of the attack, taking several blast wardens unawares.

"Powereds, switch to the other side," Thorne called, perhaps not realizing she was still in the general channel. "Let's not have that happen again."

Kaiden was finishing off several smaller spawn when the power wardens rushed past him. A shadow fell over him and he looked up, seeing one of the huge tentacles overhead. Kaiden ran out from under the shadow to safety, conking voidspawn in the head as he went.

Critical hit streak (x 4)

Two more and Onslaught will trigger.

Perhaps the pressure got to him. His next swing met only air, the speedy flayer managing to dodge him for a change. The crit streak faded.

Damn it. Triggering Onslaught would make me far more useful.

A barrage of laser shots ended the flayer before Kaiden could do anything more.

From behind, a great thud signaled that the tentacle had hit the ground. Kaiden turned to look on in horror as the curling tip of it snatched at a lagging power warden. It squeezed, and the warden's health plummeted to zero. Only, he kept swinging his hammer. He should have been dead.

Kaiden locked on with his reticle.

Ability: Last Rites
When the warden reaches 0 health, Last Rites is triggered, allowing the warden 10 seconds to kill all opponents in a 50-foot radius of the point of death. Should they succeed, they will be given 1HP back. If not, they will die. Kills made during this time earn no EXP. No abilities can be used during Last Rites. Cooldown: 6 hours.

So power wardens have a kind of 'last stand' ability? Pretty sweet in a tight spot.

For the warden trapped in the tentacle's grip, it made no difference. His hammer attacks were doing no damage at all to the boss, proving they had to go for the eye to deal any damage to the titan's main body.

The boss brought the warden toward its great mouth, as though to swallow him whole. The carapace over its eye opened as the power warden neared it. He struck the boss twice, right on the iris.

The titan wailed, reeling back, flailing its tentacles wildly. The heroic power warden dropped dead to the ground, Last Rites having faded, but his death had not been in vain. The titan's health had dropped to ninety-four percent.

"Two more legs gone," Thorne called.

Already staggering, the titan swayed further, crashing against the western wall of the base.

"Powers, split up and each group hit the remaining legs with Hammer Overload on my mark. Blasters, get ready for your shots."

Kaiden saw the green arrows of Zelda and Titus on his minimap moving, the yellow arrows beside them showing they were converging on his position. Zelda reached him first.

"Get back," Kaiden told her. "You're way too close."

"It's too hard to hit it further back," Zelda said. "I'd rather we got this over with."

"Take out those legs," Thorne cried.

The power wardens attacked in unison, and the titan collapsed onto its hulking underbelly, now unable to move. It roared and opened its eye.

"Come on!" Zelda screamed as she sent a Burst Arrow, followed by a flurry of basic blasts. Hundreds of attacks converged upon the titan, many missing entirely, more hitting around the eye, but a half-dozen connected. The eye flashed an angry red, bulging, then retracted.

The titan's health fell to seventy percent.

"Stay vigilant," Thorne called. "This thing may have a phase two."

"What does she mean?" Titus asked.

"Sometimes, bosses have escalating phases of difficulty," Kaiden said. "The overall goal can remain the same, but the fight gets harder."

"Harder?" Titus said. "You have got to be kidding me."

Kaiden scanned the battlefield. The voidspawn army was greatly diminished, but the wardens had paid a high price for it. The titan itself was acting differently. Its body seemed to be convulsing all the time and it opened its maw wide, as though locking whatever counted for its jaws in place. Then compact balls of acid began rocketing up from its gullet, flying high in the air before landing at seemingly random locations.

Out of instinct, Kaiden's eyes moved to hover over the boss.

You have greatly angered the titan. Without the ability to turn, it has resorted to more rapid attacks. Its acidic deluge now has a cast time of 1 second.

Black, smoking bile was falling in a wide area in front of its maw. The titan was firing them off like mortar shots.

A faint red ring appeared around Kaiden and Zelda's feet. He assumed that was the game giving an indication of an impact radius. He grabbed Zelda's hand, trying to pull her with him, but the gob of acid was falling too quickly. Kaiden closed his eyes, not wanting to watch as they melted into pixels.

But they didn't melt. They were still standing.

Titus' green dot had made it to their side.

"Good thing I kept this ability back," Titus said. Kaiden

opened his eyes and saw a wall of energy flashing above their heads. It looked like Titus' shield, only five times the size, covering himself and Zelda like some sparking umbrella. The acid washed over it, sloughing off to either side.

Ability: Barrier
You stand still and become the epicentre of a larger barrier to defend your allies, increasing in size depending on how much charge you use. During this time your shield does not absorb additional charge. Unable to use if your shield is already overcharged. Cooldown: 10 minutes.

"I think I'm getting the hang of this gaming thing," Titus said. "Though I shoved a ton of charge into that bad boy."

"There'll be plenty of opportunity for more," Kaiden said.

"Thank you, Titus," Zelda said, her voice full of relief. "You're living up to the role of defender well."

"Keep moving," Thorne ordered. "Stopping risks death. And protect the blasters at all costs. We need that eye taken down."

Almost on cue, the eye showed itself again, allowing Zelda to fire a Burst Arrow with surprising accuracy. Her singular attack ticked its health down by two percent.

"We're not going to win by attrition," Kaiden said. "Too many of us are going down. We need to pack a punch with some hits or we'll all be paste."

If there was ever a time to try stacking, this was it. A shame his Burst of Speed was still on cooldown. Still, he wasn't going to just run around avoiding acid for the rest of the fight.

"Titus, you got enough left for a Shield Charge?"

The big man nodded.

"We're going in closer. I want a shot at that thing. Clear us a path?"

"With pleasure," Titus said.

A flash from Titus' shield told of the ability activating. A moment later he burst past, then slammed through the scattered voidspawn ahead of them with all the fury of a one-man avalanche. Kaiden followed, pumping his fist.

"Utter carnage, big guy."

Kaiden smacked some spawn on the head as he followed in Titus' wake, finishing them off.

Critical hit streak (x 2)

Titus ended his Shield Charge near an elite spitter. His large shield easily caught the spray from it and then he used his Shield Bash to interrupt the mob's next attack.

"Nice one," Kaiden said, aiming easy swings at the stunned spitter's head.

Critical hit streak (x 4)

I'm so close to Onslaught! Come on!

Kaiden had just enough energy left for a Shield Bash of his own. He used it on the spitter. The game's system of diminishing returns meant the stun would only last for one and a half seconds this time, but he managed to get in two more head shots in that time.

Critical Hit!
+50% damage (Headshot)
Critical Hit!
+50% damage (Headshot)
Critical hit streak (x 6)

Onslaught Mode activated.
Current movement speed and damage is doubled for 5 seconds

"Yes!" Kaiden screamed. He felt the same mad rush as from Burst of Speed as he took off. The spitter's health was so low by then that even Titus should be able to finish it. Question now was, did Kaiden risk trying to stack Riposte as well?

No guts, no glory, he thought. He'd make no impact on the titan if he didn't stack as much as he could.

It didn't matter what attacks he dodged. He approached a pair of basic spawn and blocked the first of their attacks for more charge. It was just enough, so he side-stepped a second

and third swipe from their flailing tentacles, the Riposte notification flashing twice. Then, in the last seconds of Onslaught
mode, he looked to the eye of the boss and used Hammer
Toss.

His weapon flew. The armored lid retracted. Hammer Toss
hit home.

Critical Hit!
+100% damage (Bloodied Eye)
+50% damage (Riposte x 2)
+100% damage (Onslaught)
Hammer Toss hit!
+100% damage

Kaiden felt awash with glee. His hammer flew back to his
hand and he checked on the titan's health. He couldn't be sure if
he'd caused all of it – blasters were still hitting it when they could
– but its health had fallen to forty-five percent.

That'd been his all.

In the end, he was half the titan's level; it was an elite boss,
and he was one player. Only now, everything but Hammer Smash
and Blur was on cooldown, and those wouldn't help with much
beside taking on spawn.

Acid still rained down. More friendly dots on his minimap
blinked off.

Perhaps the boss was simply too much for them.

Maybe it won't be so bad back in gen pop if Titus is also there.

"I've got an idea," Captain Thorne's voice rang in his ears.
"Cover me. I'm heading to the west wall."

The last remaining power wardens tailed Thorne as she
sprinted for the closest ramp leading up to the parapets. Kaiden
tried to keep one eye on her as he returned to fighting
voidspawn, just trying to stay alive at this point.

Left with fewer targets, the voidspawn converged. Kaiden's
health began to tick down, even as he darted around the
battlefield.

Thorne made it to the top of the wall, and now she was
almost of a height with the titan. Its great eye opened and swiv-
elled to look at her, perhaps sensing it was in trouble. It tried to

smash her with a lumbering tentacle, but Thorne dove aside, leaving the wall behind her to crumble.

She rose to her feet, and her entire body began crackling with energy. Her eyes became bright blue beacons. Kaiden checked it out.

Ability: Berserker
The warden does double base damage but also takes +50% damage for 20 seconds. Speed is halved for 1 minute following the ability. Cost: 50 charge. Cooldown: 10 minutes.

Next, he saw her hammer glow with power and recognised that she'd activated Hammer Overload as well.

"This invasion ends here," Thorne called. She broke into a run, much faster than before, then launched herself into the air. The momentum of her run took her higher and farther than a regular jump.

Ability: Stampede
The warden doubles movement speed for 3 seconds, causing double base damage upon impact. Cost: 40 charge. Cooldown: 5 minutes.

Her hammer fell smack bang in the center of the titan's eye.

Kaiden's jaw dropped. He was utterly in awe of Thorne. No wonder Ellenton had been so admiring of her. With that stacked damage, the captain's level and her surely powerful gear, that hit must have hurt.

The void titan's health disappeared. Its tentacles went limp, fell to the ground, and slowly, it collapsed onto its side.

Void Titan assisted kill - 3,500 EXP gained!

Achievement Unlocked!
Boss Slayer – 1000 EXP!
You have downed your very first boss in Nova Online. May many more fall to your might and may the gear drops be in your favor.

**Quest complete: Defend the Warden Corps Outpost on
Andros**
**Part 2: Defeat the Void Titan (somehow) and save the
Outpost on Andros.**
Rewards received: +12,000 EXP, +6 faction prestige

Level 11 achieved!
Max health and stamina increased
+3 stat points

Level 12 achieved!
Max health and stamina increased
+3 stat points

Level 13 achieved!
Max health and stamina increased
+3 stat points

Kaiden didn't hold back his joy, jumping and cheering in
giddy relief. They'd done it. They'd *really* done it this time. To
top it all, three extra levels was going to make subduing Jax a hell
of a lot easier.

The dust cleared to reveal Captain Thorne, her hammer
planted firmly in the middle of the titan's eyeball, or what
remained of it.

For the first time since the *Borrelly* had touched down, the
battlefield was silent. Kaiden turned to look for Titus and Zelda.
He found them also staring at their captain in awe.

"Remind me never to make an enemy of her," Titus said, his
jaw hanging open.

"Probably a good idea," Kaiden agreed. "Probably a very
good idea."

Chapter Thirty-Four

Andros station was largely in ruins, and smoke from burning acid was heavy in the air. Most wardens were now on a week's vacation. Those who had survived the raid walked quietly to the fallen void titan.

As Kaiden picked his way across the battlefield over voidspawn and warden bodies alike, he passed a familiar face. Sergeant Dawson. Kaiden felt a rush of gratitude for the man for helping him through that fight. Dawson's body, along with the others, only remained to further Nova Online's attempt at realism, but it was still saddening to see him lying there with blank eyes.

"He's probably already cracked open a beer back in the office." Captain Thorne had picked her way over to his side.

"He saved me," Kaiden said.

"Yeah?" Thorne said. "Well, he's good at his job. He likes it, too. Probably for the best he gets back to see his kids for a while this week."

Kaiden did a double-take. It was hard to imagine Dawson living a regular life outside of his role in the game. He looked to Thorne then and wondered what her life was like. Did she enjoy doing this? It was hard to tell how she felt behind that hardened expression and those cold brown eyes. He didn't think it his place to ask her.

"You did well, Kaiden," Thorne said. "And you're levelling far quicker than most. You could have a very bright future with us."

She clamped a hand on his shoulder. "Go loot the boss. You and your friends earned it. Then come find me to discuss the *special* mission you were on."

"Okay," Kaiden said, still a little dazed from everything that had just happened. "Don't you want to loot it as well?"

Thorne laughed. "I have the best possible gear a power warden in this level bracket can get, my charge capacity is much higher than most wardens. Won't be able to find better in this area of Nova Online unless Command reassigns me to a higher-level region. Anyway," she added with an air of finality. "I'd best speak to the rest of the troops. Talk later."

She moved off and Kaiden started back on his journey toward the corpse of the void titan. Zelda and Titus were already there, holding up gleaming new hammers and grinning broadly.

"We got weapon upgrades!" Zelda exclaimed. "This has way higher damage than the basic one I've been using, and it gives my perception stat a nice boost too."

"Same story here," Titus said. "Except I got strength and endurance."

"Maybe I'll get lucky, too," Kaiden said. He'd already upgraded his weapon once by finding a hammer better suited for critical hits back on the *Mochinki,* but this was a level twenty boss so he was hopeful he'd find even better.

As he approached the boss, a line of text appeared.

Loot corpse?

Oh yes, Kaiden thought.

What he found did not disappoint. There was indeed a hammer icon there, and its name was in heavy blue text.

Void-Warped Enhanced Hammer (Rare)
Quality: Superior
One-Handed
Base Damage: 15 bludgeoning, 18 smashing
+ 25% damage inflicted on critical hits
+ 2 dexterity
+ 2 strength

The hammer was more ornate than the others, with arcane symbols etched along its surface.

"Well that's a good upgrade," Kaiden said. "Certainly makes all that hell worth it!"

"We should assign our new stat points, too," Zelda said.

"Yeah, I gained a bunch of levels at the end there," Titus said.

Kaiden brought up his character sheet. He thought it was starting to look quite fleshed out – a darn sight more impressive than when he'd first logged in, for sure. Both Sola and Thorne had noted how quickly he'd been levelling, so it was safe to say the chain quest to capture Jax was paying major dividends. Surviving the raid had been huge as well, of course.

The single biggest EXP gain I've ever had at one time. Three levels in one pop and a new hammer. What more could a guy ask for?

He'd liked dealing more damage in that battle, and after his panic about dying, his desire to have some more health and be a bit less squishy had not vanished. Kaiden had nine unassigned stat points and chose to distribute them equally between strength, endurance and dexterity.

Character
Name: Kaiden
Race: Human
Level: 13
Class: Enhanced Warden
Attributes:
Strength: 28 (+2) *Intelligence:* 22
Endurance: 28 *Perception:* 22
Dexterity: 46 (+2) *Unassigned:* 0
Abilities:
Hammer Smash, Shield Bash, Hammer Toss, Shackle, Burst of Speed, Enhanced Senses, Riposte, Flash Bang, Blur, Onslaught
Perks:
Turen Tinkering

Satisfied, Kaiden closed his sheet down.

"All good?" he asked the others.

"Healed up, stats picked, and ready to go," Titus said. "Although I have to say, even though this is a game, I feel exhausted after that raid."

"I know what you mean," Zelda said. "But as much as I hate to be the bearer of bad news, we are under something of a time constraint." She lowered her voice. "Titus has...somewhere to be, remember?"

"I remember, don't worry," Kaiden said. "Captain Thorne asked to speak with us about that, actually. We'd better go find her."

They found the captain inside the surprisingly unharmed communications tower on the east side of the base. She and a group of higher-level wardens were huddled together before a three-dimensional holographic projection of the Greater Spiral Arm System.

Thorne was pointing to a swirling green nebula. "The *Anakoni* is sitting tight between the main guild forces. They've promised a ceasefire for three more days, but we'll need to get back there quickly if we want to take advantage of that and try to find a settlement." She looked to see who had just arrived. "Ah, the heroes of the *Mochinki* prevailed."

She gave them a smile for all to see. "You three just keep accomplishing the impossible, don't you?"

"Well, just like on the *Mochinki,* we had some top-notch help, without which we wouldn't have succeeded," Kaiden said.

"Flattery won't work on me," Thorne said. "Only results."

The other wardens chuckled to themselves at that.

Thorne stepped away from her officers. "Excuse me one moment. I must speak to these rising stars."

She motioned for them to follow her into the hallway, checking nobody was eavesdropping before speaking in a low voice. "How are things coming with that assassin, then?"

She's probably worried we're taking too long with the mission. We did lose a lot of time between Jonduu, Kal Reya, and the arena.

"Things are going great," Kaiden said, putting on his best confident smile.

"They are?"

Does she look a bit surprised? All the more reason to be encouraging.

"Yes, they are," Zelda chimed in. "We've identified the assassin's guild, located its headquarters, and have laid a trap to capture him. We'll have all the answers you wanted – and the assassin himself – by the end of today, with any luck."

"You will?" Thorne blinked once, then broke into a smile. "You will! That's great. You three really are well on your way to promotion. We could use a dozen more like you." She clapped her hands together, still smiling. "Really great work, truly. But don't let me hold you up. You should get back to it!"

"Absolutely, ma'am." Kaiden nodded and the others followed suit.

Thorne gave them a quick salute, then headed back into comms room.

When we capture Jax, I'm taking the evidence of my innocence straight to Captain Thorne. She'll know what to do with it. And she probably has connections in government that can help me, too.

The raid had been mentally exhausting, if nothing else. But now, the hope Kaiden had felt after his theatre performance, the hope that he'd soon have evidence of his innocence, was renewed. He was getting out of this prison, and sooner rather than later. He smiled.

"Who's ready for a trip back to Nassau?"

~

The stars that shone outside the shuttle were more varied than Kaiden had expected. Every time he travelled through the vast void Nova Online had created, he saw something new. Far-off planets, distant constellations, meteors and sometimes even other ships, often covered in alien symbols or sporting sleek, futuristic designs. It really was an impressive simulation. No loops, no cookie-cutter planets copy-pasted to fill the empty space. It was all unique.

Kaiden might even have enjoyed the trip if not for the serious nature of the task at hand. Jax was the final piece of the puzzle, the last stage of the chain quest and Kaiden's only chance of clearing his name. If they could manage to Shackle Jax, they might just be able to get him to reveal who hired him. That evidence would likely be enough for them to re-open his case. The police would realise their mistake and Kaiden would be free.

With such high stakes, things needed to go perfectly. If they didn't, Jax would know they were onto him. The assassin might disappear, or even stop logging in. If that happened, they might not get another chance.

Manson would, though. He'd get a *lot* of chances.

Turning from the awe-inspiring view, Kaiden let out a breath he hadn't realised he'd been holding. He needed to shake off the nerves, focus on something else.

"I assume I'm not the only one who has gained some new skills lately? We should catch up on each other's moves so we can better work together." Kaiden went first, quickly outlining Riposte, Onslaught and Blur for Titus and Zelda. He hadn't had a chance to do so before the raid and without his visor's analyse ability they weren't able to glean such information on the fly.

Zelda nodded along. "With these new ones, and Burst of Speed, it sounds like you're going to have a clear playstyle from here on in."

"Float like a butterfly, sting like a bee." Titus nodded. "It's a good way to fight".

"Except that if I do get hit, I won't last long," Kaiden replied. "Dodging and scoring all those crits requires a lot of dexterity. I've been dumping most of my stats into that, so my endurance is laughable."

"That's why you have me," the big man grinned. "And my new Barrier."

Kaiden turned to Zelda. "And grenades, too," he said, remembering the carnage those Kinetic Grenades had caused to the voidspawn.

"And lightning."

"Yeah, and light— wait, what?" Kaiden turned toward Zelda, who was smiling from ear to ear.

"Let's just say my new ability is rather shocking."

Titus groaned.

Chapter Thirty-Five

Hours later, Kaiden found himself perched in the rafters of the warehouse, his armour blending nicely against the gray metal beam. Everything was set; they were as prepared as they could possibly be. They had created an open area in the center of the warehouse, removing most of the stored contents. This gave them a clear view of the main entrance. Only a few boxes remained, stacked against the walls.

The warehouse doors were rigged, set to slam closed and lock at the slightest sign of movement. The windows had been reinforced and bolted closed. Any additional entrances had been sought out and blocked. As best they could, Kaiden and the others had worked to ensure there was only one way in and one way out.

They had contacted Marty from the shuttle to let him know the target was expected to be in place at the warehouse for the next three hours. This gave enough of a window for Jax to arrive, but not so much that it would seem suspicious.

The trap was set.

Titus had placed himself in plain view on the mostly open warehouse floor. He was making a show of inspecting the few boxes that remained in the partially emptied building. Kaiden hoped this wouldn't raise suspicion; wardens sometimes did such checks to ensure the proper tariffs had been paid on trade shipments.

The trap was baited.

Now, all that was left to do was wait.

Kaiden focused on the iron double doors, willing Jax to enter and end the suspense.

Then came sound of a rifle shot. Then another, and a moment later, a third. Kaiden tore his eyes from the main doors. Three red dots had appeared on his minimap, but they were on the opposite side of the building.

Jax must have bypassed their security or found another way in. He'd surprised them – and he wasn't alone.

"Behind us!" Kaiden shouted, turning toward the sound of rifle fire. Somehow, despite their efforts, Jax had managed to slip in and flank them. Now he was set up on the far side of the warehouse, firing from atop a stack of crates. Near the ground, a crate had been shifted slightly to reveal an open grate in the concrete floor.

"He brought company," Zelda yelled, ducking behind her shield as a bullet whipped across the room. It slammed into the wall just in front of her in a rain of sparks.

Kaiden's visor identified Jax, kneeling and slinging rounds at them, but it also picked up other assassins doing the same. Two of them, each at level twelve.

Was he expecting us? Has he sensed a trap? Kaiden wasn't sure, but there wasn't time to brood on it. The assassins were set up in the perfect position, nothing but clear ground between them and their targets.

"Group up!" Kaiden shouted, then jumped from the rafters. His health dropped by two percent from fall damage, then Zelda landed beside him and they rose together, stepping up next to Titus, shields at the ready.

Another barrage of rifle fire came at them, bullets slamming into their shields so hard they sent ripples through their surfaces.

"We can't hold up against this fire forever," Titus said, grunting against the strain of stopping the precisely aimed rounds. He slammed his shield into the ground and a broad Barrier materialized in front of them.

"Have a taste of your own medicine!" Zelda shouted, angling herself around the edge of the barrier and returning a volley of fire at the assassins. She led with her new ability.

Ability: Warden's Bolt

Discharge a bolt of lightning that jumps to multiple targets within range of the impact target. Initial range 50 feet, jump range 10 feet. Deals +150% base damage, reducing by half with each successive jump. Cost: 25 charge. Cooldown: 30 seconds.

A peal of thunder reverberated through the warehouse as a bolt of lightning arced from her hammer, hitting the leftmost of the lower-level assassins. The man let out a startled cry as the lightning crackled through his body, then jumped at those next to him.

The crackling electricity splintered the concrete as Jax rolled away, missing him by inches. The other assassin was not so lucky, the bolt striking him square in the chest and tumbling him twitching to the ground.

Zelda wasn't done. A volley of blasts followed her initial shot, sending the assassins scrambling for cover – not that there was much to be had in the warehouse. Crates were blown into splinters and pixels under her barrage as they darted from cover to cover.

Kaiden didn't wait to see what would happen next. His charge bar was also brimming from all the rounds he'd blocked.

Time to put that to use.

He used Burst of Speed, the world blurring around him as he darted from the safety of Titus' Barrier and rushed the assassins, who had finally found more robust cover.

They were attacking Titus' barrier, now using explosive rounds from an attachment on their rifles. Each one sent a shockwave through the energy field as they detonated.

"Barrier's going down," Titus called.

"I'm on it."

Kaiden took a long route around the assassins, flanking in from their side and, he hoped, out of their line of sight. As he rushed them, he channeled energy into his shield, preparing to use Flash Bang in the hopes of blinding them. His shield began to glow.

Jax spotted him at the last moment and spun away to cover his face.

The other assassins were not so quick to react.

Kaiden slid to a stop right in front of them and the glowing energy in his shield discharged in a blinding flash of light.

The closest assassin shrieked, stumbling backward with a hand raised over his eyes as he desperately sliced the air with a wrist blade. Kaiden easily stepped around the first blow, and then the next, stacking Riposte. Then he slipped inside the assassin's guard, swinging upward to strike his enemy's chin.

Critical Hit!
+50% damage (Headshot)
+50% damage dealt (Riposte x 2)

It took the assassin all the way down to the red. Kaiden followed up with two quick strikes to the chest and knee, which didn't crit but managed to finish the job.

Assassin assisted kill - 750 EXP gained!

Kaiden took a moment to bask in his new-found power. Extra levels, fresh abilities, a new hammer amplifying his crit damage, not to mention better stat distribution, had just allowed him to pummel a level twelve opponent. He'd come a long way.

Returning to the fight at hand, he saw Jax aiming at the Barrier. The assassin fired an explosive round, shattering the forcefield and leaving Titus and Zelda exposed. The big man wasted no time, using Shield of Fury. It struck the remaining level twelve before rebounding toward Jax, forcing his next shot to go wide. Titus was already charging the level twelve as his shield boomeranged back, while Zelda lay down covering fire.

That left Jax to Kaiden.

Sounds good to me.

Burst of Speed was out, but Kaiden took advantage of Jax being staggered from Titus' shield hitting him to rush in and try for a critical hit. But even as he reached him, Jax recovered quickly, slashing an energy dagger at him faster than Kaiden had thought possible. Kaiden was forced to roll, catching the dagger's strike on his shield, then leapt to his feet.

He swung again, but Jax fired an explosive round into the ground between them, turning Kaiden's vision white as a burst of fire and concrete exploded, spraying them both with shrapnel.

Kaiden staggered back, off balance, his health bar flashing, then barely avoided a second shot that screamed over his shoulder. His health bar had dropped to eighty-seven percent.

Jax lunged in with the dagger again, the blade blurring with the dexterity of a powerful assassin. Forced backward, Kaiden managed to block it on his shield, then was tripped up as Jax spun into a sweeping kick that swept his feet from under him.

As soon as Kaiden hit the ground, Jax was taking aim, his rifle shouldered in half a second. Kaiden pulled his shield up just in time, the round exploding against his already near-full shield. It flickered, then disappeared.

A smile stretched across Jax's face. He cocked his rifle.

Assassin assisted kill - 750 EXP gained!

Kaiden saw the notification blink. Jax's second goon had gone down.

Perhaps Jax saw it too, as he hesitated for a fraction of a second. Then a Burst Arrow slammed into his shoulder. He staggered back, then spun to find Titus in the middle of a full-on Shield Charge in his direction.

With no time to take aim at the charging shield warden, Jax jumped, aimed his rifle directly to the ground and fired an explosive round. The shockwave threw him into the air as Titus rushed beneath him. Jax landed and aimed at Titus' retreating back in one smooth movement.

Kaiden scrambled up and used Hammer Toss. It caught Jax in the side before he could pull the trigger. So far they had gotten Jax's health bar to sixty-five percent. It was yellow, but it would have to drop to red before they could use Shackle on him.

"Just die will you," Jax said, retreating to keep both Titus and Kaiden away from him.

Kaiden almost sprang after him, then stopped as an idea struck him. Jax was a better fighter than any one of them. Swift and slippery, with attacks that dealt massive amounts of damage. But they didn't need to fight him one on one.

"Zelda!" Kaiden shouted in comms. "Circle and fire!"

"Consider it done," she replied.

"Be careful though," Kaiden reminded her. "We need him Shackled not killed. Titus, get in front of his gun. Don't attack,

and breathed a heavy sigh of relief, his heart pounding from the tension of it all.

Notifications began popping up in the corner of his vision.

Quest Completed: Capture the assassin Jax
Part 4: Capture the assassin
Rewards received: +8,000 EXP, +10 faction prestige

Level 14 achieved!
Max health and stamina increased
+3 stat points

Kaiden looked down at Jax and smiled.
"Gotcha."

Chapter Thirty-Six

"Alright, you're going to talk and you're going to do it right now," Zelda said, stomping up to Jax. He ignored her, struggling futilely against the chains binding him. Zelda planted a boot on his chest and forced him still.

"A couple of weeks ago, you were hired to kill a character by the name of Bernstein_14. You remember that contract?"

Jax ignored her, eyes distant. Trying to log out, probably.

"Come on, Jax. You know better than that. You're Shackled. There's only one way out of it, and that's when I decide to let you go," Kaiden said.

"Damn you," Jax spat, struggling against the chains again.

Titus brought his hammer down on the concrete next to Jax's head, shattering it. That got the assassin's attention.

"A little more to the left next time. You just missed me," he said.

"Oh, no one's finishing you off today," Titus said with a deep chuckle. "Not until you answer our questions, at least."

"I can't reveal information about my clients. If I did, no one would hire me again."

"Well, I'd feel really bad if that were to happen," Zelda said, not holding back on the sarcasm.

"Look, Jax." Kaiden leaned over him. "Let's be sensible about this. The Warden Corps wants us to bring you in. Sparking off a trade war like you did? That's a big no-no. They're pretty unhappy about that."

"If we bring you in," Zelda said, "they're going to scan your character, find your address in real life, and, well, after that, who's to say? A nice perma-ban from the game, or slapped with a fine big enough to cover losses suffered from the trade war?"

"I can't go to prison," Jax said, panic creeping into his voice. "And I can't lose this account. I live off the money I make from it. I support my sick mother with it!"

"Well, it's awful nice to hear you say that, Jax." Kaiden crossed his arms and leaned in close. "Because we don't particularly care to take you to the Warden Corps." Kaiden shrugged. "As long as you answer our questions, that is."

Jax swallowed hard, then nodded.

"What choice do I have? Ask away."

"The Bernstein_14 contract. You remember it?" Zelda asked, crouching down next to him.

"Of course I remember it. It paid ridiculously well."

"You looted an item from his body. What was it?"

"Just some encrypted file. I was instructed not to mess with it, so I didn't. Just handed it over, like they said."

"Like who said?"

"You really don't know?"

"Would we be asking if we did?"

"No, I get that. It's just..." He paused a moment, frowning. "I just assumed you'd know. That's why you were coming after me, right? They wanted to keep me quiet about the whole thing? Figured I'd become a loose end? I knew that contract was too good to be true."

"Who hired you?" Kaiden demanded, tired of half answers.

Jax met his gaze, eyes wide.

"Captain Thorne, of course."

Silence. Complete silence for at least five seconds.

What?

The thought hit Kaiden like an assassin's bullet.

No, he's lying. That can't be true. He's trying to mislead us so he can...so he can...

"Don't lie to us," Kaiden said. "You're wasting time I don't have."

"It's no lie. She posted the hit, signed the contract, and paid me herself."

Kaiden wasn't ready to believe it. The implication was too

far-fetched, too terrible a thought. But as he considered it, he realized Jax would be making things much worse for himself if he was lying to them.

"If that's true, then that means..."

"Holy crap." Zelda looked as shocked as Kaiden felt.

"No," Kaiden said. "That can't be true. Can it?"

He looked to Zelda. She mumbled for a moment, eyes distant as if she were thinking deeply.

"It was a double bluff," she said finally.

"What?" Kaiden and Titus said at the same time.

"Bernstein's murder, your arrest, all of it." Zelda's eyes went wide. "Oh, jeez. That's a ballsy move. A brilliant move. And it almost worked." She shook her head in disbelief before speaking again.

"I'd been thinking criminals killed Bernstein to auction his information back to the Party. That seemed the only logical explanation as to why the Party was making such a big deal out of your arrest, Kai. No one would expect them to draw so much attention to a murder they committed. They drew media attention to their own crime, the last thing any of us expected them to do. And it worked. It completely threw us off the scent."

"That's twisted," Titus said. "Even the Southside Boys wouldn't do something that messed up. Jeez."

This is nonsense, Kaiden wanted to say. *More of Zelda's rebel conspiracy theories.* But even as he opened his mouth to say so, he knew she was right. It all made sense. He *had* been framed. But not by criminals; by the Party themselves. Bernstein had information that could hurt them. They couldn't risk it getting into the wrong hands. Couldn't risk it being released, either. So, they'd taken it back. And made Kaiden take the fall for it.

The revelation dawned on him along with a growing horror. He'd been played from the beginning. A moment later, a second realization hit, this one even more horrific than the first.

"There's no clearing my name," he said, barely managing the words. "That's been my hope since I was first put in here, but...but now I realize I was never getting out. The game's been rigged since the beginning."

"I'm sorry, Kai," Zelda said with a sad nod. "They're monsters. This is how they operate. They're just so good at hiding it, no one believes it until they see it for themselves."

"Yeah, now I know how that feels." He was feeling dizzy. That had never happened in-game before. The VR pods were supposed to suppress the real world's inner ear while you were in them. Apparently, the feeling of crushing despair transcended such trivial barriers.

"Even if we succeed," Kaiden said, looking at Titus, then Zelda, "it won't matter. I can't clear my name. The Party runs the prison; they'll never let me out. I'm going to be stuck in here for the next fifty years."

His stomach felt like it was going to drop out of him. A wave of nausea hit and he stumbled backward, vertigo overtaking him.

Fifty years in prison. Even playing Nova, that's half a lifetime. I'll be an old man by the time I'm free. The better part of my life just...gone. Thrown away by some politician I don't even know.

Another thought struck him and his despair hit even harder.

"I'm going to die in here. Out in the real world, I'll never escape Manson for all those years. He'll get me eventually, one way or another. I'm sure of it".

"Kai." Zelda stepped over to him. "Kaiden," she said, voice comforting but firm.

He looked up at her.

"You're not going to die in prison."

"How can you know that? I can't clear my name. That's been my hope from day one. That was our agreement. I help you find out the truth about Bernstein's murder, and you help me clear my name. But that's impossible now. The Party will never let me out − they're the ones who did it."

"Then maybe the Party isn't who you should turn to."

"What?"

The mad thoughts spiraling in his head paused at that.

"I didn't just put myself into prison without a plan." She smiled. "Come on, Kai. You know me better than that."

"What are you saying?"

"I'm saying the rebels are on standby to break me out. As soon as I have Bernstein's file, all I have to do is post a coded message on a Nova forum − which I can do from in-game − and they'll come get me." She smiled. "Come with me." She turned to Titus and gave him a sharp nod. "You too, big man. If you want."

"What in the stars have I stumbled into?" Jax asked from where he lay on the floor. "This is insane. No, this is beyond insane. You're all going to get yourselves killed. And I don't just mean in-game."

Kaiden's emotions were going wild, switching back and forth so fast he didn't know what to feel. And then, suddenly, there was clarity. He made the decision without really thinking about it. There wasn't anything left to think about. He was done thinking. Now, he was going to act.

He wouldn't be the Party's plaything. They intended for him to rot in prison for the next fifty years. Had tortured and murdered his friend, and framed him for it. But enough was enough.

"Jax," Kaiden said, drawing the assassin's attention and walking over to him. "Thorne hired you to kill Bernstein, yeah?"

"Yes."

"And when you looted that encrypted file from him, you turned it over to Thorne?"

"I did."

"You think she still has it?"

"Probably. She said something about needing more information to open it. But I don't know. I was just collecting a paycheck."

"Awesome. Thank you." Kaiden smiled, then brought his hammer down on the assassin's head. His health bar flashed, then emptied completely.

Assassin assisted kill - 1,000 EXP gained!

On instinct, Kaiden looted Jax's inventory. He hadn't been carrying much – certainly not Bernstein's encrypted file – but it'd been worth checking. He did have a pretty rare stimpack, though.

Agilix Mach 5
Doubles dexterity for 10 seconds, drastically improving speed, the ability to dodge attacks and the potential to deal critical blows.

Kaiden looted it and the stim automatically equipped into the spare slot in his forearm chamber to keep cool. He looked up at Zelda.

"So let me get this straight. Your people can bust us out of prison? All three of us?"

"Absolutely."

Kaiden looked to Titus next.

"Any interest in that?"

The big man laughed.

"What's the other option? Rot in prison while my brother's in danger? Yeah, consider me interested."

"We need Bernstein's encrypted file first," Zelda said. "We can't leave until we've secured it."

"And there's a good chance Thorne still has that." Kaiden crossed his arms. "So what are we waiting for? Let's go take down Thorne."

A new notification appeared.

Quest: Confront Captain Ava Thorne and locate the mysterious file taken from player Bernstein_14
Expected difficulty: Impossible
Rewards: 10,000 EXP

Kaiden hoped the game wasn't being literal in that difficulty setting, though he supposed it was an accurate description. Either way, they didn't have much of a choice.

They were going to have to try the impossible.

Chapter Thirty-Seven

"This is absolute insanity," Titus said for the fourth time as the *Borrelly* hurtled toward the *Anakoni*'s position. "Absolutely insanity." He smiled. "And I love it."

"Thorne just confirmed our meeting request," Zelda said, reading from a console. "I told her we caught the assassin and are bringing him back for questioning. I also told her he's claiming a warden hired him for the trade war hit. She's personally meeting us in the hangar to take him into custody – no doubt she would have insisted on interrogating him alone."

"Perfect." Kaiden smiled, too excited by the prospect of imminent freedom to feel any nerves. He was done being afraid, anyway. He'd lived in fear too long. He was taking his fate into his own hands.

Thankfully, by the time they arrived at the *Anakoni,* all their abilities would be back online from their cooldowns and their health would have fully recovered.

"There won't be many wardens on the *Anakoni,*" Zelda said, continuing her mini mission brief. "Most are dead, and the rest are handling the cleanup on Andros, or the trade war. The ship's running on a skeleton crew. And if my hunch is correct, Thorne's going to want to meet us on her own anyway. If what Jax said is true – and I'm convinced it is – she'll want to keep anything we learned quiet."

"Even alone, Captain Thorne is no lightweight," Titus said,

his mouth curling into a smile. He was clearly looking forward to the challenge.

Kaiden didn't share the sentiment. Captain Thorne was the highest-level player they had encountered so far in Nova Online. If they simply rushed in, hammers blazing, she'd tear them to pieces.

"We need a plan," he said, bringing up the message logs from his visor. "Here's what we know about Captain Thorne. She's level twenty-five – that's at least eleven levels higher than any of us. She took out a void titan that nearly destroyed an entire warden outpost. Oh, and she's a power warden, so front-line combat is her forte."

Zelda nodded. "That power warden war hammer gains charge by dealing damage. Which means she can gain charge both by attacking us and blocking our hits with her shield."

"It also deals twenty-five percent extra base damage," Kaiden noted, checking his visor's readout. "Not to mention the fact that her hammer is the best she can get at her level. She told me that herself."

Wish we'd asked the turen to take a look at our hammers, too.

"Also, all those power warden abilities help her deal extra damage," Kaiden continued. "Hammer Overload and Berserker are particularly dangerous as they have big damage multipliers."

"So we can assume she will be dealing massive damage," Zelda concluded. "Even Titus would probably only be able to take a few hits before overloading. How do we deal with that? The strategy we used against Jax isn't going to work. We took way too many hits."

Titus had been quiet during the exchange, but now a smile spread across his face.

"Float like a butterfly..."

Kaiden beamed.

"Of course, that's it!" he said. "We starve her out. If she can't hit us then she can't gain charge, and if we get hit we're dead anyway. If I can get her to focus on me, I might be able to dodge her attacks for long enough to wear her down, with some help."

"I guess that makes you the new tasty piece of bait," Titus said, clapping Kaiden on the shoulder. "Dancing around is not my strong suit. If I'm up front like usual, she'll go straight for me to build her charge."

Zelda chimed in. "I'll be 'floating' a bit further away, but if you can keep her distracted I can still sting like a bee." She started smirking. "With that tiny buckler of hers, I'm sure I can land some decent hits without giving her much charge."

"I guess that leaves me waiting in the wings to save your squishy hides if something goes wrong," Titus said. Kaiden should never have taught him that term for the more fragile classes in gaming.

"Let's hope it doesn't come to that," Kaiden said. "I still have one stimpack left, which should help. How about you two?"

"I'm out," Zelda said. "Used my last one during the raid."

"Me too," grunted Titus. "Jax and his boys nearly made Swiss cheese out of me in that warehouse."

Kaiden chewed his lip. "Okay, that's not ideal, but we still have the turen shields as a last line of defence."

Zelda nodded with an air of finality. "It's the best plan we have and our best shot at getting the cipher. I'm in."

Titus simply tightened his grip on his hammer.

It was decided.

With the plan set, Kaiden opened his stats screen to allocate the points he had gained from capturing Jax. It was only one level, but they were going to need all the help they could get.

Given the plan was for him to act as the 'tank' via dodging, a few points into endurance for health or strength for damage wouldn't help much. He would have to dodge nearly all of Thorne's attacks and needed every drop of dexterity he could get. He allocated all three points to dexterity and reviewed his stat sheet.

Character

Name: Kaiden
Race: Human
Level: 14
Class: Enhanced Warden

Attributes:

Strength: 29 (+2) *Intelligence:* 23
Endurance: 29 *Perception:* 23
Dexterity: 50 (+2) *Unassigned:* 0

Abilities:

*Hammer Smash, Shield Bash, Hammer Toss, Shackle, Burst of Speed,
Enhanced Senses, Riposte, Flash Bang, Blur, Onslaught*
Perks:
Turen Tinkering

Happy with his choice, Kaiden refocused on the conversation.

"If – I mean, *when* we pull this thing off," Titus was saying, "your people are on standby to bust us out, right?"

Zelda nodded.

"The plan is ready to go. Has been the whole time I've been in here."

The *Anakoni* appeared on the consoles, still distant, but drawing closer by the moment.

"It sounds like we're all set, then." Kaiden clasped his hands. "Let's do this."

Titus laughed in agreement.

"Nothing makes you feel more alive than a suicide mission, eh? Even if it is just a game."

Just a game, Kaiden thought as they hurtled toward their target. *Nova is a game, but now, the stakes are real. Deadly real. This has become much more than just a game. If we attack Thorne and don't get that data file, we're dead. In both worlds.*

Chapter Thirty-Eight

"Ensigns!" Captain Thorne greeted them with a smile as Kaiden and Titus walked down the rear loading ramp of the *Borrelly*.

She'd come alone, as Zelda had predicted.

Good. That means the plan is still viable. No complications. Now we just need Zelda to kick things off.

Kaiden found he had unintentionally tightened his grip on his hammer, but now he forced himself to loosen it as he raised his eyes to Thorne.

"You've done it again, against all the odds," she said, crossing her arms as they stepped down onto the hangar floor. "You must be three of the most talented ensigns we've had in a long while." She paused. "Speaking of which, where's Ensign Zelda?"

"She'll be with us in a moment," Kaiden said forcing himself to keep his eyes on the captain and not the distant figure of his squadmate, sneaking from the cover of one shuttle to the next.

"She's on the shuttle? With the assassin?" Thorne's smile had fallen a bit. She leaned to peer past them and into the *Borrelly*. Kaiden moved to block her view. Thorne frowned at that.

"So what's all this he told you about being hired by a warden?" she asked. "Odds are he's just trying to protect himself, but on the off-chance there is a traitor amongst us, I want to hear about it."

"He *did* name the traitor," Titus said, poorly concealed tension in his voice as he hefted his hammer onto his shoulder.

Thorne seemed not to notice the aggressive move. Playing dumb, perhaps.

"And who has he accused?"

"You," Titus said with a scowl. "He accused you of hiring him to kill a player named Bernstein_14."

And there it was, out in the open at last. Kaiden would have sighed, but he was too nervous for the fight ahead of them. Not to mention there was still a bit more of the truth left to tell. And Zelda still needed a bit more time, he realized, sparing her the briefest of glances.

"And while Jax killed Bernstein_14," added Kaiden, "your real-world counterparts tortured and killed the character's owner – my friend and neighbor – then framed me for it."

Thorne's smile was gone entirely now, replaced instead with something approaching a look of regret. Not a look he'd expected. But it didn't matter. Thorne had done what she'd done and helped to ruin his life in the process. That was the truth of the matter, whatever she had to say for herself.

Her look of regret sank into a long sigh as she shook her head slowly.

"For what it's worth, Kaiden, I'm sorry. I didn't know anything about what was happening in the real world. My job was to arrange the assassination of the player's character in-game. A player, might I add, with known rebel affiliations. All I did was follow my orders."

Following orders? That's her excuse? Seriously?

"That doesn't absolve you of guilt. Furthermore, it's a poor excuse for ruining someone's life," Kaiden said, anger rising inside him now.

Thorne shrugged, then sighed again.

"You're not wrong. But, you see, that's the luxury of your generation. You've only ever known this peaceful world, this ordered and structured paradise the Party has created. It's a beautiful thing. It means your generation can be hopeful, can pursue their own wants and dreams, because you weren't alive for the Great Test." She spoke more quickly now, a fire burning behind her eyes and passion fueling her words.

"You didn't fight, didn't watch your friends and comrades die to bring order back into this world. I did. I've seen the evil, the injustice, the wanton waste and death that chaos causes. I fought to conquer it once, and now I fight to keep it at bay. And I know these rebels – well-meaning though they think they are – teeter on the edge of bringing chaos back. They threaten everything we've accomplished." Her tone softened, then, and she took a step forward. Titus raised his hammer and shield, but she ignored him.

"Look, Kaiden. It's not fair of me to ask you to understand this, but sometimes sacrifices have to be made. My entire generation dedicated their lives to ending the war and rebuilding what was left of society. Do you think we wanted to do that? Don't you think we had dreams of our own? Families? Hopes? We did."

She took a deep, shuddering breath.

"But we were forced to abandon them so we could bring that Great Test, that war, to an end. We sacrificed everything to create a world in which our children, and our children's children, would be free to dream again."

She looked at Titus, long and hard, then back to Kaiden.

"Sacrifices have to be made for the greater good. Order and peace must prevail."

Her logic makes sense, in a twisted sort of way. But she's wrong. Nothing justifies what she and the Party have done. She has to see that.

"We owe your generation a debt of gratitude," Kaiden said. "Of that there's no doubt. We're only here because of you. But what you're defending isn't order and peace. Order and peace doesn't kill innocent people, doesn't frame others for it. There's a clear distinction between right and wrong, even if you've lost the ability to see it."

"It's you who's lost the ability to see clearly, Kaiden. But you can still make things right. You've made real progress as a warden, and could have a bright future in the corps."

Is she serious?

"I just need something to show the Party you are a team player. I looked into the three of you on my way here; the files were quite enlightening. Perhaps if you had knowledge of someone working to undermine the Party. Someone who had an axe to grind after the Party bought her employers. A little digging might even show that a known dissident by the name of Bernstein was a colleague of hers. Her misguided anger may have driven her to become a dissident as well. If you were able to name such a person, help confirm certain theories, I'm sure the Party would be very grateful."

Kaiden's heart pounded as he realised what she was saying. She knew what Zelda was. A rebel.

"You would be the ensign who uncovered her plot to infiltrate a government institution. You would be greatly rewarded – be put on the warden fast-track, and shave years off your sentence. All you have to do is name that person right now, and the Party will take care of the rest. I can't change what's been done, but I can try to make things better for you if you do the right thing, right now. I won't make this offer again."

The story she was selling sounded good – a chance to go back to his normal life. Even if Zelda's plan worked, Kaiden would be on the run. A prison escapee always looking over his shoulder.

But he would never betray Zelda like that. Even if he wasn't sure the rebels could be trusted, he trusted *her*. And after everything the Party had done, giving in to them would only ensure it happened to others. He might save himself, but how many others would suffer down the road? No, there was no joining Thorne.

"If you truly felt bad about what you've done, you'd give us the file you took from Bernstein. *That* would be the right thing to do."

His words must have struck a nerve as Thorne's expression finally bent toward anger, regret now replaced with the stirrings of a scowl.

"You think you know right and wrong, boy," she said, anger simmering in her voice. "But you've never seen true chaos. You weren't there when the bombs fell. You didn't watch your world burn in front of your eyes." She breathed heavily for several moments as if fighting to calm herself down. "If you want the file, you're welcome to try to take it from me."

"Give us the file, Thorne," Titus said, stepping forward with his shield hand open. "You've lost your way. You can't see things clearly."

"Says the man who beats people to death with his bare fists. You might make a good warden, but you're no moral compass, Titus. You've no right to judge my actions."

"If you knew more about him than what his criminal record

says, you'd know that couldn't be further from the truth," Zelda said, shouting from across the room.

She was in position.

Thorne turned to look at her.

"What are you doing all the way over...oh. I see."

Zelda reached out and pulled down on the hangar's emergency depressurization lever. Sirens flared, red lights flashed, and in the span of a heartbeat, the entrances and exits to the hangar snapped shut, massive metal doors descending from the ceiling to seal them off.

"You know," Zelda said, looking around at the transformed room. "I've been wanting to pull that lever since that recruit almost did it on our first day."

"Clever," Thorne said. "Now we're all trapped in here until the techs can manually open it. That'll take, what, an hour?"

"We don't need that much time," Titus said, flicking his shield on and raising his hammer.

"It really is a shame, you know? You three are good wardens. You could have done great things here. Could have easily been promoted to Command, earned your early release, maybe even been offered real jobs in the corps. Instead, you've chosen to throw your lot in with rebels and dissidents."

She raised her own hammer, the sleek but massive weapon's reflective surface turned an angry red by the flashing emergency lights.

"If you won't name the rebel, then I'll have to secure the confession myself, along with her two accomplices. We have an hour, but this won't take a minute."

"It's three against one," Kaiden said, activating his shield. "I'll take those odds."

"Give me a moment," Thorne said. "I'll even them out."

On Kaiden's minimap an angry red dot appeared, indicating Thorne. The game knew they were hostile to each other now. And then there was no going back.

Chapter Thirty-Nine

Thorne went for Kaiden first, a calm confidence in her features as she charged, hammer raised.

"Remember, keep your distance," Kaiden said to Titus through the comms. "We don't want to let her build charge by hitting you."

And then her hammer was streaking toward him. Kaiden dodged to the side, thankful his class excelled in dexterity as her blow fell just off target. Her heavy hammer shook the ground as it struck, but her attack was slow. Or, relatively so compared to the dexterity of an enhanced warden.

She reared back for a second blow and Kaiden backed away a pace, declining to block with his shield. He didn't want to find out exactly what would happen should one of her attacks connect.

"Show some courage, traitor."

Thorne swung in with a two-handed blow this time. Kaiden leapt backward, just outside the range of the attack. The hammer swooshed by, coming dangerously close to his head. It missed, but the attack had been too close for his liking. A head-shot would likely have ended him in a single blow.

He needed to focus. One or two mistakes was all it would take for Thorne to pound him into a pulp. But at least he had gained a Riposte buff on his next hit.

She went to strike again, but a shower of sparks exploded on her back. A Burst Arrow. Zelda had joined the fight now, a good fifty feet away and unleashing a barrage of basic laser blasts interspersed with larger Burst Arrows. Even with all the attacks combined, her health had dropped by a whopping three percent.

Jeez. She's just eating those ranged attacks and taking virtually no damage at all. Unfortunately, Zelda deals the least base damage of the three of us — she's put all her points into perception to keep her accuracy up.

Another laser struck. Thorne growled, then spun to face her attacker. She raised her shield — tiny buckler that it was — and Zelda stopped shooting.

It won't be long until Thorne figures out we're trying to charge-starve her. I need to keep her distracted and attacking me as long as I can.

With her back turned, Thorne was oblivious to Kaiden's swinging hammer.

Critical Hit!
+30% damage (Spinal Fracture)
+25% damage (Riposte x 1)

Her health dropped to ninety-six percent. Kaiden wasted no time, however, attacking twice more before she could react. The next hit was also a crit, but the third missed its mark, dealing only normal damage.

Torn between the two targets, Thorne swept back around and tried to catch Kaiden with a flurry of attacks, her hammer thrumming the air with each swing. Kaiden dodged and ducked, dipped and dived, then dodged again, always a step ahead of her attacks, if only just. Whenever the moment was right, he Riposted, dealing more damage. And all the while, he did his best to keep Thorne's back to Zelda, affording his squadmate constant clear shots.

Zelda kept firing, hitting nearly every time with impressive accuracy. Every so often a laser would catch Thorne in a critical spot, dealing extra damage and drawing her attention. It was in these moments that Kaiden lashed out. Nothing more than basic hammer attacks — he'd no charge of his own, either — but every bit of damage counted. Before long, the captain's health had dropped to seventy-eight percent. Something Kaiden would have been happy about, had they not already poured enough damage into Thorne to kill pretty much any other foe they'd faced so far, void titan aside.

"You're slippery," Thorne said, lowering her hammer for a moment. "Consider me mildly annoyed." She fiddled with the buttons on the stimulant chamber on her arm for a moment.

Applying a health stimpack? Already?

They'd been doing damage, Kaiden knew, but he'd expected her to drop lower before using one of her precious two stims.

The chamber on Thorne's arm hissed with the distinctive sound of an injection. Her health, however, didn't budge an inch.

Her hammer did.

It came in so fast Kaiden had no time at all to dodge. He raised his shield on instinct, felt the power of the blow reverberate through his whole body. His charge bar filled to sixty out of one hundred and ten.

More than half!

He shouldn't have been so shocked. Thorne was more than ten levels above them, not to mention she was a power warden with amazing gear to boot. One more hit and his shield would overload.

She lunged again. Kaiden tried to dodge but her attack connected easily. Too easily. His charge bar filled and then his shield flickered and died.

"Some stimpacks are good for more than just regaining health, you know. Shame to waste my hit chance stim so soon, but I'm tiring of your ballet feet. Oh, and now I finally have some damn charge. Allow me to show you the shortcomings of your class."

Her hammer began to glow. He recognized her Hammer Overload ability all too well and hastily started backpedaling, trying to put some distance between them. If her next hit landed, he'd take three times the damage and would definitely die.

His only chance would be to dodge, but her increased hit chance from the stim had thus far made that a hopeless prospect.

Except I have charge now, too.

Without wasting a moment, Kaiden activated Blur.

Blur activated – dodge chance +25% for 10 seconds

Hopefully, that would negate Thorne's hit stim. It wouldn't do anything about AOE attacks, though

Thorne came at him like a freight train. Kaiden spun aside at the last moment and her attack slammed into the floor just behind him, buckling the metal.

There's a one-minute cooldown on that ability, so I'm fine for a little while, Kaiden thought in relief.

"No!" Thorne screamed, face burning an angry red. She rushed him, hammer swinging quick and sloppy. With Blur active, neither of her attacks came close. Kaiden danced past them without difficulty, consciously easing Thorne back into a position where Zelda had clear shots on her.

"Got anymore increased hit stims? Looks like you'll be needing them," he laughed. He probably didn't need to taunt her – he had her full attention after making her waste one of her strongest attacks – but the anger seemed to be making her sloppy. And in this fight, he needed every advantage he could get.

Zelda kept firing, still using Burst Arrow whenever it was off cooldown. Kaiden did a quick check of Thorne's health to find her down to seventy percent.

We're making progress. Slowly, but surely. The strategy is working. He looked to the corner of his screen, then felt himself frown. Blur only had three seconds left. Once it ended, he'd be in real trouble.

I'll still have twenty seconds until my shield is back online.

Thorne then did what he'd feared she might. She used Jump Smash and leapt into the air. That move had an AOE effect, and she only had to hit the ground near him to catch him. Blur wouldn't help him.

Kaiden tried to run —

Thorne crashed into the ground —

The AOE damage hit like a tidal wave. The force of it knocked him tumbling, and he slid several feet away. His health bar flashed, then plummeted from green all the way into yellow, stopping just before entering the red.

I'm almost at critical health already. From one base damage attack. One more and I'm done. Come on, shield, I need you!

And then Thorne was looming over him. She appeared as tall as a titan from where he lay, looking up at her.

"Shortcoming number one of the enhanced warden class: you can't take many hits. One or two is all it really takes." She raised her hammer, lining up a killing blow.

Blur's on cooldown. My shield is still gone. Burst of Speed won't help me as I'm not on my feet. Kaiden mentally went through anything he could do to himself and came up empty. Thorne had him. He'd put up a good fight, but it was over.

Her hammer fell.

And slammed into a blue, shimmering shield just above his face. Kaiden blinked once, then shouted.

"Titus!"

The big man had saved him.

"Get moving," Titus grunted, then squared up to Thorne and used Shield Bash. The attack caught her full in the chest, stunning her for two seconds and buying Kaiden time to roll to his feet and back away.

"Thank you," Kaiden said. "I thought she had me."

"Don't thank me yet," Titus said, sneaking in an attack, then ducking behind his shield as another of Thorne's blows came streaking down, driving him backward. "I'm about to give her a ton of charge."

"Titus, get back," Zelda shouted.

"I'm too slow," Titus said. "Besides, I want to give this a try."

A surge of energy swirled around him, then solidified into a force field, hugging his body. As Kaiden watched, it crackled and hissed with electricity, tiny arcs of lightning lashing out as if itching to shock Thorne.

This is new.

Ability: Volt Field
Send a current across your armor causing 30% of base damage as electrical damage to all melee attackers. Cost: 30% of total shield capacity. This ability is passive when activated and is toggled on and off.

Thorne either wasn't aware of the ability's effects, or – more likely – didn't care. Despite Volt Field being active, she brought her hammer down on Titus with full force. He stumbled to the side in the wake of the blow, and Thorne's health bar inched further down. Not that she seemed to mind.

"I was going to take out the pesky enhanced first, but if you'd like to offer yourself up, I'm happy to pass that honor to you, Titus."

We need a plan, we need a plan. Kaiden's thoughts were racing.

While Titus and Thorne exchanged blows, and Zelda blasted away, he took a deep breath.

Step one: use a stimpack.

He activated the item and his health rose back to the upper end of yellow. Almost into the green, but not quite.

Thorne's own health was down to sixty-four percent. More progress, but not fast enough. Now that Titus was tanking, he and Zelda would have to take her out fast. With her back to him, it would be easy enough to get crits. For now, he'd save Burst of Speed for when he *really* needed it.

He swung his hammer up then rushed in behind Thorne, speaking into his comm. "Zelda, keep firing. I'll stay low so you can still hit her torso easily."

"Can do," Zelda said. Another Burst Arrow flashed past Kaiden's shoulder to explode on Thorne's back. He followed it with his own attacks, alternating between the backs of her knees and her lower back, praying for critical hits to build to Onslaught.

He landed one, then another. Paused a moment to aim, then struck out to land a third.

Thorne pivoted to face him. "Didn't your mother teach you it's rude to interrupt?" She activated an ability. It caught Kaiden unprepared.

Hammer Sweep damages you for 35% of player Thorne's base damage.

Moves with some form of AOE were truly the bane of Kaiden's class. His health dropped right down to forty-eight percent.

Thorne wasn't faring much better, however. From Zelda's continued blasts, Kaiden's well-aimed crits, and the electrical damage from Titus' Volt Field, she was down to fifty-one percent.

"Half health, huh?" Thorne growled. "I haven't been that low in ages. Once again, you three continue to impress." It was the angriest compliment Kaiden had ever received, and as he watched, Thorne followed it up with an ability. Her eyes lit up an electric blue as she spun to attack Titus. Kaiden remembered it well: one of the moves she'd used to finish off the void titan.

Ability: Berserker
The warden does double base damage but also takes +50% damage for 20 seconds. Speed is halved for 1 minute following the ability. Cost: 50 charge. Cooldown: 10 minutes.

"My shield can't handle this," Titus said. "I'm just going to blow some abilities to keep it from overloading."

He led with Shield Charge, locking onto Thorne and surging forward. They connected with a crash, but the power warden pushed back. Together, they cancelled out each other's momentum. Thorne caught his shield with a rising blow then, mid-strike, whipped around and followed with a smash.

Titus' shield flickered and died.

"What's a shielder without his shield?" Thorne raised her hammer, preparing to deal double damage with her next attack.

She swung. Titus didn't even try to avoid it. Kaiden was ready to watch his health drop into the red, and probably right down to zero – but the blow dealt no damage.

Then Kaiden saw a green force field buzzing around Titus.

The Turen Personal Defense Force Field!

"Looks like this shielder has another shield," Titus said, all too smug.

Thorne positively howled.

Berserker lasts for twenty seconds, Kaiden thought to himself. *Titus just burned five of it with that force field.*

"Where did you even get tech this good?" she screamed, giving Titus no chance to answer as she brought her hammer down on him again and again.

Zelda kept firing while Thorne attacked, her Burst Arrows doing more damage thanks to Berserker's debuff, but it was hardly game changing. And, all too quickly, Titus' backup shield was done.

It had hardly flicked off for a second before Thorne's hammer slammed into his side and spun him around. Titus had stacked endurance, so he had impressive hit points, but it wasn't enough. She hit him again and he collapsed, his health bar plummeting into the red.

"Titus!" Kaiden cried, not knowing what could be done.

Thorne didn't strike a killing blow, however. She simply tapped her hammer to the big man and smiled.

"Shackle," she said, softly, sweetly, almost a whisper. Chains materialized around Titus, snaking around his arms and legs, then in the blink of an eye, snapped tight. Titus was left on the ground, arms trapped at his sides, with his health in the critical.

"Stay here. I'll have questions for you later," the captain laughed.

Thorne's eyes were still glowing blue. She had ten seconds left on Berserker.

Her eyes fixated on Zelda. "Your turn, now."

To Kaiden's dismay, Thorne used Stampede. This gave her three seconds of double speed in which to close the gap with Zelda.

Luckily, the distance was great enough that Thorne's Stampede wore off just before she reached Zelda. It gave Zelda precious time to get her shield up. Thorne's blow fell – empowered by Berserker – and promptly overloaded Zelda's shield. Thorne's next attack sent Zelda crashing to the ground.

Her health bar flashed frantically, then dropped deep into the red. So deep that, for a moment, Kaiden thought she'd died. But no, she was still alive; just frighteningly low on health. One or two percent, at best.

Then Zelda activated her Turen Personal Defense Force Field.

"Damnit!" Thorne roared. Instead of just hammering away on the force field, this time she turned to Kaiden, snarling.

"I bet you've got one of those too, haven't you?"

"Actually I've got three." Kaiden grinned.

At last, Kaiden's warden shield came back online, though what good it would do he didn't know.

Zelda wasn't done yet, though. Even as Kaiden replied to Thorne, she'd activated an ability. Kaiden recognized the glowing, charging ball of energy on the end of her hammer. Kinetic Grenade.

"Excuse me, Captain?" Zelda said, holding her hammer high.

Thorne spun and found herself looking at the grenade, a mere foot from her face.

It detonated with all the fury of a miniature supernova, a blast of light, then sound. Thorne crashed to the floor, taking masssive damage in the process.

Fifty percent more damage taken due to Berserker, and that grenade hit close enough to get its max damage. Might even have crit, too.

Thorne's health bar showed it. As she pulled herself to her feet, Kaiden focused and saw it had dropped to twenty-five percent.

His joy was short-lived, however, as Thorne staggered over to Zelda and, just as her turen shield wore off, tapped her with her hammer. Just as had happened with Titus, chains materialized around Zelda, then snapped shut, binding her in place.

"We'll have words later, rebel" she spat.

Thorne turned to face Kaiden.

"No one can say you three didn't try. And you even came close, too. Got me down to one-quarter health." She smirked. "Oh, but there is this." She pressed a button on her stimulant chamber and injected a stimpack. Her health bar filled back to fifty percent.

Kaiden's hope sputtered out. This was insurmountable. How could he deal fifty percent damage to her on his own? All their combined efforts, including Zelda's trick with the grenade to the face, had only done damage equal to three-quarters of her health.

His shield was back online, so that was something. Gave him some hope of surviving maybe three hits or so.

He sighed. The fight was lost. They'd given it their best and come up short. What would happen to them now? He'd never let himself consider failure as a possibility. Had been sure they'd prevail, one way or another. But now, reality came at him like a raged berserker, dispelling his foolish illusions.

Thorne advanced slowly, dragging her hammer behind her. "You really should have taken my offer. I'll give you one more chance. You're a darn good warden, Kaiden. And with my help, you can become a legendary one. Think about it. For your service in exposing Zelda as a dissident, you'd be handily reward-ed." She flicked her shield off. A show of trust, perhaps?

"Your sentence would be shortened if not revoked entirely. I can't change what's been done to you, but I can help fix your future. Let me help you, Kaiden."

He didn't even consider it. Didn't need to. He'd made his mind up and no promises from Thorne would change that. He'd seen the true face of the Party, and he wasn't going to be a pawn in that game, an accomplice to their crimes. Maybe it'd cost him everything – really, it already had – but he had made his choice. Even in the face of impossible odds, he wasn't going back on it. One way or another, this ended here.

"No," he said quietly.

"Kaiden, think about this. There's no reason to–"

"No." He raised his hammer and shield. She seemed to be taking forever to reach him. *Is she stalling?* Kaiden frowned, and then he remembered. *Berserker has a debuff after use.* He moved his reticle onto Thorne to check.

Player Thorne is affected by a debuff from the move Berserker. Movement speed is reduced by 50%. 20 seconds remaining.

I can work with that.

Kaiden felt a spark of hope reignite inside him. This fight was still winnable. He hadn't lost. Not just yet. Her movement was slowed, and he was fast. Weaving around her would be easier, as would dodging. But he could make himself go even faster. Faster than he'd even gone before. To win this fight he was going to have to stack like crazy.

Sola would be so proud to see this.

Kadien still had the stimpack he'd looted from Jax. He'd been saving it, and there was no better time. He pressed the injection button in his forearm and the stimulant entered his system.

Agilix Mach 5 injected. Dexterity doubled for 10 seconds.

Kaiden swore his feet felt lighter already. Doubling his dexterity greatly increased his dodge and crit chance, but also effectively doubled his base movement speed as well. But that wasn't enough. No, there was more he could do.

Burst of Speed.

Kaiden watched the last of his charge drain as energy swirled around him. Thorne was moving at half speed, but between the dexterity stim and Burst of Speed he was moving at something like quadruple his original speed. To him, it looked like she was moving through water.

And he knew of one way to get even faster – if he managed to get the crit streak.

Kaiden smiled.

He exploded forward, so fast he passed her before she'd even had time to react. Whirling around, he was upon her again immediately. The room turned to one big gray-colored blur. Time seemed to have slowed to a crawl everywhere around him.

Now this is speed!

Behind Thorne, Kaiden aimed a strike at the back of her head.

Critical hit!
+ 50% damage (Headshot)

That's one.

There was barely a need to think about dodging as Thorne hadn't even finished turning to face him yet. He struck her again, and again, and again.

Critical hit streak (x 4)

Thorne finally finished turning. He darted around her faster than an eyeblink. Burst of Speed still had about five seconds left. Two more easy headshots followed. He wasn't even able to stack Riposte – Thorne was too slow for her attacks to even register.

Critical hit streak (x 6)

Onslaught Mode activated.
Current movement speed and damage is doubled for 5 seconds

If Kaiden was correct, he was now moving at eight times his original movement speed. Thorne all but stopped moving. He thought he'd been moving fast before, but now, well, he didn't have words to describe how fast he was moving. He felt like a god. Thorne wasn't even an opponent to him. All she had become was a training dummy.

He began hitting her at will, his attacks flying out quicker than ever. Combat text rolled in faster than he could keep up with. Crit after crit after crit.

Thorne didn't stand a chance.

Kaiden was laughing. The feeling was intoxicating. He was unbeatable. How could anyone counter this? All his worries, all his fear, all his despair at the fight had washed away. It was irrelevant now. He'd won and he knew it. Thorne was done. Her health would have vanished many hits back, but he didn't care. He just kept laughing, all the while attacking. An unending, unavoidable stream of damage.

As the timers on his stacked abilities ticked down to the last second, Kaiden dashed to stand before Thorne, a smile stretching across his face as he prepared to see her shocked expression.

Agilix Mach 5 fades.
Burst of Speed ends.
Onslaught Mode deactivated.

Thorne did look shocked. But something was wrong.

Kaiden frowned.

She was still standing, seemingly frozen, her health at zero.

And Kaiden remembered the ability he'd forgotten. The hallmark of the power warden class.

Ability: Last Rites
When the warden reaches 0 health, Last Rites is triggered, allowing the warden 10 seconds to kill all opponents in a 50-foot radius of the point of death. Should they succeed, they will be given 1 HP back. If not, they will die. Kills made during this time earn no XP. No abilities can be used during Last Rites. Cooldown: 6 hours.

Kaiden swallowed hard. His stacked abilities were gone. He had no more. Blur was still on cooldown.

"My turn," Thorne growled.

She charged him and Kaiden immediately activated his turen shield, buying himself some time. He'd won. Had been that close. But in his victory, he'd forgotten Last Rites.

He could have accounted for this. Could have used that last second of speed to sprint all the way across the hangar. But he hadn't. He'd been too intoxicated by his supercharged condition. And now...now he was trapped.

Thorne's Berserker debuff was gone, and she was on him in an instant, hammer slamming down over and over. Blow after blow staggered him, dealing no damage, but keeping him from being able to focus.

But Kaiden had to do something. His turen shield had bought him five seconds – three left, now – but Last Rites lasted for ten seconds. Thorne would have plenty of time to finish him as soon as it wore off.

Another blow sent Kaiden stumbling to the side and his eyes fell over Zelda, Shackled and still on the ground. Titus was in the same condition.

What's going to happen to them? What will the Party do?

They were Shackled in-game now, but soon they'd be shackled in the real world, once Thorne was done with her interrogation.

And that's when it hit him.

With his last second of shielding, Kaiden reached out, touched her with his hammer and said, "Shackle."

Thorne frowned, her eyebrows furrowing, but even as she did, chains materialized in the air around her.

"You're in Last Rites, at zero health. That's critical health as far as Shackle is concerned," Kaiden said.

Thorne shook her head, then the chains snapped tight and she fell on her side. She strained at her bonds, but it was no use.

"Clever, Kaiden. Too clever."

She shook her head as the timer of Last Rites counted down to its final seconds. She looked up at him. Cool and calm once more, but significantly more frightening.

"See you in a week, Ensign."

The ability expired, and Thorne lay still. Dead.

Warden Captain assisted kill – 4,000 EXP gained!

Prestige with the Warden Corps: -300
Faction Status changed: Warden Corps now hostile
toward you.

Across the room, Titus pulled himself to his feet. Closer by, Zelda did the same. They both approached cautiously, eyes locked on Thorne's body.

At first, no one spoke. Then Titus looked at Kaiden, smiled, and raised a hand for a high five.

Kaiden couldn't help but laugh as he obliged him.

"I can't believe you did it!"

"We did it," Kaiden said. "Somehow, we did it."

"Congratulate each other later. We have to hurry," Zelda said, then knelt next to the captain. A moment later there was an item in her hand. A simple, polished brass padlock.

"Is that...?" Kaiden said, leaning in for a closer look.

"Bernstein's file? It's a representation of it. Since the file isn't native to Nova, the uploader was allowed to choose an in-game object to represent it."

"But that's it? That's the file?"

"Yeah. This contains the information they killed Bernstein for," Zelda said, nodding. She pocketed it.

Quest Completed: Confront Captain Ava Thorne and
locate the mysterious file taken from player Bernstein_14
Rewards: 10,000 EXP

Level 15 achieved!
Max health and stamina increased
+3 stat points

"A nice level up is the least we could get," Titus said. "What's that you've got there, Zelda?"

She was holding a matte black shard of metal. Kaiden frowned, then looked closer. It wasn't a shard at all. It was a key.

"Thorne had it on her," Zelda said. She pushed it into the lock on her own warden collar and turned it. The collar snapped open and fell away.

"Jeez, but that feels good," she said and handing the key to Titus.

He did the same, grinning, then handed the key to Kaiden. A moment later, his collar clattered to the ground to join the assorted rubble left behind in the wake of the battle.

Congratulations! You have been released from the Warden program and are now a free veteran warden. You retain your character, gear, money, and experience collected. The *Anakoni* will no longer be your respawn point upon death. Enjoy yourself and try not to get thrown back in prison again.

"I have no intention of returning," Kaiden said.

Zelda smiled. "I guess this makes us jailbroken wardens. That's pretty badass."

"I'd take freedom in the real world over this, though," Titus said, excitement in his voice. "Contact your people already. Get us out of here."

Zelda's eyes darted back and forth as she accessed her in-game menu.

"I'm about to trigger an immediate evac by posting my code word on prearranged Nova forum. As soon as I do, things are going to get nasty out in the real world. There'll be chaos. Use it to your advantage. Make your way to the cafeteria, then head into the kitchens. I'll meet you there."

"The cafeteria?" Kaiden frowned at that. "There's about a dozen locked doors between us and there."

Zelda smirked.

"Not anymore. See you in the real world, boys."

Chapter Forty

Kaiden's VR pod opened with a hiss and he stumbled out to a world in chaos. The emergency lights were on, flooding the pod farm in a brilliant light. From outside the entrance, he could hear distant cheering.

Around him, more pods began to open, spilling their occupants back out into the real world.

"What the heck did Zelda's people do?" Kaiden asked as Titus emerged from the pod next to him.

The big man blinked a couple times, waking up from the daze of so much time spent in-game. He cocked his head to one side, listening to the commotion.

"It's getting louder."

A short jog later and they'd exited the pod farm and were inside the central corridor of the prison.

"Holy crap," Kaiden said. "A riot is breaking out."

Everywhere he looked, doors were open and inmates were fighting, or running, or destroying anything they could reach. Rival gangs, usually kept apart by bars or the presence of guards, now had full access to each other.

"Zelda's people must have hacked the prison and unlocked all the doors at once," Kaiden whispered, watching as men stumbled out of their open cells, looking around in bewilderment.

"The rival gangs are going at it," Titus said, nodding to a group of tattooed men circling each other with makeshift shivs.

"They didn't waste much time," Kaiden said. "We don't want

to get caught up in it, what with your affiliations. We need to get out of here. Now."

"Let's go find Zelda."

Titus took off sprinting and Kaiden followed.

"If we go this way, we'll have to go through cell block E to make it to the cafeteria," Kaiden said, slowing down as Titus led them around a corner.

Titus whirled about. "C'mon, Kai."

"E block is Manson's block." He could almost feel the presence of the madman looming ahead of them.

Titus grimaced. "It's his, alright. But look at this chaos. How's he going to find you in it?"

Kaiden nodded, steeling his nerves. They'd made it this far and they had to get out, else they were dead men anyway.

They ducked and jostled their way through another hallway until they reached the giant room that was block E. Level upon level of now-empty cells rose above them, while just as many stretched below. At the far end of the block, however, Kaiden could see the hallway that would lead them to the cafeteria.

Things were turning even more violent now. Guards in riot gear attempted to pacify the inmates, batons rising and falling. Bloody bodies lay on the ground from both sides.

"You ready?" Titus asked.

"I think so."

"Stay behind me," the big man said. "And don't stop moving for anything. I'll clear a path."

"Let's do it."

Titus burst into a sprint, and Kaiden half expected it to turn into a Shield Charge. *But this is the real world*, he had to remind himself. *Not Nova.*

The press of writhing, fighting, screaming inmates was crushing. Titus did his best to clear a path, lowering his head and bowling down anybody in their way.

Someone slammed into Kaiden's shoulder and he was thrown to the side. Titus didn't notice, disappearing into the crowds ahead.

Kaiden ducked under a flailing arm and sprinted to catch up, weaving through the gap Titus had cleared, even as it collapsed inward.

They were halfway through, then two-thirds, then one

hundred feet away. Even with the rioting mass of inmates around him, Kaiden could make out the exit. And beyond it, the next hallway. Two more corners, and they would get to the cafeteria. And their ticket out of here.

They were almost there.

Titus rushed by a thick pack of inmates, but as Kaiden moved to follow, one of them turned around. And smiled.

Kaiden slid to a stop.

Manson.

The maniac hitched a thumb over his shoulder, then shouted over the noise of the riot.

"Was that big ol' Titus? I wonder where he's off to?" Manson waved away the thought. "Never mind. You're here, and that's all that matters, huh?"

Fear paralyzed Kaiden, kept him rooted in place. Everyone around him was moving, jostling, fighting, but he couldn't even take a step. Not forward, not backward, not to save his own life.

"You're going to die, Kaiden," Manson shouted, taking another step closer. "You're going to die in here."

Kaiden's pulse thrummed, and for a moment, his eyes slipped past Manson and focused on the exit, just beyond. And then something snapped inside him. His fear boiled away, replaced instead with a burning anger.

Manson raised a guard's taser baton and switched it on, the weapon crackling in a series of sharp, violent snaps.

"Any last words?" he asked.

"Shield Charge," Kaiden said, looking at the ground.

Manson frowned.

"What?"

"Shield Charge," Kaiden said again, then scooped up a discarded riot shield by his foot, let out a primal battle cry, and charged forward. He ran with everything he had, fueled by the injustice of his sentence, of Bernstein's murder, of everything he'd been through.

Manson lunged, stabbing with the baton, but it slid ineffectually off the shield as Kaiden plowed into him. The blow drove the criminal backward, stumbling and off balance. Kaiden didn't let up, however. He pushed even harder, leaning into the shield until he felt Manson slam into the railing, flip, and fall over the edge.

Manson's scream was drowned out almost immediately by the roar of the riot as he plummeted several stories down, slammed into another railing, and was sent tumbling away, lost in the carnage of the riot below.

Maybe I missed my calling as a shield warden.

Kaiden dropped the riot shield and sprinted the rest of the way to the exit.

A smile crept onto his face, but happy wasn't the right word to describe how he felt. More...relieved.

He caught up to Titus at the start of the hallway, a look of concern plastered across the big man's face until their eyes met. He breathed a heavy sigh of relief.

"Cafeteria's just around the corner," Titus said, then led on.

They reached it after a mad dash, then pushed through the cafeteria's double doors.

It was immediately obvious something was wrong.

Rubble coated the floor, great chunks of stone and burned plastic, and smoke lingered in the room, burning Kaiden's eyes and nose with its acrid scent.

Something caught under his foot and he fell, landing on something soft. Something warm. And wet.

A body, he realized, rolling away in horror.

It was a prison guard. But he hadn't been killed by the inmates. He was wearing full body armor, but nonetheless, a hole the size of a baseball had been blown through his chest.

More corpses were scattered across the room. All of them armored guards, and all of them apparently dead from bullet wounds.

"This was military grade stuff that put them down," Titus said, inspecting one of the dead men.

"What happened here?" Kaiden asked, taking in the bodies of several inmate cooks now, their white aprons stained with soot and blood.

He'd become so used to seeing digital bodies in Nova, he almost wasn't affected by these. But then the smell hit his nose. The smell of blood, coppery and sharp, and the smell of burned flesh, disgustingly similar to that of an overcooked meal.

"Is Zelda here?" he asked, a terrible thought striking him. "Do you see her body?"

A panic-filled minute followed as Kaiden searched the floor, dreading that any moment he'd find her lying amongst the other corpses.

"What are you doing?"

Kaiden froze, then turned.

Zelda stood at the back of the room, very much alive.

Relief flooded through Kaiden as he let out a long breath. He realized that he was seeing her for real for the first time. She looked exactly like her avatar did, same dark hair, same face, same eyes. The only difference was in the real world she was panting and sweaty, and her eyes were wide with what he thought might be fear.

"Come on!" She waved them over. "We have to leave. Now!"

"Where are your friends?" Kaiden asked as he jogged over. "I thought they were meeting us here?"

A soldier in full combat gear stood up from among the corpses, and Kaiden found the barrel of a rifle in his face before he even had time to blink. Several more soldiers followed, training their guns on Titus as well.

"This them?" one of them asked.

Zelda nodded.

"Very well." The soldier turned to Kaiden, his eyes hidden behind a reflective pair of smart combat glasses. "Congratulations, you're being rescued. Give me your hands." He produced a pair of handcuffs.

Kaiden recoiled and Titus cursed, stepping back as well.

"This is just a precaution," one of the soldiers said. "You're being rescued."

"Funny. It feels exactly like it did the day I was *arrested*," Titus said, snarling as he spoke.

"Do it," Zelda said. "Just trust me, please."

Kaiden sighed, then extended his wrists. Titus cursed again, but did the same.

*What choice do we have? It's this, or back to prison. We've sided with the rebels, for better or...*He looked at the bodies around them. *Or for worse.*

"Did they kill all these people?" Kaiden asked Zelda as the handcuffs snapped around his wrists, then auto-tightened uncomfortably tight.

Zelda frowned, remorse in her eyes.

"It wasn't supposed to go down like this."

"Alright, time to move. Let's go!" The soldiers led them into a supply room. A hole had been blown in the wall, revealing an open courtyard. More dead prison guards were scattered throughout. At the center of them, a tank-sized hovercraft waited, engines whirring with a high-pitched whine so loud Kaiden could hardly hear himself think. An enormous military grade mounted gun faced the prison wall, it's barrel still spinning as it cooled down.

"Focus on the good," Zelda said, pausing a moment before they headed out. "We're getting out of here."

Epilogue

The hovercraft lifted up and out of the courtyard, the prison dwindling beneath them, then disappearing entirely as they shot off toward the horizon.

"I thought we agreed not to kill anyone!" Zelda shouted as soon as they were underway. "This was supposed to be a quiet extraction!"

"They fired first," one of the soldiers grunted. "We answered back."

"I saw civilians in there. Shot all the same."

"You ever heard of collateral damage?" The soldier shrugged. "Sometimes people get hurt. It wasn't you or your friends, so what's the big deal?"

"W-what's the big deal?" Zelda spluttered, disbelief clear in her face. "I'm taking this straight up the chain once we're back."

The soldier laughed and several others joined him.

"Have fun with that."

Zelda cursed, then snatched a portable VR headset from a nearby soldier's hands.

"I have to open this file, but you haven't heard the last of this."

The soldier waved her words away and turned to talk to his friend.

Kaiden frowned at the whole exchange. Clearly Zelda was not as high-ranking as he'd assumed. She'd given him the impression — or maybe he'd just imagined — that she was someone important among the rebels. But from what he'd just seen, he was a lot less sure.

"Hold still," one of the soldiers commanded, standing over Kaiden with a knife in hand.

"Why?" Kaiden asked, recoiling from the imposing figure and his even more imposing blade.

His question was answered only by a firm grasp as hands reached out and secured his shoulders, planting him in his seat. Another set came in from above, forcing his head to the side and exposing his neck.

"What are you doing?" he shouted. "Stop!"

From across the hovercraft, Titus shot up from his seat. A rebel stepped forward and slammed the butt of his rifle into his chest, knocking him back down.

The soldier above Kaiden leaned in and jabbed the tip of the knife into his neck.

Kaiden yelled in pain. "What are you doing?" He squirmed as the cold steel bit into his skin. A trickle of blood rushed down the side of his neck.

"Got it." The soldier pulled back, withdrawing his knife. Its point was tipped with blood.

"Got what?" Kaiden spat, clapping a hand to his bleeding neck as the hands released him.

"The tracker chip they put in your neck, kid." The soldier turned his hand toward him, revealing a small chip stained with blood. Kaiden stared at it for a moment, then the soldier crushed it. He turned toward Titus.

"Your turn, big guy."

Titus made to struggle but several soldiers held him down, just as they'd done Kaiden.

"This is ridiculous," Kaiden said, turning toward Zelda. "Are you sure we escaped, Zelda? Because it still feels like we're prisoners to me."

"They can be a bit...gruff," Zelda said, the top half of her head covered by the VR headset. "Look, Kaiden. Not everyone's like this. There are good people with us. Well-meaning people."

"So you keep saying." Kaiden crossed his arms and looked to Titus as a tracker chip was cut from his neck as well.

What have we gotten ourselves into? These are the people we've cast our lot in with? Maybe Titus was right when he said, we should be wary of the rebels. The Party was fine just to lock me up before, but now that I've stolen that file...who knows what they'll do if they catch me? And my only hope, my only allies...are these people? Kaiden swallowed the feeling of vomit rising in the back of his throat. *Maybe I've made a mistake.*

Across the space, Titus' tracker chip came out of his neck with a series of sharp inhales from the big man.

"Great. Awesome," he said, voice dripping with sarcasm as he rubbed at his bleeding neck. "Now we've got that out of the way, would you mind dropping me off downtown? I have to talk to my brother." He rose out of his seat, turning toward the back of the hovercraft.

The same soldier hit him again with the butt of his rifle.

Titus fell into his seat with a grunt, then locked his eyes on the man and growled.

"Don't let me catch you in a dark alley anytime soon, friend."

The soldier only laughed, nudging one of his friends as if sharing a joke.

Zelda was still fiddling with the VR headset. Old tech, from before pods allowed for full immersion play. Based on what she said, Kaiden assumed she was in Nova, examining the file they'd stolen.

"This was Bernstein's, alright," she said. "But this thing's encrypted so tight I don't think there's a computer powerful enough to break it."

"So you're telling me, after all of that, after all of *this,*" Kaiden nodded to the soldiers, "you can't even open the file?"

"That's not what I said." She spoke slowly, as if she were working on something at the same time. "He was a creature of habit – his password is the same as when we worked together. Nobody else knew it."

She frowned. "No. Wait. There's another security measure here."

"Just let us know when you've actually got it open," Titus said, clearly aggravated. "Oh, and if you happen to find the keys to these cuffs while you're in there, that'd be cool, too."

"There's another password," Zelda said, biting her lip. "And there's some text – a riddle."

She sighed and pulled off the headset. Her gaze was vacant, and Kaiden could see a deep sadness there.

"It's a clue only I'd understand. I guess, in the end, he thought I was the next best person to have it." She spoke in barely a whisper, the reminder of her friend's death seemingly overwhelming her.

"So what's the riddle?" Kaiden asked.

One of the soldiers slapped him on the back of the head.

"Quiet. This is our business now." The soldier turned to Zelda. "Out with it. What was Bernstein sitting on?"

Zelda sucked in a deep breath before answering. When she finally did, some of the old grit in her voice had returned.

"He's hidden the next password in Nova Online," she said, shaking her head with a nostalgic smile. "And you're not going to like where."

Afterword

Hello, Alex Knight here, author of *Warden: Nova Online*. If you've reached this far, it means you finished my book (hooray)! Writing *Warden* has been a real labor of love and I'm so grateful you gave my book a chance.

As a thank you, I have written a free bonus novelette for all you readers that made it to the end; *Survivors: Nova Online*. Please go to:

www.subscribepage.com/survivors

Plug in your email on the landing page and my publisher will get your new book to you straight away!

I also have a favor to ask of you. Reviews make a huge difference to authors. More reviews means more readers will discover my books, which gives me the support I need to dedicate more time to my writing.

If you've enjoyed *Warden: Nova Online*, it would mean the world to me if you would consider taking the time to leave me a rating and write a short review, letting me know what you thought of it, be that on Amazon or Goodreads.

For those of you that want to discuss my books further, you can check out the Portal Books Facebook group:

www.facebook.com/groups/LitRPGPortal/

For more general discussions about the genre, these two groups may be useful to you.

www.facebook.com/groups/LitRPGsociety/

www.facebook.com/groups/LitRPGGroup/

Thank you again for taking a chance on my book. I hope you enjoyed reading it as much as I did writing it.

Best wishes,

Alex Knight

P.S. Look out for *Occultist: Saga Online*, coming from Portal Books in 2018!

About the Publisher

Portal Books is a LitRPG focussed publisher working with authors to create and distribute great books to readers.

We bring authors' stories to life, providing editing, proofreading, formatting, cover design, print distribution, concept art and marketing.

We're deeply passionate about the books we publish, and we hope you enjoy them as much as we do.

For more information visit:

www.portal-books.com

THE WARDENS
ILLUSTRATIONS BY DAVID NORTH

just keep your shield in front of him. Block as many shots as you can."

"On it."

Three versus one has its advantages, Kaiden had to admit as he rushed forward to attack Jax from the side opposite Zelda.

With his shield still down, Kaiden couldn't absorb more charge. And he only had enough charge left for one last ability. But what to use?

Before he could make a decision, Jax pulled grenade from his belt and rolled it toward Titus. A suffocating plume of pitch-black smoke burst forth, spreading at speed across the room.

Just before Kaiden lost sight of Jax in the smoke, he saw him activate his cloaking ability. In less than a second the assassin faded, then disappeared entirely.

Stuck somewhere in the choking smoke, Titus was unable to cover Zelda. She raised her shield and backed up a pace, eyes watching the smoke for any sign of the assassin.

"We won't be able to see him until he decloaks," Kaiden started to say, then stopped. But that wasn't quite true, was it?

He channeled charge into Enhanced Senses, just as his shield came back online.

The warehouse around him faded into the background as three heat signatures filled his vision, burning bright as day.

The first was Titus, turning wildly in the smoke. The second was Zelda, spinning this way and that, desperate to block whatever attack was inevitably coming.

The third was Jax, standing tall atop a pile of crates beside Zelda. He raised his dagger, preparing for an assassination.

Kaiden was already running, wishing Burst of Speed wasn't still on cooldown.

"Above you!" he screamed.

Jax descended, his stealth flickering off as he reentered combat. Zelda spun, but she was too late. Luckily for her, Kaiden wasn't. He near threw himself across the last few steps, catching Jax's attack on his shield.

"Run, Zelda!"

Roaring with rage, Jax lunged again. Kaiden's dexterity had greatly increased since their last encounter but it was still not enough for him to dodge Jax effortlessly. This time, the blade sliced into his calf, carving a chunk out of his health bar and dropping it to red. The damage from one hit was insane and that wasn't all.

You have been Hamstrung – movement speed is halved for 15 seconds.

"Weapon mods," Jax said grinning, ready to go in for the kill.

Being slowed, Kaiden would have a hell of a time dodging Jax's rapid attacks. So it was the perfect opportunity to activate Blur. A soft glow surrounded him, creating an afterimage as his dodge chance increased by twenty-five percent.

Whatever the disparity there was between their stats, it tipped the balance. Although slowed, Kaiden ducked and side-stepped Jax's flurry of stabs. A Burst Arrow impacted on the back of Jax's head, scoring a crit for Zelda and bringing his health within sight of the red.

Kaiden hesitated in attacking, worried that a double stack of Riposte as well as a crit would kill him outright by accident. He was also painfully aware of Blur's timer counting down, which would leave him slowed and exposed for five seconds afterwards.

Then he stopped overthinking things. He didn't *have* to go for the crit if he didn't want to. Shield Bash was still available to him, but he needed charge. So he blocked the dagger next, losing his Riposte, but gaining the charge he needed. He used Shield Bash, praying it connected. It did.

Player Jax stunned for 2 seconds.

Free to aim, Kaiden thrust the head of his hammer into Jax's belly. Not an area likely to crit, and that was exactly the point. Jax's health crossed into the red and Kaiden - taking his lead from what Sola did on *Mochinki Station* - pressed his hammer into Jax.

"Shackle."

Ephemeral chains materialized around the assassin, wrapping around his legs, then up his torso, pinning his hands to his sides. In less than a moment he was bound head to toe.

His momentum carried him forward another step, then he face-planted onto the warehouse floor. Kaiden fell to his knees